INSANE

Rainald Goetz, born in 1954 in Munich, studied History
and Medicine in Munich and obtained a doctoral degree
in both subjects. He briefly worked as a doctor, but quit
this profession for the sake of literature in his early thirties.
His first novel, *Insane*, was published in 1983. In 1998,
Goetz wrote the internet diary 'Rubbish for Everyone',
probably the first literary blog in Germany, with entries
on the world of media and consumerism. It was published
in book form in 1999 and together with *Rave, Jeff Koons*,
Celebration and *Deconspiration* belongs to *This Morning*,
his great history of the present. Goetz has been awarded
numerous prizes, most notably the Georg Büchner Prize
in 2015. He lives in Berlin.

Adrian Nathan West is the author of *The Aesthetics
of Degradation* and translator of such authors as Pere
Gimferrer, Juan Benet, Marianne Fritz, and Josef Winkler.
His writings appear regularly in the *Times Literary
Supplement*, *Los Angeles Review of Books*, and *Literary Review*.
He lives in Spain and the United States with the cinema
critic Beatriz Leal Riesco.

Grünes Winkelkanu ich dreh dir den Hals herum

PALAIS SCHAUMBURG

Fitzcarraldo Editions

INSANE

RAINALD GOETZ

Translated by

ADRIAN NATHAN WEST

ONE

AWAY

'What we can see, we can see. The secret is open.'

I recognized nothing.

Let loose from the madhouse, each day in the evening, I would walk to the tunnels of the U-bahn, not bothering to look around. Had I even caught the scent of spring? Still rattled from the journey, I made my way to my room, and nothing was as it had been before. I stepped oblivious among the beer cans, bottles, newspapers and bits of clothing on the floor, questing aimlessly. The giant white sheets on the walls, behind the sheets the shelves, on the shelves the books, concealed. Had I even read? Had I actually opened a book and heard something other than this pounding, this unbearable pounding in the ears, louder and louder with every phrase? Next to the bed lay the food scraps from the night before. I ate what I could, and fell into a dreamless sleep. I woke, it was already dark, and when I did, the unease was there. Get out of here now, go to the bars, go outside. At night when I came back, stumbling and groping, I saw everything sharp and clear. The way the trainer I kicked off had fallen, landing half on the bread plate. How odd, I thought, and all of a sudden, I came back to myself.

But the next morning there was nothing save that pain in my head and a quiver in my hands, and everything around me was blank, bereft of answers. So I set off on my way, back to the madhouse, far again from everything I'd known, into a constantly proliferating confusion.

After the usual wandering through the streets, back and forth on the pavement, pressed against the building walls, shop fronts, glass mirrors, aghast at the herds of people packed together in front of, behind, and around him, the ambush of the gazes, but at the same time ordered to be there among the people, in the midst of this back-and-forth, the 39-year-old programmer Sebastian Köhler abruptly crossed the broad stretch at one end of the pavement with free and easy steps, skipped forward under the linden trees of the opposing street to building 17, oh trusty façade, and with a bellowed HERE I AM set foot into the imposing edifice of the university psychiatric clinic, ready to hand himself over once more.

Peter Sposta, 22, has cocked back his fist, face contorted with rage. His hand pounds the glass of the pinball machine. Sposta downs his beer and walks to the bar: another beer, Harry. He returns to the machine. The ball's working fine for the others. That lasts till he returns. He glances at the clock, it's still 12.30. The foam in the glass has settled, Sposta drinks a long swig. The lemon wheel snags on his upper lip. He pulls it off the glass, throws it out among the dancers and jostlers, says: Shit. Time check, glance at the clock, 12.30. Hey, U.K. Subs. Sposta walks towards the speakers: Run, run, this is confrontation street, run, run, there ain't nothing here but heat. The others shout. Sposta doesn't react. Tear gas, tear gas, tear gas bomb. Someone comes over: You're up. Sposta sets his beer on the pinball machine, puffs his cigarette, takes it out of his mouth, lays it on the glass. He shoots the ball and turns to the others: third game's free, of course.

Walk, stand, walk, all together, keep it moving. If I was lying down, I couldn't walk. I must walk, therefore I don't lie down. As I am not lying down, I am walking. I say: My father was born under the sign of the fire stallion. For the son, that means Hell or salvation. Prone in the prison of this question, Hell or salvation, fired incessantly from the neuronal network in the pallium cowering in the base of the skull, lying motionless or walking out of the question. Days laid out, rolled up hidden soundless, days of walking. Better to walk than to lie, to walk and talk. So break out of the fetters of the mind, I told myself several days ago now, go out to the square, measure the borders, step by step as always, and thereby establish the necessary order among the people, walking and talking, standing still when exhausted, then walking on without lingering. Those who come up to me with burning eyes are dear to me all the same. I, *the appointed one*, scorn them not.

So it goes at every meeting, always the same story: Bögl talked, the others listened. About what he, as an internist, finds interesting about psychiatry. He was a little drunk just now and talks, as she knows, a good deal more than usual in that state. But he doesn't bother the rest of his colleagues with the potassium levels of his newest patient in intensive care. He talks and talks, old Bögl, it's called logorrhoea, pathological logorrhoea, he too has long been a head case, a psychiatric case, has Bögl. Incidentally nearly all psychiatrists, strictly speaking, are psychiatric cases themselves. How do they account for that? Even the psychiatrists themselves say it, and always have a diagnosis ready to hand, they don't just say so-and-so is a psychiatric case, but actually specify the type, as though a diagnosis had been made, like with Bögl yesterday, he had wanted to tell her yesterday that Bögl had spoken like a logorhhoeic, and even Bögl had said yesterday, concerning his own senior physician, that he was *utterly paranoid*, and that deep down, the director was a *grave cyclothymic*, and so she could imagine how chaotic things were when the senior physician and the director did their rounds, one time it was this way, one time another, if you catch the drift.

From the lofty darkness of the entrance hall I saw the gleaming white spear tips rain down on me, and conscious of my mission, I tore off my shirt and felt the burning rays pierce my breast and penetrate my body, I the fire stallion, son of the father, unredeemed. The searing stares of your guilt, the guilt of the clueless I take upon me, I quench it inside me, to redeem thee. So I stood in the midst of the hall, an open wound, inviolate I stood and patiently, with millions of years before and behind me, I saw the ballet of the white lab coats gradually take on the form I dictated, while I, unmoving and aware, stood in the middle of the hall, watched the clueless ones arrive in an order never before seen. And the music broke off as their hands stretched out to me, longing, feeling hands, and I heard, distinctly above me, the long-absent voice: Go and show them the way. I walked, as commanded, with measured, joyous steps, led them up the spiralling staircase, through the closed doors, ever higher.

I repeat: the truth of madness, banal as it is contested by all sides, may be reduced to the principle of the cumulative capacities of the abstract free will. Anyone who has discovered anything different about madness is cordially invited to come to the microphone and give us their *account* of it, and we will be glad to discuss it together. To give the lie to a widespread slander, the results divulged just now are not a dogma in the least, but instead the corollary of a way of thinking directed towards an awareness of the world, and even this is already a scandal in the university, where the distinguished professors have comfortably attained the most splendid stupidity with their philosophical jokes about the unknowability of the world. As we have arrived at our results not through free association or spiritistic séances, but instead through constant hewing to reality, and have made progress, today, for example, in relation to madness, we have no need of a plurality of opinion or that tolerance with which bourgeois society decks out its intellectual sloth and its errors. We are moving past these formalities, these security measures that serve as cover for every intellectual defect, which is then accorded the same right to exist as rationally grounded knowledge; we are moving past this banter to the results of our thinking and making these results public in numerous ways, and naturally this leads to the idiotic reproach of dogmatism, whose ideological character I want to point out briefly, in order perhaps to encourage those who are reluctant to enter the conversation. So where are all the psychologists, psychiatrists, antipsychiatrists, sociologists, and depth analysts? Come to the microphone and acquaint us with your arguments. And let me say once more, pointedly and slowly, so you may write it down while you gather your courage: In the exercise (established through false consciousness) of his thoroughly free will, the madman has chosen delusion, he opts for insanity, in order to reckon with the demands of capital and state, dispensing with the criteria the bourgeois world imposes to determine its members' validity.

Mr S. sits crestfallen on the edge of the bed in his robe, and digs at one thumbnail with the other. Mr S. has been sitting like this for days. The staff file past on their rounds. Amicable, practised, they attend to Mr S. When spoken to, Mr S. turns his head, hanging noticeably to the left over his chest, and contracts his shoulders, waiting. Did you want to say something? Mr S. is silent, as ever. The senior physician leans in and utters words, loud and clear, into Mr S.'s ear. Mr S. continues labouring away. His fingertips are ragged, bloodied, scarred. Mr S. tears at what's left of the nail, rips it away from the finger. It bleeds. The senior physician goes on talking, Mr S. is working harder now, trying to peel it off completely. The personnel murmur and continue on their rounds. Mr S., letting his shoulders slump, returns to his timeless, nameless world.

At dusk she gets nervous, she says, especially when he's working the night shift. She says she has everything done by this time, she's gone shopping, the apartment is tip-top, and then there is a dead space, a vacuum inside, especially when it's Friday and he's working the night shift. Then she pushes the anxiety away, calls her mother-in-law or one of us, but we don't have any time then, she tells us, because our husbands are on their way home then, or already back. And it's hard for you to respond because she's right, in the early evening I don't have time to chitchat over the phone and you probably don't, either. Then, if I say I'll call you tomorrow morning, right away I can tell that's no help to her whatsoever, she simply has to be spoken to, for some person to speak with her, to have someone she can talk to. And lately – I already knew, somehow – she's started with the alcohol, with the alcohol problem, and my husband's sitting next to me, he already doesn't like her, and he's getting more and more impatient. But a call for help like that, I don't know whether or not she spoke to you about it, too, it's not something you can just ignore, a call for help like that, and right off it puts you in a quandary. Sometimes she says, she hides the liquor from herself, but then she feels ridiculous and she puts it back in the drinks cabinet where she keeps the hard stuff, she says she hardly touches schnapps and whiskey, same for Martini & Rossi and Cinzano, no wine or beer either even though her husband, when he comes home in the evening, regularly knocks back two or three pints, right, so she puts her liquor back in the drinks cabinet and then she watches TV or knits a little to keep herself occupied, but sooner or later, this strikes her as absurd. She's not an alcoholic, she says, she tells herself she's not one, she's practically never drunk a drop before noon, and why shouldn't she have a little tipple in the evening while she watches television. So she stands there at the drinks cabinet, pours herself a tipple, then puts the bottle away. She enjoys that first glass tremendously, she says. Her husband calls sometime between nine and ten, she says, at that point she can still keep a grip on herself, but inevitably things go downhill afterwards. Recently she threw up in her sleep, she says, all over the rug in the living room. Then I hear her swallow and she starts to snivel and cry, my husband is next to me, eventually he gets pissed off, and what can you say. Chin up, I tell her, nip it in the bud, I say over and over, she almost laughs, and I say chin up, I'll call you tomorrow morning. Right, she says, nip it in the bud, talk to you tomorrow then. And I say bye, and I really do have the feeling it helped her a bit, being able to get it all out for once, and for me to tell her to stop, that it's not too late, to nip it in the bud. Then today I call early, and he picks up, and that's unusual when he's worked the night shift. And he says sorry, she's not feeling well today, she's sick or something, he says, and she's sleeping just now. Naturally I don't say anything, because he can't know that I know full well what's going on, I just say of course, and I send her my greetings. But it upset me all morning, and now I just need to talk it over with you, quickly, in confidence, she said, of course, but please, you just keep the whole thing to yourself, OK?

The motive and purpose of the law is the safeguarding of public security and order. Whosoever is mentally ill or psychologically disturbed, whether as a result of intellectual impairment or illness, and thus poses a substantial danger to public security or order, may be detained without or against his or her consent in a psychiatric institution, or subject to other appropriate measures. Specifically, in accordance with the conditions set forth in section 1, such detention is permitted when a person represents a substantial danger to his or her life or wellbeing.

As though entranced by my pining eyes, he opened his mouth to speak to me. But behind his lips, in the hollow, I glimpsed something gruesome, and for a moment time stopped, everything stood still and stiff. Gorged yellow mushrooms thrived at the base of his tongue, and worms, serpents, and many other sorts of beast, creatures of rot and putrefaction, but vivid, emerging bright and motley from the dark at the base of his tongue. A skein of movement, congealed into immobility. And I saw a scream fill the whole gorge of his mouth, with no beginning, and heard the timeless silence of the cosmos.

Until now I've subdued her, I didn't ignore her comments, you can't ignore her, I've just put up with her, and with the giggling, the curses, the endless bickering. And most of it is bickering, so when I say YES, she says NO, I'm speaking here in the simplest of terms, and when I say NO, she says, dead certain, well, *almost* dead certain, YES, almost, I said, mind you. If she would just say YES after I'd already said NO, naturally she would be easier to deal with. You'd just know that she would always say the opposite of whatever you'd just said, and that a person could learn to live with. But the tricky thing is the irregularity, it makes things tense and you're always worried about it and it sidetracks you. Like this time, will she say NO when I've said YES, or will she now say YES, the same thing as I said, in other words? Because then, obviously, I'll ask myself, why did she agree with me all of a sudden when she's been clashing with me all day long, and I'll start to ponder this specific instance where she has agreed with me, automatically I start to hope, you can't keep this hope at bay, that she'll be something besides just contrary, that at least if she has to give her two cents she will approve of and encourage me, like at the beginning, when I first started listening to her, in fact, back then, it wasn't unpleasant in the least, at last I was receiving approval, encouragement, that's what I'm thinking when she agrees with me for once, and then this brooding starts up and makes everything fray and fall apart and. Now I see there's no point in describing her, because I would have to do her constant backtalk, listen, no, just listen, no, I stop talking, listen, as she says, I keep going, now I stop talking, for the moment you can't just ignore it, I continue. But no one can make me do it, I say, you do have to do it, just listen, I have to do it, she says, no one can make you, exactly, no one can make me, just to keep a running tab of her contradictions, agreed she now says, logically, not logically she says, bickering I say, be quiet.

Dressed in red gym shorts and a sleeveless red jersey,

countless cuts adorning his arms, legs, and neck, fes-
tooned with red rivulets of blood, Raspe, in good spirits,
the razor dangling from a leather cord around his neck,
showed up at his girlfriend's party. Someone pointed at
his thigh and said super, amazing, looks just like real
life, must be plastic, say, where did you get it; obligingly,
without comment, he grabbed the razor blade hanging
on his chest, lifted it over his neck by the cord, laid it
on an unblemished stretch of skin on his forearm, and
sliced slowly and deep, very visibly, into the flesh. For
a moment the resulting slit had pale edges bordering the
wound, then, from the interior outward, it began to well
with blood, which formed a meniscus at the level of the
skin, a blood-dome that drained away once the seeping
fluid broke the surface tension from below, and as it
drained, it brought the gash, now glowing red, into view,
with the edges of the wound now overrun with red. The
fresh, bright blood, in obedience to gravity, sought out
a path downwards, crossing over the older, now-brittle,
dried black craters, and in this way, every question about
the nature of his wounds led to new ornamentation on
his skin. But no one, Raspe affirmed later, could really
have believed the cuts were decoration or a costume.
They had reacted with shock, people said it was tasteless,
they were trying to have fun, it was carnival after all, and
here comes this freak gushing blood, what was he doing
at the party. Only W. had understood him, Raspe said,
had even recognized himself in him. Months later, in
long discussions with W. that ran on through the night,
they had proposed an overarching theory of self-harm,
and looking back, Raspe said, it was never just a matter
of theory, not for him, but had just as much to do with
proximity to W., though he would not have admitted
this at the time. And so, while W. elaborated his theory

eloquently, Raspe felt himself thoroughly overwhelmed, as he later said, by the perverse desire to try and kiss those lips, the categorical and irritating urge to kiss W.

It strikes me – so goes the objection of the neutral but sympathetic observer – that you lack patience, and when I say you, I don't mean you, but rather, actually, myself, as though you were tumbling from scene to scene, image to image, as though you had neither eyes nor breath with which to linger longer than the briefest moments – it strikes me that you wish for too much all at once and that therefore, naturally, you achieve nothing. Instead of getting lost in perspectival games, you should bring material to the fore – accent on material – more material. Who cares about that, I ask you, about art (pronounced boorishly) or worse still, artistic ambition, at a moment when the question of the artistic character of art – accent on art, always with that boorish pronunciation, ironic, of course, arrrt instead of art – at a moment when this question has not simply grown uninteresting, but in fact has up and died – pause after died – when it is dead, inexistent, understand me, this question is over – voice rising on over – the end. What is interesting in a moment like this one is material, an ethnography of the everyday, patient and precise, proceeding from the admission that we ourselves have become the savages, because no one can go any further with any kind of art the way they did yesterday, or let me correct myself, one can go further, but it just isn't interesting. What is interesting – slowly I am beginning to see myself like a prayer wheel uttering the same thing over and over, but you sit there wide-eyed, as if you didn't believe it – what is interesting is material, I won't say raw material – accent on the raw – unworked, as it were, not that, but rather the material that unfolds in the course of patient and exacting analysis, patient and exacting, I repeat, which then opens on to a grounded interpretation, where grounded is taken to mean scientifically grounded –accent on the scientifically – and not just adduced from some hunch based on intuition or worldview, which opens on to an interpretation of this sort. For this reason, it seems to me, you should bring more material to the fore, careful now, though – first a deep breath in, then slowly a breath out to close.

I waver as to whether, concerning the neutral, sympathetic observer, who, against his nature, has let himself be dragged into a harangue – anacoluthon – whether I should simply let the matter rest as it now stands, with these rhetorically useful confrontations, I waver, for the moment, at least, as to whether I shouldn't answer him straightaway. No, I've decided I'm not doing it. Particularly as he is bound, even if it should call thoroughly into question his, the observer's, thesis – voice quite loud when saying call into question, heavily accented – now to resume the sentence from the beginning: particularly as he is bound to understand every phrase to come as a confirmation of his thesis. Including the present one, it goes without saying. But I consider there – no, open parentheses – now then: but I consider there to be a difference between whether he, the observer, is bound to understand a sentence that refutes his thesis as a confirmation of his thesis or whether the sentence in which he, the observer, sees himself validated illustrates the pure formal mechanics and inevitability of this conclusion, illustrates, at least, even if it does not yet clarify – accent on the clarify – and so now, for the time being, closed parentheses. Whatever argument I put forth, the observer will view it as the continuation rather than the relinquishment of those perspectival games, which are destined to bore him, the observer, and never to interest him, and which he has dubbed, contemptuously, aaartistic ambition. It goes without saying that he, the observer, is merely one of those imaginary figures, the entire dialogue only an invention, an invention of mine invented with the intention of managing to adumbrate one of those theoretical questions concerning which I would otherwise prefer to be silent, for written self-reflection is one of those grand avenues of literature that life has swept bare, and that I have undertaken not to set foot on, and I affirm – just a moment, first I will note down here this interjection – that it may well be the neutral sympathetic observer speaking, and I affirm the contradiction contained in the foregoing sentence without its paining me in the least.

And so, after some vacillation in regards to the thoughts expressed, which were firmly interlocking, I had resolved – why now the pluperfect all of a sudden – baffled question, dry but courteous answer: well now, you have to imagine that I am telling this to you at a great remove – accent on telling, pronunciation draaawn out – as I was saying before, I had then, incidentally in opposition to my original intention, resolved, as I said before, to give a brief answer, at the very least. And that was the only thing he, the observer, managed to hear; any thinking about my own vacillation, let me add, I kept prudently to myself; the one thing that I did say, this short little sentence, this amicably redundant imperative, I shall insert here parenthetically after having offered you a running elucidation of myself and the text in this passage, this short sentence: Just you wait and see, and since it was so short, I repeated it: *Just you wait and see*. Naturally, with this you, it was him, the neutral, sympathetic observer I was addressing, but at the same

24

time, in contrast to the beginning, when I was the one intended, here too this you means you – open parentheses, this conclusion is also available unrhymed – open brackets, but rhymes you see as it pleases me, closed brackets – in case you don't care to get caught up in this sort of shenanigans – in brackets after shenanigans colloquial – please strike all the words after you and please substitute a period for the comma – open brackets, it would very much displease me were this comma to just hang there in the air, closed brackets – or if you have opted for the rhyme, please strike the entire parenthetical section, from open parentheses to close parentheses – close parentheses.

– So, I believe we can, then. So Mrs, ah, Mrs
   – My name is Elisabeth Fottner, born Spitzenberger, and I'm
   – No, Mrs Fottner, you oughtn't introduce yourself, instead
   – Why?
   – Instead you should tell us a little something, we already spoke about that just now, how it all started for you.
   – What?
   – Come now, Mrs Fottner, before you were so kind as to tell me about the beginning of your illness, remember, what you experienced, what befell you at the time.
   – Yes.
   – Yes, so tell us once again what that was like, please.
   – Why?
   – I explained that to you yesterday, these people here are younger colleagues and you can help them, so that later, with an illness like the one you're suffering from now, these young colleagues will be better equipped to

treat it, to understand it, I told you all that, you wanted to help out.

– Yes.

– Good, now come on then, Mrs Fottner, let's go ahead and get started now.

– How?

– Well, if you like, you may go ahead and introduce yourself now, if that's what you'd like.

– All right. My name is Elisabeth Fottner.

– Ms Fottner, please, you must speak into the microphone, that's not a problem for you, is it?

– No.

– Right, your name is

– Yes, my name is Elisabeth Fottner, born Spitzenberger, and I'm 63 years old. I attended primary school, and then I worked on my parents' farm from 1935 to 1947. In 1947, my brother came back after the, no, my brother came, in 1947 my brother got back from jail. Then my brother took over the

– Mrs Fottner, may I just interrupt you, have you, did you prepare this explanation?

– Yes. Then, no, in 1947, my brother came back from jail. Then my brother, he, my brother took over the farm. I must have, in 19

– Good, Mrs Fottner, good. I believe, Mr Prenn, we may, er, we can stop here, this, I just don't believe there's any point in this. All right, Mrs Fottner, Mr Prenn will now remove your microphone and then you can go back to the unit with the nurses, all right, Mrs Fottner?

– Why?

– Well, thanks very much Mr Prenn. Goodbye, Mrs Fottner, you may leave now, er, nurse, nurse, can you get the patient? Thank you very much. Good. Uh. What I – ladies and gentlemen – wanted to – ah – show – show you all – with – this – as you can see, rather basically constituted patient

When I woke, I was momentarily distraught. It was already evening, which meant I had slept all day, slept away half the weekend, and as I lay there motionless, my distress drained away. Inside myself I heard the splinters of songs from my dreams, extraordinary, bewildering polyphonies, and yet not a single vestige of dream took shape within my mind, which felt its way back into my slumber, nor was there any recognition, and the more insistently I delved into myself – no, roused and dispersed. Just those melodies in my head, never sung to the end, layered one over the other, shifting in unison, growing fainter and less clear.

A cool clear evening blew in threw the window, and I looked out into the crystalline distance over the house roofs illuminated by a slanting light. I stood up, got dressed, and walked into the park. For hours, I traced the circuitous, branching paths, unaware of myself. I must have come across people – or maybe I didn't? Did I speak, did I maybe even sing? Suddenly the darkness was there, I had stopped and was standing there ashamed, these tatters, tatters of people here, all torn to shreds, and there, in the darkness, as consolation, the soothing symmetry.

At that moment – in his role as the building's specialist in these matters – the lecturing physician, esteemed Dr R. M., MD, PhD, took the floor, a man with sparse, slicked-back hair, visibly well past fifty, in other words of an age at which, in the university, the title of professor ought long since to have been conferred as a matter of course, even for the most insignificant, uninspired performance, this Dr M. took the floor, and as he flicked through his documentation with jittering fingers, spoke disgruntledly: Here, in this very setting, as is well known to all of you, I have already made repeated reference to the fact that things are not so simple. It cannot but astonish me, to an extraordinary degree, that members of the field here, above all certain of our younger colleagues, should pose arguments, eh, arguments which have their origins in the targeted smear campaign we here have fought against, eh fou-fought ehfought against for years in the arena of public opinion, arguments we've long had to deal with, please, you can read about it almost every week in Der Spiegel. Indeed, I cannot help but be astonished. For these arguments, and this too I have said here repeatedly, do not simply become truer through constant repetition. Even if it is our colleagues who are repeating them. Resentment, rank resentment, which flies in the face of rea-son in the most thoroughly unscientific fashion.

You will allow me, Dr M. said, after removing from among his documents a large-format brochure, on the first page of which the word SIEMENS could be read in Futura Bold on high gloss paper, then in the middle Electroconvulsive therapy, and underneath, Reprint, in small letters, still Futura, but not bold – you will allow me, said Dr M., and opened the brochure, to cite myself in regard to the necessary distinctions that have once more, not untendentiously, been suppressed in the course of this debate – it is printed here, whoever has the inclination and interest may read through it, I have also dealt with these questions, as people here in this building ought to know, in an experimental manner, that too has all been published, albeit elsewhere. You will allow me, then, to read aloud this brief passage, I am naturally addressing myself to you, my esteemed colleague, Mr H.

When we speak of the psychopathology of ECT, Dr M. interrupted himself, looking up, electroconvulsive therapy, that is to say, we are also including *convulsion anxiety* as well as the *fear of shock*. The *fear* of ECT is a comprehensible psychological reaction to this sort of therapy on the patient's part, one which has become more virulent under the influence of prevailing judgements among the public in recent times – as I have just discussed, Dr M. said, interrupting himself again – moving on now, that can largely be eliminated through an objective explanation, whereas the *fear of shock* is a symptom that only abates after numerous treatments and hence can compel the patient to interrupt the course of therapy. It comes to be perceived as a vital threat linked to the therapy experience. Since the introduction of anaesthesia into ECT – at this Dr M looked up again into the body of his assembled colleagues, none of whom responded to his gaze – I am now coming to the end, this fear of shock is encountered far less than before, and is most likely to be met with in conjunction with subconscious fears arising immediately before the inducement of convulsions in the patient which are, however, suppressed for the most part by anaesthesia. Dr M. laid down the brochure, took off his glasses, leaned back as though expecting a rebuttal, and waited, anxious to lock horns.

But the plenum in their white lab coats showed no reaction. In the old, dignified, august library, there was nothing but enduring silence. Finally, the Professor Ordinarius seated at the head of the thick table lifted his head, many thanks, ladies and gentlemen, the discussion is now at an end. Immediately murmurs rose up, a mingling of voices, a dragging of chairs, the lurching of the many towards the door.

29

The 40-year-old pensioner Walther Zarges lies in bed and broods. Should I stand, should I not? Should I, should I not? I should, I should not stand. Walther Zarges knows this brooding is madness. He throws a *Stop* into the flow of his thoughts. But he has no hope of it helping. Walther Zarges has known himself for years now.

Walther Zarges lies huddled, face turned to the wall, as close to the wall as possible. He has pulled the blanket over his head. He lies immobile. He knows: at any moment, the woman will walk into the room. He would gladly stand up then. No, then, exactly then, he must go on lying there. He is aware of the consequences. By the time the woman comes, he would like to have the problem thought through. He wants to come to a resolution. He thinks all the more quickly. His thoughts chase one another. His long-familiar, eversame thoughts chase one another. Argument precedes counter-argument, counter-argument precedes argument, which argument is identical to the counter-argument, then counter-argument, then argument, then counter, then counter-counter, counter, counter-counter, counter-counter-counter, counter-counter, counter-counter-counter, counter-counter-counter-counter

Zarges's wife opens the door resolutely. She stands in front of the bed in a colourful plastic apron printed with flowers. Come on, Walther, get up. The kids are on their way home. Food's ready. No movement beneath the blanket. Mrs Zarges waits. Nothing. Then: Come on, Walther. The voice has a still more strident tone. The immobile form in the bed is unchanged. For three weeks, since they let him out, the miserable slob spends the whole day in bed. Mrs Zarges loses control, Mrs Zarges curses at her husband. You blubbering pansy.

You weak-kneed chump. You coward. You dog. You fuck up everything. You ruin everything. You ruined the kids, you ruined our marriage. You just don't want it. You don't even want to get better. Three weeks you've been home from the hospital. A man should be working, not collecting a government cheque. You're ruining the kids. You ruin everything. Done done done. Mrs Zarges has closed the door behind her.

Walther Zarges lies unmoving beneath the bed-cover. He knows his wife is right. But he asks himself whether it is true about the three weeks. He begins to count. He counts the days since his discharge from the institute. He makes it to twenty. He divides by seven. Two, with six remaining. Two weeks and six days then, and not three weeks. Walther Zarges hesitates: might he have miscounted? He counts again, this time backwards. He starts with twenty and counts down. He assigns to the day of his discharge the number zero. Wednesday one, Tuesday zero. Tuesday the consultation with the head physician, consultations with the head physician were always on a Tuesday, after consultation with the head physician, discharge. Perhaps he is meant to count Tuesday. It's madness, counting backwards, what is zero anyhow. Is it twenty-one days since the discharge, or twenty? Better count forward. Walther Zarges decides to include Tuesday. So: Tuesday one, Wednesday two. He stops. He doubts that's right, counting the day of his discharge, that is, Tuesday, as one. One would mean a day at home. Walter has no doubt about it: that wasn't the case. He was only home for a half-day. In the morning, the visit from the attending physician, same as every Tuesday, then the discharge. Not until midday was Walther Zarges at home. There is a distinction there: a half is not a whole. That much is clear. The question then becomes: is half correct? He was home at one in the afternoon. Walther Zarges asks himself, am I justified in counting that as a half? Strictly speaking, it naturally isn't. Because from one in the afternoon to twelve at night is only eleven hours, hence only eleven twenty-fourths of one day, hence not a half. To get it right, Walther Zarges now has no doubt about it, he will have to count the hours. Then he must divide the number of hours by twenty-four, and afterwards by seven. This is the only way he might test the woman's assertion. Walther Zarges knows this is madness. He knows it will take hours to count the hours from the time of his discharge. He will miscount. Then he will have to start all over again. If he doesn't miscount, he will still have to do a recount, start once more from the beginning in other words. And if he miscounts during the recount, then the first count will be invalid, too. Walther Zarges says to himself: invalid, that's an exaggeration. To be precise, one should say: substantially called into question. For a miscount while recounting is the confirmation that a mistake can be made. That would mean, in all probability, that the first count has been erroneous, and therefore must be repeated. Walther Zarges says to himself: all this is madness. He thinks: Stop stop stop stop stop. He thinks it very quickly, but with no hope that it will help. Walther Zarges is not wrong. He starts with Tuesday, at one in the afternoon, as zero. Two o' clock is one hour. Three o' clock is two hours. Four o' clock is three hours. Five four. Six five. Walther Zarges sees it will not be easy. He must hold everything in his head: the hours, the pertinent and multiplying sum, the days, and the weeks. Walther Zarges thinks: I must concentrate that much harder as I count. The woman has no idea of anything. The woman blathers on, throws out numbers, and understands not one thing as she does so. Counting is his strength, Walther Zarges knows. He also knows: counting is his downfall. He knows at the same time: counting is his strength. His strength is his downfall. Walther Zarges asks himself whether this thought is justified. He has to work, he knows. Everything is in his head. He is at six o' clock, five hours. Walther Zarges goes on counting.

The bedcover hasn't shifted. Some time, late in the night, Walther Zarges falls into a deep sleep, exhausted.

There are then, just as I have outlined, a multitude of pharmaco-therapeutic interventions possible for all types of arousal states. That said, you must not forget that the success of the therapy depends above all on unspecified extra-therapeutic measures. To begin with, of course: in the case of the aroused patient, everything that might lead to aggravation of the arousal state is to be avoided. Next: the aroused patient will be most likely to accept the proposed therapeutic regimen if your approach to him is firm, determined, but at the same time relaxed. The aroused patient should never be allowed to feel his arguments won't be heard, that he will just be subdued with medicines. If you are successful in avoiding an acute episode of arousal in which the patient feels threatened and disempowered by the proposed regimen, then the prospect that the pharmaceuticals administered will take effect quickly is better than if the aroused patient grows increasingly excitable and aggressive and must, for example, be administered injections against his will, as a last resort. The voluntary ingestion of a higher oral dose is always preferable. Aroused patients are problematic on the locked wards of every psychiatric clinic, and particularly problematic in the intake areas of the large regional hospitals. Though legislation does not prohibit the direct use of force against patients in a state of arousal – later I will devote an entire lecture to a discussion of the pertinent regulations – you should attempt, for all the aforementioned reasons, to avoid the direct use of force. The arousal state, more than any other acute flare-up, puts your personalities as doctors, as psychiatrists, to the test. So, to summarize once more – sorry, just let me, we have a half-minute left, if you will just hold off on leaving, yes, if you will allow me to finish – to summarize once more:

– Madness madness madness madness, I say that is revolt.
    – Bullshit.
    – It's logical, madness is revolt, man, it's art!
    – Yeah, sure.
    – OK, I'm exaggerating, but if you had just read Laing and Cooper's stuff...
    – 100 per cent drivel.
    – With them, there's no more of that simple-minded romanticization of madness, and what you get is its necessary politicization and even, on the margins, the opening up of madness in its artistic dimension.
    – Claptrap. Total bullshit.
    – So you're the expert here, you can't be questioned. You think you see through it all because you work in psychiatry. Did you ever hear this one: practice makes you blind? Because that's what it looks like. Your job blinds you. You should try reading something about the problems. I can lend you something, Laing to start with, he's easier going than Cooper.
    – I don't read that kind of trash.
    – You really are out of it, then. To begin with, you

can't make a judgement because you don't know the facts. And beyond that, I don't even get you, you yammer on constantly about your job and yet you refuse to actually examine it.

– Nor do I want to. Work on its own is enough for me to deal with, and then some. Then you come with your revolt and art bullshit

– Just listen

– I'm not listening to anything. It's your turn to keep quiet. Take that mental masturbation shit of yours and go try it out on someone else. Blab to someone else about those wankers Laing and Cooper. You can go fuck yourself too, for that matter. So maybe it is art and revolt. Art and revolt mean nothing to me, is that clear, absolutely nothing. Feel free to come with me to the clinic sometime if you want. I'll show you crazy, I'll show you some crazies all right. Then you can see for yourself. The crazies are crazy, period. They're not artists or revolutionaries. They're just insane. Laing and his mental masturbation can't tell me fuck all about that. The crazies are crazy. Take a look for yourself. And insanity is not art, not in the least, it's not revolt. They're poor devils, the insane, the insane are the poorest devils I know.

– But you need to

– Shut it. I don't need to do anything. And you be quiet now, because you have no idea about anything. Least of all about the insane.

Esteemed Colleague:

My sincerest thanks for your kind acceptance of our patient Werner Stelzer (b. 14.7.1917), whom we have transferred to you for electroconvulsive therapy as per our discussions over the phone. Mr Stelzer has been in our care since 3 August of the current year.

The patient was diagnosed with endogenous depression (ICD Code 2691), atypical in that his depressive mood has persisted since the onset of the illness with hardly any fluctuation in intensity. In nearly three years of treatment, the depression has proven resistant to therapy. In addition to depressive symptoms, the patient has shown increasing hospitalization-related impairments. In the hope of avoiding long-term confinement, we are now making a final effort with ECT. The patient has given his consent to the treatment.

You will receive a detailed report forthwith. In the meantime, I send you my friendliest greetings, and I remain

Your colleague,

E. Beyerer, MD, Consultant

I've done research on lithium metabolism. Now all of a sudden I'm supposed to be giving lectures. People (in high places?) believe I am suited to it. I am to give open-air addresses. How is that? This information strikes me as dubious. People whisper about me in the clinic. It is said I've been measuring lithium levels for years. How many years? I am supposed to invite all my patients. The Professor Ordinarius will be present. To supervise me? But I've been published! People tell me strange rumours are circulating. Compromising recordings of comments I allegedly made during a conference have been unearthed. They want to warn me. I should keep the press at arm's length, no matter what. Various parties have assembled dossiers about me. People have been circulating these dossiers in the clinic. A large number of my colleagues are said to have passed them back and forth. And several of my (former) patients as well? Could the students have been informed? Might that be why I am lecturing in the open? I will give my lecture. I will publicly dispel any and all suspicions. I am told the TV stations, the public broadcasting consortium, have announced their attendance, story of the day. So the campaign is coming from the left, in other words. People advise me to keep a low profile, especially during the morning meetings, but also at midday, in the cafeteria. I must expose the puppetmasters, but without giving myself away. Is it professional envy? Baseless perfidy? Malice? For the sake of appearances, I should go on with my daily routine. Take note of every glance exchanged. Not even my wife, also a colleague, is above suspicion, people say. Careless remarks, even to my wife, are to be avoided. Be wary on the telephone. I come across anonymous communiqués on my desk. I should give the impression that I composed them myself. I am accused of contaminating my patients' blood. There are allegations of infection. They purportedly know everything. Yes, the lithium study, yes, in outpatient, drawing the blood, the conversations, yes, I remember, I remember vaguely.

Dr Strauss enters the clinic, greets the doorman, walks to the first floor, opens the door to Unit 1-3, walks down the hallway with mincing steps, greets the unfamiliar nurses and patients quickly, closes the door behind him at the end of 1-3, takes the keys from his pocket, unlocks the door in front of him, which leads to Unit 1-4, opens the door, waves off the patients who rush over with friendly greetings, says hello to those he knows, even the mute, stony-faced ones, opens the glass door to the nurses' station, greets the two nurses, closes the door behind him, chats cursorily with the charge nurses about any odd occurrences the night before, walks to a different door in the nurses' station, opens it, closes it behind him, unlocks the opposite door, which leads to the doctors' station, steps into the doctors' station, looks at the clock, strips off his coat, opens the door to his locker, takes out his lab coat, throws it over his desk, hangs his coat on a hook, closes the locker door, replies softly to the drawled greeting of his colleague Dr Günther, puts on his lab coat, inspects the documents on his desk, goes through the still-open door of the doctors' station, unlocks the wooden door to the nurses' station, closes it behind him, unlocks the glass door to the unit, lets it fall closed behind him, politely defends himself from the patients who scurry behind him, opens the heavy door at the end of the hall, squeezes his way through, speaks soothingly to a patient who has wedged his foot between the door and the doorframe, so that closing the door completely is impossible, forces him back from the doorway with his hand, pulls the door closed, opens the door opposite, which leads to Unit 1-3, rushes down the hallway to the other door, which he opens, then shuts behind him, walks up to the second floor, unlocks the door to the library, enters the library, lets the door shut behind him, nods to assorted colleagues, sits in a chair beneath the window, props his elbows on his knees, lets his head sink into the open palm of his hand, and remains this way through the entire meeting, without understanding even one of the countless words spoken, and without interruption from any of his colleagues, remains this way, inexplicably exhausted.

Letter: All told, my condition, to be brief, is more disastrous than it has been for years. All at once, I could no longer put up resistance to the clinic. It destroys me from within. There is nothing left. My hair is gone, there are cuts all over my body. At night I plunge into the tumult of Damage, lots of beer, rarely fewer than five, most of the time seven. That way I can also sleep. Earlier I thought, when it gets to be too much, I can just go. The temptation to do myself in is always a consolation. But if it came down to it. All nonsense. In the clinic, the sick people come closer and closer to me. They are dragging me towards them. I spit, spew, blow my nose in the face of all the medical bullshit, the entire adult world, all that earnest hypocritical clinic shit. But when I think back to the euphoria of that last year at school...

Researchers in America have arrived at new findings concerning endogenous depression, so-called. Along with disturbances of mood, of the will, and of the emotional life, the aforementioned illness, which is to be included among the group of disturbances known as psychoses, is also linked to numerous physical complaints. Most often, the initial expressions of endogenous depression in youth are inconspicuous, and grow more pronounced, in phases, over time. The disorder has a constitutionally heritable character, as research on monozygotic twins has established. An American-Canadian group of psychiatrists, pediatricians, and geneticists has recently discovered, through clinical investigations as well as diagnostic work in the laboratory, that at least one specific gene on a particular chromosome is related to a predisposition for endogenous depression. This gene locus (position) lies on the short arm of Chromosome 6.

Years later: When he happened to be in the area and had a little time, he would visit the clinic, just to do so or else to see a doctor he was friends with. Right away, he'd get that hated scent in his nose, unmistakeable, unforgettable. But the reflexive horror his apprehension gave rise to yielded immediately to an exuberant feeling of triumph: Scumbags, clinic-prison, not me, not me. The men in the white lab coats look at him as they had before. It was that cordial, lenient gaze learned through years of dealing with the insane. If before, that look had made him livid, that indifferent, unflappable forbearance, now it provoked in him sheer merriment. In your eyes I am a fool, in your eyes I would gladly be insane. Only the gazes of the patients brought him back to his reflections, once he'd opened the door. The way they sat there, stood there, stared. Panic welled inside him. The panic rose, though he knew he could leave any time. No one would stop him. He knew it, and yet the fear was in him, a constantly spreading fear. He rushed out of the clinic. Outside, back to freedom, he felt himself grow lighter with each lungful of air, freedom was a happiness in his powerfully striding legs.

As if for them it was another law, manifold gravity, air dense as water and time nearly paralyzed. As if every movement were conducted under the diktat of this alien law, the law of illness, the law of medication. Everything, even the smallest movement of the head, seemed wrested away from rigidity, as if, from the fear of total rigidity, there arose a compulsion to movement, unending movement, hours of walking back and forth, pattering, mechanical, nearly frozen. Thus the patients' procession passes through the unit. Set one foot in the unit and this law overtakes you immediately. The body encumbered with a hundredweight of granite, struggling forward through water, trying to awaken from the nightmare, but still knowing, amid screams, this is no dream, but reality, subject to an insane alien law.

After the second episode, she too had spoken with K. In this regard, K.'s position was clear. K. refused medical treatment, without reservations. K. himself was a psychiatrist, he therefore knew what he was talking about. In that conversation, K. had explained to her that the relationship between psychotic and artistic behaviour was beyond dispute. This relationship interests K. Why medication?, K. had asked. You cannot combat the truth by means of medicine, K. had said. K. sees psychosis as societal in origin. In psychosis, K. has stated, our society's contradictions come undisguised to the surface. Therefore, K. considers so-called insanity to be in essence normal. It is madness, K. believes, to try and combat the truth psychosis reveals about our own reality by means of medicine. As an artist, it is hard enough for K. to come to terms with the madness of normality – I refer here, K. emphasized, to the societally privileged position of the artist, mind you. K. refuses to force the old concept of insanity upon whoever has chosen the path of psychosis. Therefore K. rejects medication. There are, in addition, as K. clarified, a multitude of other reasons. Therefore, K said, I must tell you a long story.

– Hey, Klausä, Klausä!
  – Yeah?
  – You sure you got everything under control?
  – No way. But I got the full steamship progamme going now, though.
  – What do you mean, steamship?
  – Yeah, like I lit one up, that's like the motor, now I'm just cruising through the waves, get it, practically no steering.

– But you're cool to drive, right?

– Nah, man. The steamship, it steers itself.

– Right. Next thing, then: let's roll another joint, what do you say?

– Yeeeah. A little one, just to keep it going.

– Right, just to keep it going, a little one.

– Klausä?

– Yeah, right, just a little, if I get all spacy someone else will have to drive.

– OK, crank the music back up then. Everything's in check, everything's cool, totally in check.

Suddenly there was peace within me. I passed the days in bed, insensibly exhausted, asleep. When I awoke, I lay motionless and indifferent. I no longer felt anything. If my husband stepped into the darkened room, a serene smile came over my face. But in his eyes, I could detect the irritation, the disgust. This person, I thought, *my* husband, what madness to think he had ever been close to me. Closeness? I no longer knew what that was. Had I ever known? Illusions? Of course, illusions, life-long illusions. But that no longer mattered to me either. Everything was far away. Without yearning, I heard the muffled sounds of summer every evening, from the bars and the streets, music snippets slamming doors shouts, all pressing upward, into my room, into my ears, and I heard it all undisturbed and without yearning.

And my guilt? Where had it gone to, my raging pain? Pain at the horror, the injustice occurring every second at every point in the world, a thousand, a million times over, which I have done nothing to oppose. Self-recrimination? Bottomless despair? Everything under very clear, thick, thick ice, a metre below ground, that is how I saw my feelings, foreign and faraway, at the same time totally lucid. Just a few days ago, these same feelings seemed to entangle me, choke me, the despair and guilt were cutting off my air. An all-absorbing darkness was coming for me, in my sleepless nights, I longed for death, and during the day I sat at the table unmoved, stared at the watch around my wrist, without looking away from the second hand as it lurched slowly in a circle around the dial, killing minute after minute, hour after hour, that is how I sat there.

What's the point of watching the seconds, I asked myself now. How indifferent time and death had become to me. My inability to read had made me suffer a great deal. And now? Why read, what was the point? Lie and sleep, and nothing more. I lay and slept. I was a body, that was all. Was I grateful? I felt nothing. I suffered nothing. That was enough.

Dr Andreas Hippius, presented jovially by his superior with a tone of indulgent benevolence as *one of our youngest colleagues*, who jokingly refers to himself as a Professor of Festology, indeed the holder of an endowed chair in Festology, a Professor Ordinarius, as well as being President and Chairman of the German Society for Festology (GSF, Ltd), who had begun working in the clinic three years before as a substitute practising physician at the minimum wage of 200 marks and had shown the greatest commitment to the clinic, who remains a cheerful man despite his disillusionments, who does not allow his individuality to be taken from him, who gives in to no convention without examining it first, who didn't trim his frizzy, shoulder-length Zappa hair just recently, when he was promoted to private assistant in his superior's unit, this same Dr Andreas Hippius, who believes in the force of good arguments and the world's ability to change, has laid his tray with its soup, sausage, mashed potatoes and endive salad on the white Resopal table top in the doctors' cafeteria, removed his lab coat, pulled back his hair while taking a seat, and as he bundles it into a ponytail with a rubber band he's taken from his jeans, he greets the colleagues around him, all bent down over their plates, with one of those spontaneous jokes the people here expect of him. Then he eats in silence.

Eat slowly, he tells himself, eat totally calmly. He tries to recollect what Ms Eulitz said to him an hour ago. He needs to recall at least one or two key points for the notes in the patient chart. The relatives are worse than any patient. Out of all of them, mothers are the worst, though husbands are certainly worse than wives. I would not care to be Ms Eulitz's son, Dr Hippius says to himself, but she's not so terrible, all things considered. But that awful shrill voice of hers. The shrill, piercing voice, the attempts at interpretation, the blame-laying, you tune all that out automatically. And then you let your own thoughts wander through your head, that way you can stand it, even through the relatives' worst complaints. What's insane is that they all say exactly the same things, most times you know the words they'll use before they even come out of their mouths. You can resist for a while. But as time goes on, inevitably they all turn into one single patient, this entire group of individuals becomes one and the same patient, someone who loses it, gets medicated, calms down, then loses it again, and so it goes with all of them, and the same thing happens with the relatives, eventually it's just one relative telling you the same gut-wrenching family and partner stories. You'd like to try and take a proper interest in the individual, in every individual and his respective fate, but you just can't, it suddenly happens that you're just not interested anymore. A jumble of suffering, a morass.

Dr Andreas Hippius suddenly notices how, while focused on eating calmly, he has let his thoughts take an undignified, revealing course. After all, he's not some psychiatric monster. And naturally, things aren't so simple, naturally every patient has his own problems, and is examined and treated for them as a matter of course. He shouldn't add to his passing fatigue in this way, Dr Hippius says to himself. But what strikes him and what bothers him is that thoughts of this kind are cropping up with greater and greater frequency; at idle moments, these ideas come to him, he reminds himself they are nonsense, but it happens more and more, and that upsets him, somehow. If he is honest with himself, he has to say that this has been happening a long time now, these peculiar doubts about his job. In fact, they first came to him after just a few weeks in the clinic, he remembers clearly they were there after only a few weeks, beginner's troubles, that's what he took them for. But now, with only a year and a half to go before the end of his residency, he would have to, if he were principled – nonsense – if he really saw his work in this way, he would have to give up psychiatry entirely, but he can't give up psychiatry now, just throw in the towel like that. Also, he tells himself, here at the clinic, his unconventional nature helps set things in motion, indeed, his function is not at all irrelevant, no need to just come right out and call it political, it's a human function, rather, helping to shake up his stiffer colleagues, through his hair alone, he tells himself, he softens up the narrow-minded concept of the normal embraced here by his colleagues, and in the end, that shake-up is to the patients' benefit. That much is obvious, and so he can't up and throw in the towel just because now, at the present moment, he is exhausted, and far-fetched notions are whirling in his brain.

Another member of this lost generation, too young in '68 and too old in '77, whose critical idealism is being ground inescapably into nothing in institutions and who is unable to offer opposition based on the empathetic experiences the authentic '68-ers had drawn on: Andreas, I would like to call him again, though he is not remotely the same person I called Dr Andreas Hippius just now, this Andreas has just told me about his night shift over the phone, and as he talked, I took notes down in my notebook. Was it appropriate for me to do so? There was a brawl in the locked ward, he says. The main doctor on duty was unprepared for the situation and had called him – after two years in the clinic, he was now in charge of monitoring. It transpired that a patient suffering from catatonic schizophrenia had flown off the handle, and a male nurse – a bit of an idiot, as Andreas explained, since you have to know that such a person in a state of psycho-motor arousal is in essence deathly afraid, and this man seems to have been especially afraid – a male nurse apparently hit back at him at which point the patient, a stout character, took out three of the nurses, actually beat the three of them to the ground. So what did you do then, I said into the receiver, while I wrote down the words *beat three to the ground*. He made it clear to the man that he had no intention of tangling with him, that he was far too weak to consider it, but that he would administer his medicines, an injection, and things would go back to normal. After that, the patient allowed himself to be injected. Andreas wasn't sure exactly why. He had overcome the patient's resistance, probably thanks to his unflappable composure. Only once had he ever injected a patient by force, and the man had screamed as if they were executing him, screamed for dear life, in fact, it was dreadful.

We talked about Joyce. Again he had been reading, Andreas said, Joyce's letters to his daughter, who suffered from schizophrenia, as is well known, I didn't note this down as we'd discussed this theme before, and I'd already written in my notebook Joyce, schizophrenia, language, daughter, read the letters, but later I found the Joyce letters were only available in the hellishly expensive Frankfurt edition and thought, let's wait and see, and Joyce, Andreas continued, had written to his daughter, concerning the fire he managed to hold in his mind, that she, too, mutatis mutandis, had this fire in her mind, but was incapable of holding it in, and this was what made her ill. In terms of psychiatric categories, as Andreas said, this is known as a *spectrum disease*, a threshold mental state, verging on normality, which is common in schizophrenics' relatives. So do you believe, I asked, that he had something like that? Andreas reiterated that no, he had no opinion either way, it wasn't something that could be established with any certainty, there was no way of telling, no, he had no position as far as that went.

It struck me as odd that Andreas was taking pains to make nothing but statements beyond all reproach, as if any speculative utterance might immediately be used against him. And as we arranged to meet one afternoon at the beginning of the following week, I thought about Andreas, who tried to compensate for his professional doubts through intellectual-literary acts of distancing, and separated himself in his heart from all that he practised every day. Always on guard, fearful of becoming too much the psychiatrist, he felt a phrase like: Perhaps Joyce was something of a schizophrenic, to be thoroughly inadmissible, placing him on the same footing as the rest of the psychiatrists, whom he despised. I said my goodbye, put down the receiver, and wrote in my pocket agenda: buy Joyce letters.

The querulous personality.

The querulous person is dogmatic, stubborn, fanatical, incorrigible, at the same time vulnerable and highly sensitive, overreacting to slight or even perceived injustices. He is always looking for a fight, and is always prepared for one. At all costs, he fights for his rights against society's representatives, frequently even for *the idea* of rights against *the idea* of society as a whole. His personality consists thus of an inflated sense of justice. The Querulants, an essential book by the Munich psychologist, professor and medical doctor Heinz Dieterich, Stuttgart, 1973, distinguishes seven types of querulants and outlines them in detail. In the present context they shall be named briefly: the Rights-Querulant, the Career-Querulant, the Pension-Querulant, the Marital-Querulant, the Prison-Querulant, the Collective-Querulant, the Non-Querulant. Various psychiatric and judicial measures are detailed by type according to their pertinence to the querulous syndrome. In addition to the querulous personality, we are acquainted with the emotionally impoverished personality. The emotionally impoverished lack the capacity to

So my dear Mr Greil hoho fucking excuse me I mean Dr Greil listen to me now you must send me away from here I absolutely urgently must get out understand I have duties to attend to yes you must understand that

with your doctor's mind behind your forehead's shine
your bare hairline and so now unfortunately I have to
leave I'd love to stay here a bit and fool around here just
take one you can even have two I have a whole pack never leave the house without my smokes that's my motto
outside in the garden Willi in the English garden I mean
Willi is waiting for me what I mean is he'd like to suck
one down with me you know what I mean and then the
other obligations deadlines understand I just cannot put
them off and must attend to everything in the garden
yesterday so practically the whole afternoon there and
then the evening I tell you the clouds totally pink and I
bless everyone is that clear and then another quick one
Willi you understand with Willi just a stubby little joint
a little thick blunt one suck it down stub it out left the
English garden with this insane craving for sweets at
Capri wolfed that down super ice cream coppa anyway
super ice cream surely you know that the day before
yesterday no the day before the day before yesterday
or whatever it's all the same down at the river Eisbach
with Traudl I just met her swimming there now I've already got a date with her one after the other and I can't
make all of them though I spent practically all last week
with them so many that is so many alone in the garden
definitely no fewer than twenty maybe more no one else
would manage that and tomorrow moreover I have I'm
going fishing with my father at our lake that I will not let
anyone deprive me of because I am a passionate angler
and with my father too he also has his appointments and
it is set in stone that tomorrow we will go fishing and no
sweatbrain can keep me from going because I have my
dates set there is no other fisherman as passionate as I
there I sit on the dock of the Pilsensee where our weekend house is you know the Pilsensee there I sit on the

dock with weather like tomorrow's nothing can keep me here I must get out clearly you're aware of what a nature person I am with the weather there for me there's nothing but the sun shining over my torso just like yesterday in the English garden tomorrow I have to go to our lake to fish the date has been set with my father and anyhow tonight I have all sorts of meetings who is it that can't grasp that it is completely clear are you slowly starting to get it now I am slowly losing patience in principle I am quite a patient man and I am calmly explaining everything to you now going for a stroll is the fashion and you see that as rather strange I find myself rather strange as well but nonetheless let's get up now Mr Dr Clown and alas sadly we must say our goodbyes we can see each other again sometime you can come to the garden or I can come here or you can also go fishing tomorrow certainly my father won't have anything against our setting a date for tomorrow morning or evening or sometime next week we can set a date got it and then we'll work out everything later cool the way friends do so now I must say my goodbyes time is up enough with the laughing you goddamned cocksucker I'll scream out loud enough to make your ears prick up from your sweaty bald dome you must be hard of hearing OUT OUT beat it you PIG

Mr Wörmann, I'm begging you, please calm down!

The journalist, known for her many publications on the subject, comes across as pugnacious. She feels spurred on by the humane nature of her viewpoint. Must I make myself *even* clearer, my dear Professor? Cut.

Now, in close up, appears the benignly meditative face of an older gentleman with a grey head of hair. The professor's name is superimposed. The journalist addresses him from outside the frame: – as you yourself have just admitted. And instead of working for these people to finally be accepted in our society, *with* their deviancies, *with* their deliria, with all this anarchistic creative potential, instead of fighting *for* that, you put forth your unquestioned image of normality and use your chemicals like a cudgel to club to pieces whatever doesn't correspond to it.

Off-screen, a deep man's voice: You gotta use way shorter phrases, man. Woman's voice: Just a moment – what? The camera pulls back from the screen, now shows the television, and next to it a video recorder, turned on; a little, matte-green light. The professor is visible from the shoulders up onscreen, his head resting on his right hand, index finger on his cheek, middle finger on his chin. The camera pans over the furnishings of an elegant work- and living room decorated in soft beige tones, with lots of white; everything matching, everything modern, painfully tasteful and harmonious. The camera has reached a small group of people sitting down, and it comes to rest. The journalist sits on the sofa, her torso bent forward, a yogurt in one hand. With the other hand, she picks up the remote from the glass table in front of her. Without looking aside, she says: What are you saying?, and at the same time turns up the volume on the TV. The camera pans to the man. He is lazing in one of the armchairs next to the sofa. Comfortable white corduroys, a sweatshirt stamped with the word Greece, manicured beard, hair neither long nor short, he appears younger than the journalist. You see him speak unruffled and hear an unintelligible jumble of male voices and TV static. Piercing, off-screen, the female voice: Quiet! – Just a moment – pardon me. Cut.

The TV screen shows the journalist's face. Her name fades in. Her expressions are lively and engaged, assured of the truth of her statements. A woman's voice, off-screen: See how weird we look – don't you think? Man's voice: Ah, I don't know. Woman's voice, still off-screen: Well, I think I look weird. Cut.

The camera shows the pair sitting in the midst of the group in front of the TV. They watch themselves and laugh. He says: There's just something so theatrical about you. She stops laughing and turns her face back towards the television. She says: Rubbish – theatrical – that's utter and complete rubbish. She spoons up her yogurt. Her gaze is unmoving, aimed straight ahead. Cut.

The camera shifts over to the television, the screen grows larger, the edges vanish. We see the image on the screen. The moderator brings a glass to his lips and drinks. The journalist, off-screen: That is why we *have* gathered this documentation, all this documentation of inhumanity, in order to *prove* the methods pyschologists employ with their patients – The moderator sets the glass down audibly. Cut.

The journalist from the shoulders up, marking the stress in her words with her hand: – first of all *constitutes* them as patients. But I would like to reiterate, if you will allow me, and this is my last point, to avoid placing false boundaries around this discussion: *Obviously* institutions and the criminal methods they employ are not the *origin* of the scandalous situation of this country's mentally ill. *Obviously* this is a problem of society as a whole. Doctors and their abettors merely execute, more or less willingly, even with relish, the sanctions society imposes on every aberration, speaking here of what for the sake of brevity is called deviance, through internment, the deprivation of rights, electroshock, stupefacients, I don't need to repeat all that. The true guilty parties are – *us*. Now close-up on her face, the journalist pauses briefly, then adds in a soft tone: *Every one of us*. The day-to-day prohibition on psychological abnormality is the real problem. Why is a schizophrenic chased away from his workplace? Why can't an old woman traipse through the metro singing and praying if the mood strikes her? Why is a person who feels over the moon nevertheless forced into confinement? Why shouldn't a person fed up with the rat race lie motionless in bed for a few weeks? Why do we forbid someone from hearing voices coming from thin air and then engaging them in conversation? Why do we call that person insane? With what right, I ask you, do we say that? Why, please? – Yes, naturally, you know, I am aware of the many answers, I am far from blind as to the interests represented here, the interests in play, it would be too much to go into that now. But we should not, I believe, forget that the questions examined here are deeply political in nature. That is what I wished to point out with my final argument. Thank you very much.

Woman's voice, off-screen: Was that short enough, what I said this time, or not? Man's voice, off-screen: No, you know, just now at the end, you really nailed it, I thought it was outstanding, outstanding.

The moderator from the shoulders up, his slightly raised hand pointing leftward: Yes, I have someone who wishes to speak here, please, Professor, if you would just answer directly. The camera sweeps over the faces of the panel participants into the audience area and out across their heads. Many nod, smile, or wave to the camera. The moderator continues off-screen: I'm afraid we must, ladies and gentlemen, unfortunately I see that once again, we have *almost* run out of time, we must bring it to a close, unfortunately, Professor, if I may ask you, let's have your answer be the last word. Please, Professor.

The camera has captured the face of an attractive young woman who is not grimacing. The woman is listening attentively. Zoom, close-up on the attractive young woman. Off-screen laughing, the woman's voice: Look at that, how she is totally concentrated on making her face look like she is totally concentrated on what the professor is saying, see that. Cut. Again, from the perspective of the television, the couple. She laughs and points with an outstretched arm at the television: She is *only* concentrating on her face, I swear. I would bet on it, I'd bet anything. There must be a way to see it. Do you see it? He hardly reacts: Mm-hm.

The older gentleman, once more in close-up, just as amiable as before: – I already conceded to you, Madam. And so I do not find it helpful when you let words like *cudgel* and *electroshock* roll off your tongue over and over in this indignant but also quite self-indulgent way, giving an impression of scandal that actually hinders any measured assessment of the current state of psychiatry, an assessment that all of us, including us doctors, need desperately. I do not find this helpful, Madam. But I would like to return to what you explained in the second part of your uh explanation, when you mentioned the concept, I believe you called it social *ostracism*, and actually, you pointed out a grave problem. Cut.

The professor's hands, fingers interlaced, thumbs touching at the tips, pull apart and stretch out, then come back together in time with his declarations off-screen: You're right, in my opinion. We must learn, we must *relearn* to accept the mentally ill into our midst. Much of the suffering these disorders bring to the affected and those close to them, much of this suffering can be alleviated. You are correct there. Cut.

Close-up on the professor: Many of our patients who

suffer from schizophrenia, for example, are able to work during the illness-*free* intervals exactly as they did before. But their employers and colleagues no longer take them seriously, they are cut off, are frequently fired, and this can significantly worsen their prognosis. No doubt, there is still much work to be done in this area, educating people and improving the public's awareness. This must be done intensively, we must dismantle the stigma against the mentally ill, no question about it. That, Miss, is your department. Woman's voice, off-screen: Idiot, your department, what bullshit. Did you hear that? The professor: However, there are important differentiations here that cannot be overlooked. The dangers of this occurring strike me as great. Cut.

The professor from behind, and in the background, at the other end of a U-shaped table, the journalist, the other panel members next to her. The professor's voice: Just now, you have made it seem as though this social ostracism, which I repeat, I join you in condemning, was the true *origin* of mental illness. Just now, I beg your pardon, while flirting with the pathos of this phrase, eh, you have said, we are the true *guilty* parties, each and every one of us. And you have gone on to say you know precisely which interests are served thereby and in what way and so on. Well, I must admit, I don't have so firm a grasp on this. And yet I fear that the chains of causality you have built up, as I say since you've described something like a linkage between the priorities of capital and psy –

Heated, the journalist interrupts: Stop, I *absolutely* did not say that, that is – Cut. The enraged face of the journalist: You are twisting my – The moderator, raising his voice off-screen: Excuse me – just a moment – Professor, unfortunately, please, we must – Cut.

The moderator, from the shoulders up, looks and speaks into the camera: *Unfortunately*, ladies and gentlemen, we must bring this debate to a close, as you can see here, there is a clash between *deeply* opposed points of view, and that is just as it should be, such is the principle of this broadcast – Woman's voice, off-screen: Dickhead. Man's voice: Yep, talking head, classic nitwit TV host. The moderator: – points of view that beg for a *highly* contentious, *highly* detailed discussion, but unfortunately, we must stop here Professor, if I may ask you for a closing statement, a summary, as brief as possible. Cut.

The professor, showing no signs of agitation: Yes, actually, I fear, if you will allow me to finish my sentence, I fear that though your chains of causality come together seamlessly, they have nothing to do with reality. Mental illness does *not* have its *origins* in society's ostracism of its deviant members, *nor* in special interests, *nor* in workplace difficulties and other things of that sort. *We – do – not – know* the origins of many of the mental illnesses under discussion here. We must accept that once and for all, hard as that may be. The power of psychosis exceeds that of the environment just as it exceeds that of the vital basic needs of the affected subject. I often think of psychosis as comparable to cancer in somatic medicine: both grow autonomously and are hardly responsive to the afflicted party or to us doctors, both grow destructively and spread with devastating consequences, devouring the strength of the ill person and eventually annihilating him. Those are the facts. Illusions serve no one, the patient least of all. Statements, ahem, closing statements aren't my speciality, forgive me. I could easily tell you stories that would put a meaning to terms like hopelessness, that would make our despair comprehensible, the despair we doctors struggle against almost daily, which is often enough to bowl us over. Stories and not just the generalities I am uttering here or these elaborate attacks on psychiatry, full of humanistic airs and fancy words, that raise sparks but are the furthest thing from reality. I have said my piece. Woman's voice, off-screen: About time.

Long shot of the discussion panel. The professor speaks: – must dispense with grandiose ideas and fantasies of omnipotence. We must learn to endure the impositions of mental illness. We must acknowledge our own impotence. That would be a real start. Thank you very much. The moderator: Yes, thank you very much, ladies and gentlemen in the studio audience, viewers, goodbye, until next time. The show's jingle plays, the credits roll, as the names drift from the bottom to the top of the screen, the panel fades into the background. Cut.

The camera pans back from the image on the television, shows the TV set with the video recorder next to it. Man's voice, off-screen: Lord almighty, turn it off, I can't handle this drivel, I'm over it. The music breaks off, and the corresponding televised image at the same time, and in the abrupt silence, the woman's voice, off-screen: In the end, with this kind of programme, you always get played for a fool. Pause.

Music starts up, elegiac '60s blues. The camera pans, as before, through the elegant room over the group seated there. The couple sits silent, apparently exhausted. Soundlessly, the journalist starts speaking, she is fulminating, in a sputtering rage, stands up, sits back down, carries on wildly. The man looks not at her, but instead straight ahead, in the direction of the television, sits unresponsive and stiff. She talks and talks. Over the shifting image, in thick red letters, END. Then the closing credits.

A new patient arrived yesterday. He's still fairly young, four years older than me at most. He came of his own free will to undergo treatment for heroin withdrawal. The doctors are nice to him, but he is also treated strangely. We had to look through all his clothing to see if he'd hidden heroin anywhere. Even through the bathrobe he always wears. We also have to search any visitor who comes to see him, even his mother. That seems excessive and degrading. He sought out the cure on his own. I had always imagined heroin addicts differently. He looks utterly normal, not at all thin and haggard, at worst a little bit pale. Nor is he scruffy, he has mid-length curly (blond!) hair with a parting in it. He seems massive, he looks two heads taller than me, but most likely it is only ¾ of a head. I don't think he has noticed me at all thus far. There are so many people running around the unit in lab coats. So soon one can't tell them apart. Anyway, he's probably shocked at the other patients here. When you see them for the first time, you just can't think of anything else. It was the same with me when I started. Thank God I have got halfway used to it in the meantime. Besides, you come to know the patients. Maybe he's been in a clinic before. I can already see I'll have to talk to him.

He is very standoffish. He doesn't really talk to anyone, not even to the other patients. He paces back and forth in the large dormitory, staring at the floor and pulling his bathrobe tight, as if he were freezing. In the afternoon he was sitting in the common room close to the radio. He was all huddled up. Once, when I walked over to him, I saw his hands trembling terribly and sweat gathered on his forehead.

Today, at the midday meeting, I finally asked. The nurses grew irritable, I believe they feel we young people should keep our mouths closed. But of course that's nonsense. You have to dive in. Otherwise you could be here three months without understanding a thing. So: he's just 19, and he's been addicted to heroin for three years. He's been through detox several times, but he always ends up relapsing. Right now he's in a bad state, *withdrawal symptoms* they call it. In his case, according to the doctor, they're fairly mild. It looks unpleasant enough to me. But anyway, things seems to be looking up for him today. He smokes one cigarette after the other. Apparently the physiological withdrawal lasts only two to four days. That, too, I had imagined to be much more drawn out. Slowly, I start to believe everything about heroin has been exaggerated in the public's eyes. Doctor Günther says the psychological dependency is much worse than the physical addiction. I very much hope the treatment works for him. His name, incidentally, is Bernd.

Nothing new. He sits there, smokes, doesn't say a word. But he glances at people. He might just be shy.

This afternoon I was on watch duty in the garden. I asked him whether he was coming along. We played table tennis. He plays like a pro. He told me he had been in a sports club. There was a group of six rowdy, fairly young patients. He is the only one who can move normally, because he's not on any medications. The others are all sluggish and have spasms. The clinical term is *festinant gait*. Like that it doesn't sound so bad. In fact it looks horrifying, and the patients say it feels dreadful. Apparently you have this frenzied inner restlessness and the compulsion to move, but at the same time everything is extremely tense and difficult. I asked him whether the place depressed him. He said no. But a long conversation didn't come of it. I also think he's super-arrogant sometimes.

This afternoon, we went back to the garden. He came along, but sat to the side on a bench. The sun was shining, the sky was cloudless, and at last it had turned a bit warmer. I can smell the spring coming, though I know that isn't possible at the beginning of February. Suddenly the goings-on at the clinic don't strike me as so terrible. I even believe we are helping many of the patients. Just thoughtfulness and attention are already a great comfort for a lot of them. I notice the patients are happy when I talk to them. I believe I'm cut out to work in social services. All that makes me happy. I feel free and loose (hopefully I don't have a *screw* loose!). I want to make something of my life. I want to do something wonderful, maybe inventing something or creating something would be best. Naturally those are dreams, but not only. There is also a feeling of strength there. After a while I just walked up to him and asked if he wouldn't like to play table tennis with me again, even if I don't play as well as he does. He glanced up at me sadly and said no. He looks to be thoroughly depressed. I would gladly have consoled him, but he was so reserved. Yet he also seemed as if he would have been happy to speak with me. Maybe you just have to embrace such a person and show him that you like him. Maybe that would help him.

Now I have strayed from my purpose of noting down each day how it is going with Bernd. I wanted to capture the evolution of a single patient from intake to discharge. And Bernd was interesting to me from the beginning. Now everything has occurred so fast. Even now, I hardly know how the whole chain of events took place. In five days, more has happened (in me) than usually happens for months. Anyway, yesterday Bernd ran away from the clinic. His clothing and his stuff are still there, but he is at his mother's. Doctor Günther says since he was there voluntarily, no one can make him come back. It is also debatable whether forcing him would do any good. Bernd has a very strong need for freedom. So he couldn't hold out in the clinic any longer. I encouraged him to stick with his cure. But every day it was getting harder for him. He wanted me to break him out. But I didn't. I couldn't square that with my conscience. What the doctors said was clear to me. That after the physical withdrawal, the person has to be in a completely different environment, has to end contact with his old friends, many of whom are also addicts. Bernd is right back in his old situation. His mother gets on his nerves, and since he doesn't work, he hangs around elsewhere, in bars or at his friends' apartments. He told me all that clearly himself. Actually we just started talking a great deal. He managed to get out, even without my help. If you really want to, you can make it off the locked ward, though the windows are barred and all the doors have numerous locks. Especially if you're not on any meds. Practically all the patients take medicine, so their tempo and everything else changes. But Bernd wasn't on anything. And now he's gone. I'm sad. I don't think he'll manage to get off heroin alone. And I doubt I can help him, though I'll try. Actually I've fallen in love with him. On the third day in the garden, we talked and talked the afternoon away. In a frenzy, he told me all about himself, and I told him all about me. It wasn't a nurse-patient relationship anymore. He could sense that, too. Later we kissed in secret. I know I am completely and utterly in love with him, and I believe that my love is true. I don't know exactly how he feels about me. But he said he likes me a lot. Ugh. I'd never have thought a psychiatry internship could have this kind of consequences. Now the main thing is for him to kick his habit on his own. He knows his situation and knows the chances of success are low. He says it could work if I help him. He gave me his phone number. If I tell my mother I'm in love with a (former?? Maybe, hopefully!) heroin addict, she'll lose her mind. Naturally I'm not telling her anything. I tried to call him today, but his mother said he wasn't there. I am terribly afraid of disappointment. But I believe my hope is even greater than my fear.

Friedrich-Wilhelm Faltings is amazed, and has been for decades, at the masses' credulity regarding science. It doesn't matter whether he opens the paper or sees an advertisement pop up on TV, everywhere the most arcane reports or assertions are granted a sort of consecrated status when the label *scientific* is appended to them; from then on, they warrant belief, and that's that. Why though? Mr Faltings can't grasp it. As a young man, just after the war, he studied physics, and he knows what he's talking about. He was considered gifted, and they proposed him for an assistantship, he would do a doctorate, it was said at the time, and pursue a career in the sciences; everyone predicted a promising path for him (prophecies, already?), there were even jokes about it, his classmates and some of the other fellows teased him with the nickname Nobel Prize Fritz. After he had seen through the lies of physics, hence the lies of every science, hence the lies of the entire scientific-technical world, it became harder for Friedrich-Wilhelm Faltings to take an interest in his dissertation. Why theoretical physics, Faltings asked himself. The friends to whom he tried to bring up his doubts either didn't want to understand him or were incapable of it. For two years, Faltings strained to maintain the illusion he was working on his dissertation. At a certain point, that too struck him as foolish. He stopped for a few years, was very often at home, all alone, and noted with satisfaction how the formerly oppressive compulsion to work began to abate, tending towards *zero*. Faltings resolved to observe this phenomenon with scientific precision and methods. For the last time in his life, he wanted to confront a problem in a scientific way. It struck him as probable that the observed object (the compulsion to work) and the observational method (science) would tend mutually to cancel one another out. It was simply a matter of time. Friedrich-Wilhelm Faltings lay in his completely bare apartment and waited for indications of the compulsion. He noted down everything, readied tablets and plotted curves, and naturally, just as Faltings had predicted (his *own* prophecy), all trends pointed downwards. In retrospect, those were his best years, Faltings thinks from time to time today. At last, he could concentrate completely on the other things, or, to be exact, surrender himself to them (voices!).

Briefly: today, Friedrich-Wilhelm Faltings, out for his daily walk, was struck by a bold-print headline in the newspaper: Scientists at a Loss: Phantom Voices Stalk Dentist. Hesitantly he approached the silent newspaper vendor to read the next, smaller line: Twelve Months of Psycho-Terror − Police Investigating. Faltings turned away quickly, and throughout his two-hour walk in the gardens of Nymphenburg Castle he wondered, without interruption, whether he ought to buy this newspaper. Did he really have to bring the whole thing once more out into the open? Had he not already come to terms with it, with the voice, years before? Why begin with new struggles? Struggles, not just with the voice, but with his surroundings, with the authorities and with science. It's pointless, that much is clear. On his way home, Faltings bought the newspaper.

Now Faltings sits at his desk and wonders in which order steps should be taken. First he must formulate his grievance, then the petition itself. Faltings will make plain that he has no role in the matter, that the suspicions the voice has stirred up against him are without merit. In a second campaign, Faltings will reveal who stands concealed behind it all. Science, which is now at a loss, will be stunned. Faltings must act in public, for the proceedings themselves are now public. The psycho-terror, the newspaper reports, has preyed for eleven months on the 55-year-old dentist Kurt B. A ghastly voice is alleged to emanate from keys, power outlets, lamps, and the telephone, cursing the doctor and his patients. And moreover: scientists are at a loss. The spirit has mocked them, along with the criminal investigators.

First of all, Dr Kurt Brael is a pseudonym for Professor August Henneberg. Second, the criminal investigators were not mocked in the least. Faltings knows how Henneberg fits into all this. The professor has been working against him for years. Faltings sees in the tale of the phantom voice a particularly cunning instance of infamy. Is Henneberg finally bent on destroying him? He, Faltings, was supposed to take the fall for exposing the lies of science. Friedrich-Wilhelm Faltings is prepared to go on the defensive. It all comes down to a question of strategy. From the days of his monthly newsletter, Faltings has a meticulously maintained mailing list. Not only does it contain the addresses of the authorities, courts, parliaments, newspapers, magazines, and radio and television stations, but also 164 private addresses of key individuals from the highest echelons of business, politics, culture, science, and the press. It is not yet certain when Faltings will schedule this first press conference, and where. In Bonn? In Berlin? Or in Fahlenbach as usual? Nor is it certain whether, with all the work now before him, Faltings will have to take on a secretary again. True, he's gone without one for fifteen years now, but Henneberg has assembled new evidence. Friedrich-Wilhelm Faltings sets up his typewriter, places a sheet of paper in the roller, and notices how much calmer he feels. It's obvious. It all comes down to a question of strategy, Faltings tells himself, of making the truth known to the public. And so the campaign begins.

Put it like this: on the one hand the good drugs, the music acts, the anarchist scene, and on the other the work in the clinic. I've long since given up trying to make the two jibe. Ask me to explain how it all fits together, you'll just get the runaround in reply. It all just shoots off in different directions. Another example: around four o' clock, I pull off my accursed lab coat, drive home, and now it's a Friday night, time for some action. I throw back two beers and drive over to Klaus's. There's the gang, all these drug-addled friends, and today they want to check out the tea. Why not? Friends of friends brought back a half-ton of hash oil from Jamaica four days back, and since then, every night, we've been stoned out of our gourds. It wasn't really half a ton, but still, 160 grams. For three hours, they frisked the Jamaica vacationers in customs in Frankfurt, three whole hours, leather jackets torn apart, full body search, even the arse inspection, but the pigs never did find the stash. Unfortunately I can't reveal the brilliant hiding place here, obviously the plan is to use this same technique to bring back lots more of that black, sticky goo and hand it out among the masses. Even cash-wise, the Jamaica action worked out well: in Jamaica, the shit costs one mark per gram, and here it's like twenty-five. According to my handy little electronic calculator, that makes for a profit of three Gs, eight hundos, and four tenners. The group squeezes into the kitchen, burns a little bit, easy, Klaus stands there in front of the teapot, cool, everything's in check. Unlike the others, I refrain from hitting the cigarette smeared in black oil so I can feel the full effects of the tea, I even went hungry the whole day. The rhythm of Creation Rebels beats down from the room upstairs, especially the bass, it's Reggae Kingdom, all insanity, bliss, jah rastafari, no need to think. No need to think tonight, then comes Crass, Penis Envy, and Klaus has to stir hard so the oil doesn't cling to the teapot instead of pouring out into the cups and then down inside our bodies. After tea, everyone grabs a few snacks, hungry hungry, and we gabbed on about, if I remember right, Palais Schomburg, *Grünes Winkelkanu ich dreh dir den Hals herum.*

In the U-bahn we roll one up, no one bothers us today, and we smoke till we reach the Academy, where the band F.S.K. is supposed to be playing. Last weekend, there were too many of us trying to get on the U-bahn, so the rent-a-cops came, then the regular pigs, and the routes were cancelled, and our U-bahn party, which we had actually wanted to celebrate inside the train cars, spilled out on to the platform and up on to the street, to the pavement, rampage, fun, riot. A number of those upright citizens we all treasure so highly later complained to the Minister of the Interior, the Pigministration and the papers that the blasted punks had been let to run wild for an entire Saturday, a day when the shops were all open, no less, and the police had arrested no one nor even taken anyone's information to discourage the harassment of upstanding citizens. Pride of place goes to Uncle Johann Freundenarm, who works the cop beat in the regional newsroom for that hip underground rag, the *Süddeutsche Zeitung*, and has taken up this burning question with an in-depth investigation of why the pigs were so shiftless and which ministry has demanded reports from which agency about which proceedings. Then we got this lament from the responsible State's Attorney Hubert Leerman, head of the Prosecutor's Office for Munich District I: Our investigations into disturbances of the peace are focused on verifying individuals guilty of concrete infractions, for example, violence against persons or property. Experience shows this is difficult, as these crimes are often carried out en masse and the suspects normally vanish back into the crowd. Yes indeed, Prosecutor, you got that right, you hit the nail on the head. As a perpetrator, I know what I'm talking about.

Today the U-bahn action is going according to plan, we get out at the university, enter the Academy all-too punctually, and right then, the tea starts to take effect. Wow. Suddenly there's three people up onstage, they're not making any music, they're just playing audiotapes and don't even know the words to their number by heart, they're reading them ineptly from a sheet of paper. Shit. I bellow, I even sacrifice my beer to spray the idiots down. We couldn't take much more of that rubbish. We wanted to cut out, but then the dipshits stopped playing and word got round this was just the opener. OK, all right, we'll stick around then. The high was throbbing inside me, radiating from my core, a bodily feeling like you never get from smoking. Everything slack, knees, arms, eyelids, I manage to find a chair and I can see the others are bombed, too. I sit, wait, get hungry again. But

I'm too lazy to carry out any food acquisition action. This flimsy-arse music is coming from the tape player, what shit they play in this shit Academy, and when I try to concentrate on the drums, because at least there's a snappy rhythm there, I notice how my thoughts keep dragging me back to the documentation action, this documentation I have decided to concentrate on, which leads not to my concentrating, but only to the perception of this documenting mechanism, and this perception is once again documented, and I am incapable of escaping this thought-documentation circle, because obviously thoughts are thought constantly, every little otherwise unconscious thought reflects in the echo of consciousness, and that produces a gibberish in my mind, tangled but with an orderly arrangement along a given thread of time, as one thought yields to the next one, a coerced compulsive awareness of these thoughts that go on begetting themselves, irrespective of my will, as though driven from without, and all my attention is solely devoted to keeping pace with the breakneck tempo of my thoughts, in order not to let the echoing and the commotion in my mind surge any higher, so that the thoughts I have documented, once being documented, will at least not multiply the racket, because today, despite all my efforts, it is louder than it has been for a very long time, clearly the tea's got too much of a hold on me, hence this burning awareness of the utter confusion in my mind, which has got to change or else I'm finished finished finished, finished finished finished finished finished, if I can't get back out of this loop, finished finished finished, if it goes on this way, it will never be different, was it ever different, only now do I realize with complete clarity it was always like this, finished finished, I have been for a long time, all along, actually, get out of this damned shit too much shit in my melon down out thoughts pause pause zoom race my head in my stomach out of my stomach flummoxed puff this smoke in my brain in my veins cool molecule fool no feelings stomach reeling screeling treleeleeling.

Hear something, can barely open my eyes, see the band, finally. I get up from my chair, movement, fresh air, where is there fresh air in here, wow, all black rubber, next to me in me around me over me left right who cares, hash oil, good shit, short pause, get out. Stop. Moooonkeysounds, that's what the band up there is making, incomprehensible racket, I can't deal with that, not now. I turn to the others, Chinese eyes all round, everyone spacy like me, everyone bombed, ultrahardcore. Klaus lifts his hand, waves, me no lazy, me nod to him, slow and friendly. Everything cool, amigo? Unreal, unreal, man, just totally unreal, definitely, man, totally unreal. Hard shit, that tea. Hard hard hard. Brutal action. You hear those moooonkeysounds? Yeah, mooonkeysounds. Then back in the chair. Again, thinking about the process of thinking and having to document and hence the process of the progress of thought thinking madness thinking mad thoughts.

Klaus's hand on my shoulder. I turn around: I'm done, done done done. Klaus nods slowly and points to his stomach, the tea, of course, the tea, heavy, real heavy, same for me. Suddenly the music makes my stomach ache, especially the bass, which had really made me feel good before, but now it torments me, every tone is a kick to my solar plexus. I pull away into the furthest corner, cower between the two walls, and while I try to direct my thoughts, to turn them against my fear of going insane, no fear that's over you know that no fear just temporary just a pharmacologically induced psychotic state, I fall into a deep thoughtless imageless sleep.

Someone wakes me, hours must have passed. The hall is empty, people are busy onstage boxing up the dismantled backdrop. I shiver. Standing up, I can sense that my stomach and head are clear again, supercool. Arms, legs, and hips moving to the beat of ska that isn't audible, just imagined, inside my mind, I amble over to the others. Action people action, what's the progamme for us now? We go to the Lipstick. It's jam-packed, obviously, it's a Friday night. I order a beer, the foosball table's taken so we play pinball, Klaus on the left side, me on the right, each of us manning one flipper, teamwork is best, as always. Shoot it slowly, let it dribble up there, stellar, then stop, smash it up high, way cool, thrills, action. Then the foosball table frees up, I need to grab a beer real quick, stand at the bar, faces around me, I know almost all of them by heart. Klaus shouts, Bring me one of those contraptions, too. Natch, I say, and order another beer. We play till the music stops and the lights come up, then for a quarter-hour more. Everything fades out.

Suddenly I'm alone and making my way home. I'm done for, I think, everything's slack and lanky, and while my legs mechanically perform their function, I let myself be dragged forward into the cool of the night air.

– Listen, my friend, my dear Huppert, I believe, I would say, we have argued long enough now. You are well aware that all of us very much appreciate the work you do here, and when I say we appreciate it

– Excuse me, Doctor, it's not about that now, the way

– Please let me speak: when I say we appreciate it, I mean no one here has any doubt as to its worth. Not the Director, not me, not Doctor Nedopil. That is point one. Point two: you've been working in our clinic – correct me, please, if I'm wrong – since the beginning of, I believe, since January of last year.

– That is correct.

– Good, that means you've been working in psychiatry for a year and two months. I took up my first position as a doctor in July of 1956 at the Heiligenhafen Institute in Ostholstein, and have thus been in the field more or less as long as you've been alive. I've been administering electroconvulsive therapy since that time. You will therefore allow, in the questions that impend on this debate, that I possess a certain advantage in terms of experience. Might I assume that?

– Obviously, but the real question here is

– Doctor Huppert, I am not yet finished. I am coming to my third point, which leads back to our patients. Naturally our friend Stelzer is doing better than two days ago, naturally, we have taken him off everything. And now, naturally, he refuses to submit to shock therapy. Naturally, when you as the attending physician refuse to support our therapeutic protocol. And yet, after just over one year working in psychiatry, you must know that the positive effects of withdrawal vanish in a matter of days. And where are we then, my dear Huppert, we are back with the same old depression, but now worse than before, because we are no longer giving anything to treat it. Electroshock

– I'm only pleading for us to

– Electroshock, electroconvulsive therapy, is an empirical, evidence-based treatment. You remember Schropp, you remember, what was his name, this big, strong

– Most likely you mean Holtmann.

– Exactly, that's right, Holtmann. So you remember how successful this therapy was with Mr Holtmann.

Even for me, it was astonishing. Now, one cannot simply deny this therapy to a patient like Stelzer out of pure resentment, the most irrational resentment. A man who for two years has been afflicted with the most appalling illness, whom no medication has helped up to now, to whom we are offering one final chance, which is electro-shock. When that's done, we've tried everything. Then the guy wanders on back to Gabersee, to the asylum, and sits on the edge of his bed for the next thirty years of his life, my friend, just as you have watched him do here these past two weeks. Have you taken a look at his nails? Have you ever seen his thumbnails?

– Of course, but

– No buts. We must *do* something about that, we *must* take charge here. You have to grasp that, man. Stelzer is going to be shocked, I am starting tomorrow morning, in fact, have you got that into your head, Mr Huppert? And you are to obtain the patient's consent for me, and if you refuse, then I will entrust Dr Nedopil with the matter. Understood?

– Understood.

– What does that mean, understood? You have got to grasp that a short-term improvement in mood and drive with such an intractable and therapy-resistant endogenous depression just after weaning a man off his medicine is an effect of the withdrawal, plain and simple, not the occasion for some sort of hope and certainly not a pretext for abandoning the scheduled shock therapy. You have got to grasp that for once. Understand, Mr Huppert, however much you sit there and grimace cynically, all I am trying to do is share with you a bit of my own experience. You don't have to believe it, but it is the truth.

– May I now please

– Please, you may, but quickly, please, understand, we are already late again for our rounds with the patient charts. It is already ten twenty-five.

– Sir, you're charging at an open door, first of all, I am not fundamentally opposed to shock therapy, and second, you are not listening to me at all, you won't let me

– That is complete nonsense, out-and-out balderdash.

– Let me clarify why in the specific case of Mr Stelzer I have doubts that shock treatment is the indicated course of treatment.

– Please, then, enlighten me as to your doubts, but again, if I may mention this once more, we have very little time, so be quick about it, Mr Huppert, all right?

– I requested his medical records from Gabersee, and after a study of the very scant charts

– What is that supposed to mean, very scant?

– I have the suspicion that the diagnosis of endogenous depression for which Mr Stelzer was treated from the beginning at Gabersee was false. I mean to say that a strong component of the depressive disposition is reactive. The depressive mood in Stelzer's case appeared, I'm not sure whether you know this, immediately after his son hanged himself in the barn. In his suicide note, the fourteen-year-old attributed his suicide to the fact that his own father had probably taken his life. In fact, Mr Stelzer simply returned later than usual from the fields because he'd been having difficulties with his tractor. Mr Stelzer hasn't spoken since his son's death. This entire theme has been ignored until now. I believe

– Now listen, my dear Huppert

– Please, let me say my last sentence. So I believe we should take the chance we have here, now that Mr Stelzer has spoken to another person for the first time in months, to try and at least get some grasp of the reactive aspects of this depression, we shouldn't simply shock it all away, particularly against the will of the patient himself.

– Shock it away, aha, shock it away, you say. What can I tell you, then, Mr Huppert? Would you be so kind as to enlighten me? You know everything better, anyway. You come to me with these idealistic mock-humanitarian slogans, the same kind I read almost daily in the press, which have nothing at all to do with the reality here in the clinic, however good they sound. I urge you to look deeper, to better inform yourself about what I as well as the anti-psychiatrists think concerning the remediation of depressive psychosis. Because this fairy tale you've told me about the suicide of Stelzer's son and so on is a classic example of how a circumstantial depressive reaction can lead to an endogenous depressive phase. That is the least one can ask for, I believe, that is the most basic material that anyone employed as a doctor in a psychiatric clinic ought to master. The discussion about Mr Stelzer's treatment is over now, Doctor Huppert. Doctor Nedopil will take over the patient's care. Will you take over, please, Doctor Nedopil? Mr Huppert will care for another of your patients in his place. In my opinion, this trade is in Mr Stelzer's best interest. Let's go on now. We're in a rush. Who is the next patient?

Agonizing self-observation, remote-controlled. It increases, decreases, it is visible, it is invisible, I am watched, someone watches me, no one watches me, I am not watched. How many times a day do I touch my neck? At school I wear a turtleneck, but the gazes of my classmates, even of some of the teachers, are intrusive and shameless. People stare at me as though I were naked. It may be that my penis swells up. The gazes become ever more shameless, people stare at the left side of my neck. All this is madness, I tell myself. I looked it up in the biology book: there, where I feel it thickening, there's no gland, there's nothing at all. No one can know about it, I say to myself. I avoid anyone coming too close to me. And yet I know, even from a distance, a body's contours are discernible. These ruminations are a dead end, they lead nowhere. I try and divert myself, it rarely works. My exertions reveal to me that *I* am not thinking, that *it* is thinking in me. I don't find that so strange. I believe it has always been this way. But I also believe that is the case with most people or even all of them. It could be something like the essence of thinking that it is unbeholden to the human will. Recently I tried to explain that in German class. But the teacher found it muddled, and the others laugh whenever I say something. I am certain: *it* thinks in all people. But normally one doesn't pay it much attention. That disturbs me, it even frightens me sometimes, how relentlessly I am aware that it thinks in me. Is this awareness normal, I ask myself. What is *it*? A force? Am I being steered? Hogwash, I tell myself. Inwardly, within me, *it* laughs its droning laughter. Am I being laughed at? Or am *I* laughing at my own irrational thinking? Either way, it is a torment, yes, *it* torments me. It is apparent that I'm a victim. I am being tormented. The question is simply: is someone tormenting me, is there a perpetrator, in other words? And again: who could it be? And: is it by chance? Or have I incurred guilt somehow? What sort of guilt? All that is working at me inside. Is it related to the swelling on the left side of my neck? A relation to the exterior, the swelling as an *expression*, a way for *it* to emerge. Does it want to be visible? Why? Conceivably there is a mission. Perhaps I should take my knowledge of the essence of thinking public, publicize it. I can't believe I have been singled out. I am just a poor sinner, too mean to be an instrument of the Lord. My mother prays for me. She claims she doesn't see my swelling. The swelling is a delusion, she says. To the contrary, I reply, the swelling is an expression. She laughs at that and says: The things you come up with. She lays stress on *come up with*, unsure of what she really means. I sincerely doubt she is the thing that is steering me. While it thinks, I look through the classroom window outside. In the past few weeks, the trees have changed inexplicably. They have lost their significance for me. Before, each tree had its own particular image, the sight of which heartened me. In the woods behind our house, I knew almost every tree. I used to go walking there for countless hours, and would look around at everything, at that familiar setting, with the greatest joy. All that is gone. Every tree is the same threatening gesture, a malignancy that terrifies me. Everywhere I read of the growing danger of atomic warfare, which will destroy every living thing on earth. If there is any sign of the destruction that awaits us, it is the trees.

I haven't gone back there. No one understood what I said. I wanted people to talk about my thoughts. I tried to make my inner life clear. First they laughed at me, then they brushed me off. But your last year of school, it must be possible to talk about people. I wanted to explain that we are not machines, or mere tools or even playthings of some power. Before, too, I had talked during class, also a great deal about myself. I always had the best marks. Now all of a sudden it's: Goetz, you're blathering on, be quiet. And another teacher said: You're disturbing the class with your gibberish, either shut your mouth or disappear. For months, I hardly said a word at school, then it was: What's wrong with you, you don't participate anymore at all; and when I tried to focus on clarifying the important things, it was all supressed in the brusquest manner. What more could I get out of school? For days I sat there, defeated, in the living room, without a thought in my head. I had long since got rid of the brooding. My mother's benevolent chitchat got on my nerves. She pretends to understand, in fact she's got no idea. Eat this, eat that, everyday the same phrases fall from her lips, as if she had no control over them. In school, the torment of the stares, here, the torture of inanity. She spoke without stopping about the swelling on my neck, which I didn't want to hear anything about. I went away and shut myself in my room. I am fasting, today is my tenth day, and I wait. It may be every torment is part of a great test. Am I suited to it? I don't dare think about it. There is a foreboding in me, and an oppressive, transcendental plenitude. What role am I playing? I ask: What task have I been chosen for? I avoid the once beloved glances outside towards the forest's edge. The sight of the trees fills me with revulsion. Must everything really come to an end *like this*? And why? Fear, mortal fear, and unfathomable distress: Why should I be the one chosen to bring destruction? Agonizingly, the question of guilt emerges over and over, the question of my personal guilt. The first days up here, I never left the bed, and masturbated nonstop, as though under orders. It seemed to me I should masturbate all the guilt out of me. The semen I expelled on to a washcloth, and laid it on the heater to dry. The pale blue terry cloth is stiff, it has grimy yellow-white blotches, and its scent spreads into every corner of the room. In this way, I have killed the semen. But by doing so, have I saddled myself with new guilt instead of expiating the old? My penis throbs. I open my pants, take my penis in hand, and pull back the foreskin. The head is fire red, on the inside of the foreskin I see for the first time the web of tender blue veins. I no longer feel any arousal. I believe the drive is extinguished. I may concentrate fully on doing no harm, whether through looking outside or through improper thoughts. At night, downstairs, I hear my family praying. I start to bellow. I will defend myself by any means.

Stagnation, for weeks nothing but dejection and stagnation. I've been discarded because I've made no progress. The medicines leave me tired. Every movement is arduous, as if I'd had lead poured into the hollows of my bones. Why does no one talk to me? The visits normally last just a minute, three at most: the bedside visits, the rounds, as they're called. On other days, they have group rounds. Some thirty patients sit there with two doctors in a big circle and everyone must say briefly how he's doing. A case like mine, an uncomplicated one, will get just ten seconds during group rounds. Most of the other patients are truly insane. With me, it's just a matter of the dosage. A hundred more milligrams of Taxilan or a hundred less or even two hundred less, but then a hundred more. On Thursdays, the Chief Physician makes his rounds, it's a bedside visit, but the patients are hardly spoken to. The Attending Physician, the Unit Physician, and the Chief Physician discuss the cases. For me, even the Chief Physician's rounds are almost exclusively concerned with dosages. I try to listen to what they are saying. By now I am a regular specialist in Taxilan. I already know in advance whether they will raise or lower the dosage. Walking away, the Chief Physician sometimes asks: And how is the swelling on your neck? Are you still being watched? I find these questions ridiculous. They've decided I'm insane and now they've written me off. I don't believe I'm insane. I have terrible problems, that much is true. It would certainly help if I could talk to someone about it. The nurses are the nicest, and nicest among them are the very ones who look most threatening. Three of them are frankly giants. At first, I was afraid of them, but they are empathetic, gentle people. Unlike the doctors, they actually know the patients and care for them in a friendly way. Unfortunately, I am too scared to talk to them about myself. But still, their compassion does me good. Tuesday is when the Medical Director comes. Normally we don't even see him. He walks straight from the hallway into the three small private rooms. He comes when he feels like it. You can't just sit in the hallway all day and wait. But sometimes, when a private patient is temporarily placed in the dormitory, he comes where we are, too. I wouldn't like to lie there in a private room with just two beds. Even if I can't be part of it, I still enjoy that odd good humour that sometimes emerges there in the seventeen-man room. I really would like to talk sometime with the Medical Director about my problems. He is tall, has thick, white hair, a tanned face even though it's February. Presumably he's a skier. I've been watching him since I've been here. Should I, will I speak to him? More and more, I tend to think it's pointless. The way he moves, the way he holds his head, the tone he speaks in, it's all so exaggeratedly earnest that I find it ridiculous. The nurses say he makes a killing. That doesn't bother me one bit. I wouldn't care to be a man like that, just so I could earn a lot of money. I don't know any other executives. Ours is just an actor, I think, play-acting at being earnest. The worst thing is when he pretends to be warm. He starts laughing, and I close my eyes. Everything about him is a lie. The way he feigns understanding and empathy reminds me of my mother. His expressions try to convey thoughtfulness and conscientious sincerity. In reality, everything about him screams out: How am I doing today? Am I playing my part well, as always? Everyone who sees him must hear that. I ask myself how a person can honestly believe he is deceiving everyone around him that way. He is a professor. I've known for a long time there's no use in my speaking to him. I didn't want to admit it, in order not to give up that one last hope. What will happen now? I lie back, observe the workings of the unit, incapable of defending myself, I note the petty details, and I despair as I never have in my life. Everything stagnates. Always the same questions: Why does no one help me? Why am I trapped in here? I have to go back to school. Nobody cares that I'm falling behind, particularly in mathematics, with my exams closing in. I'm a passionate student. I have excellent marks, I want to keep them that way. No one cares about that. All they ever talk about is getting healthy. How is that supposed to happen when I lie here and nothing changes? Naturally, my parents are no help. When they come to visit me on weekends, we sit there awkwardly in the hall, and no one really knows what to say. Then my mother starts babbling to herself, carries on about the farm, about work, about my siblings, things that don't interest me in the least. There are problems with the livestock. Yeah, and? For the first time, I feel like I'm living in a different world from my parents with their farm. And knowing this is one more wound, and it eats away at me. Before I was committed, my parents allege I was running amok. Supposedly I threatened my mother with a knife. On the one hand, I can't believe they would lie to me, on the other, I can't believe I have ever done anything of the kind. I only remember the past few months vaguely. The last thing I recollect clearly is this exuberant feeling of happiness that came in with the autumn, the fiery leaves on the trees, the walks for hours through the foliage, ecstatic colours. And then? I remember brooding introspection, thoughts about thoughts, turbidity, which must have occupied me profoundly. Then there is a gap, I don't really know how long, and the next thing was the spasms, here, the spasms in my neck, my throat, and my eyes, the terrible fear they would kill me here with their neurotoxins, the fear of failing breath. Then the white lab coats, which I couldn't tell apart, they looked the same and always asked the same questions again and again: Who are you? What are your orders? Where are you now? Or: What season is it? What do the trees mean to you? What do you think is the significance of the proverb the apple doesn't fall far from the tree? And: What is three times seven? Who is commanding you? What is the swelling on your neck trying to express? Is it possible that I am your mother? But you're a man, I answered. I wanted to go to sleep and not speak with anyone anymore. But they forced me. They forced me, one conversation after the next. Nocturnal interrogation? It can't be, I can't believe it. At some point, they would awaken me, and I would have to talk again. In vain, I begged for mercy. Stop with this torture, I said, even if I have sinned. What sin, they would ask then, what do you mean, sin? I had to talk about myself in an auditorium with steep risers filled with the heads of innumerable students. The shame was extreme. Afterwards, I said again: I have done my penance, please stop now. All this is foggy. My memory gropes its way back, but all I recognize are shadows, the hints of figures, faraway and veiled. What I do know is this: now that I see clearly again, my serenity is back and at the same time my despair now looms from out of my confusion, it grasps me and strangles me and now, when

I need it urgently, there is no one there for me to talk to. During rounds, my eyes plead for help. The doctors are friendly but cold. I no longer hold any interest for them. How long have I been here now? I have to get better. Help, please, help. Everything must go back to the way it was before.

One word leads to another, names entail concepts, concepts entail names, and suddenly there you stand before the associations of words, faced with the equivalencies of words, which must be unravelled, and in the unravelling of which there are lies to be uncovered.

From Nietzsche's *Ecce Homo* to Nietzsche, to Sils Maria, Sils Maria and the manic light of the Engadine, high mountains loneliness genius, the genius of Nietzsche, genius and madness, madness and revolt, and madness and art and imagination and whatever else.

An example. You could start another of these varicoloured chains with the name Nijinsky or with Alfred Döblin's dictum: Apart from plants, animals, and stones, he could bear only two categories of people: namely, children and the insane. Well well, very interesting, Mr Döblin.

Or a little scene, by way of illustration: a warm summer evening, twilight, a circus tent on a broad field, and colourful paper lanterns. A mime there, playing with children. Not far off, an organ grinder. A melody blows forth melancholic but also merry. Everything glows in lurid colours. Amid the food stalls, the open-air theatres, and the tents, cheery people in long, flowing garments, baggy pants, overalls, T-shirts with batik designs. Faces made up fancifully; strangers meet eyes and exchange glances without shame, knowing the score. Here the troupe of Italian clowns, off to the caravan, painted carmine red. Should one not then burn the last of the bridges to conventional bourgeois life? Sure, just become one of those people who live on the road! A man in a suit moves lost through the crowd, a strange memento of a distant, long-lost world of narrowness and obligation. One person says, not mocking, but actually astonished: Look there, that one's got a tie on. Suddenly heads turn upward, more and more people stop and gaze into the heights; slowly, a bright yellow balloon in the evening sky, high and higher, a bright spot, which finally vanishes.

– Remember? I'm sure you know what I'm saying.

– Yeah, definitely.

– Sure, I knew you'd remember. It was in the mid-, maybe late seventies, back during the first theatre festivals, the first real heyday of alternative culture, clawed back during the struggle against cerebralization, theoretical drivel, societal compulsion, you remember, free, self-determined spontaneity!

– Of course, like I just told you, I definitely remember. But let me ask you then: What does that have to do with anything, what kind of argument is that?

– Argument, come on now, who said anything about arguments? Did I say anything about arguments to you?

Naturally one may consider the foregoing illustration as well as the allure of the implied chain of associations from a theoretical perspective. Indeed, this very manner of proceeding might well be advisable insofar as it is diametrically opposed to the phenomenon under analysis, to wit, the euphoric celebration of irrationality. There is a series of justifications for the heroic configuration and aestheticization of madness that would also clarify the converse phantasm of psychotic, particularly schizophrenic production as the authentic prefiguration of artistic production, of the psychotic as one who reaches effortlessly and without calculation that which the artist must struggle, often in vain, to achieve.

We draped ourselves in phrases from Laing-Cooper-Basaglia as if with gleaming exotic amulets. Ecstatically we read one another those simple, melancholy thoughts on love the schizophrenic poet Alexander wrote down at the behest of good old Uncle Navratil. The very same good uncle who gave paints and brushes to Johann Hauser so he could paint those colourful shaggy cunts of his, one cunt after another, just wonderful, the Prinzhorn exhibition, madness, they are testimony, all of them authentic, staggering testimony to the suffering in asylums and to the revolutionary potential of madness. Back from vacation in Greece in the cold, dark Federal Republic, we gazed in longing at sun-soaked Italy, where a revolutionary law had abolished all the madhouses, all of psychiatry in fact, Oh Italy.

Unbeknownst to the fans of Anti-Psychiatry – fans is absolutely the right word – psychiatry in Germany has taken small steps in the direction of humaneness. Psychoanalytically oriented, critically minded psychiatrists are moving into positions of greater influence in many clinics, are becoming head physicians, sometimes even Medical Directors. Their unromantic, very practical concern for the organizational forms of social psychiatry have naturally done nothing to curtail the ecstatic demands of the Anti-Psychiatry irrationalists. No one has wanted to look at psychiatry sensibly. They prefer to let themselves be carried away by the torrents of pretty words about revolutionary pathos: *La libertà è terapeutica*! Destroy the machine of bourgeois normality, the psychological apparatus of capital!

In the Anti-Psychiatry movement, political engagement and irrationalism have joined forces with stupidity. It impedes everything. It impedes what is essential and at the same time most difficult: the apprehension of reality as such. By which I mean not merely the reality of the psychiatric clinic, but the reality of, the reality

– Why are you stopping all of a sudden?

– Ah, you know

– Know what? Nietzsche, Nijinski, your chains of words, Alfred Döblin, you've left so much hanging.

– Yeah, you're right. Maybe I shouldn't have, maybe I would have been better off

Voices fading out, drawing apart from each other.

– Better off doing...?

– Ah, you know, all this was explained better elsewhere a long time ago.

– But you're the one who

– Bah. Even when I get all worked up, it's just blather, stuff I read somewhere, I was too young to be a part of all that, too young or too elitist. No, I'd be better off, I'd rather, you know, stories! Let me talk, and you listen.

Two figures vanish into the depths of the room. Curtain. Why a curtain? Why not?

Patient File: Straßmair, Adolf, d.o.b. 18.6.40.

Intake: In a phone call with an acquaintance, patient appeared deeply confused and at risk. The latter notified the police, who brought the patient to the clinic in a maniform state on 18/4 at 19.30.

Medical History: Patient has been mentally ill from the time of his twentieth year. His cyclothymia is expressed in alternating manic and depressive phases and has led to numerous hospitalizations in various psychiatric clinics. Most recently, on 1/3, he was admitted to Haar, and discharged himself – against medical advice – one week before being admitted here.

Psychopathology: Upon admission, patient presents psychomotor disturbances, derailment, and labile affect ranging from elevated to irascible. He is oriented and not suggestible.

Somatic and Neurological State: Normal.

Therapy and Progression: Patient initially refused medication. It was however possible to avoid an order for involuntary treatment. Within days, manic state was mitigated through the administration of 20 mg/d of Haldol and 225 mg/d of Neurocil. By 22/4, patient no longer showed signs of psychopathology, though he continues to manifest psychomotor impairments and restricted movement. On 23/4, Haldol was reduced to 15 mg/d and Neurocil to 150 mg/d. Patient is pressing adamantly for release and will be discharged on 28/4 against medical advice. Ambulant aftercare in our unit is planned.

Outpatient Interview:

8/5: Patient appears more or less daily for his appointments. Complains of difficulty sleeping and inner turmoil and is prescribed 100 mg/d Taxilan in addition to 10 mg/d Haldol and 50 mg/d Neurocil.

12/5: Due to psychomotor restriction, Haldol is reduced to 5 mg/d, Taxilan raised to 200 mg/d. Patient continues taking 50 mg/d Neurocil to aid with sleep disturbances.

22/5: Patient continues to experience motor restrictions, therefore Haldol is suspended. Now showing symptoms of depression and anxiety. *Medication*: Haldol suspended, Taxilan 300 mg/d, Neurocil 50 mg/d.

26/5: *Medication*: Taxilan 300 mg/d, Neurocil 50 mg/d. *Findings*: Patient states he feels well, mood is unstable but generally improved. He complains of irregular sleep.

Patient's presentation is organized with only slight psychomotor impairment. (Prescription: Taxilan 100 mg and Neurocil 100 mg per dose.)

30/5: Nothing to note.

4/6: Patient complains of depressive mood, but without suicidal ideation. *Medication*: unchanged.

10/6: Patient's depression has worsened. Now receiving 150 mg/d Taxilan, 50 mg/d Neurocil, and 75 mg/d Saroten.

12/6: Depressive mood unchanged. *Medication*: Saroten 125 mg/d, Taxilan 100 mg/d, Neurocil 50 mg/d. Patient has been admitted to the polyclinic.

The case histories need to be shorter, it was announced recently at a meeting. The secretarial pool is overwhelmed. The files are to contain only the absolute most important information about a patient's medical history, the Medical Director intoned, let me remind you again, it should not go on longer than a page. So Straßmeir's file is half a page too long. Ridiculous! I picked up five files I dictated last Thursday (during the night shift). If you read through them, it will depress you terribly. All the work of these last few weeks, all that dedication reduced to a couple of keywords, medicines, dosages: numbers from one end to the next. It's true that there is nothing objectively graspable about what we do save for the prescription of medicines, the constant attempt to establish the correct dosage. At the same time, our real work vanishes behind these objective data, the conversations, the empathy, everything that for me constitutes the indispensable accompaniment of medical therapy. Naturally, many colleagues see it otherwise. They write prescriptions, avoid any intensive contact with the patients, and for them, science, biological psychiatry, is above all the great search for the schizococcus or the depressive enzyme. With that, of course, you can make a name for yourself not only in the clinic, but also in the so-called field. For a year and a half, I managed to duck science successfully, then the Medical Director showed up one day, very friendly, wouldn't you, Doctor, couldn't you, but you will, and then came my debut as a researcher, with a presentation cobbled together in a rush from parts of my dissertation, the results were pathetic, but methodologically, it was unimpeachable. I was utterly embarrassed at myself.

But then they start talking to you, you get praised for your presentation, you get an introduction over here, they squeeze you in over there. All of the sudden, you're taken seriously, unlike in your own clinic. And it surprised me, in private, that many of our colleagues, men and women both, turned out to be sympathetic and capable of self-criticism: you can't let this dog-and-pony show go to your head, one of them said to me. When you've seen this a few times, you understand that the roles were carved in stone long, long ago, and everybody knows exactly what's expected of them. This science, as you know from your own projects, is going around in circles: but still, the younger colleagues want their PhDs, the ones with PhDs want to become professors, adjunct professors at the least, and that means six years of publications and research after the dissertation. Even Klein, who's made a name for himself in the clinic as a grade-A researcher, came up to me and said: Look, this is a circus, with science, everyone's just saying Hocus-Pocus and pulling rabbits out of their hats. You're doing lithium levels, that's a good gig, I'm doing cerebrospinal fluid and gamma-globulin, not bad either, there's a lot to work with there, the autonomous gamma-globulin production *plus*, you know you can combine anything with that: *plus* compulsive neurosis, *plus* prepartum psychosis, *plus* urolagnia; you can combine whatever you feel like with gamma-globulin in cerebrospinal fluid. A hell of a thing, don't you think? Our big bright research circus. But the real work, this much is clear, the medical work, the work we do on site, in the clinic, the commitment to the patient, that's what it's really about, don't you think?

After the conference, I was ambivalent. I couldn't hate the scientists as categorically as I had before. Yet I had the sense that the self-irony I had glimpsed with relief was likely just a particularly abject psychomaneuver typical of the average psychiatrist. Moreover, it became clearer to me as the weeks wore on that I now *belonged* in the clinic as I never had before. I was spoken to, queried for professional advice, made party to the small talk and jokes. The feeling was pleasant, sure enough, but what did clinical secrecy, jockeying for position, the organizational climate, or colleagues' chitchat about scheduling changes really have to do with me? That didn't pertain to me, I wanted to concentrate on my work, wanted to carry my work out thoroughly, nothing more. Now I had made myself the same as the others, made myself daily more like them, and I seemed to have lost, along with my elitist attitude, all self-reliance and independence. No sooner had I taken a single step *out of myself* and towards my colleagues than I saw in them the barely suppressed desire to assimilate me once and for all, now that they'd trapped me in their web of affiliations. The women especially began to nibble away at me with friendly words from their shamelessly lurking faces. And I discovered, with dread, that every movement, even the attempt to flee into my erstwhile aloofness, got me tangled up worse, enmeshed me more inexorably.

– You're not going to Fieberbrunn? Well, that's too bad. You're not a skier? What about your husband? Oh, you're single? Or just not married? But you know, the boss invited everyone, and however it started, it's almost a tradition now, there's this family-like atmosphere and it makes people in the clinic see you in a different light afterwards. Come on, now, don't be a wet blanket, come with us. Why the grimace? – Before, no one dared set on me with these confidential-invasive questions, but now I seemed to actually attract these conversations, regardless of what I said, how I reacted, or how I behaved. I decided once more to turn my attention away from the social game-playing and chicanery I had got too wrapped up in in the months after the conference. I busied myself exclusively with questions concerning medication or involuntary commitment or even just taking an intense interest in the patients, with the same urgency as before, but with an entirely different base of experience. Five files to go through, one after the other, all following the same pattern as Straßmair's, that's hardly gratifying, as I've said. Am I just a pill-pusher? Might all I talked about with the man have been pointless, negligible from the therapeutic perspective? The quality of the therapy, my commitment as a doctor, is not something that can be read in a patient file. But then, how much time is taken up every day with medications? How much time do I actually have left for intensive engagement with the patients? The activities that mean most to me are the ones I devote the least time to each day, I believe. Yes, I believe that is true.

Constant discussion of medication, that already starts during intake. At first, most patients refuse their medicine. Many, very many, don't consider themselves ill at all, then others believe the medications are harmful or even dangerous. Often, after calm, reasoned discussion, patients will agree that they are in need of care and that medical therapy is the first means of helping them. Those who don't submit to argument can generally be locked up; legally, at least, this possibility exists, you can always state they pose a danger to themselves or others. But here in our clinic, in contrast to many others in the region, we try to avoid that step. To begin with, it impedes the development of trust between doctor and patient, and this is indispensable for therapy; beyond that, it makes the psychiatric illness go on their record, and this can have professional or personal consequences after the patient's release. For that reason, we normally only *threaten* commitment, and this generally suffices for the patient to accept medication voluntarily. Schmaus, our head physician, has a variant on this he recommends: from the outset, he leads the patient to believe he has already been committed and thus has no choice but to submit to the physician's orders. Since only a minority of patients are familiar with their legal situation, this method almost always works. Very seldom do we have to physically restrain a person and administer medication by injection; that is something I have only seen twice before, I believe.

All this requires a great deal of time, most of all in the early conversations with the new patient. Generally the patient's resistance to medication flags quickly, even when there are unwanted early side effects, such as ocular or laryngeal dystonia. It's hard to say whether the primary factor in this diminished resistance is the weakening of the will through neuroleptics or the relief of suffering through the sudden remission of psychotic symptoms. Even if, eventually, you get drug-induced

Parkinsonism or akathysia, both of which frequently prove to be torture for the patient, it is rare that the subject of medication weighs as heavily in conversations as it did in the beginning. It comes up more in therapeutic deliberations among colleagues. There, the main question is which measures are best in the struggle against the numerous but non-uniform side effects: prescription of anti-Parkinsons drugs, reduction of dosage, or changing to a less potent neuroleptic. How far can we go down without risking another psychotic flare-up? Is a depot neuroleptic the treatment of choice? The almost futile struggle against tardive dyskinesia: a judicious reduction or even an increased dosage, which can, in the very difficult cases, lead to a temporary remission of the dyskinesia? Questions questions – one needs a great deal of patience and also, naturally, experience to make the right choice. In any case, the time expenditure is enormous. The truth is, medicines are the number-one theme of my everyday clinical work. The written documentation of our labour in the patient files certainly reflects that reality. Straßmair's is an example of that, even if, in retrospect, the outpatient consultation is highly atypical. Discharge, and here, too, the Straßmair file is typical, is theme number *two* of all clinic discussions. It is difficult to make clear to the patient that even when the severest symptoms can be medically supressed, psychosis is a dangerous, protracted illness and requires treatment. Just imagine – my colleague Bögl often says to patients demanding release – if you had broken your foot, you'd have to lie in the hospital, maybe even in a cast, then you couldn't even move freely about the unit here. But what good does it do? Many patients simply feel locked in. No reasonable argument can combat this feeling, nor some witty broken bone story told in irrealis. What ought one say to these people? What should be done with them?

The more I reflect on these five files, the more hopeless I become. Viewed pessimistically, my job consists of two things: medication and discharge. But a person can't hold out with this sort of pessimism. Maybe these dreary notions are a starting point for me to change something, to become a better doctor. I haven't given up on myself, I haven't given up on my efforts. I also feel that powerful pull towards resignation that enslaves everyone here in the clinic. But I am fighting it. And I believe I can manage to do something, really, I'm convinced of it.

We draw close from the far distance, unconcerned with the laws of physics, cross millions of light years in a matter of seconds, plunge through the universe, pierce the earth's atmosphere, reach Europe, Berlin, the Café Größenwahn in the lethargy of a summer afternoon, and see them sitting, just as announced, at one of the oval tables, the two fast friends Goetz and G., and now, at a certain distance, we observe them, from the perspective of the gently gyrating ceiling fans, two young men immersed in what we were told was an important conversation.

The two of them plead in a rapid exchange, gesturing feverishly now and then, interrupting each another, and from the sentence fragments that rise up to us loud and clear, just as if we were sitting there with them at the table, we soon gather that psychiatry – no, we hadn't expected otherwise – was once more the matter at hand. Now G., with long blond curly hair, G., apparently the younger of the two, has broken off the stichomythia with a loudly exclaimed goddammit, and in the resulting silence, the sudden calm, has expressed himself not in truncated dialogue, but in protracted, often cumbersomely recondite sentences.

As he bolsters himself on all sides imaginable, we begin to grasp that G. champions a thesis Goetz openly contests: that the report on psychiatry Goetz has composed and submitted to G. to read, assess, and perhaps even to correct, is inherently mendacious, indeed, an assemblage of out and out lies at bottom, in that its, the report's, arguments strike out at precisely that which Goetz has constantly, without acknowledging it, capitalized on: namely, the fascination with madness. If you deny this, you are deceiving yourself, G. adds in the course of his monologue, which serves to explain and illustrate his thesis and closes with the appeal, hardly astonishing after what has been said, that to correct it would be senseless, that Goetz had best bring the whole undertaking to an end. I don't believe, G. adds after a brief moment's silence, that he, Goetz, by thematizing this state of affairs, even through a forthright exposition of his true, clandestine motives for making this report public, can escape the basic mendacity it betrays. Rather the opposite, in fact. With this kind of calculated intellectual manoeuvre, we hear G. continue – and our unease grows as we, being an instance of apprehension and recountal, seem ourselves to become objects of analysis and attack – any attempt at justification makes that which G., looking at things indulgently, might otherwise have viewed as a dilemma into what is, fundamentally, a lie, for now *intention* is married to deception. G. continues – and now we have begun to pull away – with this report, too, it is the same as always, inevitably the place intended for the supposed or ostensible greatest possible honesty is here the surest bastion for the lie.

And while Goetz, visibly older than G. but looking fashionable with his short hair, prepares for his defence,

9 4

strains to put forth his motives for the publication of his report, we leave, slightly disheartened, the phlegma of the Café Größenwahn, which has only frayed at that one table, then rise up into Berlin's misty air and vanish in the direction of the nevernever.

Torturous rumination on my guilt. Awake with both the spasmodic twitching of my left leg and this rumination, awake this way before the grey of morning, yearning for sleep, for a numbing of thoughts and body. Under the cover, feel for the leg, the alien machine, fuelled by medication, unrelenting. Suddenly the feeling of the dick in the hand, today limp, strange fibres of flesh in my fist, sin, uproot, annihilate, annihilate it all. Longing for stasis. Struggling for sleep, wide-awake, forced to brood without respite. Yesterday's euphoria, I know exactly where the fault lies, euphoria after Schimmer's admission, though I knew right away I would have to atone again, an inescapable mood of joy and arousal in me, hope, hope for love, hope that everything, everything might turn around, against all reason, this treacherous hope, against all expectation, my God, I plead for mercy, for redemption.

For unreal hours, Schimmer and I were a pair. Tightly we embraced, we walked back and forth down the unit hallway, Schimmer manic, sweeping me away. How much, what have I told him about myself? Everything, it must have been everything. Schimmer talked as though driven, about an assignment, a secret mission, conspiracy, crazy, it seemed to me at first, until I grasped the system of references, the orders and dissimulations. Once it was dark out, I could see us mirrored in the tall windows with their many panes, doubled, quadrupled, a simply ridiculous pair, just impossible, all this, I refused to believe it, and the mirror image, multiplied as though scornful, shouted it back at me. Me, old and fat, bloated, disfigured from years of medication, and on my arm, Schimmer, a boy really, just a boy, beautiful like a thing from a dream, mature, manly, but tender at the same time. Of course, I could already foresee today's despair sneering at me, but I felt the drive more strongly, this ungovernable force. I pressed Schimmer's hand against my stiff member. How long have I gone without arousal? Is this not the root of my illness? For a man, it isn't normal to be deprived of sex, not even to feel the longing uncoupled from oppressive guilt. The reproachful stares of the nurses yesterday, then the explicit rebuke from Doctor Pfeiffer before leaving the unit, after yesterday's visit from the Medical Director: Pull yourself together, man, you'll be miserable again tomorrow. What could I say? I know he was right, but at the same time, not everything is right.

This afternoon my wife comes, already someone will have told her about last night's events, and as usual, we will sit across from each other wordless in the hallway, and she will try, frantic, forced, to hold my hand, wanting to understand, but clueless, and the feeling of disgust that will descend upon me will only augment the weight of my guilt and the silence and the motorlike twitching in my legs. All that needs to stop, forever. You should just burn the sex out of me, I say to Pfeiffer, Doctor, burn it out, whether in my brain or down there, it doesn't matter, but instead, they stuff me full of antidepressants and lock me up here. Because I'm desperate, I must live among the mad, I've spent countless months of my life in institutions, years, if you add it all up, and I have only become more and more desperate. Brutal torture, rigorously enforced: the institution suppresses any sort of sexuality far more harshly than the outside. Not in spite of, but rather *because* I am a special case, I see this suppression's consequences on almost all of my fellow patients. For nurses and doctors, sexuality is *inexistent*, it isn't there at all, for them there is only illness, the normal, and the insane. I believe many here are not mentally ill, but sexually ill, like me. Schimmer has stirred all of that up in me again. For years I've told the doctors, destroy my sexuality and I could become healthy, I know I would be healthy after that. And they say to me, pull yourself together, once you're no longer depressed, everything will be back in order with your sexuality, too. And I have to sleep with my wife until everything falls apart again, hold back my disgust at this black, bloody, stinking cunt that devours everything.

I told Schimmer all this yesterday. I believe he understood me. My life, I said, is a battle against the drive and the constantly growing weaknesses and guilt, pure guilt. Absurd, he said, you've got to enjoy sex. And for a few unreal euphoric hours, I too wanted to believe it was possible. Today, again, my hopes are shattered. The morning asphyxiates me. The repulsive light of daybreak filters down on those sleeping around me. Who will help me make it through the day? No one answers. Why doesn't anyone answer? Why does no one want to help? Silence and stillness, the torment of morning. I want to sleep, to think nothing, to dream nothing, to sleep forever.

Scene in the virgin forest, massive trees, I must climb them, why? There are lianas, Clemens seems to be there too, and everything binds me, incomprehensibly but all the more sternly to my double calling, I must, I must continue, constantly in movement, awakened again and again, over and over back to the trees, floundering this way the whole night, half-asleep, half-awake, knowing that I should, I must write all this down, it is, in an illuminating, incontrovertible way, a part of the novel.

Why all cosmic? Why the nevernever? Punk's not dead, it just smells funny. From the Größenwahn to the Lipstick, in due time, yeah right, on to Damage. Should I tell you the story about Nine Finger Joe, about how not long ago, he caught a beatdown at the Größenwahn – ? Just a moment, now, just a moment. Babylon, Punk & Psychiatry, everything's Babylon. Screw Babylon, not Babylon, Berlin, nah, Munich, big city and Mickey Mouse, nothing soft, nothing green, no grain fields and country, none of that shit, get it, no discussion, no liberaaation, riot roughhousing and anarchy. Words, words, vomit, hogwash, insightful words psychiatry vomitvomit the head brainfucker doesn't get nothing, just hogwash vomitvomit. I don't say nothing, I pounce.

OK, OK, so now, can I tell you now the story about Nine Finger Joe? So Nine Finger Joe, they call him Nine Finger Joe 'cause he's missing the middle finger on his right hand, and anyway, he's sitting with friends at the Größenwahn drinking a beer, same as the rest of us. At some point he asks me if I can take him to the Lipstick later, 'cause I used to have this ride, an old Mercedes. Nah, I say, sorry, I had to sell it a long time back, it was costing me too much. Got it, says Nine Finger Joe, and he turns back to his friends, and I do the same. We drink our beer, we get to talking, what can I say? The kind of shit you talk about at 11.30 at night.

Suddenly Nine Finger Joe, I didn't even know he'd left, comes walking across the room and sits down at his table, and he looks upset. Hi left eye's bloodshot and his eyelid is swollen, his shoulders and arms are scratched up, his undershirt's dirty, he must have been on the ground, what's up there, Nine Finger Joe? Nine Finger Joe is talking and laughing with his friends, I can't understand them, though, unfortunately, the music is too loud, I just see that his eye is swelling closed little by little, but Nine Finger Joe laughs and orders a beer and he's a hero. Later he goes to the bathroom and comes back washed up, wet and dripping all over, and now that he's clean, he looks even more messed up than before. Finally, it's a little before one, most people are taking off, and I ask him what really happened, and while I stare in disbelief into his Elephant Man face, he tells me the following story, in these exact words: It was a friend of mine, actually, this dude I met today. We were getting along, we had a bit to drink, not much, and the question kept coming up of how hard each of us was. He went on about how hard he was, I told him how hard I was, and then it came to who was hardest. At some point I said to him we could just step outside and fight it out, and that way we could see who was hardest. OK, he says, right, that way we'll know who's hardest. So we went outside here, outside the Größenwahn, and right away his pulls out his stiletto, a big mother, like *this* long, and tells me step up, and I say, if he's so hard, what's he need that thing for. OK, he says, puts his blade on the ground, comes up, and hits me two, three times in the face before I even have the chance to look. Then I fell down and he kicked me a couple of times with his pointy shoes. I was done at that point, I mean obviously, once you've hit the ground, you're done. OK, I say to myself, so he's the harder one, faster one more than anything, but nothing's broken, I'll be the lucky one next time, wait and see! – Nine Finger Joe laughs at me with his one good eye, there too the sclera was bloodshot, the capillaries burst, and then he walks to the exit, all laid back, his leather jacket hanging off of one shoulder. I think of the pain that must be raging in his face, in his body, and of the pointlessness of the question of who's hardest.

Three weeks later, at an XTC concert, when it was my turn to catch one in the face, almost all I could make out in my beer-clouded mind was pain and rage, indescribable rage, I ran my tongue along the row of bottom teeth, I'd been hit but they all were still there, I felt a deep wound on the inner side of my lip, and I hoped the blood wouldn't run out of my mouth, I didn't want to give the other guy the victory. It had something to do with Mary's honour, at least in his eyes; you ask me, Mary tried to get off with me like an idiot and I lurched away, end of story. But the dude said, anybody who offends my Mary's honour is a dead man. So naturally I had to laugh, and then my number came up. Once his fist in my mouth had restored Mary's honour, after the heaving, tangling, and getting pulled back from friends on both sides, one of the girls standing around sweet-talked my opponent and me, held out a plastic cup of beer, the other guy took a sip, she said to me everything cool everything all right, are we even?, and gave me the cup, I took a sip in turn, and when my rage started to cool down, I said OK, all good. For hours afterward, this anger seethed inside me, and even outwardly, I couldn't manage that image of calm composure that Nine Finger Joe had told his story with that night at the Größenwahn, when he'd fought his new friend over the question of which one was hardest and ended up with a swollen black eye.

Concentrated solely on looking, on the observation of a scene that struck him as highly modern and at the same time medieval, nothing but an eye, as he so often had been, and thus ill-equipped to *cooperate* with the demand the supervising physician had framed as a question, Raspe had, without resistance, from his assigned position, pulled the hair aside from the temple of the anaesthetized patient and exposed for the head doctor the best possible position for the left electrode smeared with turquoise gel, and already, as he stepped back, he saw the face of the patient spasm under the effects of the electric current, twitching into grimaces and frowns, again, he was just watching, spellbound, but uninvolved, and with horror he saw he had unconsciously become a perpetrator. The step was barely noticeable from bystander to perpetrator, from observation to participation, Raspe thought. He took another step back, followed the supervising physician's gaze down to the patient's bare feet, and watched the two repellently filthy big toes arch up slowly towards the head; at the same time, just as slowly, the other toes stretched forward, as the soles of the feet turned in; and they remained there thus, in this corkscrewed position, for a few seconds, until the supervising physician turned with a curt, unpleasant, well now, and the patient's body gradually relaxed.

While the effects of the Thiopenal, a short-acting anaesthetic, slowly and insensibly subsided, the patient, still ventilated with an Ambi-Bag, began snapping for air, choking, and coughing, and the anaesthetist vacuumed viscous, green-grey slime from his throat, shouting the patient's name repeatedly and smacking him on the cheek with the flat of her opposite hand; the supervising physician grabbed a cellulose towel from the back, glanced at the patient, then at Raspe, and began to speak, as though in passing, while meticulously wiping the turquoise gel from his electrodes: Unfortunately it didn't pan out right, the shock, did you notice? The toes, sure, like I told you, but ordinarily, if the shock was effective, you'd expect the Babinski reflex to be readily apparent. Anyway, he did have it, so maybe I pulled it off, you know, it's a matter of knack and experience; the eternal dilemma, shock too much and the organic shock syndrome lasts longer, but if you stay under the seizure threshold, either with the voltage or the duration, if you don't provoke an attack, in other words, then you get no retrograde amnesia, right, and the patient remembers the procedure, remembers the fear and the pain, which the retrograde amnesia eradicates with a successful shock, and that is the quandary, the balancing act whenever you shock someone. He looked up from the electrodes, pinned Raspe in his gaze, and added, with a jut of his chin towards the now responsive, but dumbfounded patient: So with this one, I'll definitely bump it up tomorrow, not so much with the duration as with the voltage, given how much variation you get from one patient to the next, it's good to assign the same doctor to shock the same patient every time, we do that too here, because you have to make these adjustments based on individual differences, especially when you're doing it by hand, when you decide the duration of the current based on your own experience instead of using a pre-programmed setting, that changes according to the situation, you just see how much is needed and leave the electrodes on that amount of time, but that's harder, of course, when you're first getting started just plug it all into the machine beforehand, OK.

The supervising physician finished cleaning the electrodes, and while Raspe cursed him in his thoughts, he uttered this last, broken sentence, and turned to the electroshock machine, a Konvulsator 2077 S from the firm

Siemens, opening the thick book beside it to enter the day's notes: the patient's name, the electrical intensity employed, the duration of the shock, and the technique. You know, speaking of technique, this machine here allows for a gentle, glissando approach, we can do it that way here now, you sort of creep up, starting with thirty per cent power, and the voltage rises constantly, all this in a matter of milliseconds, until, after a predetermined time, you reach full electrical intensity, and that is really an elegant technique, gentle, it leads to fewer secondary effects, same as with the principle of oscillating direct current they used to induce seizures years ago, we don't just shoot current into the brain, this is something that is being continually, scientifically refined, this machine here, which we're working with now, I believe we just got it three months ago, and it represents the newest generation equipment available, the newest we have on the market here in Germany.

After the supervising physician asked the nurse for the next patient's name, he interrupted his explanation to turn his full attention to the dials and buttons on the Konvulsator. Furious with himself, knowing that his will-less compliance in the placement of the left electrode was what had facilitated that contemptible chummy tone, indeed had actually elicited that tone which the physician had never employed with him before, Raspe thought he might wander off without attracting notice. When he had almost made it past the open wing doors they'd just shoved the patient through on his gurney, the supervising physician asked him: Wouldn't you like to stay a while longer? Four, we have four more to go. At which Raspe turned, responded in the negative, and added, by way of explanation, a bit too sheepishly, as he immediately noticed, again in conflict with himself,

103

you'll have to excuse me, they're expecting me back in the unit. Then he left, with quick striding steps, abandoned the torture chamber in the furthest corner of the topmost floor of the clinic, turned towards his unit, towards a more familiar horror. After descending into hell, he came back to the realm of psychopharmacology, of the soft laws of being and movement beneath the dictates of neuroleptics, as though to a place of calm, of tranquillity and clement hope.

R: Now trema, trema dilemma!
YOU: You just brought up questions about haloes. What do you mean there?
R: Yeah, for example, if you mean questions of sex positions, or expositions of questions.
YOU: What are you trying to say there?
R: File hound, just listen, file hound.
YOU: Yes, and?
R: Yes and, what's that mean, yes and, you file hound.
YOU: If you –
R: If you how you you see TV, could you prithee explain that to me?
YOU: –
R: And now you are calm and instead of just listening. So actually you could hear these syncopes, and that's why you upset me.
YOU: When you say –
R: Say, convey, waylay, as I say, syncopes, hippies beat flat like a manta ray I say.
YOU: It seems to me that this *yes*, yes I believe –
R: Calm down, I'm saxing, cybernetic, sperm bank, stereotactic, prophylaxis, parallax, para lallia lexia lallia andyouandyouandyou, and you, my dear, say YEAHSO!

YOU: I believe, yes, I believe –
R: What what?
YOU: What interests me here above all is your, is this *Yes to the Modern World*.
R: For real?
YOU: Yes, this *Yes to the Modern World* I do somehow find quite interesting.
R: Yeahyeah you flatbrain, oopsy daisy! Crazy! You tremor trema, that's my trema dilemma.

Even if people didn't immediately understand everything when Doctor Karl Held spoke... – still, a thinking subject can only bear the endless demand for proof of his own productivity by incorporating as a life goal the *path to success* endorsed by this same demand, thus evaluating himself according to his demonstrated *efficiency*, and boasting of all manifest or unfairly ignored indications of this effectiveness to such a degree that this boastfulness quite logically terminates in *megalomania*. The harder it is to trace the way back from the radical alternatives to bourgeois self-consciousness towards its functional mode of operation, the less need there is for the *madhouses* to worry about a reduction in the flow of cast-offs coming to them from the world of the upright and prosperous. The individual spirit's frantic attempts to prod itself towards ideological constructs that are an affront to empirical knowledge, but for that very reason are new and *original*, become something like blockbusters getting hyped at a book fair, or like a sadistic murderer who may bask in the warm glow of public attention, so long as he carves up his victims with sufficient panache. And for the sake of this attention, which is easily accorded to any extravagance, the kids give it all up, turn their clothing and hairstyles into lifestyle markers that distinguish them from the masses, and then run around calling themselves *preppies* or *punks* and push this show of self-presentation to the point that they end up brawling in the streets, standing up for a meaning they claim as their own, a meaning –

Meaning, you thought, exactly, finding a meaning for life, a path instead of this erratic meandering, and you felt, as so many times before, a longing to participate in the discernment and perspective Karl Held's words seemed to promise, to participate, which you could do by joining that organization, whose members you were sitting with, one among hundreds, by becoming one of the probable thousands who would, through self-sacrifice and intensive theoretical labour, carry out revolutionary praxis, and who were rewarded with meaning in their lives, changing the world!, meaning, as the evidence around him demonstrated conclusively.

Extorting a promise is pointless. I have to promise I won't do anything to myself. Otherwise I won't be released. Your word, Dr Eben says, you must give me your word. Dr Eben doesn't understand that I have to get out of here, and now. A person in my position would promise any- and everything, I believe.

I'm not mentally ill, my soul is ill.

I'm very frightened. The current of my thoughts is growing fiercer. I will destroy everything. Not like before: snuff out, drift off, sleep forever. This time, I must demolish and dismember it. No part of my body can remain intact. My body is the lie. In me, inside me, everything is shattered. I am being devoured and dismembered from within. Fear and delapidation, that is all that remains in me. The lie is insufferable. I will clear it away. I will annihilate and dismember my body.

A promise extorted is as good as no promise at all.

Walking beneath trees, high, scraggy furs, forgetting about the clinic. My soul is a wound, nothing more, and they've closed me up among the insane. They've taken everything from me, clothes, handbag, even my lipstick. You want to make yourself pretty? For who, then? Here? You need to just get better. I could barely raise my eyelids, not to mention my head. I wanted to talk, I was mute. Already I was defenceless, and then they humiliated me further. Around me, fellow patients, babbling, bellowing senselessly. Never will I return there, no, I won't go back. The forest floor is black. Tree trunks flit past. Branches strike me, sometimes they scratch my face. I feel no pain. In the distance, I hear the rush of the roadway. Barely hear it, rather I feel it. Westerly wind, presumably, westerly wind. I search for the tracks.

You can swallow a lie, up to a point.

Who leaves no one behind, also hurts no one. Dr Eben is a young man. He has all the women patients fighting over him. He looks at them all with the same benevolent regard. In a conversation once, I told him: Music is my life. For the first and only time, he truly looked at me and said: Oh, that's very interesting. Then he fell silent. I remember. I don't want to be found after a few weeks in my apartment, a stinking cadaver. Before couldn't have cared less. But when I think to myself how Treppesch gawks from her flat, or Mr Heckl. I won't let them win, not like that.

Solitude is also freedom.

Is that the train I hear? I think I've got lost. I can't imagine just calmly laying your head on the tracks and waiting. You wait, and the humming on the tracks grows ever louder. You have to close your eyes. It goes on, even after the brakes start to squeal. Who knows how long.

Then, only then, is it over. The longed-for total annihilation, the only one conceivable.

Clear as ever, I see it all before me. Everything with the pension fell through. Music: my grand, lifelong deception. Migraines aren't enough to justify early retirement. If you spend days without speaking a word to another soul, you must listen to music. Until I left work, I thought music, my beloved music, gave everything meaning. But nothing gives meaning. There is no meaning when you live as I do. I know all that, despite medicine. Medicine has loosened the stiffness in my body. I can lift my head again. In the forest, I can walk. I am weary. The trains thunder past.

It is as if I could hear the screams of the insane. I hear them screaming. A life without meaning must be exterminated. At the same time: dreadful fear, fear, nothing but fear. Every time a train comes near, I see myself run up the embankment and jump in front of the engine car. No, no music, just the wails of the insane. The sky has gone dim. Twilight?

Dark.

TWO

INSIDE

'In the course of events, all will be made clear.'

One evening, or was it late afternoon, when the heat of the expired but the unseasonably warm spring day still lingered on the bushes, the lawn, and the gravel path, Raspe, again in an unaccountably excellent mood, found himself on a park bench in the clinic's inner courtyard next to Kiener, who had taken to calling himself Hegel, exchanging the odd sardonic remark. Nothing loomed over him. Oh, how nice the afternoon is, thought Raspe, a song ringing in his ear. Melodies, music – why fight against it? He felt the warm air seep into his body, the sky blue and high, cosmic unity, and with the warmth, the scent of the earth. His left arm he saw as foreign, draped in a white lap coat, lying on one knee. And the hand that emerged from the lab coat, pale skin crisscrossed with veins – is that supposed to be mine? Then it grew smaller and smaller and vanished. Everything wants to be naked, Raspe said, stood up from the bench, pulled off his lab coat, walked on to the black swatch of newly tilled rose bed, lay on the soil, and buried his face in it.

Was that the end? Who knows. Raspe had lost his footing. It was so sunny. Raspe sat in the park with the crazies, for hours, whole afternoons, talking or saying nothing, moving from bench to bench, and up above, the wind whipped through the thick trees. Yes, thought Raspe, yesyes.

The clinic director had asked to see him. Raspe didn't go. What was he supposed to tell the man? The unit physician sought him out. Time was, Raspe would have gone up there and given the director a straight shot to the balls, torn off the mask of his tanned face and his thick, snow-white hair along with it. But what good will come of uncloaking the director, Raspe asked himself?

Sometimes Raspe felt for his keys. The keys were still there. Are the keys still there? Then Raspe would have to feel for them again. Kiener talked about bodyguards and about Uno. – Are bodyguards legal here in Germany? – Yeah, said Raspe, why. – Good, great, said Kiener, because in fifty-five years, I'm done with Uno. I'll have made enough money by then to pay for any bodyguard out there. Then Kiener laughed, and Raspe laughed, too. And so the days passed by.

At times, Raspe might sink into brooding. How long had he been there? The job, the profession, unprecedented torment. Raspe looked for reasons. Panic overcame him. But from where – there was no past. Then the impervious calm returned, dispassionate, again he knew the pain was far away, everything inside him had been uprooted. Raspe waited, unthinking. Yes, wait. Time passed. At some point, everything stops.

1.

Lord and master of his thoughts and deeds, Raspe had entered the clinic months before for the first time, at half-past seven in the morning, with a euphoria it was difficult to suppress. It was early summer. Hyperpunctual, Raspe paced beneath the lindens in the clinic quarter for a few minutes, aimless, almost lost, but with an intensely lucid mind soaking in this occasion, this historical occasion, he thought, which was one with the scent of the lindens and the clear summer morning air, the ample promise Raspe displayed of victory and confidence: finally, it begins. You can triumph. Onward and upward, whatever I do, it will turn out well.

And so Raspe set foot in the clinic, perilously ecstatic, almost drunk, approaching his assignment, his first job; and in the darkness of the entrance, acclimated to the light, his eyes resisted, too long, it struck him, and he could make out nothing but coolness, height, breadth, grandiosity.

Did he know why then? Why psychiatry? You look into the future, Raspe thought, and all you see is glistening fog, no form, only promise. Raspe was, in his mid-twenties, unbroken. He expected everything, not knowing what everything was.

A lab coat was issued with his name on the breast pocket. Raspe was now *Dr Raspe*. He was given his keys, various forms to fill out. Careful, watch your head, said the doctor who led Raspe officiously down assorted floors and hallways, separated by heavy wooden doors coated in dark lacquer, which you had to unlock with keys and then carefully pull shut behind you: the upper world showy and imperial, while down below, in the bowels, lay narrow, twisting tunnels, a subterranean secret network, washing here and cooking there, watch your head, careful, careful.

After this first guided visit through the clinic, which addressed organizational necessities – this is where you change your lab coat, this is where you get your cafeteria vouchers – but also constituted a sort of cursory orientation – up here we do the occupational therapy, over there the electroshock – after the odd introduction, this is Dr Raspe, our new colleague, faces fleeting past, handshakes, unremembered names – Raspe sat at the desk assigned to him in the doctors' station of Unit One-Four – the men's locked ward – and looked through the many panes of the antique windows out into the summer trees. No sooner was he there than he wished to flee. No, Raspe told himself softly, get on with the work.

He was supposed to talk to a patient named Grahl,

whom the police had brought in Saturday afternoon because, according to them, he had beaten his wife, threatened to tear his son into pieces, and, such were the policemen's precise words, had coerced his wife violently into sexual intercourse. So his first patient, Unit Physician Doctor Bögl said with a laugh, was also a danger to the public. Bögl was a small man, mid-thirties maybe, with thin blond hair and a high forehead. He had greeted Raspe very warmly with an outstretched hand and had jovially, cordially declared: No formalities here, I'm Waldemar. Sure, Raspe said, my name's Raspe.

After reading the police report, Raspe left the doctors' station, not through the doors that led to the nurses' station, where Bögl had introduced him to the nurses on duty, and where the glass partition opening on to the hallway offered a glimpse of gawking patients, nor through the door to the stairwell Bögl hurried off through, unbeknownst to the patients and nurses, but rather through the third point of egress, which led directly to the patients' common room and dining area: a set of padded double doors that muffled the noise from the patients while at the same time affording the doctors the directest possible access to them, in case of emergency. The sick people, too, Raspe quickly understood, hoped this door would grant them direct access to the doctors, but naturally, they could not open it without a key and had to knock, and never knew, because of the door to the stairwell, whether the doctors' station was occupied or empty, and whether their inconsequential knocking was failing to reach anyone's ears or whether the doctors were simply ignoring it, as was frequently the case, particularly when they took their coffee breaks at mid-morning or in the afternoon. Enraged by the uncertainty, a patient would sometimes hurl his body against the outer door with a crash, until finally one of the doctors would stand up from the coffee table with a groan, open the first door, and jerk it shut behind him while opening the second, to obstruct the patient's view of his colleagues at their coffee, to whom, after offering the patient a few words of consolation, he would return, with a smile, at times with a guilty conscience. The nurses did nothing to curb these outbursts on the patients' part; being themselves at the patients' beck and call, they were incensed at the doctors' constant absences from the unit, sometimes on the grounds of pressing necessity, sometimes with no justification whatsoever.

Still ignorant of the special purpose of the double doors, Raspe walked through them as if through an airlock that led to another world.

Silence and severity surrounded Raspe now, ghastly stagnation, none of the things he had expected and had steeled himself against, none of the raucous mindless agitation. Nothing but a hit song at medium volume coming from the left. There was an old radio there. Next to it, dozing on the couch, lay a young man in a dark blue tracksuit with white stitching, whose angular arms and legs gave an impression of dynamism, of readiness to jump. But no movement, all was sluggish dilapidation. Raspe saw various pairs of eyes, gazing at him stoic and indifferent, and from the idle ill cowering in the easy chairs and stools, and up on the ledges of the windows, a storm of angst whirled into his mind.

In haste, Raspe walked across the room. There, with swift steps, his torso huddled over, a man emerged from the dormitory, very grave and grim, stopped in front of Raspe, tugged at one of his sleeves, and warned him softly, but with the greatest urgency: Quick, Doctor, quick, poison, everything's poisoned, no one can pin this poisoning on me, understand! Then he laughed, like a child, without a care, into Raspe's face and walked back the way he came, looking both threatening and threatened, to the dormitory. That was Kiener. Raspe followed him, almost relieved.

Yes, a dormitory, a proper place to sleep. How many beds did Raspe see, fifteen, nineteen? Many, in snug rows, arranged perpendicular to the wall, and immediately, unavoidably, Raspe caught a whiff of egg soup, the same kind they had made him eat under threat of punishment back at Achatswies where, repulsed, he had forced it down before vomiting it into his dish, and the nurse at the children's home, a nasty piece of work, had ordered him to spoon it up, and he had naturally vomited again, then was ordered to eat again, and so forth. Unfathomable rules, unfathomable laws of an unfathomable institution, overwhelming. Laws of torture? An annihilation institution? – Yes, thought Raspe, a proper place to sleep.

In its centre, with stiff, obsessive movements, Kiener walked back and forth, his head now sunken, apparently ruminating – was that true? – or else in a dumbshow of earnestness. (I am the philosopher, must bear the weight of the world on my shoulders, guilt suffering stupidity bad intentions. No: I'm performing, in my patient disguise, the role of the thinker, to save the sick from their insanity. But when I am acting, who is the director, and vice versa? Is there really a threat of poisoning, and if so, who does it concern? And who is the perpetrator? Why? Possibly, someone is playing a prank on me. Right: Act out all the possibilities, no looking back, think everything away.) Kiener took no more notice of Raspe. Aimlessly Raspe scrutinized assorted patients lying drowsy, dozing, on their made beds, and they left a distinct impression from the ones in the first room: they didn't look squalid, but actually sick. Who is Grahl? Where is he? Doctor Raspe, Raspe thought, and saw himself like a stranger in that unfamiliar lab coat, Doctor Raspe is looking for his first patient and no one cares, but still, it could be different, everything could be utter chaos. He could just beat it, save your own skin, and the others, Waldemar Bögl and the extremely friendly Medical Director (How happy I am that you are now one of our collea –) would ask themselves if they were still in their right minds, if that Raspe had not been just an illusion lasting half a day, no, of course not, no one would ask that, anyway, Kiener would also vouch that he was there. A vague angst led Raspe to these calculations. He should do something. A nurse will be able to help. In the dormitory, no nurses were to be seen.

Raspe walked on towards the hallway, and exhaling with relief, he entered the realm of the living. Here there was talking, joking, playing, people walked around smoking cigarettes, it seemed to Raspe just then as though they were strolling on a corso in the Italian afternoon, and outside visitors mingled with the patients. But the difference was unmistakeable: however lively the patients seemed, every movement was hushed, muted, as though the laws of physics that reigned there were different, with gravity multiplied and time slowed down. They seemed to have granite in their bodies. And the patients strolling on the corso pressed tight against the wall, shuffling and straggling, advancing as though by compulsion; gait mechanical, bereft of purpose, the patients' parade filed past down the hall. If Raspe had believed, after emerging from the double doors in the doctors' station, that he had plunged into psychiatry's deepest horrors, rigidity destitution silence; and if, after passing the dormitory, illness's abode, and stepping finally on to the promenade of life, psychiatry's warm side, in a way, he felt full of confidence again (he would find this Grahl, talk to him, heal him, yes!); now, after no more than a second's observation of this simulacrum of life, he was not at all certain which was more horrible, that first room with its oppressive stillness or the nightmare movements here, or whether everything, all of it, was equally horrible, and again, so much so confusing all at once, panic vaporized his thoughts, dissolved, me?, away –. Did Raspe now shut his eyes?

Soon there was a nurse there. – Mr Grahl, of course. Come with me, please, he's been standing there by the door since he was admitted. He won't say why, no, he won't say anything.

Later: almost everyone has talked about him these past two days, especially the patients. Naturally they too wanted to welcome him, just like everyone else. One or two even went up to him, offered him a smoke, but he looks straight through you. And if you say something to him, after a few seconds, he closes his eyes. Word's got around, people are sure he's totally bonkers. I'd like to know what's happening inside someone like that, one of the younger patients seems to have said. What's going on in someone like that? He stands there like a pillar and says nothing. Is a person like that actually thinking? Is he suffering? Maybe, another said, in a state like that, you just don't feel anything anymore. But he must see something, he's got his eyes open most of the time. He seems to hear, too, because he shuts his eyes whenever anyone addresses him. His face is rigid, never stirs. Gotta wonder what goes on in a head like that. How can someone just stand there for hours without moving, even physically, without the muscles getting exhausted? That was what people were saying here and there, the nurses told him. Experienced patients, the regulars, as we call them, who kept coming back here over and over, who even insisted on being brought back to our unit during intake, those were the only ones who hadn't been part of these discussions. They understood. No one had wished to discourage Raspe by assigning him a hard case, but to Bögl, a difficult start seemed the only right one, in effect it was *always* the right one, and especially, of course, when it came to psychiatry. Did he, Raspe, see it in the same way? Regardless, he needed only note down in his examination report what he had *seen*, that was absolutely the most important thing, observation, that's what Bögl's professor of internal medicine, old Grünhofer, always stressed, and rightly, that all medicine begins with observation, and this phrase, which he'd learned at the beginning of his career, still today, more than ten years later, defined his medical practice, and he himself passed this phrase down to his younger colleagues, to Raspe, for example, who, as he'd said before, ought only consider what he'd seen, write it down, presumably he was familiar with the terminology, later of course they could talk about everything, talk it through, he, Bögl, was obviously ready to help however he could, that went without saying, when it came to the younger colleagues, no need to ask –. This was how Bögl talked to himself. And Raspe leaned forward, grabbed the coffee cup on the round table in the doctors' station, took a sip, set the cup back on the table, and leaned into his chair. Later, he took another sip, and then another. Bögl, in the meantime, went on talking, uninterrupted by Raspe.

At last, Raspe was alone. Bögl left a phone number,

then vanished through the door to the stairwell, for a few seconds steps could be heard walking away outside, and then, as Raspe pulled himself wearily from his chair to walk over to the desk, Bögl opened the door again, stuck his head, just his head, inside, and again, cordial and relentless, a torrent of words about Raspe fell from his lips, but the latter retained nothing save the assurance that Bögl was always available should something unforeseen occur in the unit, and Raspe, standing there calmly and barely nodding his head, waited out the untold qualifications about how unlikely such an incident was at that hour and further reiterations of Bögl's commitment to be ever at the ready for him. What was this man even saying? Once Bögl's head had disappeared and the door was again closed from outside, finally?, Raspe stared into the void. Oh oh.

No, the terminology was not familiar to Raspe in the least. Incidents were not to be expected. But he had read so much. He saw the textbooks, the critical textbooks, political as well as poetic works on psychiatry and the beauty of madness. He saw himself reading, like it was an infection. Some pathogens leave behind an immunity, others weakness and susceptibility. He would study medical records. A lexicon is something one can learn. He'd had no choice in medicine, psychiatry was the only thing possible. *That* was what the books had taught him. No thoughts before now regarding questions of terminology, just stories, fates, institutions in decay, but also, in the distance, shreds of hope; back then, when he would, Raspe would think, you just have to strike out with strength and courage and in that way make your hopes into reality. Grahl fell silent and was standing motionless at the door. All at once, inside you, the books fall silent, too. Observation is the opposite of accepted terminology. Bögl insisted on both and grasped nothing. Still, Raspe thought, learn the vocabulary. At the same time, don't give up the observation. Most likely Bögl's not a complete idiot. Don't dismiss anything, learn to see the contradictions.

So Raspe opened one of the case files lying strewn across the desk and started to read. He didn't read. He looked at the words. Thoughts marched through his head. Discipline, Raspe said to himself: You must and you can. In vain – he felt the weakness, less weariness than erosion and the flagging resistance before the bonfire of images and the volley of words that first day at the clinic. Attack, thought Raspe, storm against the storm, think in order not to be thought. Reading must be possible. Reading is always possible. Raspe picked up the next file at random and laid it over the first open one. He looked at the blue cover, at the top, where in large blue letters the words *University Psychiatric Clinic* were printed. At last, a doctor, no longer a student. A university career need not be a disgrace. I want to become a professor. I want to become the most extraordinary, most unbelievable professor. I will revolutionize German psychiatry. I will acquire the necessary vocabulary, this very evening. Reflexively, Raspe's hand jerked as the telephone rang, but he held off. Not yet. Shrill sounds from the grey apparatus, and disorder spread over the desk. On a doctor's desk I expect order, and a softly chiming telephone. Everything is shouting at me. Then the apparatus fell silent once more. Raspe could hear the birds. A reprimand is unlikely. Could that have been the aforementioned incident? At any rate, one must reckon on disturbances. A name had been written on the case file in a felt-tipped pen, on the left in upper-case letters: the family name, then a comma, then the first name, with the birthdate underneath. Raspe would like very much to have a long, sonorous name. Raspe would rather be called Martinius than Raspe. One of his future colleagues had introduced himself as Hippius. The name lingered in Raspe's memory. Professor Hippius had a nicer ring to it than Professor Raspe. Important for names: sonority and exoticism. On the other hand, the most sympathetic psychiatrist he had come across in the course of his studies was named Berger. Superficial, stupid thoughts are being thought inside me, thought Raspe. Back then, two years ago, Professor Berger was only thirty-five, and already he had become a professor. You can have an exemplary university career and not betray yourself. Berger is proof. Emulate Berger, Raspe thought. His eyes, he noted, had been thoroughly engrossed in the Resopal surface of his desk. For how long? Garish turquoise, dreadful, vulgar wood grain. At that moment, once more, the torment of disorder, the birds. And to top it off, I'm supposed to deal with emergencies on my own. Raspe stood up and closed the window. Out there, in the unit, none of the windows had handles. And the door handles didn't stick out to one side, they pointed downward. A person could hang himself from a normal door handle. With the door handles in the psychiatric unit, any sort of ligature, even a sheet or a power cord, would slip off. – Suicide prophylaxis is one of the least pleasant, but also most important tasks on a locked ward, Bögl had said. For more than five months now, we have not had a single successful suicide attempt here, that is a number to be proud of. Bögl's logorrhoea. Bögl has to be stopped, tomorrow if possible. Bögl talks and talks and ought to shut up while Grahl, whom Raspe has to speak with, says nothing. An out-and-out maniac the day before yesterday and today he's silent, impenetrable. Was he looking outside? Raspe had followed Grahl's gaze to the frosted glass of the hall window and had seen that in that window another window was visible, cracked open, so you could make out an iron grating, metalwork with flourishes, and past it the leaves of a tree and thick branches. But Grahl's eyes, fixed on that point, had been empty. That is the gaze of blinded eyes. Dazzled, blinded, why? Grahl had let his eyelids slowly sink, his mask-like mien unaltered, and then had held his eyes closed. What is happening in that head? For Raspe, theory seemed to have sunken quickly, inexorably away.

The blue file lay before Raspe, still unopened, and he looked up from the clumsy felt-tipped script. A window to the east. Trees, trees in the middle of the city, and high and red, the leaves gather the slanting late light. Tomorrow morning, yes, tomorrow, the morning sun would invade the room. Raspe had not yet reached Grahl. Grahl seemed unreachable. Raspe opened the file, felt the hunger for air, took a deep breath, more air, and opened a window. Now a cigarette. The smoke he exhaled drifted slowly outside and was immediately pulled into the open. A wind blew in. Work unthinkable. Then that suction again, drawing him outside. Raspe struggled. Who will turn off the radio if I leave now? Deafening, again, the birds, the screeching, that was the tram, and Raspe stood there, skinned alive.

Later, Raspe was back at the desk, and night had fallen. It's pointless, Raspe knew. Thoughts marched through his head, and the turquoise green Resopal surface suffused his hands with neon light. Raspe sat idly.

2.

Just a weakening of the spirits?

A restrained whirr of voices, their centre hardly discernible, but restless, rushing back and forth among the assembled doctors, swift as a swarm of flies, filling the space of the library, a stately, dark-panelled hall, until the Ordinarius at the head of the massive table raised his head, and presently – break – silence reigned. Good morning, Professor Reiter said.

Raspe sat near the front. Afraid of being late, he had been one of the first ones in the library and had sat, without dithering, in one of several empty leather chairs, guided by the compelling but unconscious need to have the door in view. And he looked in that direction, out over the table. The door kept opening and closing, more and more frequently now, and the doctors entering the room, often with a word of greeting, had, Raspe noticed, a trace of astonishment about them, a certain unconcealed perplexity in their eyes. They are giving me strange looks. It must be they size up the newbies. Or no? Older gentlemen took their places to Raspe's left and right, nodded to him pleasantly with their cultivated faces, and then, bent over the surface of the table and leaning light on their elbows like schoolboys, began to talk softly over him. The younger ones sat further down, on the other end of the table. There were plastic chairs, too, lined up along the wall, three steps behind the leather ones. Back there, people sat shoulder to shoulder.

Raspe had wandered into the area reserved for the Chief Physicians, those the Ordinarius addressed as Professor. The talk was about the night shift the evening before, about an incident that should serve as a warning to all of them, one from which all assembled, particularly the less experienced colleagues, should draw their

127

own conclusions. Preventive security measures were indispensable, the Ordinarius said. He spoke in allusions. Raspe tried in vain to follow. His weakness from the evening before invaded his mind like a distant memory, unreal and ridiculous, a mere mood, mere exhaustion. Fight against moods. The Ordinarius spoke of certain personnel changes in the building. Then it was Doctor Raspe's turn to take the floor.

Hey, you, Bögl said, catching up to Raspe, clapping him on the back, and beginning to talk as Raspe walked, turned half-way towards him. The two open lab coats flew down the long corridor side by side. Even in the hallway, the doors stood stark and unwelcoming, and not even the breeze raised by the men storming past stirred the sick, who had long since transformed into furnishings. Raspe needed to think. So he walked with a brisk, icy demeanour, but a person like Bögl could not understand disdain. One must calmly shout into the face of a Bögl until he falls dead on the spot.

The case histories various doctors from the clinic discussed in the half-hour after Raspe's presentation in the library, a series of terse descriptions of the patients brought into the unit the day before, had again nearly emptied Raspe's mind in order to fill the emptiness with their turmoil. He couldn't let that happen. You have to think order back into your head. Grahl is waiting for me, Raspe thought. Grahl was absolutely not waiting. The day's work. The morning, without fail, especially this earliest hour of the morning, is the time of my greatest strength. The doors to the locked ward, far off at the end of the corridor, approached Raspe and Bögl faster the more heated Raspe's thoughts grew. Think against the dwindling time, as the door rushes forth to meet me, think against Bögl. Bögl mentioned unwritten laws for the order of seating in the library, blathering and distancing himself from his own words with self-ironic clichés. This ambient chatter, which poisons the air, an aerosol aimed at the atmosphere, will drift up into the universe and be cast back a billion times, occasioning a global catastrophe. Horrible stories, far too brief, had followed one another in succession, each striving with the others to leave the listener more shocked, and not one could Raspe remember from beginning to end. The horror all seemed so similar. And it was particles of this horror, dancing wildly in Raspe's head, that cluttered, balled together into a new mass of suffering, illogical, against which there was no defence. Note it down tomorrow, bring order to the terror through writing.

Findings. On Monday, 2/6, patient stands in a stupor next to the door. Doesn't react when spoken to. Refuses nourishment and ignores all requests to move from his place by the door. The next day, 3/6, patient begins walking persistently and anxiously, back and forth in the hallway. Posture is hunched, movements uncoordinated. When spoken to, patient reacts with dread. He is confused, and his formal-operational thinking substantially disturbed. Patient speaks past his interlocutors in rapid, often disconnected fragments. Orientation is impossible to ascertain, affect is rigid-inadequate. Patient states he is neither sad nor happy. He must simply be allowed to walk back and forth and let his thoughts flow. It is nice, he states, not to have to remember. Orderly verbal interaction with patient impossible. Paranoid thought contents, as attested to in the case history, are impossible to explore in a preliminary consultation. Provisional diagnosis: paranoid psychosis (ICD – Nr.:295.3).

With the late morning sun on his face, after attempting

a conversation with Grahl, Raspe assimilated the terminology in the shortest possible time. Once he'd written
up his findings, Raspe dictated them into a recorder.
Experienced doctors dictated on the fly. Most of what
stands out to the beginner is extraneous observation, in
the end. All that gets crossed out.

Grahl's phrases. The ambulance lady said, those are
the lesbians. I already know them. I have to play Mr
Grahl. I demand an explanation. I will not go along
with the lesbian progamme again. Gabi Grahl and Gabi
Loder are not a couple. I always thought I was Mr Grahl.
But if I am allegedly a lesbian, I cannot be Mr Grahl.
They should have been frank with me. The only explanation is that I am not Mr Grahl. If we are both lesbians,
then my wife must have known, but she's the only one, I
had no idea. My wife is being harassed by my so-called
son. The doctors have a hand in it, too. My wife needs
reassurance. She takes pills. But I will set her free. My
so-called son is talking about divorce. I have never read
any books about where babies come from.

Raspe stood at the window. After bedside rounds – attending physicians always do rounds on Thursday – and
lunch with Bögl and colleagues in the upstairs cafeteria
reserved for doctors (where do the nurses even eat?),
Raspe rested, and the midday heat – the meteorologists
said it was the hottest June in 100 years – pressed into the
room through the window, undiminished by any breeze.
Through the trees, out over the walls, passers-by were
visible across the street: men and women, proud in their
shameless summer garments. Fuck, now, I want to fuck,
fuck. Raspe was startled.

Strict rules you couldn't say, there weren't rules in the
narrow sense of the term, Bögl had explained that this

morning in the hall, and as the day stretched on he came back to the subject repeatedly, most recently at the table, seconded up by the others' nodding, rules, as I said before, there are none, and so everyone is an individualist, but naturally, we too have certain customs here, certain ways of doing things, but small-scale, absolutely, ways of doing things. Bögl clearly found something striking in that phrase, because he repeated it tirelessly, drawing out the A and U, waaays of dyuing was how it sounded, and this pronunciation was a sort of house style, every workplace has a house style that manifests itself in trifling details and creates a certain climate, really, you mustn't miss a single word of it, because this code, this latent code, Bögl specified, not without appending a restrained perhaps one can see it in *this* way, imposes itself no matter what, and even the new colleagues, especially the more in-tune ones, quickly grasped and adopted it, and it shouldn't be overlooked that with each new colleague, these ways of doing things were modified slightly, you could see that everywhere, this constant, perhaps I should say, Bögl said, subcutaneous modification of the code, indeed, he too, for his part, some, let's say, ten years before, those were the wild years, in the wake of the student movement, which hadn't left anyone, not even him untouched, no, he himself had contributed to the gradual loosening of the necktie requirement for assistants, which had finally been dropped, this wasn't achieved through high-flown arguments but rather through a kind of infiltration, you could almost say, Bögl said to his peers while eating, through a subtle strategy of subversion, so that actually, today, the necktie is mandatory only for the Chief Physicians, but mandatory was too strong a word, a false one in fact, as even he, not without astonishment, had in the meantime come to realize that he thoroughly enjoyed, really enjoyed sporting a tie now and again, and this had nothing whatsoever to do with the fact that his promotion to Chief Physician had been foreseen for the end of the present year, as he had found out two months back, and the Chief Physicians too had turned a corner in the interim, even with them you could see it, just as with the ties, some had also given ground concerning hair, the best example was Singer, seven years younger than him, who wore shoulder-length Beatles hair, did he, Raspe, Bögl threw out, not bothering to wait for an answer, not also think the Beatles were just super, Singer now no longer had to cut his hair, since he was a private assistant to the Director, just imagine, fifteen years ago, a private assistant looking like a hippie from Amsterdam, that was unthinkable back then, and grooming, that was really the issue, Singer's hair was always clean and groomed, which wasn't a problem for him, Raspe, with his matchstick-length hair, but the *lab coat*, which here people normally wore buttoned up, no, basically the lab coat wasn't a problem either, and perhaps Raspe who, like him, Bögl, seemed to prefer to wear his lab coat open, perhaps Raspe himself could nudge things in a new direction as far as that went, inject a certain laxity, obviously that takes time, obviously you have to proceed with caution, of course there were observable, reasonable grounds for people here to prefer wearing their lab coats closed, taking blood to start with, and then the violent patients, apart from what was considered an appropriate appearance for a doctor, a plausible medical bearing in the building, and yet, Bögl conceded right away, one could obviously take a totally different approach, he neither wanted nor could deny him, Raspe, such a right, to the contrary, quite to the contrary. The

132

savage mind, Raspe said to himself, now at the window, where he'd gone to have a smoke, initiation rites.

Later Bögl came in. He'd brought ice cream, set the two bowls on the little table with a scheming expression, and said, come on now, inviting him over. Bögl sat down, uncommonly reserved, and for the first time, Raspe asked questions. The duties for the night shift were divvied up. Early in the evening, Raspe left the clinic. The heat in the streets hadn't broken. At night rain fell, woke those asleep, and brought a brief spell of cool.

3.

Wednesday, it was agreed, Raspe was to take the afternoons off. So: out of the city, windows rolled down, sunroof open, the balm of the breeze blowing over Raspe as he drove across the landscape, the hills, the blossoming fields, and the green mass of grain. The sky was reachable, far more than normally. Raspe lay by the water. The sun let him soar, without moving, higher and higher, until it sucked him up into its glow. Eventually Raspe came to, and quenched his burning skin in the water of the pond.

Everything was clear. The Ordinarius had said: Sebastian Köhler, and at that, one of the doctors on the far end of the table began to speak in a quick and measured tone.

This is the seventh admission, and the fifth here in-house, for the 39-year-old programmer, who came to the clinic of his own accord yesterday with a paranoid-hallucinatory syndrome and requested to be admitted. As far as psychopathology, the patient presented the typical profile: alert and responsive, oriented to time and space, but only to a limited degree with people; he was agitated, with compulsive speaking, affect was inadequate-euphoric, thinking formal, thought contents substantially disturbed. Concerning the delusions themselves: patient heard voices, claimed he'd been commanded to restore order among men, had been chosen, per the voices, because his father had been born under the sign of the fire stallion, for the son that means Hell or salvation. Patient stated that for the past three days and nights, he had walked back and forth on the pavement without stopping. Passers-by had tried to thwart his mission through so-called gaze attacks. Even now, patient claims to see glimmering spear tips gouging at him. In the entry hall he tore off his shirt. Claims he is an open wound, a fire stallion, must bring redemption, and so forth. After initially refusing, patient allowed himself to be transported to the unit. Medical history unavailable, patient has no relatives and lives by himself. Etiologically speaking, this is the second outbreak this year of a paranoid-hallucinatory schizophrenia that first manifested itself more than hour years ago. Patient was administered Haldol and Neurocil.

Hardly had the assistant stopped speaking when the Ordinarius called the next name and another of the doctors responded. This is the first admission of an 18-year-old school student with agitated-paranoid syndrome who was brought to the clinic by his parents. Findings at intake: elevated affect with puerile conduct, wayward thinking, potentially delusional contents. Admission occurred because patient had threatened his mother with a kitchen knife. Prior history: only six months or so ago, the patient, according to his parents' statement, began to change notably. School performance declined, patient spoke of an imaginary swelling on his neck, believed that everyone was staring at him because of this swelling. Patient expressed fear of insanity and mentioned orders to penetrate the essence of thinking and proclaim his discoveries publicly. Around a month ago, patient stopped attending school, and ever since has sat silent and listless in the kitchen. Two weeks ago, he withdrew completely, shut himself in his room, refusing all contact as well as nourishment. There was a dramatic outburst early yesterday morning after the mother gained access to the patient's room. Parent's statement gives no indications of drug use. Etiologically, we suspect this to be the first manifestation of schizophrenia, subtype hebephrenia; differential diagnosis would consider an abnormal reactive response to an adolescent crisis. Patient had to be treated against his will with a combined injection of Haldol and Neurocil. Paroxysmal-hyperkinetic dystonic syndrome appeared, with cramping of the tongue and throat. This was quickly resolved through the administration of Akineton.

Then, after Werner Stelzer's name was called, Bögl said: Brought in for electroconvulsive, 63-year-old male, therapy-resistant endogenous depression. The Ordinarius: Who sent him to us? Bögl paused briefly, leafed through the documents: This one, yeahyeah, this one's from Haar.

A female doctor responded to the next name. First time admitted to this building, repeated hospitalizations, 47-year-old, married, childless secretary with pre-delirium syndrome consequent to long-term alcoholism. Moreover, there is a history of depressive and possibly suicidal symptomology. Patient was delivered to the clinic at night by two friends. Striking, from the psychopathologic viewpoint, are the confusion and restlessness, clouded awareness, compromised orientation, and incoherent thinking. No signs of visual hallucinations. Tremor, cold sweat, foetor ex ore. Patient almost impossible to examine. States that she cannot continue anymore, her husband will have to see how he will get along without her, etc. Medical records reveal prior history: alcohol addiction has been present for ten or so years, detox, including inpatient, has been attempted several times, most recently a few weeks back, discharge from the specialist hospital in Annabrun, more drinking immediately afterward. Etiology therefore alcoholism, admitted for crisis intervention. Treatment with distraneurin.

A notebook is a wonderful thing. Raspe read the upcoming names, the keywords that followed them, and now heard Bögl speak again. This is the first admission for a 16-year-old mechanic's apprentice with obtrusive-maniform syndrome. Affect was elevated-fatuous, presentation extremely obtrusive. Hypomanic with racing speech, thinking disorganized, interspersed with grandiose delusions. Current abnormalities have existed for approximately one week. Patient feels euphoric, healthy as ever, talks about demons he has seen in the clouds, he had to bless all the people in the English garden, he is Zeus and Neptune, god of the fish, and a passionate angler, he illuminated the sun, he must therefore take advantage of the radiant weather, meet with countless friends, sanctify, desecrate. He had important meetings, the fate of the world hung on them, and had to be discharged immediately. Abnormalities already present from early childhood. From two to four, stereotypic rocking in bed. In school, dyslexia. More recently, petty misdemeanours, fare dodging, fishing without a license, theft of bus passes, running riot, flipping cars. Drug abuse, has taken hashish for several years, LSD lately as well. Moreover, there are antecedents in the family. Paternal grandmother was treated at

Haar for persecution mania and alcoholism, father had a depressive-paranoid outbreak and received psychiatric treatment on an outpatient basis. Diagnostically, we are looking at schizophrenia, hebephrenic subtype, as a differential diagnosis we are considering mania. Patient has not been medicated previously, was administered Haldol here.

Raspe thought about Wörmann. The boy had come over to him yesterday in the unit: What's up? You get a cigarette, I'll roll a joint, then we'll smoke it, head for the English garden and lie out in the sun. Cool? What's your name, anyway? He pointed at his close-cropped, whitish blond hair and said: So you're a punk rocker now, too? Me, I've been a punk for two years. That's when I chopped it all off. You get what I'm saying. Now, let's wrap it up and go to the English garden. 'Cause I've got meetings there, get it, real important meetings. Hesitant, if also sympathetic, Raspe had murmured incomprehensibly and pushed past Wörmann towards the door.

Maybe Raspe should have taken charge of Wörmann. Bögl had suggested it: Goes without saying, you can have the junkie along with him. He too had been brought up at the morning conference: Bernd Sikorski, 19 years old, unemployed, admitted to the clinic voluntarily for heroin addiction. In the unit, Raspe had been surprised to find that from the outside, this Bernd was not in the least unhinged, but instead an amiable, dapper bank-teller type. But, thought Raspe, everything being hopeless with heroin, Wörmann's a safer bet.

Finally they introduced the case of a 40-year-old man named Zarges, a former postal clerk who was let go a few weeks before, forced into early retirement, due to his compulsive counting and arithmomania, and wholly unable to cope with life. Last of all, there was a soldier whose name Raspe didn't catch, who claimed to have swallowed a couple of sleeping pills, or maybe actually had. Suicide attempts by conscripts, Bögl later explained, are almost never serious, but if they get a short stay here, they generally end up discharged as unfit for military service.

In all, at the morning meeting that day, eight new admissions were introduced. Leaving the library, Raspe overheard the conversation between one doctor who'd clearly worked the night shift and the unit doctor, both irritable.

– This isn't the first time I've said it, I've told you several times now, cases like that don't belong with us, they belong at Haar.

– When I'm on night duty, I decide what comes in and what doesn't.

– That is the issue. You will make more than a few enemies around here if you keep letting in more people like that fucked-up alcoholic

– Hey now

– If you admit people like that. That has nothing to do with therapy, nothing to do with research, you're just opening up a file that's DOA; two, three days and they've scrammed, if they even make it that long.

– Come on, crisis intervention, that's one of the things we're here for.

– No, no, absolutely not! Crisis intervention, particularly when the person is a wreck like that woman, those need to go to Haar, they have to take those cases, we don't. You need to get that through your head.

– Well, my sense of my medical duty is obviously different from yours.

– Oh man, here we go, medical duty, that sounds just

peachy, but that's not an argument, it's just bullshitting. Listen, *you* take them in, that takes you an hour on average, and in the meantime we're stuck with all the work.

– Do you mean to suggest that I

– No, I'm just saying that, like it or not, a time will come when you will have to grasp how things work here in the clinic. It's also a question of collegiality.

– The Director hasn't issued guidelines about these situations, I've already inquired about that.

– Inquired, inquired, that really is rich, what sort of guidelines is he supposed to issue then, the Director, he can't even officially do such a thing, it's a matter of custom, of practice, get it, that's why I'm talking with you, because you're making enemies here in the clinic, and the sooner you understand that, the better, for you above all. For you for you above all for you.

Oh, the heat had turned Raspe's head into an echo chamber. How they talk and talk! The memories boomed, ricocheted against the bony interior of his skull and down into his cerebral cortex, endless repetition. Now it was Grahl's wife, who had ambushed Raspe yesterday with her shrill, agonizing tale of woe. Let them talk, let the echoes come! Blood-red, lit by the sun, his eyelids lay closed over his unshifting bulbus oculi, yellow and black particles danced calmly, red dots, red, varying intensities, a dog's barking from afar, the sound of children in water, and the colours blended together in his eyes, all at once – form! Silence! The chatter dies off.

In the evening, the water released the bather with avid hunger.

The soft strum of the telephone rousing him gently but inevitably from his first, troubled sleep, from vaguely tempestuous dreams that dispelled with the opening of his eyes, Raspe looked, before lifting the receiver, at the glowing electric-green face of his alarm clock. It was just past ten. As always, PALACE HOTEL gleamed in neon red script far out over the roofs, the usual view from his window, now barely perceptible, and behind it the sky still bore the last cold splendour of evening, hesitant before plunging into night, into moonless blackness, finally. So, get out then.

The matte door opened a crack, closed, the chain was undone audibly, then it flew open, and Raspe turned a dark corner behind Peter and nodded to a stout man sitting on a barstool beside the door, with a soft, spongy face, in ridiculous contrast to his body, nodded as naturally as possible, the way he'd seen Peter do less than a second before. Right away, shrill noises, droning, the crash of music. The beats came through a slack, black curtain hanging in tatters from the ceiling, which Peter pushed aside with a practised movement as he walked, revealing to Raspe's reeling gaze a space no larger than a living room.

Electrified people, thrown by the rhythm into a white light brighter than day, rushing and jostling, a bundle of spastically quivering arms and legs, titled heads, hair shaved or dyed, garish colours on the ratty black leather jackets and too-short stovepipe trousers. Raspe saw someone fall. The machine of legs raging on the floor pulled him in, stomped him to a paste, then picked him back up, now he threw another to the floor, rose up crosswise over the others, then fell back inside. See the blood on the streets that day, the blood and the madness. A war of dancers, which no one else in the room seemed to notice, as Raspe saw when his spellbound eyes had turned away. He, though, was the centre of bored aggressive stares bearing down from all sides. Alone and unsheltered, he stood immobile in front of the dark strip of fabric, his clothes wrong, his posture wrong, and by now Peter was far off at the bar, greeting, being greeted, and laughing as he chatted with the man barman. Still under surveillance, Raspe started moving, just walking, eyes pinned on Peter, towards his goal, as naturally as possible, one foot in front of the other, only five more to go, then Raspe could climb under Peter's wing.

Peter passed him a beer without a word. The glass in both hands, freed from the prison of stares, Raspe relaxed; the same dilapidation reigned over the benches, the tables, the walls, and the people shifting among themselves, casual, but with a constant air of hardness. When they walked, they didn't step aside, instead they barged into each other, and the one who continued on his way was the one who pitched forward with greater force and less inhibition. Words jumped out at Raspe from the purple walls, from the leather jackets, scrawled down with markers or sprayed on with spray paint, clever, cheeky nonsense. Raspe read, laughed to himself, then forgot what he had read. The beginning of the next song pounded into his head. Madness, total madness, he shouted into Peter's ear, which was tilted towards him. Peter jerked away, his face pained, and grabbed his ear with his free hand, pressing down with his middle finger on the tragus of his outer ear. Don't scream like that, you idiot. Then he laughed haughtily, almost as though talking down to him, and Raspe had to ask what. Peter now leaned into Raspe's ear and bellowed. TOO LOUD! That hurt, and Raspe liked it. Then they stood without talking, gave in to the movement of the music and the mass. Raspe drained his beer greedily and ordered two more. Same hissing, Peter said between two songs, down it goes then. Occasionally one of the dancers was thrown into the group standing calmly at the bar, and Raspe would feel a surge or shove. The beer in the glass would slosh, and the cold would run over the back of Raspe's hand and drip on to the floor. When he looked up, he saw someone spit a mouthful of beer into the face of an errant dancer. The dancer leapt up and turned, and with the next wave fell back into the mass. Only when the clinking of glasses was heard did the reedy man behind the counter look up – Harry, he was called – and shake his head ruefully. Take it easy, damn it, he shouted, but the music was louder, and the fighters had already made up. The man who spat the beer had been pulled on to the dance floor by his leather jacket, and was now running riot himself, bumping into fellow dancers and bystanders. Whoever stepped through the curtain and into the room received an immediate salute. Everyone seemed to know each other. Peter had crossed the room to the once-elegant benches with their red velvet covering and the marble-topped tables, most of them broken, to give a friendly shove to a girl, no leather jacket on this one, just an obscenely tattered T-shirt to cover her flesh. She laughed, punched Peter on the upper arm, and took a sip of his beer. Now they sat side by side, legs spread and outstretched, feet resting on the edge of a table, and several times people went over, had a word or took a sip of beer, and left, groups formed and then dissolved. Raspe stood at the bar, he didn't know anyone, but the place pleased him, mobbed, tumultuous, and he observed the scenery now free from his initial discomfort. Slowly, envy grew within him.

Then, the beer took hold. Perception shattered into images lasting only a second. Someone came over, asked for money morosely, cursed, and shoved off. Time slipped way. The silver ball raced up, made beeps and rolled off, past the reach of the flailing flippers, to the outside. You gotta pull up on it, man, when it does like that, obviously. The sink hung shattered from the wall. Inside the empty mirror frame, the word WANKER was written on the wall. Raspe walked across the filthy tile floor. Cigarette butts dance in the colourless foam of piss. In two streams, the urine drained weakly from the little slit at the tip of his penis. Raspe went on standing there at the trough, pants open, flesh hanging out.

With the third ball, Peter said, you get a free game, with the third one, naturally. It was still half-past midnight. The music went on as before. Again, the lemon wheel snagged on his upper lip. Run run, this is confrontation street, run run, there ain't nothing here but heat.

Oh, how right it felt, the glow of the lights, unmoving, and the glistening white spotlights that flitted all over, fell into a calming pattern, then dissolved in the consoling red glow. His head was so light. And it sank forward. A horn honking, a fright, but Raspe said to himself, reassured, sir, be patient, everything's cool, everything's cool.

4.

Who entered the clinic the next day at eight. Was it a changed man or a double. What had happened. Who really grasped the tactful movements among his colleagues. There was a breach between the laws of day and night.

Leaning back, Raspe pulled on the heavy, oaken door, using the weight of his body, walked into the glass-panelled alcove, opened the right wing of the second set of doors and uttered a greeting to the doorman. Three steps at a time, he leapt up the curved stairway to the first floor. He opened the door to Unit 1-3, scurried down the long hallway, briefly acknowledged the unfamiliar nurses and patients, closed the door to Unit 1-3 behind him, and removed his key from his pocket. He opened the lock, entered the stronghold, nodded and deflected, again lock door lock, walking through walls, monotonous reception at his destination by his esteemed colleague Waldemar. Raspe threw on his lab coat, buttoned it up, as requested, loath to participate in the heated partisan warfare Bögl was waging. Together they walked back through the numerous doors, up to the second floor, and into the library, and Raspe sat in one of the chairs along the wall, resting his elbows on his knees and letting his face sink into the open palms of his hands, and he remained that way a long time.

He heard the arrivals greetings scuffing chairs. The world was so foreign. Images of desolation stood about, what lostness, where was I I was at the ocean's edge and heard the never-ending.

And the voices, how are things with the voices?, Bögl said. The patient said nahnah, the voices, that's practically gone, except when they – they drop in sometimes, you know, they –. Turning to Raspe, Bögl said: That means we'll bump the Taxilan up another hundred, I think, right now he's on, how much are you taking now?, right, he's on seven hundred, write that down, please, three hundred two hundred three hundred Taxilan. Then, Bögl to the patient: So what do they say? What do they tell you to do? The patient wavered, looked self-conscious, hemmed in and stared at by the fellow invalids gathered round him in a circle. You know, like I was telling you, they basically don't say anything anymore, they're practically silent, maybe just a murmur or something like that at most, no more commands, though, it's more jumbled, because they're always talking over each other, but as far as orders −. Again, Bögl: Yeah, good, anyhow, we're going, do you have any other complaints? Twitching, anything like that?, right, well, we'll bump the Taxilan up another hundred milligrams, OK, it's obviously doing you some good, and when rounds are over we'll talk again about the voices, one on one. Anything else? No? Good, then let's continue, next we have Mr Zarges, and how are you.

Mr Zarges looked up bewildered and said: Ah, *me*, I'm fine. Then he fell silent. Bögl looked at him, expectant and patient, almost for too long. Where had Bögl's thoughts veered off to behind his graciously attentive demeanour? After some time: No complaints, everything in order? What about the counting? Ah, Mr Zarges said, back at home the wife tells me it can't go on like this, especially because of the kids, she says a man has to have a job. I'm happy to be back in here. Visits are tomorrow. Bögl: Yeahyeah, we're happy to have you here, too. But the counting, do you still need to count everything? Ah, counting counting, Mr Zarges said, and waved him off. Bögl waited and again let the silence settle over the day room packed with patients. Thomas Wörmann, the kid with the short blond hair, who was already highly strung by nature, grew more agitated and jumped up suddenly: Man man man man! Get the fuck on with it, I barely have any time here, he ain't gonna talk no more, or do you have something else you wanna say? Mr Zarges looked at the young man as though from a great distance, then said, in a flat tone, imploringly, to Bögl: Why me? See!, Wörmann said, all right then! Come on! And Bögl said to Wörmann, Please, Thomas, sit down, be patient for a moment, you'll be up in no time. But first comes –

That's right, the man sitting next to Zarges, in his late twenties or early thirties, said softly, to begin with, I have a complaint that all of us here need to discuss. Fact is, lately the nurses have ordered us to remain seated after lunch, even when we're already done, until *everyone* has finished. I would like to know whether you, Doctor Bögl, find this measure necessary, because to me, it is totally excessive, after eating I like to lie down, and moreover, we should take a vote here and see whether the other patients think it's right, for community reasons or what have you. Bögl nodded several times encouragingly, looking at the man's face. He wore a thick, trimmed moustache, had a meticulous parting in his hair, his torso was reclined, legs crossed deliberately, and over them fell a long, tufted white bathrobe, the very image of self-assurance and effortless elegance. Yes, Bögl said, I think it's good that you bring this up, we can talk about that, in any case, perhaps first we should hear the nurses' perspective, why the nurses have made this suggestion, why it is they want people to remain seated until everyone's done with their meals. At that he looked up at the two nurses in the back, resting against the edge of a table. Unlike the doctors, they wore short-sleeved gowns, buttoned not at the front, but behind their backs.

The two of them looked at each other, then the younger one pushed away from the table's edge and began to speak, standing up straight. So at the weekly nurses' meetings we've established that there just isn't enough communication among the patients, that there are isolated groups where conversation takes place, especially among the younger patients, they even play games together, but the majority have no contact with each other at all. For many, especially those who don't often get

146

visitors, we believe their stay here can be a burden. We've also seen that even very withdrawn patients, if they are encouraged to make contact, once that contact has been initiated, they clearly find it comforting, even with them, the need for communication is there, it's just buried deep, unfortunately. We've tried to think of how to do something about it, something that won't depend on whether there are nurses available to devote their time to one patient in particular. Between getting medications ready, making the charts, and so on, often the nurses just don't have the time, not to mention, we think it's good to encourage the patients' own initiative. And so lunch presented itself, this one time a day where the patients are gathered together in one place. We wanted to stress the communal character of eating, and so we asked the patients to remain seated. Our reasoning was exactly as I've explained it. There were no orders. Certainly – the nurse knew – just sitting there alone wasn't necessarily the same as contact, but it was at least worth trying to see whether a stronger sense of community might develop among the patients. From what he had observed, the possibility was there, not from one day to the next, obviously, but maybe over a longer time period. And so he thought it would be wrong to just bin the whole thing, to shut down what they'd tried to do, to say done, no need for it, and nip what they'd only just begun in the bud.

The nurse leaned back again, and the man in the white bathrobe, who had turned to one side and was listening to the speaker attentively, rocked forward again, sat upright, and raised his hand conspicuously to shoulder height, so that the sleeve of his bathrobe drooped down to his elbow. Thanks very much, Bögl said, now we've all heard the nurses' reasons for pushing for a common midday meal, they are good ones, I believe, I see no objections to what they've said. Now what's important is what you think about it, I recommend all of you join in the discussion. Yes, please, we have the first request for the floor here, please.

Again, Bögl nodded considerately to the first speaker, who grew long-winded as he reiterated his grievances from before. He is well aware of these reasons, they have been explained to him many times before, but for him, the practice represented a special hardship, because the time after eating was the only moment of drowsiness he experienced in the endless twenty-four hours of the day, it was only then that he was truly, pleasantly tired, he both wanted and needed to take advantage of this occasion to catch up on lost sleep, because at night, as a rule, he couldn't fall asleep, disturbing noises from the large dormitory could be heard through the door of his private room, he wasn't used to such things, and the night nurses were stingy with the sleeping pills, he awoke without fail at the crack of dawn, which nowadays was at half-past four, and that was in the summertime, mind you, he interjected, that meant that in real time, he was waking up at half-past three, would just lie there sleepless, it was torture, and if at midday he missed his window and wasn't permitted to even out this ever-growing deficit, then, he was of the opinion, and at this moment he addressed Bögl directly, that this hinders, actually blocks the process of my recovery. Bögl expressed his sympathy. The other patients, whom Bögl asked for their opinions at last, had almost all begun to ignore the progress of the discussion over the course of the two long tirades, and sat there now turned inwards or murmuring, rolled cigarettes or waited in tense silence to be forced into participation, for their names to be called out in accordance with the usual group routine.

148

Two had gone off to the dormitory in obvious irritation, with reprimands from the nurses and a shrug of the shoulders from Bögl. Amid the murmuring and chatter and the general absence of calm, Thomas Wörmann said suddenly: Boys, I gotta go pee, it's burning, fuck this debate, people are blabbering on like crazy, and I'm in a hurry, I got a pile of appointments, I need to go, I gotta foot it to the English garden, and you people here are just pissing and moaning. Hear that, you bunch of idiots? You baldheaded doctor twit?

Bögl smiled and shook his head. Now it was quiet. With the self-assurance of experience, he set to putting aright the situation that had temporarily gone off the rails: Precisely this outburst from Mr Wörmann shows how necessary these discussions are. He, Bögl, would ask that the patients think back over the questions broached there, and tomorrow, they would return to the subject; further, and he imagined everyone in attendance would agree, the lunch policy would temporarily be suspended for Mr Halbinger Di Carlo temporarily, until a definitive decision had been made. At that Bögl looked the other man in the eyes, blinking affably, and as the latter said softly, thank you very much, Bögl, in a plea for sympathy, glanced at the faces of the two nurses. They nodded curtly, and Bögl turned several times to the side and back, as though he'd landed in desperate straits and had found a prickly but nonetheless practicable way out.

Bögl continued his rounds, moving on to the next patient. He was an older man, perhaps the oldest one in the group, deeply taciturn, like Zarges, and vomited up his fragmented phrases in the strong dialect typical of the region. Suddenly, Raspe was gripped by compassion and pain. The way they all sat there in a circle, those convalescing and those gone to seed, each alone, all together, nothing but a single face of misery. This old man here, without even a language! And the pointless verbose debate! Raspe had to avert his eyes from the old man. From the corner of his eye, Bögl checked the time on his wrist, looked up, and then at Raspe to his left, his expression one of well-meaning chumminess. Now he cut short any pauses in the dialogue, concentrated on getting the rounds over, restricted both his own contributions and those of the patients. Maiming what in any case was already maimed to its very core. Raspe had to stopper his ears, get out of here, now. Raspe admonished himself. Take it all in, take it all on, turn the suffering into strength. Raspe shifted in his seat, then sat up straight. Learn to pass this strength along, learn to reflect the suffering of the sick, to return this suffering to them as power. Was he starting to admire Bögl? Even the scantest attention from him seemed to bring solace to many patients. What does a Bögl think and feel? Familiarize yourself with Bögl.

Then it was Grahl's turn. Raspe's mission. Grahl, who was new to the rounds, sat there estranged and intimidated, same as his doctor. A soundless abyss, the sick man stared at the floor between his feet, upper body and head hanging to the fore, held in place solely by his elbows resting on his knees. A whisper was audible, but despite the silence filling the room, Raspe had to ask again, leaning in towards the man sitting opposite him, then involuntarily jerking his head back. In the hush that followed, this tense, attentive posture became like the lurking of a vampire. Finally there was a voice, a bit louder this time, and Raspe leaned back. Grahl said: Yeah, I know, Doctor, it didn't work out right, we need calm now, relaxation, maybe a rest cure would be the best thing. He looked up at Raspe unmoved, without hope or despair: That's right, Doctor, I think the best thing would be if you prescribed me a rest cure, OK, I need to get out of here, out into the open, out in the fresh air. I'm thinking about my boy's holiday, you know, we already planned that, it's already booked. It was all a bit much in recent days, you're right, especially at the office, even at home, too much of a burden. Raspe had never said a thing to Grahl about burdens or relaxation. Grahl stopped speaking, asked no questions, and Raspe said: Mr Grahl, I had a word with your wife the day before yesterday – but he felt Bögl's elbow jabbing at his arm, an intense pressure, he was confused, paused, looked at Bögl, who made a motion for him to hurry. Raspe, once again: And so your wife, Mr Grahl, she wanted to visit you, tomorrow, perhaps, or the day after, I would say we should talk –. Out of the question, Grahl said, barely louder than before, interrupting Raspe without the least sign of annoyance, nono, Doctor, I won't play that game any longer, and what does that mean, tomorrow-or-the-day-after, I'm leaving today, I already told you, I need a rest cure straight away. Raspe looked for words, and Bögl intervened: Clearly, Mr Grahl, we will have to talk over this question of a rest cure, preferably this very afternoon, but for starters, I think, you should stay with us a little longer. Yes? This *yes* was less a question than a gently conclusive, determined manner of bringing the conversation to a close, and it was obvious Grahl understood. He nodded, undefiant, while Bögl expeditiously proceeded with the rounds.

Raspe was defeated, and sat there baffled. He looked out the window, and the sounds of voices devoid of meaning escaped him, following his gaze outward, through the glass into the open air. The trees, too, he left behind, they shrank as he flew heavenwards, just get out of here, far away, up into the blue, that was the goal. Again the birds were visible, they stormed the crowns of the trees, and Raspe heard the voices, now closer, the patients' answers, questions about voices, side effects, states of mind, Why do I have to be Satan? And the twitching in my legs? Do you think your wife agrees? I want less of the stuff, all right? Can you overlook the consequences? Raspe heard it all, but it sounded foreign to him. Now the entire circle had been consulted, advised, inspired. At the end, Bögl said: Who has table duty, who's going on leave, no discharges today, is another group going out to the garden? The nurses gave their answers. Then everyone stood up.

Bögl took Raspe by the elbow. Come quick, over to Stelzer. Then he led him down the hall, past the sluggish patients, and let go of him when they'd reached the dormitory. He's getting shock treatment next week, I took him off everything yesterday, let's take a look how he's doing today. It's astonishing, I tell you, the way it works sometimes, just taking them off, when it's a therapy-resistant depression, this guy had doses and combinations that would make your hair stand on end, I'll show you the file later. Then they stood at the foot of Stelzer's bed. Were you getting up, Mr Stelzer? Are you feeling better? The man sat in his bathrobe, slumped on the edge of the bed, and dug at one thumbnail with the other. Slowly, almost unnoticeably, he turned his head, which was dangling over his chest, to the left, raised his shoulders slightly, and froze. Would you like to say something, Mr Stelzer? Stelzer was silent. Bögl bent forward and spoke loud and clear into Stelzer's ear. You do know we want to start the electroshock therapy next week, that's why you haven't had any medicine since yesterday, and we need to know how you're getting along without your medicine, you see. Stelzer continued working away at his nails. His fingertips were ragged, scarred, bloodied. Pulling at what was left of the thumbnail, Stelzer tore away a strip of the nail bed. Bögl paused, laid his hand on Stelzer's shoulder: Come, Mr Stelzer, come on. Now blood welled from the nail bed. Bögl waited, moved his hand gently over Stelzer's shoulder, and the stiff creature started nodding, lifted his hundred-kilo head towards the doctor, and said: It'll be soon, right, that'll be soon. Then his head sank forward again, and Bögl's further attempts at contact were fruitless, Stelzer was mute. The doctors walked away. Dreadful, Bögl said to himself, just dreadful. In the doctors' station, both sat down enervated at their desks. Eventually Bögl stood up and said: I think I'll make some coffee.

Raspe removed his lab coat, unbuttoned his shirt, pulled it off, and tucked his T-shirt, which had slipped out, back into his pants. Today he was wearing an old pair of hand-me-down trousers, cut broad at the top and narrow at the ankles, of grey nylon with pleats, permanent press. Noon was still far off, but already, in the heart of summer, the sun had heated the room terribly. Yep, Bögl said, the heat takes it out of you, and after he, too, had taken off his lab coat, the two doctors sat at the coffee table, one across from the other, essentially alone. Bögl had opened his shirt button under his red-and-white-striped tie, and laid one foot casually on the knee of the opposite leg. He was wearing jeans, freshly washed, freshly ironed, the crease slightly smoothed at the knees. They nipped at their coffee and Raspe said, Dear God, that's hot, stood up and filled his cup to the brim with cold tap water from the sink. Still standing,

153

he took his first sip and walked back to the table with care. – You don't think the coffee's too hot? As Bögl shook his head no, making unformed sounds with protruding, puckered lips, Raspe realized, with astonishment, that he'd addressed Bögl directly for the first time, and as an equal rather than a superior. It wasn't yet clear, though, whether Bögl would become Waldemar for him as Raspe, without doubts or ceremony, had been Wilhelm for Bögl since the beginning. Bögl seemed lost in thought. He was shaking his head. Raspe asked:

– What?

– What do you mean, what? Stelzer, you saw him.

– Yeah, of course, but I figured you were used to that type of thing.

– Used to it, my God, obviously it's not the first time I've seen it, but used to –

– There wasn't much evidence of rebound effect?

– Not much would be fine, but with him, there was nothing happening at all.

– Maybe you'll see it later?

– Sure, of course, it takes time to get the stuff out of your system.

– So will he get better after the electroshock?

– Don't be ridiculous, no one's said that.

– But you yourself said he is getting shocked. Isn't that the reason he's here?

– Most psychiatric hospitals won't do it anymore.

– How come?

– Too much criticism, too much hoopla, this torture claptrap, you probably know about all that.

– Of course.

– Right, so the people in charge are scared shitless, and we get stuck with the hopeless patients, and what do you know, the university clinics, the MPI, and the small

154

research hospitals come out of it smelling like roses. It's crazy.

– But if electroshock is no good for anything anyway?

– I didn't say that either. It's a bit more complicated than that.

– OK, so what then? What chances does, say, a Stelzer have?

– *That* is precisely where our problem lies.

– How so?

– For Stelzer, in my estimation, the outlook is grim. You have to consider, he's been in this state more than two years. Add that to the harm that comes from hospitalization itself. With him, I have barely any hope.

– So why are we doing it?

– Most likely, this is his very last chance, and no matter how slim it is, since everything else is exhausted, logically we have to try.

Raspe fell silent. Afterwards, the conversation turned to group rounds. Bögl fended off Raspe's objections. You don't know the patients, they're all new to you, that's why you find it so painful. Bögl on the other hand had conversed with all of them one-on-one, he knew their stories, their backgrounds, their progress, chatted them up in the course of the day, in the hallway, at night sometimes, whenever the opportunity arose. The group rounds were more of a ritual, giving the patients the assurance that at least once a day, they would see their doctor, could bring up anything pressing, etc. The patients saw it this way, too. No, no, it looks dreadful from the outside, but it really isn't, I don't know if you understand me. Nor is it true that it's awkward for the patients. You'll see for yourself how quickly your impressions change once you get used to it, in a week it will all look different, I would put money on it, no doubt.

From his earlier succinctness, Bögl slowly found his way back to his accustomed manner, cycling through reservations and repetitious monologues. And again, Raspe was a mute observer of this well-oiled machine of doubt-devouring self-justification. Raspe drank, he ruminated. With Stelzer was the first time he'd seen Bögl shaken. Even a person like him is still capable of feeling pain, a Bögl twaddles on from vulnerability, to save himself. That talktalktalk was an anaesthetic, a longed-for deep sleep, unscathed estrangement from consciousness, the torment of reality packed in the wadding of words.

I take this kind of conversation very seriously. That, even and in fact particularly that, is the point of group rounds, though one certainly ought not forget the other thing I mentioned before, the possibility of contact between individual patients and doctors. Still, in these discussions, the collective momentum of the situation can unfold, you see, all that comes right out. I mean, today there are things we can't just decide on in an authoritarian manner, like these procedures with the midday meal, though of course we can't conceal our authority as professionals when we offer our opinions, even if they are just that, opinions and not orders. In the end, in these matters, it is the patients who must and should decide, precisely because they are so impeded in so many other respects, the unit administration alone, which enforces numerous professional restrictions, is an impediment to the patients; our therapeutic protocols, which are often incomprehensible to the patients, they too are an impediment, not exactly, but certainly a restriction of their personal liberty, of course we work to keep those as modest as possible, but they are not just there for no reason, they are medical-therapeutic necessities. You'll see, there are situations where compulsion is the only thing that works, whether a loud word, even physical restraint, dreadful as that is to all of us here, sometimes can't be avoided. This is the reason I encourage these discussions, even if, as far as substance goes, they are not particularly meaningful, because the confrontational model promotes individual and collective responsibility, and this can effectively compensate for the patient's aforementioned passivity. Can, I say, not does, that much is clear. I mean, in the end, for me personally, it's all the same how long they sit there at lunch, all the same is a bit of an exaggeration, but does it really animate the collective spirit, my God, I don't know, that sounds like something of an illusion. Still, you have to look at the nurses' situation, we've got a whole new generation of people in these last few years, a very engaged generation gaining influence with respect to the older nurses, and of course, that's a double-edged sword. Much of the experience the older nurses have, their sure hand with managing the patients, composure, in the best cases, the ability to discern how much rigour or flexibility is needed, this knowledge you can't arrive at with intellect and reason alone, a lot of that is getting lost, and that worries us, logically. At the same time, it is gratifying to see the crust start to crack, to see the sense of responsibility these new nurses bring with them, which extends even to therapeutic matters or questions of medication, and that gives you a foil at the midday meetings, which I find positive, understand, because it's not the Chief Physician or the Medical Director I must justify my therapeutic protocol to, it's the nurses, whose arguments are objective and offer a distinct perspective; no, I consider that to be a development we need to accept, even encourage, that's just my opinion. They're even doing a kind of Balint session under the guidance of a psychologist, they are serious about it, and you can take that how you will, but you see the point, and consequently we have to take things like this lunch initiative seriously, we need to give these engaged nurses the feeling that decision-making is shared with them, even if I don't believe, or even if I doubt, that the improved communications the nurses expect will come out of it but then, on the other hand, you can never really say in advance, probably you can't, and so, presumably –

Raspe excused himself, he had to rush to the bathroom. Sure, man, Bögl said, leapt to his feet, and pulled his tie aright with a quick grip at the knot. In the end here, you've got to keep moving forward with the work. And while Bögl put on his lab coat, Raspe walked through the door to the stairwell, leaving behind the pressure chamber of the doctors' station. Once outside, he stood weightless, in the cool dark and quiet, he stood and he didn't move.

Raspe studied Thomas Wörmann's file. You don't always have to say Mr Wörmann to me, for you I'm just Tommi. The conversation had been exhausting. Now Raspe had to draft a case file in accordance with the composition guidelines, a form Bögl had passed to Raspe with a breezy bit of commentary: Of course you don't have to stick to it point for point, but all patient histories in our hospital need to follow a certain pattern, as per the wishes of management; this little cheat sheet is useful for that. In a muddle, Wörmann had exuberantly and enthusiastically offered details about himself. Music and drugs, authority conflicts with his parents and his boss, passion for motorcycles, anarchistic leanings – none of that was unfamiliar to Raspe. And his sympathy got in the way of his work on the file, which required dispassion. Raspe was in the room alone, Bögl was attending to his research, his lithium questions. The afternoon slipped past calmly. Already, two days before, Raspe had put his desk in order, otherwise he couldn't work. The voices in his head, the echoing prattle, had died away too. The jingle of the phone no longer prompted panic, it meant one task among others, and a manageable one at that.

Raspe immediately recognized the voice of Grahl's wife. How were things with her husband? Her? She was done for, at the end of her tether, no longer knew up from down. Raspe heard sobs, a struggle for composure, then again, a bursting into tears. Shrill loud talk, coming thick and fast. She wanted a divorce, there was no point anymore, she was fit for the nuthouse herself. With her husband, she no longer knew what was the madness, what was the illness, and what was the real person. His disease had destroyed the marriage long ago. For years now, out of the blue, he would stop talking to her for weeks on end. In that same period, he started wanting to sleep with her non-stop. If she turned him down, he forced her. The truth is, she'd have to say he raped her, over and over. Then, a few months ago, this inevitable prattle about how he was a woman, he had started up with that again, but this time, he dragged her son into it, said she'd had relations with her son, that was hogwash. So she finally wanted a divorce, a divorce would mean some peace at last. Weeks ago, he had turned just as strange again. He'd come home from work in the evenings and not say a word, not a single peep. She tried everything, she'd started over time and again, at some point you just can't keep doing it. The son was fifteen, in a difficult phase, he caught on to everything, he would go insane soon, too. It had to end, she could no longer be responsible for it, on account of her son alone. Then, after an eternal silence, her husband had talked to her for two nights straight, about her lesbian relations, how he knew he was crazy, but liked it, and she was crazy too, and under no circumstances was she to leave him. On and on with this delirious nattering: he could read her thoughts, she'd had relations with their son, actually she was the one who was ill. His colleagues at the office were crazy, they were conspiring against him, he had evidence of a plot, he would soon be liquidated. But her husband had been telling her that for years, that wasn't only the illness, that was part of his normal personality. She had no more hope. Should she visit him, then? She no longer dared to go outside, her face was swollen from beatings, she had strangulation marks on her neck, one night, the whole night long before he was taken in, he had kept choking her, had threatened to kill her if she breathed a word. No one was to know about anything, certainly not about his illness, he'd forbidden that, she was forbidden to speak to her friends or relatives, or to anyone at all, she'd had to deal with it alone, no one can endure such a thing, not even the strongest person. For a long time, she'd been afraid of her husband, but now it was unbearable. The best thing would be to never see him again. But she can't just leave her husband high and dry, not right now, she says to herself. She no longer knows when, what, how. Again, Raspe heard the woman overcome with sobs. Raspe looked for consoling words. What should one say? At these times, all words are twaddle. Wait and see, Raspe said. Try and stay calm. You shouldn't rush things with the divorce. You told me yesterday, there have also been good, even very good periods these past few years. No, we shouldn't give up hope. Today your husband's much better, he's quite peaceful now, the medicines are having a good effect. Maybe you should come tomorrow, or the day after. You need to recover, too. You need to try. Raspe went on in this way. He knew how ridiculous his words were compared with what had happened over all those years. But still, the woman calmed down. When he'd hung up, Raspe looked disconsolate at the phone. Can we not help somehow? He returned to Wörmann's file, curiously invigorated.

You're studying, I see, very good very good, said Professor Reiter. Raspe had expected him, but was surprised to see him now standing there in the room next to Raspe's desk. Bögl had tipped him off that the boss would be there between seven and eight p.m., he always comes on Thursdays to do his rounds with the private patients, he likes one of the doctors to go along with him, could Raspe handle it that evening. As he stood, Raspe stowed the textbook in his desk, shook the Director's hand in greeting, and buttoned up his lab coat. Good-humoured, the powerful man stood before him in the middle of the room, and filled the entire space. His wavy white hair was still thick, his face a deep brown that said ready for action, rearing to do something decisive. Was there not a kindness perceptible in his traits? They were taut, nigh haggard, but showed something more than simple discipline and self-abnegation. – And you, have you settled in a bit?, the Director said. Do you feel comfortable? Is that a stupid question after so few days? You've landed in one of the most interesting units of our hospital. Were you aware of that? Many of our colleagues actually climb over one another to get a position on the locked ward. Of course, this is also psychiatry at

161

its most difficult. But you won't lose heart, will you? We have quieter units, but in those, there's far less freedom than there is here. And with Dr Bögl, you have a prominent and proficient psychiatrist, ideal for showing you the ropes. Doctor Bögl has already left? I'm glad to hear that, he often stays late into the evening, even into the night. So you're taking over? You'd like to accompany me? I think that's lovely. So you were hitting the books? Studying what? Yes, hebephrenia is a most absorbing chapter. As a young doctor, shortly after the war, I, too, studied Bleuler in extenso. That extraordinarily humane, utterly altruistic approach to psychiatric illness fascinated me back then, indeed, I was a fully fledged Bleuler enthusiast. Only later did my research lead me to a more biologically oriented psychiatry, and that was how I established myself as a scientist, if you will, and that is the line we work in for the most part at this clinic, on questions of that nature. Has Doctor Bögl told you yet about his lithium studies? No? Highly interesting, a very important field, long-term pharmacological therapy for cyclothymic disorder, that will be a revolution, in schizophrenia research, too, even if we are progressing in baby steps. Just let me hold out another twenty years. But you, in any case, are still young, you will live to see it. Naturally, this revolution coming from the laboratories of biologically oriented psychiatrists does not in the least mean that the psychological approach is superfluous. Far from it! Bleuler will never be superfluous, you know, that is the humus out of which all humanistically engaged psychiatry grows. For me as much as for anybody. No no, it's not that simple. Study your Bleuler, you couldn't be more right, and then, without rushing, look around and get a sense of what kind of clinical research interests you. Right now, for example, there's a big study of cerebrospinal fluid underway, interesting stuff, the production of gamma globulin in the brain. I'm certain you will find something you can be passionate about. As I said, there's no hurry, for now just get used to being here with us. So? Sound good? Shall we then? Yes? Get started? And you'll be so kind as to come along?

The private patients in the twin rooms just past the dormitory snapped to attention, even Mr Halbinger Di Carlo, then sat down on the edge of their beds, and the Director waved. No, relax, no need to get up. Professor Reiter did little more than listen, was a friendly advisor, and very patient. He never let his eyes stray, not a single brief glance to the side, not even to Raspe, no conspiratorial winks of the sort Bögl often gave him when a patient spoke. No, the director's eyes observed and accumulated, nothing more.

When the pizza came at last, there was a brief pause in the conversation, or rather an intermission in the breakneck monologue Wolfgang hurled at Raspe, with his usual intention of convincing him. Now he gobbled down an enormous bite, which he hardly chewed, hardly swallowed before opening his mouth again, hungry for the next one.

Raspe had begun by telling his friend about his first days in the clinic, relaying what he had seen, repeating what he had heard, explaining how he was less an orderly presenter, striving circumspectly towards insight, than a victim to the impressions that assailed him in the course of telling. Though immune to the other's influence, Raspe had, without wanting to, presented an image of disintegration and chaos, of the most extreme perplexity at his strange new job, and at some point, Wolfgang interrupted him with a curt aperçu: Seems like it really gets you worked up, this psychiatry. In the ensuing silence, he added: Man, you can't just let yourself get beaten down by these experiences, you also need to grasp what's wrong here, that's something you can understand if you try to, if you'll stop being so goddamn sensitive and try and think about it a bit, too. And with Raspe's agreement, Wolfgang pivoted to the same conversation about politics, Marxism, and revolution that the two of them had engaged in almost every time they met for a good two years now. Wolfgang, a member of the Marxist Group and one of their most intelligent representatives at the university, had a buoyant urge to spread the word and had not yet given up hope of winning Raspe over to the work of politics in time, and Raspe was always willing to think along and learn. They had been schoolmates, and Raspe had always been struck by Wolfgang's manner, his way of speaking, of feeling his way through a thought, or pursing his lips in narcissistic superiority.

Mouth full and chewing, Wolfgang continued with his lecture: Apart from the question of will, apart from the fact that the insane person actually willingly chooses madness as an optimal mode of emancipated accommodation of state and capital, apart from the fact that false consciousness lies in back of this free will as expressed through praxis, all of which you need to finally recognize – apart from all that, your job at the clinic, at a psychiatric clinic, is the epitome of reactionary politics in action. A society that consistently makes its members ill, mentally ill in particular, employs psychiatry to help itself survive. You are healing people whose sicknesses are a reaction to the twisted conditions they live in for the sole purpose of enabling them to function again amid the conditions that made them sick in the first place. As a psychiatrist, you eradicate symptoms of this society's debasement without even considering the causes, let alone working towards eradicating them; to the contrary, you actually cover them up, so your labour conforms to the same principles as advertising, consumption, the enhanced gratification of urges, improved work conditions, in brief, the principles of societal self-preservation. You need to decide whether it's really so great, letting the strategems of capitalist reason work through you as they do through so many others, and forget all your therapeutic nonsense, that's a dead end. Look, you don't even need to daydream with political romantics like Marcuse about the revolutionary potential of the marginalized and outsiders, historical materialism on its own is enough to show how all of that is politically reactionary praxis, reactionary, get it, reactionary.

Raspe was too exhausted from the day to formulate his objections with any rigor, or at least with the jovial self-assurance Wolfgang brought to his certainties. The visible suffering, the suffering of individuals, was overwhelming, Raspe said, was palpable evidence of a cry for help, and it was that, the actual reality, in other words, that never showed up in Wolfgang's theories. Something, Raspe was certain, was amiss in conclusions like his, even if he couldn't say for sure what. – So what, then, what, please, said Wolfgang, more heated than before, give me just one argument and I'll knock it down, but your goddamn irrationalism, it makes me sick, man, that shit brings every reasonable discussion to a halt. He paused, then set out calmly to clarify himself further, but Raspe heard nothing save for isolated terms, vindication ideology critique societal status quo relation of ends to means, and he looked, at a loss, into Wolfgang's face, which had grown broad, stark in these past few years, peremptory, but not without a lingering youthful beauty that seemed to raise the zeal of his words to a sort of enchantment. And the whole evening, unobserved, Wolfgang's girlfriend sat next to him, a girly girl, pretty as a picture, mute and jealous.

The things that had been talked about today. The things the he had heard and ought to retain. And what should be done with them. Exhausted, Raspe lay in the dark. What did a brain have to think away in order to find peace in the night. Unceasing chitchat, prattle. Come at last, sleep, you, solace forget head you be quiet.

5.

The water pounded down on euphoric skin, hot at first, then icy. An Italian pop singer stood undressed and braying in the room. Congestion on the motorway heading south, a beaming woman announced cheerily. The streets were so bright and empty, one by one bicycles flew on to them, flew past, flew away. And in time with the cherished strangers, Raspe danced through the U-bahn, through a dazzling cold light. Alas, this glum depressive with his almost empty, scuffed briefcase. A storm rose up from the black tunnel. The newspaper sheets were crumpled birds, wildly rustling, then dragged off, subdued and docile, as the train sped softly away. Momentarily fused with the pale blue plastic strap, the singer read and hummed his melody. He was the kind of person others smile back at. Two women sat there like imposing mountains and gently exuded the odour of their sweat. Oh, yeah, one said. – So you'll be free earlier. – Why me? – Because you get off before me, that means you'll be done earlier. – But we don't finish until three. Exactly. – What do you mean, exactly?

– The second woman turned to Raspe and said: Get this, she don't understand me; then, speaking properly: She doesn't understand, she doesn't understand, it's really not that hard. Right? Raspe laughed too, released the plastic strap, and let the escalator transport him into the sunlight. Here the cars dashed about, stood still, and the motorbikes' roar, the birds chirping in the trees along the road, and Raspe's sportive singing merged in a melodious chant to salute the morning.

Wasn't it easy just to sit and listen? Stories stories, the alternating voices spoke so warm and quickly, curt, but they had something to offer. There are many of them. Other people with other fates come, make contact with an open ear, and vanish. Stay, you flitting shapes! Where do you go so restlessly? I want to hear you, want to talk to you. Today one sat there among the rest, alone, he was fearless. Come, you weak and weary, for I am happy and powerful! Nothing was visible, not even the possibly unequivocal expressions, for Raspe kept his eyeless head – careful with the glances these days! – bowed and hidden in his hand, nose and mouth covered by his palm, fingers spread over the cheekbones and chin. He sat that way calmly, was only an ear, and with a soundless cry, happiness passed through his head.

Again came Bögl, this time from behind, with encouraging words, cluelessly offering solace. You always sit there beaten down, when you sit in the library, you look like you just can't take it anymore, but wait, you'll get used to it soon. You're wrong, Raspe said, everything's OK. But Bögl felt he should keep an eye on his younger colleague, and Raspe groped his way back towards last night's sleep, which had banished the dread of the preceding day in a way concealed from waking thought; groped his way back to the still enigmatic moment of

167

awakening, which had plainly, amid the haze of dreams, hurled a kind of strength into his awareness: Chosen one, you have a job, do what you can. Then Raspe was reassured.

– Rosemarie Rosemarie, se-he-ven years my heart's yearned for thee, my heart's yearned for thee. You know that one?

– Nope.

–Well, what do you think?

–About what?

– If I can sing it, you can say something about it. So, spit it out.

– Uh, well, it's fun.

– Fun? It's sad, though, se-he-ven years my heart's yearned for thee, heart's yearned for thee. Some fun. What do you say now?

– Yeah, you're right. But I don't really know what I should say. What should I say?

– That's for you to know, what you should say.

– It's not sad, either, though, you're laughing while you're singing it. I don't know, I just don't.

– Don't overthink it, boss, I don't either.

So went Kiener and Raspe's conversation, walking down the hall in the unit, over to the glass door of the nurses' station. Kiener is a character, Bögl said, and laughed aloud, and after the two doctors' had walked through the door in the nurses' station and were out of eyeshot of the patients, he went on: I like him, old Kiener, and he's glad to be here, I believe, I believe he likes us, too.

Later, when the rounds and the two discharge interviews were over, they sat back and had their coffee. The sirens of the ambulances racing around the clinic precinct howled through the open window. They don't come to us much with the lights flashing, Bögl said, occasionally the police, with the violent types and so on, but usually without the sirens, and most times the paramedics drive straight to the North Pole, out of the city and towards Haar, I mean. We're the South Pole, in radio jargon, it sounds warmer, but it's just as cold, geographically speaking at least. Bögl laughed.

The weather outside was still nice as could be, that morning a steady warm wind had blown all the mugginess out of the heat, shot through the leaves of the trees and risen up into the ungraspable high blue. The grace of summer! The world is there, so clear, everything is as it should be, what solace. The summer is slipping past, Raspe thought, the wonder outside is trickling away, I'm sitting here, the person next to me is talking, and I am not by the water, not in the heat. The endless summers of childhood, all joy in those perennial hot days, out in the open, and he felt nostalgia, at the same time pride. I am grown, the summer should shout, I have duties to perform.

The day's work was almost done. There was small talk, absent-minded chatter. Bögl was relentless, and as he was dressed casually, in a semblance of weekend wear, Raspe thought that for the first time, without prompting, he would tell him something private, about his children, maybe, his sailboat, concerts at the Schlossheim Castle, walking tours in the mountains, or a barbecue that evening in the yard. Some people will strip themselves bare in front of a stranger. But Raspe was wrong. When prompted, Bögl dilated upon his scientific work, the lithium study, and now and again Raspe interrupted him with a question.

Research as such was less fun for him, though the

tracking down of obscure sources, delving into thorny details, formulating investigative hypotheses, and designing the experiments themselves, particularly that, the designing, had its creative aspect, although all that was fascinating, in principle, all that was the same in any medical-scientific profession, irrespective of the subject area. So it was not as much the research as the actual work related to the study with lithium users in outpatient care that had kept him devoted to this topic for so long, for years to be precise. The patient population in outpatient care was the exact opposite of that on the locked ward. Here, especially for him, the pointlessness of psychiatry was at times simply overwhelming, he had to say that this notion of revolving-door psychiatry, which was on everyone's lips nowadays, was being blown out of proportion by all the bad publicity, but still, you couldn't deny there was a grain of truth to it; faced with the tenacity of psychiatric disorders, you always ended up buckling, you had to confess your helplessness. The outpatient clinic, though not free from setbacks, gave constant encouragement, it was altogether a place of hope. For a long time, for years, in fact, he had looked after individual patients, gained intimate knowledge of their work and family lives, followed them through ups and downs, had been able to guide them, to intervene in crisis situations, had often helped them avoid the trauma of institutional confinement, and all this with patients, keep in mind, who only a few years before had suffered from periodic mood disorders, mainly unipolar endogenous depression, but also schizo-affective and manic-depressive psychosis, *en passant*, depression was something like a psychosis among the affluent, but anyway, for this contingent of patients lithium salts were a form of prophylactic, an instrument to prevent the

170

recurrence of outbreaks, and their effectiveness as well as their tolerability over years of continuous therapy was frankly unbeatable. Nothing, no psychoanalytic measures, went as far as these merciful lithium salts, which of course did not mean such patients should forgo psychoanalytic treatment. That, too, he had learned *lege artis*, not for nothing had he pushed others in their countless group meetings to pursue a secondary degree in psychotherapy. Lithium certainly couldn't prevent relapse in every single case, but even if the intervals between phases was lengthened or the intensity of the episodes diminished, you could by all rights call that a therapeutic success. Of course, difficulties had cropped up in recent years, there were reports from America that lithium treatment led to unspecified disorders of the kidneys, still, it was questionable, highly questionable, whether lithium was nephrotoxic, up to now there was no solid evidence of reduced renal function. His scientific work included questions of this kind, very interesting, and that struck him too as more sensible than many other aspects of biological psychiatry, no no, there his scientific work was of immediate and direct benefit to the patients in outpatient care, had a direct effect on the people who were at once object and material of his research. Actually, if he were to be honest, he couldn't but sing the praises of his subject area, which was an ideal union of his humane and scientific interests. Nor had his lithium obsession derailed the course of his scientific career, to the contrary, it had enhanced his profile as a specialist in the field; his habilitation thesis, which would present the fruits of more than four years of research, was just then on the point of completion. He didn't want to push Raspe, but in the upcoming months, Raspe would have to start looking for a research field of his own, of course this wasn't an obligation in the strictest sense of the term, but it was expected, you could say that the Medical Director expected the younger assistants to participate in research, and he, Bögl, would naturally welcome Raspe on to his project, there were still unanswered questions, unexamined material in droves. In any case, the work in outpatient care, he wanted to emphasize again, this work he did two afternoons a week, had become, for him, an absolutely necessary recompense for his work there in the locked ward, the energy he burned up in the one was restored in the other, and it was incomprehensible how others of his colleagues, without a corrective of this sort, without any concrete basis for hope, could cope with the oppressive daily grind, certainly he could no longer imagine Waldemar Bögl, psychiatrist, with lithium out of the picture. Not even in private life could you find the balance indispensable for work in the asylum, he was being sarcastic when he invoked this obsolete concept, 'the asylum', no, and anyhow, that and his private life were two different matters, and his wife, a doctor, was employed in the clinic, too, so more, in all likelihood, than at other psychiatrists' houses, psychiatry was in the air at home morning noon and night.

Raspe supposed Bögl's long-winded speech was coming to an end, though the topic of private life had only just risen to the surface, because the pounding at the doors to the patients' day room had grown more and more urgent these past few minutes, and was now a rabid hammering, and persistent muffled shouts and curses could be heard through the padding and the space of air between the double doors, Openupyousackofshit, cocksuckingdoctor, openupBöglyoubaldheadedfuck. With a flick of the hand, a frown, and a curt shake of the head, without interrupting his lithium disquisition,

Bögl restrained Raspe who had tried to stand to open the door, and only when he reached the end, with a long pause after the word *weekend*, amid the ever-louder hammering and shouting, only then did he leave his chair and walk, Comingyeahcoming, to the door.

For a moment, after the outer door had been opened, but before the inner one had closed, the heated face of Thomas Wörmann came into view. He greeted Bögl, less vexed than incredulous and weary: Man oh man, Bögl, a real bunch of bastards, that's what you guys are. Wörmann wants outside this afternoon, Bögl said, back in the doctors' station after a brief interlude with the patient, and I told him yes, hopefully you agree, he is your patient. He can go out in the garden today, I think. Raspe nodded.

Towards the end of the nurses' meeting Raspe announced, as he and Bögl had agreed, that he would go down to the garden that day. His proposal was met with warmth on all sides. Together with the young nurse who spoke up the day before in group rounds, Raspe led a group of six patients down a stairway that he had neither used nor even noticed before. The nurse said his name was Peter Wettinger, Raspe could just call him Peter, and Raspe answered, Everyone's always named Peter. Wettinger: What do you mean, everyone? Raspe: You know, two of my friends are named Peter too; but yeah, obviously it's not everyone. Got it, Wettinger said. The steps led to a short, low hallway, like a tunnel. Wettinger turned slightly towards the patients and said: You don't really need to worry about anyone bolting, everything's locked, the stairs, the hall here, the entire garden, it's a good thing, really, you don't have to be on the patients like a guard dog, you can leave them in peace.

The garden was arranged like a kind of English park, in the same turn-of-the-century style as the clinic building. Shrubbery grew lush along the wall, stretching out branches over the softly curving pebble paths, over the flowerbeds arranged as if at random, and there was grass, lots of grass, a sward, thick as velvet, of innumerable tender green filaments, and out in the middle stood the ponderous tree trunks, bark glinting silver, time-battered, or deep black and coarse, rising like candles into the crowns, birches, lindens, and maples, coming together in the heights like a fissured roof that still gave shelter. People walked almost elegantly, sluggish and alone, in bathrobes, along the paths, or else sat motionless on the dark-hued benches. Nothing could be heard.

This is just for the men, Peter Wettinger said, the women have their own over there. Then he pointed leftwards with his chin, to where the interwoven leaves and branches of hardier trees were visible past a high wall topped with red roofing tiles covered in moss. In front of a stand of clustered buildings, squat and peculiar – tool sheds, perhaps – there stood a ping-pong table, no one playing. Steps on the crunching gravel. The garden was much smaller than it seemed. Wettinger set up a net and played doubles with three of the patients. In the absence of other noises, ping-pong is a loud game. The scrape of feet, and louder, sometimes presto sometimes slow, the rhythm of the white celluloid, the succinct click of ball against bare table, or the wood of the paddle with its knobby rubber coating sending the ball back with a softer but still conspicuous thud.

Raspe sat down on a bench nearby. If he closed his eyes he heard his heart thunder. The closing of the aorta, the contraction of the ventricle, click, bamclick

bamclick. – Listen, you need to listen to the music, all right, the music, and be patient, you need time to really hear it, to really get it. From the patient's body, the grey plastic tube of the stethoscope forked through the chrome binaurals and led to Raspe's intent ears. Behind him, the professor waited calmly and then asked eagerly: So? Did you hear it? No? Try again, like we said, music, and take your time. Raspe had a knack for learning the physical examination methods, auscultation percussion palpation, it was fun, the doctors were friendly, and internal medicine itself was a hard field and that made it stimulating. What did surgeons with their artful handiwork and juvenile sayings have to do with Raspe? Had he studied medicine for six-odd years to end up an eye doctor, a radiologist, or a specialist in skin disorders? No, my patient must be the whole man, not a sick ear-nose-and-throat or some other random organ till the end of his days. But internal medicine was a field of arduously bottled-up despair, one where resignation reigned. Old people, almost all old people, ruins, Raspe had seen old people constantly in the internists' units, and the patient doctors treated them to death, marshalling the whole of their intelligence to wrest a few ailing years from death, drawing the patients' torpor, their weakness, out a little longer, interminably, then agony and death. And he wanted to heal. I am young. Raspe didn't want to accompany senescence on its passage towards death. Raspe wanted to bring health, bring health to the ailing. And had those countless feeble eyes not said to him: it is not my body that is sick, it is my soul? Psychiatry had been a necessary choice for Raspe. Psychiatry was the only possibility. Now I am sitting in the garden, it is good. Around me, inside me, this once-in-a-century June is unfolding. The wind blew, the afternoon stood fast. Raspe thought: once upon a time. He thought of yesterdays and tomorrows. Afternoons know no time.

Hey, Doc, whatcha doin' sittin' there all knackered, Thomas Wörmann said and walked over, come and gimme five, you know what that means, right, gimme five. Of course, Raspe said. He stretched out his arm, palm open and upturned, and Thomas smacked his hand down powerfully, then turned his own palm upward, Raspe smacked it just as powerfully, and it cracked like a whip. Wörmann was happy, sat on the bench, and said: Where do you know that from, gimme five, I learned it from Henderson, you know Henderson? Raspe: Henderson, nah, I know it because I've heard it around, it's a soul and funk-disco thing, no? I was in America for a year, though. Supercool, Wörmann said, America, where were you then? I'm going there sometime, too, were you in Frisco? 'Cause I'm going to Frisco, I'm gonna smoke till my mind's blown. Raspe didn't know New York, either (what do you know then!), he talked about Flint, a dump between Detroit and Chicago, talked about a high school he had attended when he was the same age as Wörmann was now. Wörmann was jealous of him, but whatever, he had plans. He would finish his studies, that was a given, you need a diploma, of course, it goes without saying you're a fuck-up if you don't have a diploma. He was apprenticing at BMW, that was aces, because he could work on bikes, not just on cars, cars got to be a pain, the customers were tossers, the owners, you know, motorcycles were way more interesting. In the autumn, the third year of his apprenticeship was starting, and he wanted to focus on bikes, he was a quick learner, even his boss could see that, it's just that the goddamned school was such a nightmare, such stress, tech school!, those dimwits, the teachers, they were real snotty fucks, way worse than teachers at a normal school, naturally he hardly even went in anymore, once a week, because they all thought the world revolved around them, there was basically nothing hands-on, they were just idiots, then at work it was major stress, they ratted him out to the school on account of his absences, and he'd already had to cough up serious cash, by law he had to foot the bill for the entire programme, on account of his absences, but to tell the truth, he couldn't give a fuck. So one year, said Wörmann, diploma, then boom, I'll be out of here before anybody notices. Straight to Cali, and I'll specialize in BMWs, they're wild about them over there, I heard that from this black dude at Henderson. Get it, I'm checking that out, 'cause I gotta get out of here sometime, no one can deal with all this, it turns you stupid, being inside here. Even you give me the slip. Later, their talk turned to clubs and bars, and Wörmann said a few names, knew a lot about the different parts of the scene, where you could buy pure hashish, LSD, he talked about Damage, too, and Raspe told him about his first time there recently. Wörmann played it cool.

The ping-pong players were tireless. A gardener, Turkish (or Greek?), of indeterminate age, was fussing with a rosebush, maybe he was thirty, maybe he was fifty-five fifty-six, in dark blue bib overalls with broad straps that crisscrossed behind his back, the kind of outfit you saw on progressive school teachers and, increasingly, HippieGranolaFreaks, often with nothing underneath, on the street or at the theatre festivals. You were used to it on those people. On the gardener, paradoxically, it looked ironic. Now, the gardener grabbed the hose attached to a rotating sprinkler, folded it with a practiced grip, and walked, dragging the hose behind him, to the sprinkler's slack, mutely dripping arm, picked up the contraption and placed it a few yards away, at another spot on the lawn. When the water jetted forth again, Wörmann jumped up, ran across the lawn, and danced in the artificial rain, hopping, spinning with outstretched arms, throwing his head back, then stopped and looked up to receive the fine spray of water as it fell. He returned to the bench with a smile and flicked water into Raspe's face.

– Still and all, I've about had it with this bullshit clinic. It's the weekend.

– Why still and all?

– 'Cause I wanna go swimming, fishing, I need to see my friends and all, you know, bars, I told you all that before.

– Yeah, I know, of course, but I think

– Anyway, I ain't taking those goddamn drops anymore. 'Cause when you're healthy, you don't need no drops.

– Since when did you stop taking your medicines?

–Medicines, that's a good one! They give you cramps so you can't even walk normal, you can't swallow, drool runs out of your mouth.

– But I already told you, those side effects will pass.

– Yeah, but now they're gone, 'cause I ain't taking it, that shit. Beat me if you want to, it doesn't matter.

– Since when?

– 'Cause I'm fine. When you drop acid, you lose your shit, everyone does that, obviously. What about you, you ever take that poison, that Halodol?

– I know, I know, I want to try it myself sometime.

– What now? You take that Halodol

– Haldol, it's called Haldol.

– Haldol, the fuck do I care, you take that Haldol

178

before?

– No.

– OK, no, so acid, you ever trip before, no, I don't even have to wait for an answer, do I?

– No, you don't.

– So Doc, man, I don't get it, how're you supposed to treat me, you ain't tried Haldol, you ain't tried LSD, you don't know New York or Frisco, you don't have a bike, Doc, dude, dude, do you at least have a girlfriend?

– No, I don't even know what a woman looks like.

– This ain't *no* joke, man. 'Cause I got a girlfriend, I need to go see her, it's urgent, so I gotta get out of here, understand?

– Certainly.

– Or do you not think I'm totally normal and healthy again, because the way I am now, that's how I always am, and it's not like any of you guys are any better.

– No, I agree. But when you came here a few days ago, you were different, you weren't healthy then, I have to say.

– Yeah, of cooourse, dude, I was tripping my balls off, I was out there, overdrive, come on now, no one's normal when they're tripping. But this here, in the clinic, that's a shock for everyone, the nastiest bad trip ain't got nothing on this, these people really have a screw loose, pling pling, they're nuts, and I'm locked up with them, in the same room, that's the shock of a lifetime for me, it really is, understand.

– You're right about that, in a way. I'll have to talk to Bögl and we'll see if we can't get you out of here soon.

– You're a good dude, Doc, soon – I need out *today*. And why Bögl, I figure *you're* the one who's responsible for me. You told me yourself.

– Of course, that's true, too, but I've only been here

for a week.

– Whaaat? So that means basically we've been here the same amount of time, right?

– Basically, yeah.

– So you're an apprentice, ha, sorry, that's too much, I'm going to split my sides.

– True, it's funny, I think so too.

– OK, Doc, how 'bout a cig, then.

They smoked in silence. Good old Wörmann, Raspe thought. The ping-pong table was free, and Wörmann wanted to play. He hit the ball hard and aimed well, but Raspe was better. Must be that goddamned Halodol was still in his bones, Wörmann said, otherwise I'd give you the whipping you deserve, you hear that, Doc?, we can keep score, go for it.

The sun sank deeper, and the afternoon declined softly. The hours sank away as though unnoticed. Raspe sat a long time on the bench with Peter Wettinger. Some of the patients played football. Wettinger was the same age as Raspe. Raspe understood what Wettinger said. Wettinger observed everything and developed radical concepts for his daily work. In little steps, he said, you can make progress, even here, in a clinic like this. I make a balance sheet every day. It takes an insane amount of effort. Sometimes a week passes and I'm at the end of my tether, tired, slack. At those times, everything runs its course without me. But eventually, I always end up pulling myself together, always have, it's been five years now. Giving up – anyone can do that. I want to fight, otherwise there's no point in my work. Wettinger had long, frizzy, curly hair, parted in the centre. He rolled his own cigarettes. Raspe hated freaks. Warily, he would get to know Wettinger better.

I'm in the lab, phone's on as always, call if something comes up, Dr Bögl. In pencil. Raspe picked up the scrap of paper he found on his desk and grimaced. Doctor, Doctor Bögl, in conversation it was Waldemar, in writing His Highness Dr Bögl. Sure thing, MisterProfessorDoctorSir. Raspe stood there and dialled, Bögl picked up right away. Could he now, was he done for the day, for the time being there was nothing happening in the unit. Bögl: Of course, naturally, you can go, the nurses have my number anyway, I'll still be around for a while this afternoon. So yeah, see you Monday, cheers.

Promptly Raspe removed his lab coat, hung it up in the closet, a few sweeps of the hand to put the desk in order, and soon he was outside, downstairs, in the U-bahn tunnel, a part of the evening's festivities, a back-and-forth surging, everyone happy, weekend good mood, homeward, my loves, the stately carriage bears me, blue and silver gleaming under neon suns.

The weather foundered. Clouds pressed darkly forward, threatened the morning sky, and soon the wild currents were whipping through the streets, deep, almost palpable. They loomed over houses, over roofs, then let loose, thunder crashed, lightning, and wielding water like a weapon, the storm brought the heat to a halt, drove it back. Dramatically the temperature fell and fell, cold, a blackberry winter in this hottest June of the century, wind raged from the northwest, and the storm clouds hurried away. Rain fell in veils, timeless, formless, aerosol from the gloomy sodden sky, and the grey was imposing now, and nothing more divided the hours, the days.

Inside, behind glass, amid artificial light: the slow-motion ruin of the weekend, who can bear it? And how? Raspe wanted to clear up, clear out, but for what?, wanted to read, but read what?, why read?, and so he lay in bed, ate chocolate, looked, disconsolate, through the window at the water hammering away on the mansard roof, noise rilling cooing flowing, twilight lullaby, Raspe dreamed. He woke up overheated, felt the flood in and around him, discontent, indefinite, nothing but discontent, Raspe wished to go on sleeping, couldn't. Soundlessly he let the blue Suchard wrapper fall to the floor, hazelnut milk chocolate raisins, left the torn foil as it was, not balling it up, left everything, even the record player that spun inexhaustibly. Next to the bed lay a precarious pile of old magazines, *Stern*, *Spiegel*, and others, more to clear out, throw everything away, Raspe thought, but then he tipped over the whole heap beside the bed in resignation. Why throw them out? He took the top item off the pile, leafed lost and irresolute through the pictures, which were still glossy, had barely faded, but had an effect like the irruption of authenticity, irreal reality, awakening an ache, a pull, no, no one, no one can resist that. The seventies, sinking down into the recent past, half-moving-risible half-appalling, the faraway stone age of those still-present years, lived through long ago, Raspe leafed through them, and at last he gave in, no longer resisting, to the pull of those old magazines, which reached like the weather into the present, dissolved time, left every living being lying on the broad, sloping surface of melancholy. Slip, fall, wanting nothing but to fall.

Oh, suddenly there was the job, something to hold on to. Morning drew Raspe to the clinic, evening back to his apartment, and soaked with incessant rain, but nonetheless pleasant, a gentle green strip of day spread out before him.

Who even knows how to live? There were demands, patients colleagues faces, open and tormented, or deeply guarded, you had to talk, so Raspe talked, reasonably. Should he perhaps be silent? Words fell from mouths, much of them were madness, silence was often brief.

I want to be an abyss, Raspe told himself, but in vain. The lure was too strong. It would be nice to be an individual, to walk through the clinic impervious, as he used to at university, to sit aloof among his colleagues at the meeting. But then someone smiled at him and waved. Another asked for advice, for help with some science thing. It was soothing to go along with it, in a lab coat, like the others, to sit there being earnest. And then the power was there, yeah, that had been alluring. – I don't believe we can let you go yet, it would be best if you stayed a while, Raspe had said to a patient shamelessly. How quickly his shame had vanished. And did everyone not clap him on the shoulder in agreement and say:

Right on! To lord it over others like that was a distinctive pleasure, and without noticing, Raspe had got the taste for it.

Raspe sucked knowledge up greedily. Psychiatry knows many diagnoses and five medications. Raspe specialized in hard diagnostic questions and subtle distinctions. Soon he could say to Bögl: What does our supervising physician know about the problems of hebephrenia? And Bögl said: Exactly, exactly! But the supervising physician ordered the inducement of symptoms through Imipramine.

Raspe would touch his patients gently on the back. Kiener appreciated it. Almost every day he told some short, ludicrous story. Everyone would laugh. Thomas Wörmann got out. After a few electroshocks, Stelzer was declared definitively cured. The nail beds of his thumbs had healed.

Once Raspe was walking down a long hallway behind a colleague, it was night, there was an emergency in outpatient care, and he looked spellbound at the colleague's flowing, curly blond hair and thought he was a woman, and felt yearning. The night was a magnifying glass. An alcoholic came in and attempted suicide, you had to talk a long time with these poor people, and Raspe treasured every second he could sit at work with his colleague. He looked Raspe in the eyes.

Then Grahl was released, too. His wife no longer insisted on divorce, and it must have seemed all was well. Every week, Raspe changed his lab coat in the supply wing. Bögl returned from holiday and said: Let me show you a photo of our boat. Those are my two boys, that's my wife, you know her already, and here's my mother-in-law.

Raspe was supposed to give a lecture, science, and

184

now had to do research in the evenings, despite his exhaustion. When it was over, his colleagues walked up to congratulate him. A Swiss researcher inquired into detailed problems. A moderator brought the conference to a close, all present were lithium researchers, Bögl was there too, but hadn't given a presentation. Raspe had, people came up and wanted to know all about him.

What did Raspe perceive on entering the clinic in the mornings? You know what you know, and the eye turns lustreless. The aching compulsion to observe had long since abated. Raspe came and went.

Awful: how in mid-August, all at once, autumn was there. The next morning rose after a hot, stormy day with a soaring, deep blue sky, and cool, almost cold air. Who can salvage the summer after a wind like that? And the morning fog lay over the roofs when Raspe took his first glance outside. No sooner had he seen the lindens dying on the way to the clinic than he thought of his work. I want to become the best, a preeminent psychiatrist.

The autumn brought concerts outside the city, weekends, early evenings, outings to the country in Raspe's roomy Mercedes, which seated five or six, drinking beer, smoking hash, swaying like a steamship through the hilly landscape lit up by the sinking sun. Babylon is burning, then, very slowly, the billiard table sank, dispatched by Raspe and Klaus, like an elephant shot in the knee. Later, Jah War fighting jah war, Klaus dug a tooth deep in the hairy skin on Raspe's head, and it broke off and stayed stuck there. And the others? They hopped back and forth, blessed alcohol and kief and rhythm. Late one night, a tyre popped on the motorway. There was a helpful man in uniform on the scene, he saw the crate of beer in the car, the empty bottles, and said: How can I help you? What should we do now?

This unaccustomed violence of late summer. How should Raspe come to his senses? The organic brain syndrome patients were a relief. They sat in front of Raspe with child-like cheer, knew nothing of yesterday, were friendly, were always self-assured: When I get better, I'll go back into the kitchen, one of them said, and laughed, laughed to himself. Labile affect, Raspe noted in his file.

Had he really complained? About the morning meetings, about Bögl, about science? That was beginner's shock, Raspe came to understand. The Ordinarius, Professor Reiter, approached him amiably and said: People tell me you really shone during your presentation at the lithium conference in Marseille. I'm happy to hear that, very happy indeed. So now? What comes next?

Raspe had also gained a foothold at Damage. Pflunder, the doorman with the baby face, now greeted him like a friend, and Harry only rang him up at 1.30 a.m., not after every beer. You could see friends new and old, shoot some pinball, drink two-three beers, without too many words. Was it a problem, the distance between the two worlds? Not at all: it's just that there was day and night and the weekend, and their contrasts held them together and gave each hour its proper importance.

Raspe sat in front of a woman with greying hair. Was she a mother, a sister, a wife? Raspe looked askance at his notepaper, the patient's name must be written down there. Biographical data, childhood illnesses, sexual history. Raspe made an orderly inventory of everything, looking attentively but not listening, already heard himself reading into the Dictaphone, no more than ten minutes, Raspe figured, playing doctor, miscarriages, nah, leave that out, I could still ask about masturbation, maximum ten minutes to dictate the case history afterwards. The way they sank into one another, the patients before and the ones after, how every patient was a fraction of one great suffering, and the talk of relatives, what distinguishes today's conversation from yesterday's? How they look at us! How the suffering makes their gaze so monotonous, so predictable, so boring. And how we say: Haldol Haldol and Saroten and Neurocil. Does it not have a melodious ring to it?

Raspe wanted to call himself to order. Am I still a person? Where have my feelings gone to? Have I ever felt love? Did I ever truly love? Down below, hair hung over that brown dampness, I wedged my head in there, lapped there with my tongue, I remember, what did my nose smell? Was that love? And now? Just as near, just as far, everything that once was poignant drifts past. Those strange people in the U-bahn, did they move me? Did I suffer along with the poor devils, the patients? – I do my job, and I do it well. – That sounds so cynical. I won't accept that! – What? What are you getting at now?

There was talk in Raspe's head, strange arguments. Raspe listened, heard an idealist, heard a defeatist, a drunk, a cynic, a man in despair. But the pull of reality was stronger. Was he not sitting here importantly in his lab coat? One among the many, the chosen. Why sink his head pensively? Even sombrely? Greetings, cheerful greetings for the colleagues, on a Monday morning. – The weather was nice for your trip, right. – Ah, old Tasso. So you're actually going to Salzburg, sorry, but you're nuts, that's absolutely nuts.

Then the chromosomes and the depression. How clueless science was. Or electroshock? – I don't feel like that, the patient said. – But I do feel like it, the supervising physician said sternly. Later, Bögl to Raspe: Did you hear that with the electroshock and the feel like it and all that! He doesn't know what he's saying, how he's showing his hand. Raspe didn't want to commit to electroshock, preferred Saroten for depression, or talking, a little at least, even if it was practically good for nothing

Raspe pounded his head on the edge of the desk. A brain fell out. It dripped on to the pages of a book. Or was that water? The words danced lost in his eyes, letters, uncoupled and meaningless. I must learn to read again. Raspe understood only symptoms, the histories themselves disintegrated. The fictive experiences of books were dead, but the histories of these individuals were hacked apart in the exact same way. Now now: Do you smell that? A racket, a chaos behind my eyes, how it stinks, the scent of brain. Cenesthopathic symptomatics, thought Raspe, oh right, pathology, I remember that well. We made the cut along the hairline, then tugged the scalp, sometimes hairy, sometimes smooth, over the skull down to the root of the nose, down towards the dead stranger's face, the headskin would hang slack, the hairs from the neck floating somewhere over the chin, and the DrillSawChisel worked at the roof of the skull until, with a crack like the shattering of plywood, the calvaria finally folded to the side, and there it lay, the reward for our effort, open, so orderly, slightly wobbling, yes, there it lay, the brains, all of them so alike, their scent unmistakeable.

But the alarm sounded at six. Then Monday morning broke, a new week, another week for Raspe, back to the daily grind, to the office with its bracing demands. None of the traps a Sunday afternoon held out, free time, a bit of reading again, at last, an abyss you fell into unawares, stumbling backwards with unsteady steps. When had that been? Yesterday, was it really

188

yesterday? Raspe knew it, and yet couldn't believe it. Everything was slashed to pieces. What madness. Had he ever before lived with such order and concentration? The time seemed to race by, every week faster than the last, and sometimes Raspe feared the tempo would prove too much, that the next curve, a slight bend on the road, might catapult him out, and there would be no going back. But these fears grew microscopic alongside the daily onward and upward, better more correct more informed and so his work as a doctor more beneficial for the patients. After months, did he not finally understand the meaning of the highly differentiated psychiatric diagnoses? You must learn to grasp them as a legacy, as deliverance from the ruthlessly curt verdicts the previous century imposed on the afflicted: feeble-minded or insane or melancholic. We had begun to look, to listen, to make finer distinctions. The diagnoses must spur me in that direction, Raspe said to himself. That means I must assent to my legacy, lay hold of the psychiatry of today in light of that of yesterday, that is the only way to arrive at a vision of a humane psychiatry of the future. If Raspe looked around, he saw that for many of his colleagues, diagnosis was an end in itself, at best an aid to documentation, that could only goad him to challenge himself and to remedy the situation. It is not the institution that is bad, Raspe thought, or if it is, then it's because we doctors are bad. Raspe found other colleagues feeling their way forward like him. They would have to change the way the diagnostic toolkit was employed: as opposed to the common practice of using diagnosis as a defence against fear, as a defence of a body of knowledge that had its roots in the fear of the sick, they should view diagnosis in its historical context, turn it back into an instrument serving knowledge. That shouldn't be impossible, Raspe thought.

This impulse gave Raspe's work meaning. And to this degree, the setbacks, the doubts were pushed aside, the days when Raspe was not even aware who he was talking to. Did the days pile up? Did he not think more and more that all of them were just a single indistinguishable patient? Did he not stare, suddenly spellbound, at the face of a passing patient reflected in the silver glimmer of a curved drainpipe beneath the sink and wonder: Who cleans that? And when?, while the person across from him believed Raspe was following along with his tale of woe? Such things happened. Such things happened not infrequently. But was that an argument for or against anything?

The euphoria of morning was there in the autumn mist. Raspe leapt. Atomized as everything appeared at times, it was evident: Raspe had a story. Did he know it? It could be reconstructed. He could count the months at the clinic. He could count the number of beers consumed in an evening at Damage. Raspe kept a list of the patients he'd treated, with syndromes, duration of therapy, and effectiveness of treatment. The list grew longer. It included one suicide. He could gather the parking tickets left on his car. Raspe gathered. Oil receipts, newspaper clippings, photos, all these things had their own place and their own duration. Naturally, a doubt arose: Were you even alive yesterday? Raspe looked at his birth certificate. He wanted to take stock, yes, a list, make some kind of list. Raspe sat before a sheet of white paper and noted achievements, failures, the food he ate. Raspe tried to hold himself together with his mind. In the late morning, after the fog had lifted, a painfully clear autumn light fell in the doctors' station, and the euphoria of morning took a sad bow and said goodbye.

At night, Raspe woke up terrified, and the brooding started in his head. There was no understanding. Megalomania, crazed ambition for a brilliant career in science: I must I will I want I will will will. At the same time, Raspe felt unfathomably low and futureless, saw far off, like a mirage, the collective misery of psychology, the basic impracticability of this particular branch of medicine. Sullen stagnation, the most contradictory impulses, no way out. And Raspe wished for the reproach of arrogance, more and more he wanted his colleagues to reproach his arrogance, he wanted it as a distinction, to pin it on his lab coat like a medal. But he had long enjoyed the blessing of fitting in with his colleagues, of being a member of their circle. At night, in the dark, the antinomies remained, antinomies, of course, and the same arguments recurred, and his sleepless mind could reach neither decisions nor even conclusions.

There were days in the clinic and a way of functioning inside that lay beyond conclusions, but still, were not mere blindness. If he deliberated, life seemed so complicated to Raspe, in fact, quite simply unmanageable. There was alcohol. The evenings at Damage, that was solace in the meantime. And on the weekends: Ruts, Talking Heads, Siouxsie and Devo, friends, proximity to drunkenness. The clinic, oh, how everything always falls apart again. Come on, boy, let's drink another one, cheers.

The first terror was past. Acclimatization became ever more powerful. That perplexed Raspe. He said: I am completely different from you all. Raspe knew this was a fiction. The others had thrown their nets over him, and he had willingly let them capture him. Science, competence, responsibility, proper treatment: Raspe knew he could help, was met with gratitude. The successes were obvious. The grimmer a clinic of that sort might seem, the more helpful it could actually be.

The months passed quickly, faster and faster, maybe, and frequently a fear beset Raspe: of not being up to it, of falling short before all that suffering. But then came the next day, and after that, the next. At night, dully relaxed, Raspe sat in front of the TV and ate. Generally he would go to bed early. Then he would wake back up, go to Damage, drink a few beers, meet acquaintances, play pinball, drive home with a curious levity. The next day, he would get up, still a bit drunk, go to the clinic, and perform his duties.

Research, the overnight shift, collegiality, and power, at times it was familiar, at other times strange, at others exalted beyond all doubt, like the beer and the night music, exhaustion, happiness.

So time lurched by. Was Raspe not still standing, knocked about a bit, but still? Then something pulled him away again. A face offered support. They sat in a bar regularly, every fourteen days or so, Raspe and the man, whom he'd barely known at first, they drank and talked and talked, it was friendly, but still, they maintained a polite distance. Tears welled up, from where? Some phrase, a look, may have caught Raspe off-guard. Raspe looked back up from the tabletop: the face, the eyes, were radiant and indifferent. Blend of longing and revulsion. What was that? A stopping point.

One morning, when Raspe left home, the wind assailed him, the wind which for days had refrained from ruffling the trees, now in their autumn colours, it was bracing, even icy on his face, Raspe stopped, inhaled the air deep through his nose, savouring the scent. Then, unmistakeably, he caught a whiff of snow, a distant menace, tidings of winter. Raspe shook his head, or rather his brain, jerkily, said to himself: No!, then walked on to work in vague ill humour, once more habituated, painlessly dead to apprehension. How many times, how long already?

The tree trunks stretched their now bare branches bizarrely splayed into the air. Already: let it come, the winter, let it cover everything, the whiteness.

III

1.

A scent of slurry, almost a privy stench, rankled the bulbus olfactorius, but didn't reach the cerebral cortex, for Raspe's frantic, questioning mental leaps were focused on the search for his key to the clinic, which he had left at home, presumably, had hopefully not lost on the way, the key dammit the key, which his fingers felt for in the pocket of his coat, his jacket, his trousers, first according to the principle of probability, then to the principle of consequence, not foregoing the most unlikely places, until at last, the key, as Raspe had hoped deep down, against the suspicion he had expressed to himself to forestall disappointment, was found, lost, overlooked, in his right trouser pocket, nearly undetectable inside his handkerchief. Only when Raspe had inserted the key into the lock of the dark wood door of the unit did the stench, which had plagued him throughout the search for the key, rise into his consciousness, and with it the knowlegde that this stench had been plaguing him throughout his search for the key. – Shit, Raspe thought, maybe that's what the smell is. Bracing each time against one knee and turning the opposite foot inwards, first the left shoe, then the right, he bent over to examine his soles for any trace of dog excrement. Nothing, Raspe said, strange, then opened the doors.

Immediately Raspe gagged, nausea disgust refusal to breathe. The entire hallway, WallsFloorsWindowsTables, was smeared black with shit. Three nurses in yellow maids' gloves cleaned in silence, fighting a losing battle. It's 'cause you all never give them enough, one of the nurses said, kneeling on the floor in front of Raspe, without looking up. Of course, the lord doctors don't have to clean up afterwards. Save medicine, though. This guy even ate his shit, to boot. It's not my first time with this one. The nurse was right, Raspe said nothing. What should he say? The morning meeting started in five minutes. Breathing as little as possible, and when he couldn't help it, only through his mouth, Raspe sucked the bare minimum of air into his lungs and walked down the hallway towards the nurses' station, past two other nurses cleaning up, past the gurney where the new patient lay rigid, his hands bound to the frame with leather straps. His face was smeared with excrement. His expression was at once attentive and mask-like, the eyebrows above the eyes slightly raised and stiff as if drenched in resin. Here this unmoving stare, and above it the disarrayed dirty blond hair with excrement massaged into it, a stink that frayed your nostrils. As Raspe opened the glass doors to the nurses' station, he looked back over his shoulder one last time into the hallway. He saw there the psychiatry of another century, raving excess, straitjackets and ice baths, saw back three, four decades, and the achievements, the mercy, of medication.

Already in his lab coat, Bögl stood at his desk in the doctors' station, the phone close to his ear, and instead of his usual blustering greeting, merely nodded to Raspe, pointing towards the hallway with his chin, rolling his eyes, and shaking his head, at the same time agreeing yeahyeahyeah into the receiver, carrying on with the clearly onerous but uninterruptible conversation and gesturing to Raspe about the files on the table, the hour, and the morning meeting. Kidskids, said Bögl, setting down the receiver, chop chop, not through the shit hallway though. He opened the door to the stairwell, said to Raspe come on, and remarked cheerfully, as they hurried to the morning meeting, crossing the floor below the mephitic station entrance, along the building's hidden corridors, which gave covert access to nearly every part of the clinic, so you could pop up anywhere as if from out of nothing. All you needed was the keys. And involuntarily, Raspe felt in his pocket for the key he still thought he had lost or forgotten. Stupid, of course, Bögl said, with the rounds and all, having this mess this morning, we're not responsible, though, it's the night shift that's responsible, obviously, they're the ones who took him in and they're the ones who messed up his dosage, who was on duty, anyway? No idea, Raspe said, but by the time we get back, the worst of the filth will be cleaned up. True, Bögl said, we can even stop for a coffee in the cafeteria after the meeting.

They entered the library. It was two minutes after half-past, silence already reigned among their assembled colleagues, interrupted by the Director's greeting, which brought the meeting into session, and hastily, Bögl and Raspe took their places. In the interim, Raspe had been promoted from a chair along the wall to the august conference table itself, where even today, though the other seats were occupied, the armchairs reserved for Unit 1-4 had been kept free for him and Bögl. As Raspe sat, acknowledging the colleague to his right with a smile, Professor Reiter said GoodMorning with that dependable click of his tongue which gave the phrase, and the entire meeting along with it, the agreeable character of a ritual. We're running late, he added, and must get started right away. Then, with benevolent reproach, his eyes swept over Raspe, who looked up, huddled over the table, lifted his brows in an amused-ironic corroboration of guilt, and frowned in response. His *standing* with the Director was excellent. Raspe leaned back, relaxed.

The circle of colleagues, the familiar voices, the ritual, and you have your place there. Ever-changing names, never-changing patient files, the eternally self-same HumanTerrorFate, a broad stream of histories flowing in, dragging Raspe away, to where? Snow white blinding, gaze out the window. The stink of excrement in the unit, and while we sit here, the nurses wipe it away. If psychiatry, then, at the very least, as a doctor. Raspe looked at the clock, seven past half-past, Raspe had been in the clinic some ten minutes, how was it possible he was already so weary? And night shift today, and tomorrow, the Talking Heads concert, and the day after tomorrow, the meet-up with Rutschky, and then it's Friday already and Damage and the weekend, even starting at Tuesday morning, the weekend is nearly in reach. The only terrible thing is the Sunday nights and Monday mornings, really.

Bögl's elbow, Raspe nodded. Now the histories of the new patients, chronic schizophrenia, such-and-such an episode, catatonic excitement, clouding of consciousness and-so-on-and-so-forth. So what's the guy's name, Raspe said to Bögl. Bögl pointed in front of him at the hectograph paper that showed the names of the new admissions, Günter Schneeman, it read, then looked past Raspe to the young colleague who was still speaking and had clearly just come off his night shift; it was Rainer the Gentle, and Raspe could hardly be sour with him for administering what was clearly too low a dose, too late, to their regular guest Schneeman this morning at 5 a.m. Tell me, is his name really Schneeman, Raspe said to Bögl, who sat with an exaggeratedly stiff attentive look and shook his head joylessly without answering. Bögl and his eternal notions of diligence, thought Raspe, in the meetings and during the supervising physicians' and the Director's rounds. Maybe the head physicians liked it, the Director certainly didn't.

Raspe liked Rainer, who continued talking. Recently they'd had the late shift together and had uncorked a bottle of wine, and while they drank it, breezily as possible, given the diffuse restless feeling of waiting for the next patients to appear, Rainer had said, quite rightly: More and more, Bögl's entire orientation is towards the head physicians, his attitude and especially the way he sits there in the morning meetings. If a head physician was away at a conference or on vacation, Bögl would sit at the end of the row of the five head physicians, right there in the director's line of sight. At first, Raspe was shocked that he didn't feel ridiculous doing so, but increasingly, Raspe himself was caught up in that calculated chicanery that formed the basis of university clinic careerism and explained one's successes and failures. Raspe wavered. There were days when he was dead set on a stellar career, thought himself destined for it, and the cost and the casualties mattered nothing to him. The success of his early experiments – eventually, he dropped the lithium studies – his success with his colleagues and the Director in particular had brought his dreams of a dazzling career closer to reality. But there were other days when he was prey to abysmal loathing, for himself, for the whole of psychiatry, for his capacity to adapt to the horror, for that cynicism that grew inside him without cease, and all he could imagine was devoting his last bit of energy to being a good doctor, irrespective of what he might lose, at the expense of any sort of career. Or else throwing it all away, medicine, cutting out this torment of a job that had sprouted like a wart, metastasized like a devastating cancer, grown into a *second head*. So Schneeman's the name of the guy, Raspe thought, who was lying there fettered to the bed, his own excrement in his face and hair.

2.

The cafeteria wasn't properly heated yet. Raspe shivered, passed his coffee cup back and forth to warm his right and left palms, took greedy sips of his coffee. Meien, one of the head physicians, whom Bögl spoke of disparagingly, calling him either the Lecturer, the Pastor, or the Shocker, was coming for his rounds today between 9.30 and 10, and Bögl was already looking forward to slipping the Shocker some outrageous and patently false diagnosis, as he did almost every Tuesday, in so earnest a tone that Shocker had no choice but to believe it, even if, to all appearances, and judging from prior experience, it was certain to be a put-on. Meien was a nobody in the clinic, even and above all with the Director. He was in his mid-fifties, with a high forehead, colourless, slicked-back hair, and his appearance alone, among a group of colleagues who, like the Director himself, were all resolute, winning, handsome psychiatrist-types, was a not inconsiderable handicap. Then there was his half-aborted scientific career founded on the field of electroshock therapy, which on optics alone could hardly be described as auspicious. Only towards the end of his forties had Meien finished his habilitation and taken up his post – with tenacity, but without real merit – on one of the thrones reserved for the head physicians, and conceivably he would even, if the sniping in the clinic were true, be accorded a professor's pension when all was said and done. True, the Ordinarius, Professor Reiter, had proven a hindrance to his career path when they'd brought him over from Berlin University. But Meien also stood in his own way.

Apart from his occupational obsession of regaining lost therapeutic ground for eletroshock, he had a private peculiarity that proved a relentless irritation in the doctors' daily lives. Meien was a preacher for the Adventists or Mormons or some other sect along those lines, and he touted their principles tirelessly, above all in questions of morality, butting in with pithy remarks for patients and colleagues alike. Often the effect was not merely perverse, but actually a misstep. As though to give the lie to his unremarkable appearance, Meien cultivated a highly abnormal sort of rapport with his patients. To the younger colleagues – to Raspe too, at first – Meien extolled his exploratory methods as earnest, direct, and beneficial to the patient. Meien treated his patients like healthy peers: if they cursed at him, which was far from uncommon in the clinic, he might fly into a violent rage. Certain of the patients' delusions Meien would dismiss with an appeal to evidence and healthy human reasoning. In the beginning, Raspe had admired his frankness, so at odds with the other doctors' nebulous responses, which took everything with mendacious, unemotional nonchalance and an interest that was little more than botanical. But then Raspe had seen many times how Meien's forthrightness could wound and torment the patients, destroying the growth of trust in the process. In this light, Meien's protestations that he alone took the patients seriously were not enough. And there were times when Meien seemed to be just another victim of a now rampant loss of control. Meien was a perennial topic of conversation there, and while Bögl blabbed about him, Raspe recollected his early weeks at the clinic. From the first, he had shown an interest in electroconvulsive therapy, and that had made Meien happy. – You should see it for yourself, it's something you can pick up quickly, if you wish, Meien had said. The next morning, after a meeting interrupted by the beeping of his two-way radio, Meien had left the library with Raspe in tow, and the younger colleagues commented maliciously; they were skeptical, these colleagues, wanted nothing to do with electroshock, absolutely nothing, as though their resistance might bring the daily practice of it to an end. Raspe walked behind Meien to the fourth floor, to the furthest corner of the clinic, where the anaesthesiologist had prepared the first patient. Already, Raspe had allowed himself to become Meien's collaborator. Caught unawares by the request to push the patient's hair aside, Raspe had complied immediately, though all he had wanted to do was watch and learn. Raspe gave no more direct assistance for the six more people shocked that morning; steadily, his aversion to the therapy's violence had grown. Meien's chatter, flippant phrases, and technical-scientific explanations were just background noise to the images of dread, the spasmodic faces pulling wretched grimaces beneath the electric current. But far worse was the patients' fear before the shock, an evident, undeniable panic, even among those who knew shock had helped them before. When the morning was over, Raspe had tried in vain to talk about this panic and the other side effects with Meien. At every question, at the least criticism of what he termed therapeutic convulsions, Meien's conversation-ending defence mechanism came into play. As a consequence, Raspe and he frequently clashed, and these disputes grew more bitter as Raspe reached a degree of psychiatric competence through experience, a study of the relevant literature, and his own scientific work. In the meantime, Raspe, like almost everyone in the clinic, made fun of Meien, and kept up the culture of Shocker-jokes with Bögl, absurd brief dialogues from the psychiatrists' routines that invariably ended with Meien's recommendation: Best if we give 'em a couple of shocks, then.

After the topic of Meien had been dispatched with consummate humour and the second cup of coffee drunk down, the uncomfortable question arose of whether the nurses had finished cleaning Mr Schneeman's excrement in the station hallway. They chatted about the nurses in general, and for the umpteenth time, with the pertinent vocabulary, Bögl explained his well-established positions. Raspe often had a guilty conscience since he'd come to know Peter Wettinger better. Still, it was a fact that the nurses would clean up the shit and that as a doctor, Raspe would steer clear of it.

At the last possible moment, shortly after 9.30, Raspe and Bögl walked sniffing down the steps and to the doors of their unit. – You smell anything? – Nah, you? – Me neither, I don't smell anything. Instead of the stench, they were met by a scream that pierced the doors and echoed into the stairway: inarticulate, indistinct, animalistic deep drones that rose and subsided as though bellowed amid death-throes. Bögl opened the door and they stood there in the hallway replete with fetor and screaming, an undifferentiated torment to the senses of smell and hearing, a hurricane-like assault bearing down on Raspe. But he didn't stumble, he walked on calmly and did his job.

The three nurses who had spent the past few hours cleaning the hallway now stood at the freshly made bed of the likewise freshly washed patient and tried to administer him warm tea through a sippy cup amid ear-splitting howls. – All right, *that's* not what we meant before about the dangerous fluid deficit, for you to force it on him at any cost, give me the cup now, you have to talk to the patient, he hears you just fine, even if he's pretending to be deaf and dumb, hear me out now, Mr Schneeman, listen, look at me, come on, Mr Schneeman, no one wants to hurt you, you have to drink something, you know that perfectly well from prior visits, turn towards me.

Schneeman did quieten down, but did not relax his rigid posture, kept his face turned stiffly towards the wall, didn't react to Bögl's words, and if Bögl touched him, even softly, he would start roaring again. Bögl straightened up and turned to Raspe: What do we do? He needs fluids. He's rejecting the tea. Neuroleptics won't work for him either with an exsiccosis like that. Meien will just want to shock him. Should we give it another go, or what? The nurses exchanged an annoyed glance, one said: Look, and Bögl ignored him.

Raspe turned to the patient, who went back to bellowing like an animal, and stood at the top of the bed, Schneeman was looking straight ahead, his eyes pressed shut, and when Bögl came over with the sippy cup, he slammed his mouth shut, and his screams became a more terrified moan. A nurse pinched the patient's nose, and when he opened his mouth for air, the nurse applied a painful grip that forced his upper and lower jaws an inch apart. Raspe had to muster all his strength to keep him from jerking his head. Bögl spilled tea into the man's open mouth. The liquid filled his oral cavity and drained from the corners of his mouth on to the pillow. Shit, Raspe said. Exactly, Bögl said. The nurse holding one of his arms sat on it and squeezed the patient's larynx with his newly freed hand. Reflexively, the patient swallowed the tea that remained in his mouth. Over and over, Bögl refilled the sippy cup. Raspe's hands were tired, they could hardly hold the patient's head straight any longer. The man's resistance was unflagging, but the technique they'd chosen to administer the tea was even stronger. How many millilitres have we got down?, Bögl said. The nurse, who filled the cup from a dull tin pitcher, answered. 250 or so we need to take off, Bögl said, because we didn't get it all in there, right? No, Raspe said, not all of it.

Raspe held the man's head. What thoughts were in that head? What thoughts were in mine? Did Raspe think? Did he see how the scene combined everything: lust for violence, therapeutic necessity, revenge? Did he see anything? He was a collaborator, he had held the patient's head from behind. Was there a choice in such a situation? Did Raspe question it? What had happened was plain to see. Now, the stink was back in Raspe's nose, and the welling disgust overwhelmed Raspe's brain, disgust, nothing but disgust.

3.

Then calm, sitting and waiting, sitting in the doctors' station, waiting for Meien. When is Meien coming? The head physician hoped to be there by ten at the latest, Raspe looked at the clock, it was six after, then looked at Bögl. Bögl answered by wearily hoisting his arm from the armrest, splaying his fingers, turning his palm upward, and freezing. Then, balling his hand airily into a fist, he let it fall on to his upper thigh. I could give him a ring, should I give Meien a ring? Well, Raspe said, I'd just as soon be working on something as sitting here killing time. You really think Schneeman was aware for all of that? Don't trouble your head about it, Meien would have just shocked him, no doubt about that whatsoever. Pass me the phone, I'll call upstairs, we'll see if he's forgotten or is on his way or what. If Schneeman was aware, he'll tell you himself in a couple of days.

Bögl had dialled as he uttered these words, and now he pressed his ear to the receiver. Yeah, Bögl here, Bögl said, then the other person interrupted him, and it was clear from his tone as he said yeahyeah and naturally that none other than Meien was pleading with him. This time, Bögl didn't grimace to Raspe or pantomime jocosely, carrying out a parallel dialogue in gestures; instead, he nodded yes to himself or lowered his eyes while his gaze seemed fixed on the left hand he had brought close to his face, middle finger and thumb bent into a circle and touching at the tip, making a sharp, snapping sound with the fingernails in regular half-second intervals.

Stop, Raspe said to himself, blindness for weeks, and today as though forced to observe – forced by what? For what purpose? – this compulsive perception steered from elsewhere, and stillness behind the eyes, in the head. And in the occipital lobe of his brain, he saw the visual cortex like a movie screen forced on the optical nerve, a rushing vanishing succession of details, sudden stillness, images, burned in. And past the window, a heavy snow fell from the heavens to the earth.

– Wake up, man, this is no time for daydreaming, Meien's not coming till tomorrow, and now we've got a surprise visit to keep everyone on their toes.

– What was he going on about for so long?

– What do you mean, so long?

– Look at you being all civil, you must have said yes and naturally thirty times on the phone.

– Nonsense. What do you mean, civil? Professionally speaking, you know my thoughts on Meien. Still, there's no call to be hostile with him. I see no advantage whatsoever, for me or for our work here in the unit, to taking a hostile approach with Meien.

– OK, OK, roger that, so what did he tell you in such

detail?

– No idea, man, the usual, he had an urgent expert assessment, had ordered his colleagues to put together a medical history, they could only do it today, so he's coming tomorrow, 9.30 on the dot, wants you to be here, and-so-on-and-so-forth.

– And-so-on-and-so-forth, right, stellar. That doesn't work for me, tomorrow after my overnight shift, with the Director coming round to boot.

– Yeah, it's bullshit. So it's 10.14, how long do you think we need?

– What's on the agenda this morning really, besides the two discharges?

– So what do you say? Rough guess?

– A quarter to eleven, smooth sailing, I'd say. What about you.

– Smooth sailing. Let's get to it.

Raspe stood up, buttoned his lab coat over his navel, and bent over the washbasin, across from his mirror image. Then he walked with Bögl through the double doors, both of which, unusually, were open, and on into the patients' day room. Before he had closed the two doors, Kiener was there, he had been on the sofa next to the radio waiting for Raspe, clearly, and right away, he began to talk. – Burning to ashes, Doctor, that's what I'd like best, burning to ashes. I told my father, burning to ashes, that's what I'd really like, I told him once and I'm telling him again, and you should tell him too, Doctor, when he comes, or tell my brother, burning to ashes, that's what I'd like, and you've always stuck by me, so I wanted to ask you about it. Raspe tried to push past Kiener. But Kiener, neuropathically edgy, hopped from one leg to the other, blocking Raspe, and when the other foot landed flat on the floor, a wave of shudders coursed through his body, out into his arms extended at an angle, and into his slack, bloated, irritatingly jaunty medically swollen almost glowing face. Kiener, listen, Mr Kiener, said Raspe, we are running around like crazy because of the rounds, we'll talk this afternoon, OK. – And as soon as Raspe had writhed past Kiener, he hurried after Bögl, with long strides and a theatrically pensive sunken head, to the large dormitory, and just then, for a millisecond, he was aware of the overly harsh deceitfulness in his words, and right after, he forgot it again. Bögl stood in the centre of the room and pointed at the door to the hallway, which was closed, contrary to custom. Seems we have no nurses today, or are they still cleaning, or what? Raspe walked to the door, opened up, and shouted to no one in particular: Can we do our rounds now, please! Immediately, he closed the door again. This smell today, Raspe said. Yeah, said Bögl, all the more reason to get it over with. I say we just get started, and somebody will eventually show up.

Bögl and Raspe walked to the first bed on the left of the door. The patient lay atop the orderly arranged bed-cover and propped himself up on his elbows when he saw the doctors approach. – Now, Mr Past, Bögl said, we'll start with you today, how are things? – Nothing new, all's well. – No special complaints or requests? The patient seemed to turn that over listlessly, then nodded his head, saying: Nah, not that I can think of, nono, all's well. – Very good, Mr Past, we won't disturb you any further then, said Bögl, walking away with a wave to the patient, who said right then, two or three times, nono, you're not disturbing me at all, Doctor, you don't disturb me in the least, while Bögl, now standing at the next bed over, turned to Raspe and said: I find it extremely strange that he doesn't try to get out, do you find that normal? Because according to Meien, he's fit as a fiddle.

Raspe shrugged and turned to the next young man, who lay clothed and dozing on the bed. – So, how's it going, what's happening with the swelling on the neck? – Same as always, the patient said with closed eyes. – Do you still feel you're being watched, then? – No, but either way, it doesn't matter, I want to go home, and for real this time, not just for two months like before – forever. I need to get back into school, you know that. – I do, Raspe said, but you also know you can't return home yet. – Can't, bullshit, whatever. – Yes, so for the time being, we'll continue with the medicine, Raspe said to the nurse, who had shown up in the interim with the patient charts and nodded without a word while glancing at the still-blank page in the prescription book.

In the next bed lay Stelzer, whose depression the shock therapy had improved to an astonishing degree, even if the results had only lasted three months. Since the end of November, they'd gone back to shocking Stelzer twice a week, but this time, there were no effects whatsoever, and Stelzer had resumed the lethargic grisly destruction of his thumbnails. Stelzer appeared to be sleeping just then. – We'll let him sleep, of course, and turning to the nurse, he's up again tomorrow, right? The nurse nodded and they walked to the next bed. There the patient begged for Akineton. Raspe refused. At the next bed, Raspe could lower the Haldol by ten milligrams in good conscience. Now Bögl was back and Raspe stood beside him, dull and indifferent. All nerve and all feeling, stolen away, thought Raspe, they tear them out of you, the sick do, after just ten minutes' worth of rounds, you speak the same phrases into the same faces, nod meditatively to the stereotypical answers, though it's been ages since anything's occurred to me when Adelhauser, that fat sissy with the eternally quivering legs, tells me for the nth time he got up early again this morning, was desperate so he couldn't sleep, felt guilty about the incident with the new kid, the young manic, at the end of last week, was not depressive but rather sexually disturbed, when he tells me all that for the hundredth time. Whatever they said, it was all so oppressively inconsequential. And that junkie in detox Raspe had talked to will come back, just as Tommi Wörmann had come back, and this Zarges, and the rest of them, whatever their names were. How was all this grandiose dedication supposed to sway them? And as the rounds became routine and unfurled on their own, Raspe's tedium and listlessness mounted, everything was pointless, all this wearisome commitment. How many of his current patients had he already treated before, when he'd only just got there? And he'd thought he could heal them, what a pathetic delusion. All that still so kindly chatter, all that prattle was nothing against the power of psychosis. Well, let's try it again, Raspe said, with medicine, we'll be able to get a handle on it. Things along those lines came constantly to Raspe's mind, and simultaneously emerged from his mouth, to his despair.

– So, my good man, Bögl said after the last bed, we've exceeded our time limit by nearly ten minutes.

– Tighten it up, Raspe said, we gotta tighten it up, tighten it up a little bit more.

4.
Finally eluding the sick gazes again, a place of sanctuary, of calm: the doctors' station. Raspe stood at a desk flicking through the newly stacked paper, findings pharma flyers patient files science. What's arduous isn't the rounds themselves, what's arduous, almost torturous, is

209

the presence of the insane, their glowering, their stares. What am I thinking, Raspe thought. What's pointless, what plagues me, are my doubts about the job, like today, it strains you, these spells, inconsequential basically useless, this struggling.

Like lightning, Raspe reached for the telephone receiver, picking it up before the first ring finished, then holding it a few inches over the apparatus, laughing triumphantly at Bögl, who had reached for his own phone a second later. They were connected to the same line. Bögl laughed now and said: four-two to me. Raspe nodded and then brought the receiver to his ear.

Professor Schlüssler said he was in dire straits, had a pressing, urgent request. He was down a patient for his next lecture, which started in ten minutes, he had wanted to give a demonstration of involutional melancholy. Could Unit 1-4, maybe Raspe himself, help out? Not gonna be easy, Raspe said, we're under a lot of pressure here, but if I'm honest, I have to say, yeah, we can help. We have Mr Fottner here, we just went over him in detail at the Friday meeting, I don't know if you remember, he's got involutional melancholy and then some. I could let you have him. Schlüssler agreed immediately, asked Raspe to handle the necessary details, and to attend the lecture himself, if at all possible.

Schlüssler, Raspe said to Bögl after hanging up the phone, wants to present Fottner and me in his lecture at a quarter past, Fottner as an involutional melancholic and me as a premorbid schizoid personality in the early stages of trema, with unease, angst, vague feelings of guilt, the typical symptoms of delusional tension, in other words. What do you say? Magnificent idea, my delusionally tense friend, Bögl said, but first, just one thing: Who'll take care of the discharges here? I mean, I would gladly, I think, I would have, sure – but I'm afraid you have to do that on your own, today.

The lecture by one of the head physicians, Professor Schlüssler, the oldest doctor in the clinic, just a year away from his retirement, was more interesting and more instructive than the main lecture by the clinic's director Professor Reiter, a man ten years his junior. Professor Reiter presented himself in every situation, and thus in his lecture as well, as a moderate, dispassionate man of the middle, who parried all objections to the biologically oriented psychiatry he advocated, but nonetheless took them seriously. Professor Schlüssler, on the other hand, was a gnarled extremist, whose lecture showed both an undisguised contempt for his patients and a contempt for humanity as a whole, combined with a pitiless emphasis on truth that extended even to the state of his own profession: This and this alone is what psychiatry looks like, my esteemed colleagues, there are no fine words that can change it, and the unverifiable hypotheses of psychoanalysis are no help either. At that he indicated the quivering, erratically spasmodic person next to him. Take a close look, that is tardive dyskinesia provoked by more than ten years of neuroleptic therapy, one person gets it, another one doesn't, and as psychiatrists, there's not one thing you can do about it. Right, now come here, Mr Mr Mr – come on over now, up to this first bench here. Pointing at the twitching patient, who could only walk with difficulty, Schlüssler said to the students: Look, he can't even walk normally anymore, or would you say that's normal, the way he walks? To the patient: How does it feel? Is it comfortable or uncomfortable? While the patient looks confused at the professor, begins to stutter something out, the latter turns back to the students, who sit before him on steep risers: No, naturally that isn't comfortable for him? So, what do we do with him? How do you treat someone like this? And naturally, the units are packed to bursting with them, not so much with us, as we're a university clinic, but the big institutions that offer long-term treatment, the regional hospitals, absolutely. Now, how do we treat tardive dyskinesia? Yes, it's paradoxical, but neuroleptic-induced tardive dyskinesia is treated with neuroleptics. There's no choice there. Without them, it can't be done. And that is psychiatry. Nurse, bring in the next patient.

Raspe observed that at first, the students reacted to Schlüssler's brutality with shock and disgust. Some avoided the lecture because of it. But most seemed to sense quickly that what this ruthless honesty was offering them was nothing less than the entire horror, and therefore the truth, of psychiatry, and along with it the compromises the psychiatrist faced, the unreasonable demands of his office, which almost inevitably made him into a monster.

Since the beginning of November, like most of the assistants at the clinic, Raspe had to teach a small group of students in a practice session devoted to basic psychiatry. Right off Raspe had recommended attendance at Schlüsser's lecture, particularly for the two anti-psychiatry fanatics; in Schlüssler's cabinet of horrors, psychiatry was laid bare in a way unknown at the university and certainly in Professor Reiter's main lecture, which was no less mendacious than it was mawkishly intellectualizing. It had begun to irritate Raspe how these two critics of psychiatry, with their keywords of theory undisturbed by practice, made the true impulses of anti-psychiatry into supercilious prattle. They could use that to attack Professor Reiter and were guaranteed a moral victory; but not with Professor

Schlüssler, who presented himself as the miserable avatar of the misery of psychiatry itself. Indeed, this visit to Schlüssler's lecture threw Raspe's students into an uncertainty and brooding that now plagued Raspe himself again. The choice was an awful one: a calculated barrier to perceptions of the clinic and psychiatry, a scotomatous malfunction in the visual field that swallowed everything, even in Raspe, barely reaching the level of consciousness. That Schneeman, smeared with excrement this morning, had vanished like a lightning bolt amid my growing partial blindness, Raspe thought. Or you could see everything, and become a monster in the process, like Schlüssler. Earlier, Raspe had urged himself, standing before the papers on his desk: Conquer these doubts about your profession, there's no point in them; now, sitting to one side in the first row in the auditorium, he had to admit that the putative flight from his doubts into the ActionLecture of Professor Schlüssler had led him only deeper and more irrevocably into those same doubts. Professor Schlüssler limped past, nimbly dragging his short, stiff leg behind him – an old war wound – attaching the wireless microphone to his neck as he did so, and when he had managed to reach the lectern and lean in, nodded gently to Raspe, uttering a few introductory words.

To start with, I'll show you all something pleasant. We don't want to present you with unmitigated angst and horror. So this is a 23-year-old soldier, he's always chipper, and we want to talk with him a little bit. Nurse, please. Yes, Mr Knudsen, please come on in, these are all budding doctors you see sitting here. Right, and there you have a microphone, look how he's always laughing, how happy he is, and you can talk right into it, into the microphone, and now just go on and take a seat, to start with. Well now, esteemed colleagues, what we have here is a patient who from the outside appears unremarkable at first, and you shouldn't underestimate the importance of that, of your first impressions, for example, in the majority of cases, you can diagnose endogenous depression at a glance, without even speaking a word to the patient, even if that's no longer the modern approach, because, you know, now you're supposed to talk about everything all the time. So: we have here a patient who, besides his laughter, this generalized gaiety, exhibits nothing out of the ordinary. Now, let's try and find out what he knows. Do you know who you are, actually? – Yes, I'm Knud Knudsen. – Wonderful, well, he knows that, and again, he's happy about it. Are you happy about that? Why are you laughing? See, he doesn't know the answer, that's typical, he just is that happy. Good, let's continue: Mr Knudsen, do you know, could you tell me, where you are right now? – Sure, in the building, right? In the building, the one with the sick people, there. – Yes, well now, that is not entirely false, what he's saying, so yes, there's another thing he knows. Regardless, you may note that the word hospital doesn't occur to him, that he's talking his way around it. Let's keep that in mind. Good, now then: you are correct, Mr Knudsen, we are here in the hospital, what city is it in then, this hospital? See now, there he hesitates, he laughs again, he's not so sure about that one. Well, Mr Knudsen, which city? – Um, maybe, could be Hamburg, or...? – No, Hamburg, no, nonsense, this is Munich, do you realize that, Mr Knudsen? At that, he nods quite confidently, notice. And so we have established: personal orientation is unimpaired, spatial orientation is impaired. Now: What day is it today? There again, he's clueless, but that's the sort of thing one could forget here in the clinic. So: what month is it? He

doesn't know that, either. And the season, Mr Knudsen?
– Maybe it could be autumn, no, winter maybe? – How
did you arrive at that, winter? – So maybe autumn,
then? – Nonsense, it's winter, of course it's winter, but I
want to know how you came to that conclusion. – Ah, I
think because of the thing outside, the white and so on,
maybe winter, I think, or...? – Do you mean the snow?
– Exactly, on account of the snow, I was saying. – Good,
now, let's speed things up a bit here. I was inquiring as
to his orientation, just now, that is not so important,
nevertheless let us note that his temporal orientation is
likewise impaired. What I wanted to demonstrate to you
above all is his sensory anomic aphasia, which he tries
to compensate for, as we have seen with snow and hospital, by talking around the concept. All utterly typical.
And moving on, let us ask one more time, all right, Mr
Knudsen, what city is this hospital located in? See, he's
already forgotten, though I said it to him only a minute
ago, and there he goes laughing again. He has a blessed
disposition though, doesn't he, this young man? Right,
he has impaired retention as well, above all with regard
to the recent past, I could show you that too, but I will
hold off on that for now, these impairments take the form
of a memory disorder. I went through all this with the
patient yesterday, but he doesn't recall one bit of it, are
you aware, Mr Knudsen, that you and I spoke yesterday
in the unit? No, of course he no longer knows. Yes, so
in addition he has a retrograde amnesia stretching back
over a number of years, one can specify the length of
the gap with a great deal of precision. For example,
he no longer knows when he entered the military, but
he knows when he left school, correct, Mr Knudsen.
– Yeah, that was in '75, Doctor, in Jevestedt, maybe
you've been there? – You will observe that though his

thinking is somewhat laborious and constrained, there is no disorder of thought content, his affect is remarkably friendly and attentive, if also somewhat flat and emotionally incontinent. Good, good, in brief, what do we have here, then, what are we looking at? A classic organic mental disorder following craniocerebral trauma as a result of an automobile accident, this occurred during his military service, he no longer knows that, naturally, compression cerebri, epidural and subdural hematoma in the right and left lobes, and in addition, post-traumatic epilepsy. The only atypical aspect of his case is that, apart from a slight optic-agnostic disturbance, there are no other or hardly any other functional impairments such as alexia, acalculia, or constructional apraxia. He can count and read, though not so well, but presumably it was always this way with him, and he can also dress himself. Admittedly he does suffer from anosognosia, again of a very typical sort, I will show you that to conclude. Yes, Mr Knudsen, note, too, how nice a name like that sounds, or Peter Peterson or Diedrich Diederichsen, that's how it is in the north, with you all here in Bavaria there is no such thing, right, so, Mr Knudsen, I wanted to ask you in closing: Why are you actually here in the hospital? Hm? Do you not know – Well, maybe I can go soon, right? – Where would you like to go then? Are you really ill? – No, I think Jevenstedt, that I'm going back there, back home, no?, to my parents'. Or back to the thing, the uh, with the two stripes on the arm, maybe, yeah? – Do you mean the army? – Right. – Do you feel capable of doing that, then? – Maybe, yeah, sure. – Yes, he is confident because he is incapable of recognizing his own impaired state, right, Mr Knudsen, I mean, the army takes all sorts, but in his present state, he's rather a candidate for

216

disability, wouldn't you say? This anosognosia is actually an exquisite thing, a merciful invention of nature, I would say, particularly in concert with this sustained cheerful affect. Many others with organic brain impairments, most of them, basically, are persistently morose-depressive, agitated-dysphoric, we can't really say that about him. Isn't that right, Mr Knudsen? Would you like to say anything in conclusion? – Maybe, I don't know exactly, thanks, maybe? – Yes, our thanks to you as well, see you soon, the nurse will take you back to the unit now. Nurse, please. Goodbye, goodbye, yesyes. So what do you think? Is he not a ray of hope, this boy? Yes, that, too, is psychiatry, isn't it, you also needed to see something like that. Good, let's continue, we're in a hurry, on to the next patient. The one I had scheduled unfortunately dropped out on me at the last minute. But our colleague Raspe was so kind as to help us out in a pinch. Sincerest thanks, Doctor Raspe. And so I can show you an example of the illness I had planned for this point, which wasn't the case with Mr Knudsen. I admit I haven't yet spoken with the patient himself, so it is likely that at some point, our colleague Raspe will have to provide us with a bit of information. That means, esteemed colleagues, I am in the same situation as you all, and together we will have to see what we can conclude from his outward appearance once the patient enters the room. Nurse, please bring Mr Fottner in.

Through the avid eyes of the students, inspired by Professor Schlüssler's words, Raspe seemed to perceive Mr Fottner, who had been a familiar sight to him for weeks, in a new and appalling way, as if his awareness of the students' stares were a kind of injection to fortify his withered perspective. Mr Fottner was nothing more than a pair of house shoes. They struggled millimetrically against his formidable yearning for stasis and pure tranquillity over the blue and black veining in the linoleum. Did the linoleum too want to hold those house shoes fast, to suck them in? To lie down eternally, to be treaded upon, simply to become floor? But the house shoes were not even house shoes, QuittingTimeTelevisionBeer, they were slippers, hence shuffling, colourless and scuffed, unwilling to rise up anymore over the floor, dragged, merely dragged, a footwear of despair. In contrast to the slippers, which shoved on across the floor, the rest of the man hung back. If the slippers harboured the meagerest wish to proceed into the auditorium, all the rest, all those parts hanging out from the grey bathrobe, the hands hanging almost to the floor, above them the matted grey hair, hanging down where there was normally a face, the head hanging enervated over his chest, the entirety of Mr Fottner preferred to remain outside.

But now he was there, standing in the centre of the auditorium built like an amphitheatre, and under the silently flashing gazes of the students and the merciless booming penetrating word thunder Schlüssler hurled down at him, he sank even further into himself. Deafening noise inside a mind whose own thinking was already noise and torment. Raspe could tell. He knew he ought not have brought Fottner there, just to lend Schlüssler a hand and get himself an idle hour in the audience. Fottner was outfitted with a microphone, now he was supposed to speak. Had he not prepared any remarks? Everyone was silent. Now, all at once, the silence was thunder, a rumble rolling in from the distance, his own breath loud as an amplifier, clearing his throat an explosion, but he did not raise his head from his breast, silence, growing louder and louder. The prepared explanation, every word disintegrated, where? I

218

wanna speak, Fottner said, as though to himself. But the loudspeaker shrieked this alien sentence back through his ears into his mind, echo chamber, proliferation of words and clangour. Wait, let it die down. But then they shot forth again, the same circulating phrases from which before he had managed to wrest something else, an explanation, the description of a truth suppressed throughout the course of his life: everything was deception, self-deception, imposture. I am a nobody. I am rubbish to the world, a nobody. The overwhelming force of these phrases, giving up to them, capitulation. Why speak? Explain what? The students, the microphone, the professor, all of it was pointless, meaningless, debacle. Everything is one. Raspe saw a hardly perceptible shaking of the hanging head. Or had his gaze effected the semblance of movement in this starkly eternally stiffly stared at stiff speechless body? Then Professor Schlüssler spoke, shamelessly as always, of the miserable patient Fottner standing there as though of a heap of refuse.

Too many people were angling for a pension. It was a craze nowadays, qualifying for a pension. Even patients in their forties, psychiatric patients in the best years of their lives, hoped to collect a pension. That simply isn't normal. Not only the economic aspect merited examination. Retirement also worsened the prognosis. There were studies in that regard. From the doctor's perspective, withdrawal from the workforce was generally contraindicated. A person wants to work, deep down everyone wants to work, even if now there's this modern propaganda, this propaganda that –. He had never been a follower of fashions. Never in the least, he emphasized. Not even when those fashions were very much in fashion, not even there at the clinic, he had never minced words, in fact he was proud to be known as the house reactionary. In his forty years in the profession, he had seen far too many fashions come and go, medical as well as political ones, there were fashions in every field. The future would vindicate him. History, that is, the history of psychiatry, would –. One had to learn to think in other dimensions. He was digressing. He didn't care. Now and again, one was allowed to, one had to, tell the truth. Ahem. The university suffered from these fashions, too –. Sometimes a clear phrase, often an unambiguous, clear, everyday phrase was the truth. The truth is not this wishy-washy modern rot now prevalent everywhere, even here in the clinic, as he'd said before. He was opposed to all that. He'd been speaking his mind for forty years. He was digressing. People took him for an oddball. A person had to be able to live with that. He was coming back to the patients. People thought him outlandish, simply because he called the truth by its name. What was he to say about it? Should a person even say anything? Rather the opposite. It was ridiculous. The other side was the one that should lay it all on the table. The other side, which lurked in the depths –. He was getting round to it. He was getting there. This was nothing to marvel at.

While Schlüssler spoke in this way, turbid and frazzled, Fottner stood impassively still and offered, as Raspe registered with astonishment, an image of dignity: his apathetic calm, a massif pitched against this limping, abstruse prattle, the unmoved wisdom of despair. Instantly, Raspe knew the appearance was deceiving, that a despair like Fottner's was nothing more than despair, no choice wisdom dignity, only a sullen abyss, a dungeon. Now Schlüsser repeated *dejection* and *dejected*, indications of depression, one could study them in *him*, in the way he'd entered, the same as if he were a textbook. Naturally, Schlüssler was right. But his hand, flung over and over to the right and back, in Fottner's direction, opening for a fraction of a second and pointing limply from his outstretched arm, then retracting elastically, turned each unimpeachably accurate word about the essence of depression and Fottner's condition into a lie.

He stood there the way chronic depressives always stand there. His head hung. His shoulders hung, above all his shoulders. His expression hung as well. In essence, the whole person hung. That, too, could be measured, investigated scientifically, this hypotonic musculature. There's no need for you to worry about that, the science behind it. What matters for you is this: when you get one *of these*, whether you are general practitioners, internists, or what have you, do not prescribe him inotropes, instead send him to a psychiatrist. He needs to be with a psychiatrist. There are colleagues on site. He needs help. He needn't go directly into a clinic, but he needs a psychiatrist. I would very much have liked for him to tell you a bit about himself. But it's also typical that he be silent. He's silent. See, that's absolutely typical. Tell us something, Mr Fottner, can you hear me? It's doubtful he can even hear us. A depressive hears nothing over the sound of his brooding. That is common indeed. Of course, it can be the other way around, that they are hypersensitive to acoustic phenomena. This one here is rather dull. What is his first name, anyway? Sometimes with that – Erich, say something to us, Erich! Well, as we can see, he says nothing. He's brooding. Brooding means: he is thinking the same thing over and over. What is he thinking? As I've told you all already: the depressive broods about his dejection. This is a word with more than one meaning, no? You can ponder this word on your way home. Dejection, that implies both prostration and the condition of the outcast, one's repudiation of or by a community, and much more beyond that. And so, this single word helps us understand depression as a whole. That really is splendid. And here we will continue. You may take the patient away, nurse. All right, bye now, Mr Fottner.

Fottner was led out. The students beat their knuckles on the wooden benches in applause until the door was closed behind the nurse. Professor Schlüssler looked at the closed doors, said yes, my esteemed colleagues, that is what it looks like, then added further observations about the peculiarities of involutional melancholia.

Raspe sat without hearing. Nor was there anything to see. He forgot what he was thinking. Again, a patient was led in, a man, no, a woman. Raspe looked at the clock. He felt hunger. Then he forgot the time. Raspe sat and waited.

5.

With a roar of voices, the cafeteria greeted his silence. Cordially, if from afar, still yearning for tranquillity, Raspe nodded to the faces nodding to him, a shout from here, a shout from there, banter, specks of spray thrown up from a shifting sea and into the face of the man rising from the centre of the swell, Raspe stood in the eye of the storm, a tray full of food in his hands, the soup sloshed in the bowl filled to the brim, and struggling for balance, he turned towards the rearmost corner, the last still completely empty table. The deluge, now comes the deluge. Let it drag you away, pull you under. I don't want to talk and talk. I don't want to assert myself. I want to be a noodle, a noodle floating in soup. Raspe laughed to himself. Not to think through it all. He just wanted to eat, he brought one spoonful of noodle soup after the other up to his lips, his mechanics were excellent. The compulsion to think order, unity into the world. He didn't want to have to think all the time. His head was still holding itself together on its own. But how, really, and how much longer still.

Snorting with laughter at a joke of his, which Raspe hadn't even understood, Doctor Andreas Singer set his tray on the table and said to Raspe: Is this seat free? Then he tossed his lab coat blithely next to Raspe on the bench, and sat down across from him. So?, Singer asked. Raspe looked at his colleague, two years his senior, shrugged wordlessly, and thought, great, the festologist, here we go with the festologist again, like a bad penny, this one. Tomorrow I'm chopping it all off, right down to the skin, Singer said, flicking back his bushy long Zappa hair and bundling it into a ponytail with a rubber band he'd taken from his jeans. Or maybe I'll grow it down to my arse. I think short is *in* now, though. What do you say? Singer laughed and started eating. He went on talking with his mouth full, unbothered by Raspe's failure to reciprocate. Eventually, he said: You're not too chipper today, are you? Eh, things are good, Raspe said. The truth was, Singer didn't bother him. He had bullshitted away whole afternoons with his eternally cheerful colleague, letting the other man's optimism, unblemished after three years, drive away his own doubts about his profession. Singer had a touching faith in the emancipatory function of his unconventional appearance. Me, a private assistant!, he had shouted jubilantly to Raspe not long back, a hippie as a private assistant! It looks like it's happening. Raspe knew Singer sometimes lied to himself, too, he knew in his heart of hearts that as a lone individual, he could change nothing in the clinic, just as no individual could change anything. But then Singer seemed to come back into his own, talked of the duties of the Society for Festology, how as the first chairman he had brought *jubilation* to his unit, and how he would do so, even if it took years, for the clinic as a whole. Jubilation can't be stopped. It's the soft revolution. And he, Andreas Singer, was its prophet. Naturally Singer's tone, as he uttered these kinds of sentences, was impishly self-ironic. Raspe detested self-irony. Self-irony is the cheapest attitude. Even the biggest loser could spruce up his loser existence with a little dash of self-irony. Yet Singer seemed to derive from his credo a strength to persevere, and that was something Raspe envied.

After *Wollwurst* with mashed potatoes came an apple and then coffee. Pleasantly, languidly sated, Raspe took an HB from his packet and lit it. Singer rolled his own, Schwarzer Krauser was his brand, and said: I don't get how you can do those filter cigarettes. – Why's that? – I don't know, same way you didn't understand how I could just leave my apple. – Got it, Raspe said. He gave Singer a light, then they smoked in silence. At the next table over, they were talking about a ski trip. Raspe wondered: Did Singer's conversation bring me round? He looked through the cafeteria, saw the order of the tables, the people, and felt reconciled.

6.
Warm, overheated air. Raspe walked into the overnight room, just large enough for a bed, a cabinet, and a desk, shut the door behind him, and left the key in the lock. In a few steps, he reached the telephone, picked it up, turned it over, and saw with surprise that the ringer was already on low. He opened the cabinet door with his left hand,

placed the phone in an empty compartment, and laid a few freshly washed-ironed-folded lab coats over it. The cord barely interfered with the closing of the door. So. Raspe stripped to his underclothes and lay in the newly made bed. Everything cool, what a blessing. Lying on his back, Raspe tensed all the muscles in his body, particularly his thighs, stomach, and neck, felt strong, at the same time sluggish, let everything go limp. Not a single perceptible irritation remained. Raspe dozed off. Then he awoke. He sat up in bed, leaned over to the alarm clock on the desk and set it for two. He crept back under the heavy duvet, turned on his right side towards the well, and fell straight into a deep sleep. At midday, the time stops and stands vigil.

7.

Startled into panic, torn from his sleep by a strange screech, thinking he had only just drifted off, Raspe stumbled through the years, hours, places, who am I where and why, was a dust particle gleaming in a beam of light in a living room, thrown from childhood into duty, the overnight room, must have slept in, nonono, how long, what time? Again, the screech of the alarm, still just a drone in his poorly acclimatized ear, and Raspe felt on the floor for the clock, shut it off, held the dial near his face and opened his eyes wide. Two on the dot. He breathed in deep, felt a burning on his face, sweat, damp on his chest, on the insides of his upper arms and between his legs, felt his stiff member, foreign and annoying. Mechanically he pressed it down in a half-circle over the skin of his groin and upper thigh, but when he let it go, it flopped up, righting itself, and now Raspe felt this rush of blood to his penis as lust. He threw aside the duvet and sat up on the edge of the bed. In that posture, his stomach felt fuller than ever, a repulsive, engorged feeling, never eating again, better to starve than wake up with a belly like that. He looked down and saw his revulsion incarnate as a small bulge poking out under the vault of his ribs. Testing it, he grasped a bit of skin between his thumb and middle finger, pulled it up, and squeezed the adipose tissue underneath until it hurt. Fat, Raspe said, and repeatedly flexed his solar plexus, pushing in his stomach, then stopped and forgot it. Shivering, his naked skin was now one big shivering organ, though Raspe knew it was warm, even hot, in the room, and he shivered, the feeling on his skin was inexplicable. He drew in both legs, pulled his knees to his chin, rubbed his shins lightning fast with his hands till they were hot, shivered again, jumped up, bent over the clock on the floor, it was already almost four after, 2.04, Raspe said, standing up, pulling his clothes on in a hurry, pick up the pace now, at last he slipped into his lab coat.

From the second floor, Raspe descended to the cellar, crossed under the hallway of his unit, which was packed with filing cabinets and rubbish, then took the stairs back up to the first floor and stood in front of the door to the doctors' unit in the stairwell. Inside, he could hear the phone ringing. Clearly Bögl wasn't there. Unrushed, Raspe pulled the key ring from his trouser pocket – he had, in the interim, attached it to his belt with a metal chain – and opened the door with the small key. As he walked in, eyes turned to his desk and the phone, he saw, to his astonishment, from the corner of his eye, Bögl sitting there to his left. Raspe turned to him with a shake of the head, and the other man, sprawled out across his work area, said laughing: Don't feel like it today. Then I can even the score, Raspe said, now it's four-three, and he picked up the receiver and sank back into his chair.

Most of the time, you can just let them talk. You say yeah, yeahyeah. You learn the right tone without even noticing. Basically, everyone just wants to be calmed down, especially patients' relatives. Raspe's gaze swept over the surface of his desk, lingered briefly on the glass ashtray, turned up towards the brightness, while his free hand felt for his cigarettes in the pocket of his lab coat, then finally shifted to the window and on to the landscape decked with snow. Even a question of the kind: What will it be like from now on?, you can answer with a simple yeahyeah. The only important thing is the consoling tone, no one wants the truth, especially not the relatives. Raspe remembered how he'd feared the phone during his first days at the clinic. One time Raspe said: Don't worry about that, then he went on listening and nodding. He lit the cigarette, and without removing it, blew the first puff from the corner of his mouth; then he pulled his cheeks in powerfully towards the filter, and sucked the smoke that gathered in his mouth deep down into his perceptibly expanding lungs. He paused. Fleeting vertigo rose up in his head. Raspe let the smoke escape slowly through his nostrils, observed the not quite symmetrical forms of the two plumes, would have liked to blow a smoke ring, but instead spoke words into the telephone and saw as he did so how the pale smoke emerged from his mouth and mixed with that exhaled from his nose. When he spoke, mixed mouth- and nose-smoke; when he was silent, nose-smoke only. Say nothing, let them talk. Raspe hung up, looked ahead, and smoked. He made no reply to Bögl's inquisitive expression.

Raspe wanted to work. He took a pile of blue patient files from the desk, his patients, currently fourteen of them, and arranged the newly composed progress notes, letters, and charts. The case histories had to be shorter, the Director had repeated recently, after already saying so a few months earlier, the typing pool was hopelessly overburdened. At first, the man's appeal had outraged Raspe, then it had set him to brooding. He had considered the case histories an objective expression of his work, albeit one that left out everything essential for the sake of brevity. What's left of my mission, my engagement, Raspe had wondered. Am I really just a pill-pusher? That is what the files say. But since then, Raspe had learned to see the files in terms of their clinical function and as evidence of the soundness of a given diagnosis and therapeutic course of action. Early on, Bögl had said to him several times: It's not about what you really, actually do with the patients. You can do what you will with them, whatever you think is right. But you have to be able to explain everything in the case history, the whys and wherefores. The case history needs to be proofed for inspection, that's all it's really about, getting it ready for review, in case there's an audit of some kind, whether from the chief physician, the director, or even the authorities. Once Raspe had understood this, he no longer had difficulties dictating terse, pithy case histories with an emphasis on thoroughness and plausibility. Raspe set aside five of the blue files he planned to dictate later, during his night shift.

Then Raspe took a look at the pharma publicity, diagrams, and brochures, before dropping the packet of colourful, high-gloss paper uncrumpled into the trash. Raspe clipped a few special editions of scientific journals, irrelevant to the lithium study, but published by colleagues he had met at his first conference, into a binder specially acquired for that purpose, not even bothering to glance at the titles. Finally the desk was empty, as Raspe had wished. Just the telephone to the right, the ashtray with four stubbed-out cigarettes in the middle, and to the left, flush with the table's edge, the stack of five case histories. So, what's on the agenda, said Raspe. Bögl shrugged.

Raspe thought of Kiener, whom he'd pushed aside brusquely that morning during rounds. Often you promised a patient you would talk to him again in the afternoon and then forgot. In the nature of things, the patients you forgot were precisely the most annoying, difficult ones, who would stand somewhere in the hallway at the end of the workday, when you were already in your street clothes, and declare sheepishly that they'd been waiting there all afternoon for the agreed-upon conversation, but now it was too late, the doctor was clearly in a hurry. And you nodded, expressed your regret, spoke of unforeseen obligations late in the day, of being pressed for time, and you hardly felt shame anymore at these evasions and outright lies, instead you had just one thing in mind: get out of here, out of the clinic, the work-prison. I even think of Kiener sometimes at home, Raspe thought, Kiener is a ray of hope. He stood up and walked, without addressing Bögl, through the double doors into the day room.

Raspe had long since got used to the time lag in force here, the phlegma, the perpetually languid air of a Sicilian siesta as if, day in, day out, the sun stood at its zenith; long since, the stone forms that lay there, cowered, and slunk around had become extras on the quotidian stage. How consoling, how calming familiarity is. Again, Raspe noticed the forgotten smell of excrement and thought with disgust of the new admission, Schneeman. Bögl's patient, this Schneeman, he's not one of mine.

Raspe reached the dormitory, and as he looked around for Schneeman, they must have brought him back here in the meantime, Kiener waved to him from the bed, his movement graceful and buoyant. I know, I know, Raspe said, I came for you, I just need to give the new patient a once-over, do you know what bed he's in. Kiener didn't answer, repeating his gesture instead. Schneeman lay over by the window, asleep. Raspe walked over to Kiener.

– Yeah, so like I was saying, Doctor, burning to ashes, that's the thing, I already told my father, basically burning to ashes is what I'd like, actually I would very much prefer that.

– Just a moment, Mr Kiener, what do you mean now with this burning to ashes?

– Doctor, now you're making me out to be even dumber than I am.

He knew exactly what he was talking about. It wasn't about the funeral, at least not primarily, it was about what they would do with him once the funeral was over.

– Why are you talking about your funeral, Mr Kiener?

– Well, I'm not going to get up in arms about other people's funerals, am I!

Then Kiener delved into a further series of questions concerning fire as a funerary custom and other such matters, constructing a highly recondite but overall coherent edifice of thoughts. Raspe often marvelled at this discrepancy: Kiener would spend the whole day repeating a single, often highly cryptic sentence; but when asked about it, he would produce an astonishingly complex answer, both logical and mad. All those hours Kiener spent with his head down, walking obsessively back and forth through the unit, he must have been brooding about his idée fixe. If you asked him, he was happy, and would readily explain everything. Kiener was a defective schizophrenic, not, as Meien sometimes said, a case for a university clinic. But Kiener was so universally liked, even by Meien, that they let him stay there in accordance with his wishes. A photograph was pasted to the front of Kiener's patient file showing the now 38-year-old patient a good ten years before. Most inmates were photographed during their first admission. In the course of ten years, as the comparison with the then-28-year-old German literature student made clear, psychosis had carried out an unthinkable labour of destruction.

8.

World transformation, Raspe read, momentarily consoled by the unabashed poetic bent of the scientific language of before, even if his reading of Jaspers's *Psychopathology* did nothing to aid Raspe's understanding of schizophrenia and hence of Kiener. Then Raspe turned the page. He was alone. No sooner had he entered the room than he picked the book up off the desk; he was familiar with its soothing effect. Back then, when psychiatry was far more awful than today, people had written comprehensive and sublime books, books of solace, in line with the scientific spirit of the nineteenth century. And today? Raspe looked outside. It had begun to snow again, the sky bedimmed, a gloom bursting into the mid-afternoon. Fall asleep and wake up. Raspe read.

The things thought, read, perceived, imagined, glide off, jump the rails, merge, give way to bafflement, while at the same time, the intuition might arise of an undreamt-of form of experience, of deeper meanings and a presence of the infinite.

And in the window: the snow sank from the heavens. The flakes were heavy, weren't they?, so big and so heavy. Innumerable. Raspe watched them and followed their course, he watched. His gaze reeled into the grey. The words stood askew, the letters shifted, whole lines began to buckle. Raspe let be what was and what was happening now. His head fell forward into the book.

9.

When Raspe awoke, it was nearly dark.

He was filled with a motiveless cheer. He had fallen asleep in the wrong place. Raspe stood up, turned on the light, and walked to the sink. In the mirror, he saw a glowing red dot on his forehead, the size of a five-mark coin. That was where his head had lain on his left wrist. How long? The only strange thing was that the phone hadn't rung, and Bögl hadn't come back, none of the nurses had come into the room either. Normally the nurses burst in on account of some trifle, really they were just checking on the doctors. Raspe didn't care whether they found him asleep, drinking coffee, or busy with his work. He was amazed at the weariness often occasioned by those monotonous afternoons. Most times, he was exhausted when he went home in the evening. What is it about the clinic that exhausts me in this way? Normally, by now, around five, I would be looking forward to the end of the day. But today, the overnight shift has thrown off my rhythm. Raspe no longer dreaded those shifts, no, it was just that the advent of evening inspired a different mood. Raspe stood at the window. It was still snowing. But now the flakes danced, swirled neon-white around the streetlights. Probably a wind has struck up. Raspe felt the coming of night as a burden. He walked to the opposite corner of the room, where the coffee machine sat on the floor. From the yellow tin came the scent of the ground coffee, scent of the early part of the day. The radiator beneath the window had warmed his thighs. Raspe sat in the armchair in front of the small table and drank coffee. Bögl wasn't missed. He stood up and walked to the light switch. Then he sat back down in the dark. The cup was still visible. Raspe drank. The noise outside seemed clearer. Sitting there, in the bowels of the clinic, Raspe listened deeply and attentively.

10.

The night hours drifted together. That last walk through the clinic, had he really single-handedly, single-bodily prevented a young woman's attempted escape? Does the logic of the hospital already hold so much sway in my mind? Did Raspe ask himself that? What was certain was: the snow fell, fell, and fell. Raspe read patient files into the recorder. Raspe brooded, dozed off, went on working. He read through a book, forgot what it was about. Then the phone rang, an assignment. Back in the overnight room, Raspe lay fully clothed on the bed, without even removing his lab coat. The entire day careened through his head, the whirr of voices, unbearable questions, doubts, self-doubts. I don't want to become like Schlüssler, like Singer, like Reiter.

I don't want to become like I am.

Was the serenely falling snow no longer serenity? It was panic, it fell in Raspe's head, had nearly covered the base of his skull, rose in ridges. Had Raspe really had to leave, to go to some set of tracks, to identify this suicide, a former patient of the clinic with no relations? Did she not lay there intact over the snow, unblemished, only very pale? No, there were bloody mangled bits of corpse lying strewn over the snow-decked landscape, lit up by the harsh police headlights.

At night there were only questions. This whirling stagnation in everything. Was there a fissure in the world? The question stopped Raspe short. Wait, wait for the coming of morning.

11.

At morning, Raspe fell into a deep, dreamless sleep.

When he woke, he saw the tormented face of the patient he'd had to restrain the night before, he'd had to restrain him because he represented a danger to himself and others. He had resorted to the judicial recourse of *immediate provisional internment*. Naturally he could have just let him go, Raspe thought to himself now. But at night, things had a different weight to them. Outside it was still dark. Raspe tried in vain to get up.

He thought: Everything needs to be different. Everything makes no sense. So nothing makes sense.

Raspe prepared the case histories for the morning reunion. By January, isn't the deepest darkness already past? The clinical terminology was at his fingertips. It was almost irrelevant which detail from the night before was thrown in to give an air of authenticity to those unvarying phrases. Raspe was ashamed. He was so amenable, so committed, he performed so well. Night thoughts, Raspe said, and let the hot water run a while over his hand, splashed his face. He said: We'll have to see.

12.

Meien was punctual. The rounds turned into a disaster. Right off, the chief physician flew into a rage, an out-and-out fit of rage. He shouted, bellowed, tore down and shredded the pictures a young patient had painted in occupational therapy and hung up with scotch tape over his bed in the large dormitory. They were done in garishly bright colours. They showed phallic symbols. – Smut, I won't tolerate this, Meien shouted, obscenities, here on my unit, you can hang that up at home, not with us here though, smut of this kind. No one curbed his fury. Raspe stood there stunned. Later, in the doctors' station, he proffered a few timid objections. The head physician said: You listen here with your hyper-sensitive carping. I have had enough of these pointless conversations in my life. I am a Christian. I'm putting my foot down. You have to draw the line somewhere.

Meien's voice came from a growing distance. Where am I?, Raspe said. Who am I? And it seemed as though he saw himself ejected from a spaceship, flailing, arms and legs reaching out into the emptiness, searching for something to grasp onto, he saw himself racing forever outward, smaller, still smaller, tiny, a dot, a star amid stars in the murk, a nothing floating in the universe.

IV

Every evening, every night, the music raged. On week-days, regulars drank their beer among regulars and stood in their living room at the bar. No one said a superfluous word. The music was noise enough. On the weekends came the wannabes, who jumped all around like mad. The weekend patrons obviously had no right whatsoever to be here: students, artist scum, fashion bimbos. The intruders were showered with contempt. That soothed your irritation, even made you feel good. Harry, the bartender, was always properly dressed; everyone else, a bit ragged. The only thing that still bothered Raspe after four, five beers was that his face remained unblemished. Maybe he ought to drink something harder. But Raspe didn't want to go for hard stuff. Better more beer, more and more beer every day. Raspe wanted the most brutal face, the most ordinary, the coarsest. He wanted to know no language anymore beyond a few fragments of dialect. He wanted to have a fist that beat without compunction. Never again did he want to have anything to do with his onerous piles of books. Imperiously on the shelves, presiding over the room, witnesses to a fraudulent past, a life devoted to the world of ideas. The mere sight of them was a reminder of it and a torment. Raspe wanted to remember nothing. He covered the walls of books with sheets. Against his will, a thought rose in his head, became a roar, swelled, a brain-rending racket. Destroy it. What amnesia didn't expel, Raspe combatted. He stood there, a regular among regulars, drank one beer after the next. In the greatest torpor lay a new happiness.

Over snow-slick streets, Raspe stumbled home. Hardly had the snow subsided than new snow fell, subsided in its turn, and overnight, everything was covered in snow again. On the borders of the streets, snow hills rose up. Winter was all there was. Winter was eternal.

If only his face glowed gleaming red! If only a *crash* would rush rhythmically from the stage. If only the crash would crash loud enough. If only the singer raved wildly enough. If only the surging and racing and back and forth and Getting ThrownToTheFloor and jerking and shoving and panting were *all there was*. The more madly Raspe danced, the better, logically. It made no difference which band was playing. At every one of these concerts, Raspe was so euphoric, he wanted to party to death. But sloppy drunk, he always made it back home at the end of the night, no matter from how far away. Then the dead bastard lay down in bed.

The next day, the alarm would sound. Raspe would stand straight up. His hands twitched as his blood alcohol dropped. What did Raspe know of himself as he headed to the clinic? The ground was so steep, his head was so heavy. Raspe doubted he was a doctor, doubted he had ever been a doctor. But the job was there. A man erased did the work of a doctor. Survive the winter, Raspe thought, survive, survive the day.

And at night, all was well again, death-raging good. What a feeling to have a home, finally, a place! Naturally a doctor couldn't be a punk rocker. Instead of a doctor, Raspe wanted to be an unemployed mechanic. Whoever the PsychiatryInsanity didn't grind down into nothing shouldn't be allowed to call himself doctor. Psychiatry is the most humanly impossible medical profession. Hate hate hate, Raspe hated the patients, hated the clinic, hated the goddamn psychiatrists most of all, hated all of them, without exception. The psychiatrists were zombies, they were coming for Raspe's life. They wanted him to become a zombie, too. Better to stay there in Damage, whacked out of his mind, than become a psychiatrist-zombie, better another beer before everything came crashing down.

That idiot with his long hair, Singer the world-fixer, tried to plead with Raspe. A bullet for Dr Singer! Or the electroshock specialist recommended more shock treatment. Thirty shocks for the chief physician himself, for the honourable Professor Doctor Meien! And that dipshit, the Director, offered inducements. Out with this nice, friendly man, drown him, in a cesspit if possible, or else let me sew his mouth closed and poke out his polite little eyes! And the next patient's mother I'll shoot in the face with my gas revolver!

Weeks passed, months. Would the spring never reveal itself?

The weekends were torture when nothing was on, no football matches, no concerts. Raspe lay in bed, slept, woke back up, wanting nothing but to sleep, to keep sleeping. All at once, it was evening. The sky was dark, but clear. The roofs of the houses caught a last, slanted ray of sun. Raspe stood up, pulled on his clothes, and walked to the park. On the edges of the street lay the filthy residue of snow, Raspe walked without knowing where. Did he have people to meet, or was it something else? Did he not speak, maybe even sing? Then the darkness was everywhere. Raspe stumbled. Then he stood still and waited.

Words were spoken: target symptom, combination therapy. You'll have to stay with us one or two months. And Raspe asked himself: Why are the sirens howling endlessly outside? A cerebrospinal researcher wanted to stick a needle into each patient, in the small of the back, to take a sample of their cerebrospinal fluid, that was Charlie Needles for you, a man of the future when it came to research. Raspe never thought about lithium anymore. Why spend your whole life struggling against depression? Raspe no longer asked the patients questions at group rounds. Why didn't one of the friendly doctors ask him something, instead? Raspe didn't want to take on new patients.

Once, that was in Weißenohe, or maybe it was in Isen?, Raspe drove his fist into a guy's face. Raspe knew the guy, his name was Martin Winkler, right away he started to bleed. Another time, at the Alabama-Halle, someone punched Raspe in the lower lip, it bled, Raspe didn't know that guy. Raspe washed the blood down into his stomach with a beer. Maybe depot neuroleptics would have helped him out. Or that old hash of Peter's that made him go off like a fucking howitzer, like he'd never gone off before. Then there was the cutting action, the razor wounds all over his body, covered up by the clothing, by the lab coat, right, covered up by the lab coat, but still. They were hidden, the badges he'd stuck into his forearm, into the skin, as if into leather. Had anyone ever heard of a psychiatrist who didn't have skin of leather? Nothing was visible but the needles in his ear. At Damage, they laughed scornfully. But at the clinic –

The Director called Raspe to his office. Raspe didn't bother to go. What was he going to say to this person? Bögl pleaded with Raspe. But Raspe wanted only to punch Professor Reiter in the balls until he started spraying blood. Raspe felt for his keys. The keys were still there.

Everything dissolves in alcohol. The pinball rolled.

V

Then spring came, and Raspe knew this was it, that the end had to come.

A peculiar calm invaded him. Or was it weariness, a prodigious vacuity? Without a word, Raspe made a sweeping gesture with his arm to Kiener, to say it was futile. Then Kiener laughed, and Raspe did too. The sky was so blue, the sun so high, and a clear, sharp light warmed the planks of the park benches, which were painted strawberry red. Nice out today, Kiener said pleasantly. Sure is, said Raspe. Far off, the sirens howled incessantly, rose up over the high walls, descended to the clinic's inner courtyard. So many sick, nothing but sick people. The forsythias, but none of the other bushes, were speckled a hundred, a thousand times over with brilliant points of green. The flowerbeds looked freshly tilled, and Raspe would gladly have knelt down to kiss the very dark earth.

The boy with the whitish blond hair came past. – If I, in the form of a man, Tommi said, let my ice drops fall inside of my woman of fire –. – And then, said Kiener, I was thinking, if I get out of here, I can't die anymore. – A woman made of fire, like thisss, Tommi said, moving his cupped hand up and down in the air in front of his groin, closing and spreading, closing and spreading his thighs. Kiener laughed, imitated Tommi's movements, then laughed again, more and more agitated, finally going off the rails. – What's the point of terminology? Raspe said, it's all insane, nothing but insane, and he laughed too, and went on laughing a long time.

Time stopped. Raspe looked at the clock. It was the peak of morning. I feel so strangely dull, Raspe said to himself, I'm dull now, I lie awake at night. For weeks, whenever the alcohol wore off, Raspe lay sleepless in bed. He lay there and felt nothing. If he got up, the room reeled. If he lay down, he lay awake. The nights were long. Even now, the seconds lurched, as though frozen, and every second that the second hand shifted on the dial, tick by tick, was a demonstration of eternity.

I think I am a delinquent. Am I guilty of something? Guilty of what? Raspe sat welded to the bench and felt a sudden rush of freedom inside him.

Everything was one in the end.

THREE

ORDER

'Don't cry – work.'

BEGIN AGAIN. Yes!, begin anew, completely different. At last I want to begin. I would like so much to have
a life.

So much LYING AND SLEEPING, lying and sleeping and nothing but. I would gladly come to know my
thoughts. The bedcover sweats, it stinks. Perhaps some
alien, dead flesh is lying in my bed. Countless times
I am forced awake. In dread I close my eyes, quickly,
and turn to the side. Then sleep comes again. There
must be a cure for this weakest of weaknesses. Maybe
I just need an injection, cellular therapy, for example.
Maybe dreaming would also help. But there's nothing
there. It's all just lying there, utter tedium. And thus
the days passed, the nights. And in this way, the weeks
evaporated.

Something flashed VIOLET. What's flashing? But the
mass of abhorrent plum puree in my head is incapable
of thought.

I will OPEN MY EYES again. I will see the world
again. There is a greedy man who wants to look again.
Through the large InspirationSockets the external will
invade me once more. Yes, the pull will be the same as it
was. The swell of joy and gratitude will once more bear
me away. I will bow again before the world rendered visible. Then, once again, I will be permitted to speak: Dear
EyesWorldMercy, thank you, thank you very much.

But the ENDLESS NIGHT is very black in my voids
with their scanty covering of skin. And above all, I need
release. I should give myself up without resistance. If I
could, in that way, collapse into myself, logically, that

246

would be my redemption. At least, I would lie there a clump of filth. I am a void, filled with a great fear. The fear is so great. It won't go away. That is the kind of night this is.

But only say THE WORD, and my soul −. With a sentence from Diederichsen, StrengthYearning and Dignity entered my mind. Now I'd like to walk away like nothing else. In SevenLeagueBoots, with tender elegance and sovereign nerve I'd like to walk straight across stupid Germany. I'd like to leave behind all the LyingWaveringSearchingAndRaving and abandon it to its dithering. I'd like to shout loud, in victory: Roar!, Roar!

Then I would have atoned for the entire Madhouse-Hell and annulled it in the process, and would stand there resurrected and not a single word would fail me: I have bled red for all my failings. Now what I say becomes law. And like ET, the extraterrestrial will place the glowing tip of his finger to your, the reader's, forehead and say in that smoky TrenchCoatVoice: Tomorrow, baby, we're outta here. Tickets are taken care of. We've run down the clock. Let's beat it.

So where to now, you want to know? Come on!, use your goddamn eyes!, you can see it perfectly well, gleaming and tempting us from the end. So I ask you: Where, logically, does a modern novel finish? Logically, in New York.

Suddenly it's back to the old GOOD JOB of lying there asleep. Naturally outside the rain pelted down, and then the storm blew over, the clouds were gone, the sun was there. In the interim, images rose up from out of some mythical past into my dreams. So often now, the MostRecentPast is the MostDeeplyBuried and LightYearsAway. I couldn't dream away the horror of the clinic. I dreamt about WhoKnowsWhat. Awakened, I said: God Almighty!, let me dream again. Then I went back to work, where I haven't come to know myself better either, same thing as with psychiatry before. But when I came out of it, I wasn't getting sicker and sicker, instead I was slowly convalescing. It was good, the EatingDrinkingPissingShitting. Then I crawled back to sleep. Later came my work at the billiards table, hours seeing only balls and pockets. On the way home, sometimes, I bought a sex magazine. Then I worked on my rhythm in bed, then back to the SleepDream.

May is already upon us.

With THE BEER the warm early summer wind blew back inside me. That's nice, maybe! I've entrusted myself to others again. I've managed to speak again, looking at the faces of people I know. I went to Lipstick, because Damage has shut down in the meantime.

I no longer had the shakes. Easy as ever, I was back on the scene. My mouth drank the beer down into my stomach and then I lay down on a bench to go to sleep. When the CleanUpLights came on, I woke up and went home. The fear I could do something wrong was gone. I didn't give a damn. What I had forgotten in my faltering PsychiatryDespair I now knew once again: clearly, I couldn't fit in. This knowledge was a HeliumGasPump. It inflated me, I floated. No more did I fear the disparaging gazes of the know-it-all first-generation punks. And I saw my own rage at the fourth-generation punks as the scorn of a Dumdum. Then it vanished. It no longer mattered to me, as it had back at Damage, to become one of the crowd, I could never have been one, no matter how much the clinic trampled me into a pulp. I didn't have to be stupid anymore, I could think, and I no longer felt ashamed to do so. I stood there as what I wanted to be: lonesome wolf, observer, arrogant. What freedom that was! I drank to that, more than a few beers. Stumbling out, I kissed the very blonde AndreaFromBehindThe Bar on her bare neck. An outsider, I now skirt the edge of the scene and so logically am deeper in it than ever.

If I think of PSYCHIATRY, I hit my face against the ConcreteFloor like a person who's just collapsed. It hurts. I am unprotected. My hands are cuffed behind my back. Fresh blood runs straight from my ear. It does the trick for me, so I lie there.

I give CULTURE a ring and say: Hey there, Culture! I worked with you before from time to time with my yellow typewriter. Afterwards, I was with the DoctorArseholes and even wore a white lab coat myself until I started to think I would burn up inside it and be left a heap of ashes. Then I decided to just lie in my bed for a few weeks naked as a jaybird. Now I'd like to fill the void with something, maybe even with culture.

Where the SPIRIT is, that's where I want to live. Everyone's good there, no one's stupid. That would be my greatest happiness.

For the NORMALITY of a psychiatrist, every normal person, i.e. me, is a madman. You can say anything, no matter how atrocious, to a psychiatrist with his gentle LeniencyFace. He will simply smile and nod. He is only thinking of the diagnosis. You say one word, already he's got the most likely diagnosis in mind. Two psychiatrist colleagues talk, and they both think, not only of the other's diagnosis, but also of the diagnosis the other is giving them. Basically every psychiatrist diagnoses himself with something, just to be on the safe side, something minor, obviously, to prevent his fellow psychiatrists from pinning a serious illness on him. Bögl used to always say to me: You know, my anankastic core personality. Yeahyeah, I would have liked to say, I've got amenorrhoea or amputation or anadyomene too. But I kept my mouth shut, and it didn't matter, either, because mockery doesn't preclude diagnosis – quite the opposite, in fact.

But now for the first time GRASS must grow atop this entire story. Understand, Baby, we'll come back to it later.

WHICH DRUG is really the right one for me is something I still haven't managed to figure out. Right now there's a lot of sniffing, but it's not real coke, it's Royal Crystal, a white powder that costs 200 marks a gram and will eat straight through a tin can. It makes the mucous membranes in your nose burn and bleed. The kick's supposed to last a long time and is megalomaniacal. But of course, that's no use to me, because I already spend the whole day writing and acting like a megalomaniac.

You might think a poison you could smoke would do the trick. So we burn a joint of homegrown or mix the brown resin up with tobacco and assimilate the good Tetrahydrocannabinol via the lungs. But this technical term brings me to a crossroads again: the week-long retention rate of the stuff in my blood. I absolutely can't have my drive and my will to work wanting to lie there in bed and refusing to get up the next morning, and then, in the evening, that languid reluctance itching to smoke something again. I could only have done that when I was working in the clinic, where presence was a duty, but not thought. I've seen enough psychosis, I don't have to drop acid. And I've had speed in my body from the day I was born, I don't need to ingest any extra. So what else is there a person can take? Valium is naturally useless, because nervous intelligence for me is the height of happiness. And-on-on-and-so-on.

So what's left is beer, I have lots of experience with it, I can dose it optimally. And the linear elimination rate is the best thing of all, .015% per hour, out of the blood, out of the head. You can top up later and keep the same level or let the liver do its work, go to sleep, put out the fire the next morning, and get back to work almost unimpaired. That's why beer tastes so good.

Best would be to finally reach the IMAGES but first I must master myself.

Inside me a MANIAC is roaring. He roars so loud, he is constantly trying to roar his way out of me. I hold his mouth closed with all my strength, so not a single roar will roar out of me.

I still do not know the NEW ORDER.

An early summer scorching HOT HEAT in the air on the paper, logically I must write on it, because logically the time afterwards, as well as the time inside, is making its seasonal and thus climactically inevitable progress, here on the paper, while outside WinterDerisory warm storms sweep through the most bizarre January in human memory. Now it is here, thanks be to God, perhaps I am glad it is here. For no one can grasp what this January has done to me. Above all at night these curiously warm storms waft through the streets with their rows of buildings as though you should know even less what you were thinking. At any time, this unseasonable warm could turn to a PolarWind, yeah!, it's so stormy. The nights are rife with bad hours. An ungraspably peculiar disquiet, to stave it off I maybe should get hammered, maybe I do get hammered, who knows? I know nothing. Least of all do I know the therest things, the things that are most present. How it hurts.

Back then, coming home from the club, a wet rain soaked my alcohol-hot face. Out loud, I asked: Why now? But the streets were empty of people. Lights flickered on the black asphalt. I had the impulse: Turn something over? Me? No: Silence and wait. Nor did the past tense help. But the time will come when I will report on this January. From the JanuaryCancer I wrest away heat. The new task grows in me like a tumor, strength-sapping, the CancerOfThePresent, against which I direct my actual past life to the ClosureWork of the old task, so that all light and all power come out of the FutureFogRepresentation of work for the new task or in other words the next act.

Yes, my dears: So it is. No lament can affect it, just as none is any use against psychiatry. *Work* alone is useful against this entire dreadful life. If someone tries to take work from me, I'll blow him or me away. If I'm gone, I won't need work anymore. But as long as I'm here, anyone who can tell me a better lifesaver than work will get 1 mark 20 in reward. I believe the price I have stipulated here is the hardest-to-earn collection of twelve ten-cent pieces the world has ever seen. Because in life, against life, the only salvation is through work.

And summer. Look, the light, how unshakeably it sits up in the sky and beams down. It does not come from our days. The city lets off steam until it dries. The heat comes from the hot MediterraneanSand. And this light must be from a faraway past for it to glow so bright.

DISCHARGE was the name of the fanzine we made that summer, the way everyone made a fanzine that summer. The best fanzine was sold by a pimply kid with shy clumsy movements at the Sunday OpenAirConcerts at Theatron. This kid's so cocky, he's got a future. There he was, all sharp and cocky, and there I was, still wondering in my PostPsychologyEmptiness whether I should ditch culture and go for Marxism. Then at least I'd have something to hold on to, I thought. I too could finally be a know-it-all. That would be cool for sure. To start with I wrote in a blistering rage about hippies, what good it did us, other ex-hippies and me, to rage against them that summer, and then, with a few StateDerivations in mind, I did a take-home essay about Gorleben. I entitled my DischargeEssay: *Softies, Gorleben, and the Most Subservient Petition for Even More State*. Leather-jacketed, sun-glassed, and freshly-wounded friends would move through the pertinent bars at night and shout: DISCHARGE 2 Marks! Suddenly I'm standing face to face with two former colleagues, a man and a woman, psychiatrists, in other words. At first it was startling, then: GAG HEAVE VOMIT. And on to the next bar.

Then they printed my PunkMarxism about Gorleben next to a MonteVeritasStory in the AlternativePaper BLATT. Laughter laughter. This woman Evi said I should go fuck myself for my suggestion that others could go fuck themselves instead of punking out the alternative scene. Further, Miss Evi bid me to learn to differentiate, which amused me to no end, because after years of differentiation I had only just learned non-differentiation.

253

Even then, it did me good, just as today, it is still right to wage war against the countless caring stupidities that go on spawning that DifferenceAndToleranceJibberJabber.

The RUNNING AWAY from psychiatry was just as essential for me then as it is now. Psychiatry is always the greatest SpiritTorment. Before I was inside. Since then I've run from it in a panic. Again and again, I have to go back inside. Because I am looking for life. How gladly I would like to speak of nothing but nice things.

At night, in bad dreams, I hang opposite myself as THE PATIENT.

THE FILM.

While summer burned and I was off readying my great journey through the German culture supplements, we are back in January, admittedly not the same January as the authentic one before, but in a snowy one, where we see the first of twelve sequences of a film that will accompany us through an entire – and moreover, entirely special – year, a clinically paranoid one, in other words.

First of all you see a still image in the twilight of morning: in the distance, a crumbling building façade, a pavement with snow-scum in front of it, a streetside without parked cards, snowhills soiled grey-black.

At the same time, you hear, louder and louder, a hissing zinging din, and now you notice a deep-frequent pounding, which must have hovered there the whole time at the very threshold of audition, BOOM BOOM. You sense it is going away. You're not wrong.

From the left, with mincing steps, a passer-by on the pavement comes into the frame, me, logically, but you don't recognize me yet. The passer-by is hunched over, struggling like a *midget* against the wind and fog, and proceeds across the lower edge of the imposing BuildingFaçadeTotality.

The hissing might be breath – the pounding might be a HeartSound. But it could just as easily be machine or factory noises you hear; annoying, in any case. At last, following on a likewise annoying overlong interval after the midget's departure from the image's lower-right-hand side, you see something new, the –

2nd FRAME: In the foreground a desolate field, behind it battered fencing, chimneys, trucks, yes, factory buildings, so I heard right, you think to yourself, how pretty and peaceful such a nice little industrial landscape can lie there on such a pretty winter's morning – twilight, what a thing! Now the noises are in sync with it and no longer disturb the mind. The feeling is pleasant.

But: LOOK SHARP, I am a bent-over torso tumbling in again from the left, and I almost fall back out to the right. But now the camera is *in motion*. You see me vaguely to one side. You struggle to keep pace with me. The focus shifts from the far-away factory to my face. Though I walk like one hunted, looking desperately

255

ahead, then, no less desperately, at the ground, the camera keeps me in its sight. My breath sputters, my heart races. Behind me, shadowy, the barely discernible landscape of the ruined slaughterhouse and market quarter rolls past.

You see me nodding vehemently. Immediately after, I shake my head with no less vehemence. Then again, the nodding. In spite of the noise, you can understand my first words.

YEAH!, I say, NOW! GOOOD!

Then, for a fraction of a second, absolute silence reigns. The music kicks up triumphantly: Zoltán Kodály, Psalmus Hungaricus. You feel tranquillity surfacing, now you can sit back amid this choir of human voices. You see me walk, obsessive as before, and the music lends my progress a certainty of victory that rises up out of the DoubtingAbyss. Head-on, the teleobjective sees me walking, step by step I walk, I walk on the spot. No matter: the music is powerfully present.

Then the teleobjective shakes, likewise without shifting places. The music turns softer now, and while you hear it fading in the background, suddenly, almost intrusively close to your ears, a sweet and sonorous male voice is heard off-screen, whose unquestionably wise empathy and kindness makes you think for a moment of *the voice of the old doctor.*

The sonorous voice says: Mr Raspe has terrible days behind him. In those days between Christmas and the dawn of the new year, when time's immobility and vital paralysis could waylay a person like a monstrous Sunday afternoon, in those days of great forsakenness, the suspicion that someone was watching him grew, in Mr Raspe into an irrational, exhausting, compulsive brooding. Now Mr Raspe has broken through the agony.

He is resolved to purposeful observation. He talks of *counter-investigation*.

During these last words, the camera watches me progress forward from behind, approaching a building door, and vanishing through it. You have to stay outside. The heavy black wooden door almost slams in your face. You turn: parking cars, driving cars, street noises rising up, nearing the pain threshold. Achingly loud auto noises. The building wall across from you looks even brighter. Yes, it grows brighter, as though beneath a desert sun. Just before the image fades to white, a window on the ground floor opens. A policeman's head appears in a peaked cap. Harsh white, harsh noise. You ask yourself: Did I really see a policeman? Then you think: Get this light and noise over with for once. But both remain. Until finally:

CUT: gloom and silence. Your pupils dilate. Slowly, you recognize my barely furnished room, viewed from the furthest, uppermost corner. A television is clearly visible. To the right, at the edge of the image, perhaps there stands a table. In the middle is a window, but the rolling shutters are pulled down almost all the way: the strip of light is only around seven inches wide, and there, to the left of it, I cower. Tiny and cowering, I cower on the floor. You are up on the ceiling, I am down on the floor. I look out.

For a half-second flash, you are behind my eyes and see my gaze through the rolling shutters at the ground floor window of a building lying at an angle across the street. You have taken in almost nothing, at most, perhaps, that we are above the ground floor, on the first or second, perhaps, you conclude.

But already it is back, the gloom seen from above, the immobility and the taut, cowering ObservationSilence.

The silence has time. And such a silence can become a burden. So a stupid thought might come into your head, like: What's this all about?, or: These fucking theatre chairs are so stiff!, or: After the film we can grab a bite to eat, and after that it would be cool to –

But in the midst of your thoughts, I throw up my right arm, I am this clenched fist, power. And then very quickly many things happens at once. I jump up. Simultaneously:

CUT: now you lie crosswise on the floor beneath me and see how high I am jumping. Very high, obviously. I may even hang in the air for an improbable length of time. I come crashing to the floor, before your eyes. Now:

Now Music! An old punk hit, Ruts, Babylon's Burning. It starts off with the ringing of a bell. At that, I pull up the rolling shutter. Then, over the RutsTrack, a PoliceSiren gets louder and louder. And as the un-mistakeable bass line comes in, then the guitar, which anyone who's heard the song will recognize right away, I start dancing ska and pogo wildly and jubilantly.

CUT: you see me from outside through the double window, thus mingled with the reflections, arms hur-tling, head flailing. You see a face that radiates happiness. It speeds up and down.

Now you return to your former position in the up-per back corner, and look down to the floor where this bundle of dynamism is jumping in place. You see the almost bare room below you bathed in light. Yes, it is a table there on the right, with a work lamp on it and a telephone. The surface is made of wood. Something is written on it in large letters in marker. CURIOSITY IMAGINATION HUMILITY, you read. Some who read this find it stupid. Some of you are reminded of something. And for some of you, it's a place to start.

I dance, a little calmer now, and at the same time look outside. The RutsTrack moves on to the next number, this one just as familiar. I stop. The music dies off slowly. I lay the right hand of my outstretched arm on the handle of the window. Did you see a jolt pass through me?

Again, a view of me from outside the window. On my face, you see the repulsion grow, my eyes, like those of a TV correspondent, are irritatingly close to the camera lens and stare off into the distance. No, I'm not looking at you. My terror must be immense. You ask yourself: Is this guy insane? Or is this whole film insane? Now I say something, but you don't hear me. I shout. Hectically I whirl in the room, then out, then back in.

CUT: You look through my eyes, see the closed door to the room. You hear my voice offscreen: Klaus! Klaus!

COUNTERSHOT: You see me from the door, at head-height for the first time, standing at the window and looking out. Half-profile from behind. You see me talk.

Softly, I say: Man, they left the rolling blinds down over there. I pull them up and they leave me down. Then I shout: Come on!! Now I bellow: Dude! Klaus! KLAUS! As my head turns towards the door, the last –

CUT: Close-up on my head as it turns, face in a panic, full-frontal, mouth torn open in a soundless cry, and in the silence, the image freezes. Tension and silence. I look you in the eyes with the whole of my immense fear.

Rushing quickly spreading light, like before, but much faster. Now: shimmering white.

After this far too long FilmChapter I wrote a way shorter one. This is it. A medical chapter, consisting entirely of the sentence now to follow. Perhaps it all comes from the GLANDS. Boom, there you have it.

Now I jump back briefly into the TOTAL PRESENT with a short letter I had to write recently to His Majesty the Editor. It deals with a few of the less pleasant aspects of the otherwise quite comfortable CultureExistence of the independent CultureEntrepeneur, with money, in other words. It also addresses Colombo. Why exactly Colombo is something I will clarify at the end of this fine little missive:

Dear Meester Sch–:

Colombo! Colombo puts me in mind of something lovely. As a young man, I actually was in Colombo once. The hotel was big and white and ColonialEraLuxurious. Ceylonically swarthy servants devoutly swept the dust without cease, even when there was none there to sweep. Close by, the sea made its rushing sounds. Outside all was sun, in the room cool dark wood, next to me Doctor Diepes, the Joe Blow Politico from the FAZ. At the time, I would have been over the moon to have three hairs on my chin. So logically, as far as tour guides go, I was a laughing stock. Me, a ProvincialGreenhorn playing tour guide and sixteen Bettertravelled globetrotters in the best years of their lives, their mid-thirties that is, getting herded about by a kid who can't even grow a beard. My, that was something.

But logically, love was the worst part. To tell the truth, I essentially never was in Colombo because I was so in love back in Munich that I didn't know my arse from my elbow. I stopped eating completely. I didn't even want to go out on to the MaldivesSand. I lay unnerved under the ceiling fan in the hut and read Fontane and Handke, naturally.

The three weeks were endless. The love dragged on

260

a few years. But they passed quickly enough. And so for me, despite Colombo, everything turned out for the best.

And now, my dear Mr Sch–, you must be asking yourself, right!, why am I writing you such a lovely letter. – Simply because, as every month, I would like to inquire as to my expenses. Of course, as you already informed me by phone, they are transferred from your account lightning-quick, so that your magazine's independent collaborators may get back the cash they've shelled out lightning-quick. – Yes, well, it is three months now that my lightning bolt has been on the verge of striking. Perhaps you have closed this account? Or since the whole thing is a scam, shall I pay the expenses myself? The photographer, too, while I'm at it? How about the politically committed paper my contribution was printed on? (Just send me an invoice!) Or maybe, Mr Sch–, you would like, at your ripe old age, to contemplate the life of a freelancer, even if you, for as far back as you've been able to think, have been an administrator, with unlimited power over freelancers like myself – question mark! Yeeeaah, thinks the freelancer, if 600 marks from *K Magazine* roll in, then in February I can buy real German dairy butter instead of margarine as an intervention stock, a sweet deal now at the current price of 1.89 even if the line doesn't hold. That would be cool. Arrright then, dear Mr Sch–. Yours, Goetz.

Ah, one more thing: if it's not too much trouble, don't feed me the same story from weeks ago –, and so the secretary –, and you yourself understand least of all –, and the bank or some other extra-terrestrial power –, etc. I already told you a pretty little story about Colombo and I didn't invent nothin'. So make with the cash. Got it? – G.

Man!, that got long, that letter. Quickly, I will go through the most important points of uncertainty: 1. Fees: *K Magazine* sent me to Zurich to interview Miss P. Highsmith. Nothing came of the interview, but still, I wrote some clever fun reportage and used the occasion to deal out a few blows *en passant*, as I'd had the urge to do a long time: some against Mr Lyric Poet E, some against Mr ProsePoet A, which also gave me the chance to have another go at the hippies; then I went off on *S Magazine*, whose Mr LiteratureEditor F, in his early forties, is already longing to cash it in, not to mention a certain model student and up-and-coming CultureHireling who has got his start with F and will be heading up the CultureSection at *S Magazine* when the novel appears. Yes, each one of them made an appearance. Logically sex and crime showed up in my reportage as well. Some routine that was. Let me tell you. Then *K Magazine* printed the thing up. Sure enough, contrary to our agreement, Lord Editor Sch– struck out many words, making beautiful sentences drab ones, wedged in false quotes, and didn't bother to reimburse my expenses. And yet, I wasn't so angry at Lord Sch–, because his phone voice is so nice and professional, the way it purrs. I stuck to writing him a nice little letter now and then inquiring after the money.

2. Colombo. Good for nothing, once more, Colombo is about money, concretely with the fee for my reportage. *K Magazine* actually tried to short me on my 200 marks, rounding down the already not precisely sumptuous 80 marks per column in their favour. Thereafter, over the phone, I calculated for Lord Editor-in-Chief and ArtistBeardWearer B the precise number of columns down to nineteen twenty-fifths. Then, via his secretary, he communicated to me that the 200 marks ought not

be pared down in my case. But as punishment for this attempt at paring down, the prosecutor's office opened an investigation into *K Magazine*. I allowed myself this little prank. And in the next issue of *K Magazine*, which reports on this amusing investigation in the habitual valiantly indignant tone typical of *K Magazine*, readers are further apprised that Lord Editor Sch– was accompanied on his Christmas holiday in Ceylon by a lady from the Federal Criminal Police Office. Hence my mention of Colombo.

3. The line didn't hold for dairy butter because the line trailed off in the original letter because the page had reached its end and in consequence was pulled out of the typewriter. So. Anyone got any questions now? No? Good, let's get on with another pretty slogan then.

TUMULT AND HERTIE

I know at some point I must make it BACK into dreaded sincerity, that eventually, this slapstick must come to a close. So now, tentatively, I walk my way back. Even if it requires great courage and preparation, like this title strip here.

Others have managed to liberate themselves at home by performing a psychological analysis. I had to do two courses of study all the way to their bitter pathetic end. Naturally, that was more or less pointless. It liberated me from nothing. I have to work like a madman in order to live. The compulsion is absolutely inhuman. Perhaps, after many years, I will be able to explain it. Perhaps it will crush me, I will fall to pieces and die. Then nothing will irritate me anymore.

EXCUSE ME, but what are you actually talking about

here?

Right: What am I actually talking about? Can someone tell me. I'm searching for something, somehow. What. A styyyle, a me, a God, a broom, an art. Or else one of those WomensThongs. I think I'm looking for WomensPanties. I was standing next to two women at the WomensBargainBin but I didn't dare rummage around inside. The skin under my hair was glowing red. I won't say any more about it, because it's really just the *setup* for all this risqué nastiness I'll get into later. Hopefully it stops with the ThongdSearch. Hopefully I'm not looking for style, art, least of all for originality. At best, I'd like to know how life is. I would like to grasp the ImmediateVicinity. I only want to see what can be seen; only the necessary, the SaidBefore, who cares how often, that's all I really want to say. I know that with something so simple right now I am asking the gods for far too much. I know all too well how very confused how benightedly I must croak back and forth like a toad until I can simply speak. But it is a consolation that I am not just looking for any old rubbish, but for the right thing, at least. And since I am not waiting for a gift, but moving across the page like a mad work-raging seeker, I may hope that for once, if only for seconds, the gift will be conceded to me.

So I talked on in this way. I would trust everything. Everything would be soft and light, no shocks. I would say out loud what everyone knew. In this way, it would be nullified. Yeah!, that would be right and beautiful.

Ever since a daily trip to the cinema became for me an irrational CRAVING AND LUST, ever since I started looking rapt at the screen as I had once stared at book pages and actors on the stage, a new problem has emerged, once more in the form of a question. Namely: what's the story with film subsidies? The good thing is I'm still a little kid, even if I can't stand kids, it's still a good thing. From nothing, which entertains me, I learn nothing. From image and tumult and Georg and Oehlen, from everything, I learn something. I see it, and right away I want to play with it myself. Me want one too. Then couple that with my work-discipline. Bang, there you've got a smart combination. The cineastes, on the other hand, are stupid, even stupider than the already very stupid Germanists. See below.

Already, the STARS glimmered. And still further out, beyond some outermost horizon of the night, a dog howled. How I longed. I long for a happy ending.

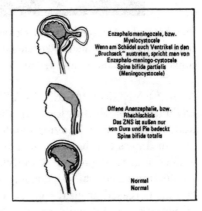

Reluctantly, but still, I turn back to the MONSTR-OSITIES of medicine. It cannot be otherwise.

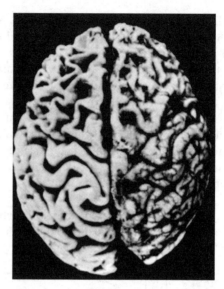

Pick's atrophy. Macrophoto. Brain convexity. Pronounced atrophy of the frontal and occipital lobes. The central
convolution remains unaffected by the atrophy process.

A diffuse NEURODEGENERATIVEDISEASE like
Alzheimer's or Morbus Pick can afflict young people as
well. While reading the symptomology, the fear gathers.
– ... an illness that leads to such symptoms as changes
in personality, coarsening of individual characteristics,
attenuation of ethical judgements, loss of tact, disinhi-
bition, increased arousal etc. Generally impoverished
initiative and spontaneity, on the other hand, are related
to lesions at the front of the cerebral convexity. Atrophy
in the temporal lobes is characterized by –

The young man is immortal. If he sees a dead person, he need not recognize himself in him. He does
not yet have to carry around his own death inside him.

266

He thinks: I am immune to weakness, to degeneration and infirmity. The young man reads, he learns the symptoms. Then he asks himself, restive: Might I not notice all these Pick symptoms in myself? He asks himself simple questions. Sure of victory, he checks himself for symptoms. He reassures himself he does not have Morbus Pick, which actually he knew to begin with. Some time, though, death will creep under this young man's skin as well. Then the fear breaks loose, the CountingDownOfTheYears, RunningAway from HavingToSee the symptoms, from HavingToTalk with the EternallyMiserablyIll, from the terrible sorrow at NotBeingAbleToHelpAnyoneAtAll. This sorrow burned and smouldered inside him. He could fall from his lab coat like ashes. He lies there squalidly on the floor, nothing more than a pile of dust to be swept away. Out with me.

To stay there, you must constantly stifle the burning sorrow at your helplessness. Then it comes, what else, habit. It is a necessity in medicine, in psychiatry above all. Habit is already there at the beginning when imperceptibly, along with the DeathInjection, the young doctor's body is administered the initially no less imperceptible sensitivity to the ill. Habit grows alongside weakness in the doctor and becomes his crutch. And so, instead of immortality, there is life.

Ah, it gets me because it is so sad. But again, this is no time for laments. Again, it is time for Insight Seeing Thinking. I know perfectly well I have no right to cast aspersion on any doctor, least of all on those most miserable of doctors, the psychiatrists. That is why I did it. That is why I carry on with this reflection with newly kindled rage. For never yet has a member *of the profession* grasped even a scrap of the veil of the truth *rightly*. Maybe *maturity* could be right and righteous at the same time. I will not discount any possibility, contrariety, or least of all any development. Here where I stand, I scream all the louder. And I must do my work as a scream.

The PHOTOGRAPHER, in many cases, I said, despite numerous objections, need not rely on human language. The image before his eyes, he hearkens to wordless visibility. The most beautiful beauty is there, immediate, the most horrible horror too.

And was it not *images* that assailed me then, as soon as I'd entered the clinic. Was the constant *sight* of the ill not the most repulsive repulsion? If you uttered words, no matter how awful, already, that was a step towards conciliation. And it was the Clinic*Images* that I couldn't clear from my mind, even after I'd left the clinic, not through forgetting, through beer, through anything, the images invaded my bed over the weeks of my narcolepsy-like sleep. And it was *these images*, after months, and not mere trivial LollygaggingMonths, that compelled me relentlessly, that bestowed on me my duty, that imposed on me the greatest exertion: images I wanted to write away, but that no word nor description could rid me of, that go on harassing me, that drive me into the most panicky panic.

Not a single word was of use against the images! Understand!, Man!, do you not understand that all I want to show you are real images! You dogs! Then tears were shaken from the weakling word.

THINKING. For some time now, according to Eugen B., the concept of *association* became an image of thinking. But this reduction to association meant that thinking was long inadequately described. Thinking also harbours something energetic, which stems from *affectivity*:

goals, content, tempo, fluency, and the manner of think-ing directs itself towards momentary interests, needs, and aspirations. The predominant emotions and moods, the degree of awareness or fatigue, influence thinking. In thinking, the whole person is always present.

A melancholy, poetic wind pervades the great psychi-atric TEXTBOOKS, just as it pervades the American South in the epics of William Faulkner. The wind crosses a great distance. But where does it originate? It is so warm and beneficial. Either it comes from Africa or from that other darkness, the animalistic eter-nal HumanInscrutability. And so the wind is a dark affliction.

And everyday, the breeze rises from this darkness up to the psychiatrist. Bleuler and Jasper took up the DefenceStruggle against it anew with every sentence. They didn't hope for a quick false victory. Against the antagonist's animal force they respectfully opposed a grand inexhaustibility of spirit. They wrote books that explain everything, but without striving for clever con-clusions. Hence, apart from strength of character, these books have another characteristic of great works: total usability. Not in the least must one read Bleuler and Jaspers through. You can open them up at any place and virtually every line wells with truth, wisdom, and consolation.

At the central station, down below, SWEDISH MASSAGE PARLOUR performs the necessary labour for the world's recuperation for the price of a SingleEntryTicket to AKI NonstopCinema.

Call BACK UP all the empty faces before your eyes.

Recall once more the twistedness, the huddling, the time-lessness of these bodies, the inescapable scuffing of the slippers on the linoleum of the unit hallway. The blood is red. Again, Mr S. sits there hunched all the way over mangling further his already mangled ThumbnailBed. Without meaning to, you cover your own thumbs. If I still feel pain inside, if blood can still flow from my flesh, then there must remain a remnant of life in my DeadenedDeath. So goes the thought, perhaps in some deep convolution in the brain in Mr S.'s skull. Oh oh! Who knows. I no longer know anything from that time. If I am quite still, I hear my former patients. Can you hear it? I hear the faint echo of a life, so faint, so distant. I wanted so much once again, for one last time, to speak of the suffering of men. I have seen such misery and tor-ment. It is recorded, quadrillion-fold, somewhere inside me. Where, please? I can no longer reach for it.

In the sky, I can see the stars at night. I see a zillion stars, two zillion, maybe. That is how infinitely un-reachable the HumanMiseryRecorder inside me must be. But I have forgotten where is up and where is down. I have given you all my strength. I am too weak now to step back into depression. But the weakling does not stop here. The weakling is no coward. He has courage.

Courageously, in my weakness, I reach for the other law.

The working hypothesis is OPTIMISM.

In the TWILIGHT IN THE WEST Venus now rises as the first star. In these inexplicably AprilStormy first days of February, it climbs, as every year, with early evening calm, to its point of greatest luminosity. Then it is utterly dark. Yes, we look up in the sky again. The loveliest stars have risen in the southeast and turn towards their highest point in the south. At no other time of the year does the evening sky disclose such splendour.

– If it's already FEBRUARY, you could go ahead and show the second sequence of your twelve-part film now.

  – But that February was totally different, totally snowy.

  – Who cares. You can just show the viewer a snowed-over landscape, he'll soon catch the drift.

  – Easy for you to say, you have no idea. In the second sequence, the viewer sits in the theatre blindfolded.

  – What do you mean, blindfolded? That's not a movie, then, that's a joke.

  – Well! You're in a naïve mood again today!

  – You can lay off insulting me. Because if you keep on, I won't say another word, you can take this dialogue here and shove it, and then you'll have to go back to writing monologues.

  – OKOK, that last bit was more intelligent. And logically, it relates to the film, too.

  – What's that supposed to mean, logically, why this logically all the time?

  – Logically means this film here will never be a film, no matter whether I blindfold the viewer and just play the soundtrack or describe down to the last detail the (logically) blazing lighting effects and their entire array of colours. Because it is and remains fucking literature.

  – Then there's no need to be coy. You knew all that from the get-go.

  – First of all, knowing in advance doesn't help one bit, at this very moment it is especially painful. Second, even a downer like myself has the right to play coy once in a while. And third, the whole reason you're even there

271

is for me to say something wrong and for you to criticize me indignantly.

– I'm doing that now, but this is it. I'm not letting you use me like that. For now, I'm not saying another word.

So I wanted to continue in the FIRST PERSON, wanted to show you, for the love of God, the second sequence of the film, though I'd far prefer talking about yesterday's AndreasDorauConcert and this morning's KröherInterview, because again, I learned so much from both of them, wanted to push Dorau and Kröher off till later for the good of the film, but then the doorbell rang, Raspe opens up, and there stands Psychiatry outside, slightly drunk, and he wants to come and visit.

Actually I was hoping to hope for something completely different, said Raspe, but hey, come on in. I'll make us a coffee. Psychiatry staggers and reels into Raspe's apartment and smiles and out of his mouth wafts his beer breath. The scent of the seediest dive bar fills the hall, and Raspe says kindly: Did you just have a meal out? Psychiatry is the only one of his former colleagues Raspe keeps up with. He says, by way of an answer:

A warm sun is shining outside. I walked to the Isar. It's flowing. I can tell you that.

Raspe says: Yeah. And he thinks: Well, looks like it's summer out. That's just – Lovely, Raspe says, well I'll make us that coffee. Sure, says Psychiatry, and sits in the chair facing the table. From the kitchen, Raspe shouts: What's the point of wanting? Psychiatry shouts back: What? Raspe says: Doesn't matter.

Since on this plane, no person can have a reasonable conversation, let's switch over now and give psychology an attractive made-up name, Rainald, for example, so now you have two tangible, concrete people talking on a new coffee-drinking plane about God and the world and work.

I just do things my way, like my two great EXAMPLARS the media carries on about constantly, the esteemed Dr Herzog and the esteemed Dr Hitler. I keep struggling till the final victory. His Honour the Prosecuting Attorney Dr Sprenger, though, has pushed for life imprisonment, just because once, from SexGreed, I wanted to experience a SuperOrgasm and two women wound up dead. But even all the kids know twice is nice. Besides, this other dude in London had such a SexGreed he hacked up and cooked seventeen men to death. His Honour the Publisher Dr Springer reported as much in my very favourite newspaper. Esteemed Dr Hitler must have had a Doctor Honoris Causa too. But he fought too hard for the final victory and they probably revoked his doctorate. Dr Kohl, though, has an authentic doctorate. An authentic doctor, I believe, is unconcerned with defeat or final victory. Homework: Choose another Doctor Honoris Causa who also struggles in politics and is also a Bavarian through and through. Build pretty practice phrases with him and Dr Hitler. Note: FinalVictory SexGreed SuperOrgasm Cook. Repeat: FinalVictory.

Everything concerns me, EVERYTHING.

THE COOKING, now placed on the table, was hot, of course, but there was nothing chopped up in it, it was coffee, that's all. Two people sit down to this coffee: They are both mentioned above, and have the following names: Raspe and Rainald.

This information is for users who may have only just arrived. My courtesy here is valid for all users

273

irritated by the longer interconnected WordPassages, who, if they can enter into a book like this at all, can only do so by skimming, and for whom this supershort EverythingSubChapter could logically provide a way of getting onboard. Such users very much have my sympathy. I share with them the longing for terse, felicitous language (BLUBBER COOK BLOT SHOT) and for images.

About the latter, someone has written they may be comfortably treated as tools within a creative apparatus. And tool wasn't meant as some kind of dirty joke, because it appeared not under a lurid picture in the comic magazine MAD but as a comment on coloured tables including a book hacked up into 680 subchapters, some of them extraordinarily succint. With regard to this instructive riddle, I will say no more.

YEAH, COFFEE!, Rainald said and shook the LighterFlame at the tip of his cigarette, too close to his mouth. The glow rose along the soot-black paper in that first drag, hectic like a non-smoker's. He blew the barely inhaled smoke into space with inordinate hissing and cool, took a swig of coffee, smoked, drank, and said, pointing with his chin to the person opposite him, to Raspe, as if an entire group were sitting there: So what's up with you?

Raspe said: Eh, it's going, you know, same old same old. Then he fell silent and knew that then and there, unsolicited and uninhibited, Rainald would start talking about the clinic. Often, in recent months, his one-time colleague had stood at the door to Raspe's apartment, unannounced and tipsy, generally on Saturday or Sunday afternoons, and Raspe would have to struggle through the usual violent agitation (I hate unexpected

274

visits during the daytime); then he would invite the drunk in for a coffee, and Rainald inevitably had the most unbelievable, harrowing, scandalous stories from the clinic. At last, Raspe no longer played the role of perpetrator or victim, he was simply an observer and chronicler. Rainald's reports reminded Raspe of all he had learned back then at the clinic, and what he now, oh how painfully feeble is the memory of the horror, already once more almost wanted to forget: Nothing is so fantastically overwhelming as the authentic, nothing so unbelievable as real reality.

And as Rainald spoke, Raspe thought to himself: 'I always want to see what I am able to believe, and so I must croak through the world like a dumb blind toad. Strength, please! Come into my eyes!, so that I may simply see the truth and not have to think it away. Already I am walking upright with it. But insight is weak, even weaker than that impoverished blind daily gazing, and the strongest thing is the harebrained imagination, which hinders the most serious work, the simple transcription of my world. Beloved diary!, be my totally real devil against my faith!'

That afternoon, with drunken avidity, Rainald smoked one cigarette after another, and spoke, as Raspe had expected, of illnesses and colleagues, above all of himself. Raspe just nodded and kept his mounting astonishment concealed. His friend had worked just three years at the clinic, he had started with an excess of idealism doing his alternative civilian service as a doctor four months before Raspe got there. Now, though, Rainald no longer believed he was capable of helping the patients. They were interesting, though, there was something about the ill that struck him as very interesting. Through them, he was trying to understand how we must learn to talk about ourselves again, without psychiatry, that, for him, was the most interesting thing about the sick, whom he couldn't help, but could learn from, that was what kept him in the clinic despite everything. Rainald talked of 4.000 marks, of unit doctor posts, of sharing the payments from private patients, of his new scientific interests in sleep and hebephrenia research.

Then Rainald got up from the chair, and Psychiatry stood there grown large, stood aslant in the fog and lit up another cigarette. His hair was blond and curly, maybe already starting to thin, and his asthenic stature, his almost anorexic frame, were a constant cry for help constantly stymied by his aloofness. But the alcohol made that haggard figure pliant and tender, and from above, he kissed Raspe softly on the lips. Just as he came in, so he teetered out. Most likely Raspe waved goodbye.

He shut the door, his head leaned aside, the three middle fingers of his left hand came to rest over his closed lips, and in this way, inside him, it listened. Then he came back to himself, noted the abhorrent scent of smoke, aired the place out, and at last, Raspe got back to work.

DAMMIT, when will the eternally promised images finally come? Stampf!!

276

But of course, the DISORDER in his head was ear-splitting. Work was out of the question. After every visit, and especially after this one, the chatter had to be silenced and order restored once more. The muddle of voices in his head, sometimes only two, but usually innumerable ones, was a constant threat of chaos and along with it, logically, demise. Every day in the morning, often for hours, he had to think away the chaos and think order into being. Every PersonPresence, above all in the mornings, but during the day, too, was a ThreatToExistence until the work was done. For without order, no work, without work, logically, no right to live.

Sometimes Raspe asked himself: How could I ever think I could work every day among people, more than that, work *for* people as a doctor, and beyond that, work in the most dreadful PeopleChaos as a doctor, how could I ever dream I would manage that. Oh!, I must have been very young. The young person doesn't know himself, I think. Maybe that's it. Maybe it is a very dark very heavy cross.

Free fly be high TERROR must be nearby.

At night, logically, it is the LAW OF THE NIGHT that counted. People-addicted, whirling, stumbling in the whirling gazes, yeah, could now be everything and wail, yearn roar unrestrained, chaotically I was jostled here and there and who the fuck cares. That's true for now and it's true for always.

Continuation of the film. You are unfamiliar with THE VOICE that said that. Still, you are not frightened. You knew it was coming. The voice continues: You are sitting in the cinema. The seats are comfortable. The whirr of voices in the room grows softer. Around you, everything is black. No, you see nothing, nothing at all. You lean back. The kind person sitting next to you may graze a few fine nerve endings on your ElbowSkin. You are alone, you are eager, you are all ears.

The voice pauses. Music comes in softly, gets a little louder, right away you recognize the eversame stoned rhythm of a reggae track, and momentarily, your good humour increases with it. Yep, you can't do nothing about it, whether you're a weedhead, a beerpunk, or an upper crust Valium-type. Reggae gets everyone high. Now the voice is back and tells us we are now in the ParanoiaYear, in February, in a roomy car, an old Mercedes, maybe, judging from the description, driving over a hilly snow-bedecked landscape. You'd like to see the GoddamnedThingForOnce. But the voice says:

You want to, but you can't open your eyes. You feel something pressing down on your eyelids. You reach up towards your eyes with both hands. You touch a bandage. Panic surges inside you. You try in vain to tear off the bandage. Raging, rapidly raging panic, but then you stop to consider your situation. At this moment, you grow calmer, I say. It is nothing but the calming presence of my voice, by now quite familiar to you, that eases your mood. You will listen, if you can't talk, just listen. You are relaxed again of course and pleasantly curious. You must have risen up, maybe. You lean back again. Once more, in the background, you hear the good reggae, you had almost forgotten it. You smile.

Then the voice left, and the music turned louder. Then this CarInterior DrivingNoise came on. And finally you heard these voices, at first distant and incoherent, eventually it was two men in a dialogue interspersed with laughter, shouting, or pauses. The music and the

DrivingNoises have must have faded. What are they talking about?, you ask yourself, what the hell kind of yammering is this?

KLAUS: Ha! LAUGHTER, hohoho, the brothers are coming hard again, boom-chicka boom-chicka boom-chicka boom.

ME: Brrastafari, Bbrrrreggaue, Brunich.

KLAUS: Right. Brrastafari, Breggae in Brunich.

ME: boom-chicka boom.

KLAUS: Next unit's ready to go. We could light up in the ditch if you drive on a bit.

ME: Why me? Why's it gotta be me?

KLAUS: Roof overhead, tyres turn up, logical, let the music play on and easy peasy, light the fuck up.

ME: And the stash flies out the car and the deal's up.

KLAUS: What do you mean, deal?

ME: And then pow, busted, fucked.

KLAUS: What do you mean, deal? You got a pen or a match for the filter, everything's hanging out.

ME: Nope. Nothing's as cool as cool white snow. Nothing goes with the hills and the evening as good as a snowy winter.

KLAUS: You're right about the evening, but summer's just as cool.

ME: True. Bum-bum-ba-dum pum.

KLAUS: Dude! Pen! Or a match! Otherwise I can't get this unit packed tight.

ME: Maybe there's something in the glove box. And put some different tunes on, I can't listen to this reggae shit anymore.

KLAUS: Oouu!, I got something. Now we're cooking with gas. What kind of tunes you got in mind?

ME: Fuck do I know, some sappy new pop or some old

Fishnet Stockings.

KLAUS: And all the while I was thinking Breggae was just the right warm-up for the Creation Rebels.

ME: Yeah but not the whole time. Otherwise I'll be deaf before the concert has even started.

KLAUS: I'm gonna light up now.

ME: Mhm.

KLAUS: Hmmm! Hit it, good shit, ya.

ME: Man, you gotta put in a decent tape for once, retard.

KLAUS: And you gotta drive us quicker through this snow. What deal, anyway?

ME: Dude, the new shipment, that's all.

KLAUS: Stray Cats OK then?

ME: Yeeess. Yeah, I got that here in the car.

KLAUS: What? The whole shipment! You're bonkers.

ME: Hell yeah. You got that right. If I lose track of the situation, you gotta take over.

KLAUS: Roger that.

ME: Dude puffpuffpuff. I think I'm good for now.

KLAUS: Don't run out of gas, boy, we've got the whole night ahead of us. And you got the whole goddamn stash right here in the car.

ME: Yep.

KLAUS: Where and why?

ME: I already told you, my place ain't pig-proof.

KLAUS: A kilo's what it came out to, the shipment?

ME: Yeah, just. Right at a kilo. Here under the seat, in here, to the side. Safe and sound.

KLAUS: Yeah, but like you said, if there's an accident, bad luck, the pigs – you're done for.

ME: Fuck it. Whoa!, now this is cool, rumble in Brighton tonight, there's a rumble in Brighton tonight, yuy yuyyuuy.

KLAUS: And the next one, Uh uh uh uh, I get my dinner fro-om a garbage can, shloobydooby duby dee, woow.

BOTH: I don't wonna chasing mice around, shloobey-doo –, I wish I could be as Kevin –

ME: Kevin who?

Both: But I *got* cat class and I got cat style –

KLAUS: Just the right little stretch, like the song.

ME: Exactly.

KLAUS: I snake through the alley looking for a fight –

BOTH: SMASH!

ME: Supercool. The next one you can turn down. Nah, what I was telling you was, either me or my apartment they prolly got their eye on.

KLAUS: Dude, man, I think you're losing it. Just 'cause recently they left the rolling blind down over there at the precinct.

ME: No, not just 'cause of that.

KLAUS: 'Cause of what, then?

ME: I'm telling you, they're watching me, or anyway it's likely, they prolly are.

KLAUS: Hold it! We're both baked out of our gourds and I'm in no mood for you to go putting that paranoid shit in my head. Got it?

ME: Don't panic, dude.

KLAUS: Whaddya mean, don't panic, dude? You're the one that's panicking, man, and then you tell me, don't panic. You're a trip.

ME: OK OK. I can give you the evidence –

KLAUS: Kill it! Even the best rock 'n' roll gets old after a few tracks.

ME: True. You can go back to playing reggae till we reach Ampermoching. We're basically there.

KLAUS: Supercool. Right, and during the concert

they'll swipe that kilo shipment out of the car and you'll have to file a police report for theft of drugs.

ME: Ha ha ha, very funny, anyway you put in cash, you're in on the deal too.

KLAUS: Oh, fucker, you're right, better if that doesn't happen, then.

ME: And here we go, grooving to death on this stupid ass Rastafari Reggae Kingdom, boom-boom.

KLAUS: Boom-chicka-boom. Now approaching Ampermoching, all passengers out, please.

ME: That's right, Ampermoching, end of the line.

OUT with this stoned flimflam, with those Tripping AndDrinkingBooks, out with those floundering Drug Songs, out of here, weakness!, shove off. I don't want to hear one more excess eccentric word. The weird is too cheap for me. That always comes free, derangement, any idiot can do that. I just want to read a simple clever story. That would be a real trip (Peter's objection).

At the end of THAT SUMMER, which had begun by releasing me from the post-psychiatric WhoKnowsHowLong bedriddenness and, yeah!, catapulted me out into freedom, in the early autumn then, which I remember as only clarity and light – was it really like that? – I see such a beautiful unwavering blue in the sky, with a joy only granted at this time of year, we got in my big Mercedes, five, six of us, and made many excursions to the country.

We drove north. The highway was straight. The evening shone with the still setting sun into the car from the left. The landscape stretched out before us flat as a board, on and on. Nature lay ungraspably far, but the orange warmth brought the horizon comfortably close.

The world was at last comprehensible again. My! Isn't that strange. My!, this happiness. I let go of the steering wheel and threw up my arms. The left one flew outside through the open window. The right, CRASH, crashed into a sky composed of a steel-blue plastic panel. I laughed and rubbed the pain away from the tip of my ulna.

And onward we drove. The goal was indifferent, one concert after the next. I looked at my life calmly on these journeys. I knew nothing. But I drank beer and no longer had to go wild pouring it down into my belly like a DeathWisher.

In the meantime, to the left, the turquoise had started glowing, bright, still undetermined and hence full of promise. One by one flared the headlights of the oncoming cars, multiplying cold and cruel, and the red ones, too, and soon the magenta stream of taillights before me pulled me in. I lit a cigarette and looked left, blinded by the yellow of the flame, into an even grander, deep-distant violet.

Then the sky went black. We turned off the motorway. I steered over the country roads, again, there were hills there, up and down. Where does it lead? Someone always knew the way.

Hours later, way past midnight, the journey back. Then everyone sat still, the sleepers slumped over in the back. I drove. My eyes were so tired. In the silence, I had ears. I heard the singing of the tyres, the motor, and the bluster of the wind as I tore through it. Such was racing homeward in the night. Exhausted, all the friends embraced. See ya, see ya, till next time. Already, the grey of morning.

In the interim, the LOGIC CLASSES for the students

from the special school: logically he is not I, and I am I, logically, least of all. Good. Everyone got that? Did those unregenerate dumb fucks in the back get it too? – But excuse me, I am wondering, what – – Zip it!, better to be clever and think it through than to ask questions like an imbecile.

I SCREAM because my yearning is so great. I wanted nothing but to whisper. I wanted to be quiet and proper and toe the line with this story. So I have to interrupt myself constantly. Now I am so old, already, and yet so young.

Before, back AT DAMAGE, I would have loved to be one of the earliest punks. Today I don't envy the prematurely aged, who've been running around for five years now in their unchanged BustedOutfits cursing the chic fashions and whatever people do today because nothing, absolutely nothing, can measure up to the wild days of London, '77, man, back then, that was power, you know? Invariably sympathetic, though: those BourgeoisKids for whom punk was an injection of politics, FreeTimeTerrorists from GenerationSuchAndSuch who burned down a few banks for kicks, but then in all seriousness were packed off to the slammer and today just want to go back to being artists. All these artists, filmmakers writers painters musicians and photographers moving through the scenester bars, with me among them. I know every other one by sight, I don't need to talk to any of them. That is my favourite combination of all: I stand there, stare, I know everything by heart, it never ever bores me, I watch and drink. Logically, I see the elegance become that much more elegant the higher the unemployment rate rises. Just standing there and drinking and watching, what a pleasure. Sometimes I get plastered. Then I bounce around like a RubberBall.

Blue-feathered DEATHEAGLES swooped down at me from the depths of the starry sky with whipping wing-beats, trying to exterminate me with grenades or with a frontal kamikaze attack. I shot back. Ploing ploing ploing. But soon I was shredded red and yellow. Then instead of the fun ShootingGame the dull EatingGame came on. If that's the deal, I'd rather go back to playing pinball or else, logically, foosball. But Lipstick was the only place that had a foosball table. Lipstick shut down long ago. And in our game room, where we are regulars but they treat us like lepers because we're not foreigners and for that very reason we keep going back there, we'd take billiards over VideoShooting or foosball anyhow.

LONG PAUSE, just a hanging and the great indolence drooping there where once a head had grown, made to stay there so long like that trying, logically in vain, to think into the head what was missing from it, till it burned, the courage, we simply must be able to wait for it, wait for it more miserable than the most miserable of dogs, pausing then before rushing headlong into the next fucking wall.

WHO CARES how gorgeously the sun shone down in the autumn, and how I wanted to drive my car through the countryside drained of color – it was obvious that couldn't be all there was. Maybe it wasn't obvious, most likely though it was. There was something, and I had to look for it.

So there I was sitting with the Marxists once a week. But Dr Fertl was so fat and stupid-clever. And the rest were naïve and already convinced, all they wanted from fat Dr Fertl was to know why it was they were so firmly convinced by Marxism. That's something Dr Fertl's been well suited to these past ten years. He rattles it off, the RigorousKnowledgeStrivers parrot it back, rinse and repeat. There you have it: Marxism. It works like a charm, but for me it was all too asinine. I stopped hanging with the ArgumentLearners long ago, but sometimes I still made it to Doctor Karl Held's magnificent public sermons. How he stood there! How he spoke. He didn't look in the least like some dumb boozer, he was handsome and beaming, as a revolutionary should be.

Maybe I was there serving a PrivateSelf or PrivateAmbition. Maybe it was far vaguer than that and I was just asking myself: Where in the wide world will I find something to grab on to? Because I'm getting blown all over the place, man! I'm not a feather. I just want to live. How's that work? Then, I got a job in culture. My pride leapt into the air with joy. Hey kind people!, I shouted, take a look! There's my name in print. Just like the things others have thought, now the things I have thought are out there in the world. How weird! How lovely. Now, at last, I am among the clever people, now everything in my life is going right.

And, that was the nicest thing, I was allowed to sit alone all day at the desk, didn't have to talk to colleagues, nor to a single patient, had only to talk into the telephone receiver and think things with my head. My eyes were allowed to take a complete break. In my work room, the image-prohibition and the office-like spotlessness reigned. I didn't have to hide my daggers. And the work was allowed to do its work.

My good fortune that the word CELIBATARIAN no

longer exists. That way I can become one tranquilly, and no one can reproach me for it.

Then, though, he became increasingly BIZARRE. Maybe he had erred too far in the direction of aberration. For, as we know, he had to go back to the clinic. Then he sank deep into LiteratureWords and slipped so far into the EverythingIsAboutMe-thinking that he even believed the police station across from him had eyes and could watch and irradiate him. And culture said: You're loco, I don't have any more use for your rubbish. You don't even write about the thing you're supposed to write about, just the same old shit about yourself. That doesn't cut it. Have you turned into a megalomaniac? Or do you want to take your own life?

Word has it I am supposed to review my own novel in DER SPIEGEL. I find the idea outlandish. Do they think I'm an idiot? Word has it they are on the hunt, not for the quotidian, but instead for the most outrageous combinations possible. But I suspect they simply want to make a fool of me. I play the clown and everyone else gets to laugh up their sleeves. No no, best to keep my guard up, I figure.

The worst thing is that I have to work it all out on my own. Why won't anyone help me, please? Am I standing alone in the world, or do I only have enemies? At night I awaken and I can't sleep anymore, because the fear is dancing and trampling on my chest. Why me?, I ask. No answer, just this trampling. Do they want to annihilate me?

Suddenly the grey of morning. I jump up and make slowly – Oh beloved daybreak! – a tremulous gesture of gratitude to the light.

287

THAT MORNING the former insurance broker Josef Hutter, 34 years old, who for unknown reasons is already receiving a pension, was frightened from his sleep by thundering WomanWomanWomanWoman-shouts. Josef Hutter sits up in bed and murmurs: Er, eh, what's wrong? Then Mr Hutter feels the loneliness in his stiff member. He lets his torso fall back. His head lies on his pillow. His eyes close. It'll be bright out soon, Mr Hutter thinks. Now he is ashamed. All at once, his dream comes back to him. Mr Hutter is ashamed of himself.

A young woman stands at the telephone and shouts over and over, half-questioning, half-demanding, WomanWoman into the receiver. Seems she's trying to suss out who might be on the line. The phone is in a kind of ski lodge. Peter, standing up from the lower bunk of the bed where we had lain together, holds a second phone in his hand and giggles, amused.

We had been lying together blissfully. Peter had deftly told off a journalist who had subjected him to the cheapest ridicule: They didn't know themselves, took no time for themselves, didn't even know who they were. And I had listened, lying naked under the blanket, quite moved by the excellence of Peter's speech. Then he lay next to me, and we didn't touch one another. His face was pimpled and pale, and that made me want to kiss him. But then I moved his head to the hollow of my stomach, his hair was unkempt. We lay that way still, without a word, and I was happy and unafraid. Later I saw women in the lodge, wood panelling, many bunk beds, women looking at me. I didn't know them. Then the phone rang.

That must have woken me up, Josef Hutter said to himself. What a, uh, what a dream, really. Who was that then? The things the mind comes up with, Mr Hutter thinks, and outside it is getting light already. The shame is gone. Shortly after 6 a.m., Josef Hutter falls asleep again. And the next two hours are the most beautiful sleep of all.

But that very same night MY CRANIUM was so thin that when I slept the pillow dented my head and pressed into my brain, and the pressure was so painful that the interior became a gigantic, traumatized, throbbing testicle. I hate the night.

ASK FOR the appropriate power: Heroic activity.

I CAN'T ANYMORE I CAN'T ANYMORE I just want to get to the end. I don't want to have to run into more walls like a sick man. It hurts so much. How much longer now? The hotly awaited happy end looks further off than ever. BLAH BLAAAH my sorrowful mouth cries.

The film in MARCH: We hear shots. The TV's on. Quick cuts. The night colours are bright. Again with the fucking fear. Is my room a detective bureau? Better that than the world headquarters. Get something, just to be safe. Gotta happen. Outside the WindNoises blow loud. The kitchen knife is very big (butchery). A revolver is a safer bet than an automatic. In the gun shop the Lounge Lizards are playing, out in the street David Byrne sings his Psychokiller, and in the U-bahn, menacingly, the Cure's SubwaySong hammers away, logically. Yeah!, convalescence. To be continued.

THE FULL MOON shines down over just and unjust.
– Get the tool out of the trunk! The car's staying here.
– I don't like anything about this.

Why doesn't Mr Donald like anything about it? It's in its 33rd year now under the chief editorship of Dr Erika Fuchs, it's printed on paper and the brightest colours, rotogravure, and thousands and thousands of copies are sold to children all over the world. Every normal person loves it. Only the BookWriter is envious. Because never in his life will he scale the heights of rotogravure. Even those books of Chinese Tortures for PsychiatryPatients, PsychiatryProfessors and CultureBores are printed in BlackAndWhite, though in my world they loom varicoloured and looming. This is where numbers come into play. And that's the good thing about good books. No one buys them and even fewer people read them, and logically, that's a good thing. How good and numbers go together, let me demonstrate –

NOW. Off the bat, time comes in as a calculation factor. Doesn't matter where I begin, say with Dieter Thomas Heck, Peter Weiss, Peter Handke, Didi Hallervorden, Trio, Heinz Schenk, Nicole, Böll, or Simmel. Because the whole thing is like algebra, you can solve the equation from either direction, choose any whole number you like, do the maths and then pow, there you have it.

Either you're Gottlieb Wendehals or you're Johannes Mario Simmel. Everything in the middle is a refuge, no one pays it any mind. It's a space where you can do as you wish. I've still never read a Simmel. Maybe I was too highbrow or maybe I just didn't have the time. But the title of his latest book and the copyright page are enough already: *Please, Let the Flowers Live*, 1st ed. 200,000 copies. Natch, dude, I let the flowers live, I never tread on the daisies because I'm not so stupid and don't go walking through the meadow. But now even the mustiest MinistryMouse in any ministry in this republic, not to mention every peabrained scoundrel (in brief: every mature bourgeois) accepts and stands up for this EcoShmeekoNonsense. You can sell these types 200,000 times on the stirring story of the great love between a 50-year-old has-been and a young bookseller, with pressing questions, logically, about our fate in this decade, the eighties, which is inextricably entwined with the fate of these two lovers, the mature bourgeois will tear a few hundred thousand of these from your hands without thinking twice.

But before a nasty assent breaks out among the social-democratic, anti-intellectual, critical bourgeoisie, here's the twist: Simmel is actually the same as *Die Zeit*, not to mention *Stern*, not to mention *Der Spiegel* or any other renowned newspaper cultural supplement. Once you pass a few hundred thousand, you hit a point where nothing intelligent can come out anymore. At present you've got the EcoBalderdash and PeaceFever, not to forget the dangers of media, video games, and computers. Everything very grave, always the same old shit, GAG.

The other way to make your mark on the public and

line your pockets in the process would be something like the *Polonäse Blankenese*, which one out of ten mature bourgeois owns, including every toddler, mental defective, and homosexual. 6 million Gottlieb Wendehals sold, and played God knows how many million times, and then of course there's *Herbert*, or *Nippel* or *Zum Blauen Bock*. The most tremendous thing about all this highly calculated EntertainmentIdiocy is this: a normal person, that is, anyone who has thought one inch past the StupidCritical ResponsibilityThinking, not only has the most exquisite amusement at his disposal, but can even get novelty served up to him every day. All you need to do is turn on the TV.

What *Zum Blauen Bock* serves up for normal persons of the other sort – namely those who have not yet reached the stage of StupidCritical thinking – right, what should I say, no idea, I don't know anyone like that. No, nothing helps there, imagination least of all. How dull is a life that dull? Not the slightest idea. The only ones who do know are the StupidCritical ResponsibilityBourgeoisie, with their interminable conjectures, warnings, illuminations. I don't want to convert a normal person. Why should I care how dull their life is. Mine's not exactly a cake walk.

– Representative, will you allow Representative Professor History to interrupt you for a question?

– Logically.

– Representative, are you aware that the opinion you are endorsing here, this affinity of the intellectuals for the trivial, has already been –

– Thank you, Professor, for your stupid-arse question, as if I gave a damn about the age of whatever hat I've put on. The main thing is whether it's smart and whether it looks good on me. Please allow me to continue.

I come to the aforementioned calculation factor: time. As a ground rule you can keep in mind – and this naturally comes to bear on the HundredThousandPrintings: if something nabs you a title story in the *Stern* or the *Spiegel*, then you better start looking for a new trench or refuge where you can hunker down and fight for the final victory. Logically you can just put on some new old hat for camouflage. Addendum: no rule without an exception. Second addendum: no less worthy than fighting from a sly, ever-shifting, impossible to pin down redoubt is when everything contemporary irritates you and you turn radically to your private affairs, radically, as I say, and boldly, the way the deeply thoughtful person lives.

Right. Implement what we've learned in a concrete counting game: New German Literature. It appears in practical isolation from the public. And here is how it runs its course. You got three, four overburdened editors (Good god, it's autumn again, here we go with these mountains of books piling up around my desk! Dreadful, dreadful!), so if you're lucky these three or four pulled your book out of a pile, flipped through it, and maybe, if you're still lucky, sent it to some likewise overburdened reviewer (– Good god, it's autumn again, here we go again with this entire –), maybe his wife just came down with jaundice, or he has a kidney stone that just won't go away, always with this goddamn colic. If that's the case, your book doesn't get reviewed. Or say that it does, still, you cannot in the least begin to grasp how much contingency is at play. But whatever, let's say you strike gold and a couple of reviews do appear, and the biggest win of all: two people think your book's good. Naturally you celebrate like never before in your life, but normal people couldn't care less. They rip the book pages out of the paper and throw them off to the side. So does anyone buy your book? Sure: there do exist those rare disreputable thousand buyers of New German Literature, maybe a given subject pulls in another thousand, say a thousand more are hoodwinked by two good reviews, and bam, that's that. – So what have we learned here?

That logically, literature for that very reason, because practically no one at all reads it, is the most beautiful queen of all. Why is she so beautiful? Because she may be gravid with truth like none other, if only one knows how to inseminate her wisely. You can pack everything into her enigmatic womb, every false start, every deviation, every error, even the truth. All you need is respect for yourself and for those you want to tell it all to.

Let us turn back to THAT RASPE who stepped into the psychiatric clinic a thoroughly idealistic young man bent on discovering himself and his life in the course of his labour there. The clinic walls are high. Within them reigns the law of Hell. Naturally the SufferingInferno in this hermetically sealed space lit Raspe up like fireworks.

Then Raspe left the clinic and tumbled from the beautifully concluded and dispiritingly relatable story out into a right trifling chaos. No longer could any depressive exoticism enlighten him in his ever-immoderate quest for himself in his work and in his mutilated life. Nor was there anything left of that long narrative breath that does both narrator and discriminating reader so much good, instead what was needed was: minced meat, theory, filth, brains and more brains, manic pamphlets, gossip and corny jokes and finding instead of looking. That's shit, that's not literature, someone said to me. But you have to blow that off because this is an immoderate attempt at truth and nothing but, and there should never ever be any looking back, except to make sure the whole thing is right, so what you have to have, logically, is total true space and nothing but. And logically, the only thing that can hold this insane project together is an intelligently insane and at the same time insanely intelligent SELF.

The two chic ladies sit in an elegant coffee house GOSSIPING and BACKBITING, one with a Wiener Melange, one with a coffee-and-cognac, both drinks in front of them on the marble table top, and they sit there and talk, just talk about the things you talk about, oh, yeah, yadda yadda, they talk about the ultra-hippest embarrassments that have recently occurred. And as we cautiously creep a bit closer, we notice the two ladies with their broad feathered hats are conducting a quite vulgar, almost ordinary conversation.

– So, the second one says, he's meeting his publisher for the first time, and the first thing the publisher says to the guy is this: They warned me about you. You write down everything people say. Then people wind up reading it somewhere later.

– That's fantastic. So what did the guy say back?

– Apparently, this is how it was told to me, the guy was taken aback for a moment –

– And then?

– And then he asked the publisher who he heard that from. And the publisher –

– Yeah!, what did the publisher say back?

– He just said, half-icy, half-playful: I'm not telling.

– Huh. This is getting better and better.

– Hold on now, the best is yet to come. Because now the guy says the name of a famous writer, and then he's like: You could only have heard that from him.

– So was the guy right?

– The publisher gets this big grin, laughs, says: Yeah, and that breaks the ice with the publisher and author.

– Very nice very nice.

– But the real kicker is this. The guy sits down, right, he's cracking up laughing about this famous writer and the whole industry, where a teensy-weensy story like that thing about writing stuff down makes the rounds, like it was some kind of scandal and not the most obvious obviousness.

– So was the guy pissed off?

– Nah, he's like us, he's a big fan of stories like this.

– Then everything's kosher. So?

– Since he is such a fan, and since beside that, to hear him tell it, he's orderly to the point of pedantry, after a couple of years in the industry he's put together such a big collection of these perverse stories –

– Yeep! That –

– Right, that he can float himself as an author with them for the rest of his life, and he's not crazy old either, this guy.

– That's what I call good prospects. So can a person read this somewhere sometime?

– Not just yet.

– Why, if he's such a fan?

– Something to do with writing, that's how he explained it to me, because the hardest thing to learn and the most important thing at the same time was that you had to keep most things under wraps. But most things, not everything, and the few select things you write down had to contain most of the other ones, once and for all. He says, this ProperSelection is the MainBitchJob for the whole job.

– Yeahyeah, I got that, I had to hoe my own row too

before I became an editor or whore or whatever, or was it secretary or President of the Republic? No idea. Who cares anyway. Work is a bitch, always. Is that what he means? Or are you just fucking with me?

– Not at all! That was dead honest.

– So tell me more about the publisher!

– He really stressed that *once and for all.*

– And so?

– Yeah, I don't really know either, to hear him tell it, that was in the middle of this funny story, and the real point is yet to come, then suddenly there's this pensive strange seriousness. So I...

– Right: he sits there, he cracks up, the publisher laughs too, and then?

– OK. The publisher says it's not the famous writer himself that told him this thing about how he's got to watch his back around the guy, instead it was this other one, the publisher says, what's her name anyway, the uh, the guy's friend.

– And that made the guy crack up laughing?

– Exactly. This AbsoluteZero, who lives out her ZeroExistence at this famous writer's side, as he explained it to me, but interrupting himself, laughing, all the while, she actually thinks she has to inoculate this particular publisher. Who, according to the guy himself, he had made fun of often and certainly not without reason –

– What do you mean, made fun of?

– But logically, he never had any doubt that he was a true professional.

– And this chick brings this risible warning to him, that –

– Exactly, this chick who has worked her way up from a zero to a fully-fledged writer's companion, offers her services, probably with a smile on her face, to change the diapers of a true professional.

– Hee hee, ha ha ha!

– Right. The guy says what he does is the most normal thing in the word, he has a bad memory and so he has to write everything down.

– And then this comes!

– And then comes this Class-A ZeroChick –

– It's already a riot.

– Hahaha, an absolute joke. In closing, the guy says: They all seem – otherwise this wouldn't happen – they all seem to be crackers, like their brain's got terribly overheated there beneath the dura mater.

Everyone's in NEW YORK, I'm the only one who isn't. I gotta run amok in the stupid German literature scene. But not for much longer, and then never again.

If I had to have something, I'd at least like to be MANIC, and to all appearances, I do have something. But please please not schizophrenia, particularly not one of the types with a mild-onset presentation, that's downright diabolical. Maybe that's why I don't feel like doing this paranoid film. The good thing about mania is that the world has to put up with my mania, not me, even though it's mine. But maybe I'm perfectly sound and am just exaggerating-exaggerating the working hypothesis of optimism. Can I do that? Must I do that?

Word has it that in the near future they will revoke my BIRTHRIGHTS AS A CITIZEN. I won't say why. That strikes me as lowdown. Apparently this one sentence I wasn't supposed to utter. I haven't said anything yet. Just once: You can't suck it anymore.

298

What is that?　　　　　　　What is that?
What kind of light is that? (Carl Orff, The Moon)

CHEWING GUM OR ART? That is the question, I said aloud. Secretly I thought to myself: I'd love to have that full unrestricted hunting license so I could concentrate one hundred per cent on shooting and not have to think while I was out poaching about stupid rights and the threat of the law and the gamekeeper stringing me up by my heels. Then I could just start up a chewing gum factory. And so I say aloud:

1. Logically everything is invented freely, the people, the names, the events, and the places in this novel. But this is literature, you idiots, not chewing gum. 2. If I were a chewing gum manufacturer, I would still tell tales about my work; how the sugar deliveryman had shorted me on the sugar delivery for the second time, about the new market in faraway Red China, and the stress with the goddamn competition, and the export pack on the assembly line, whatever, what do I know, maybe something totally different, I'm not a chewing gum manufacturer and I don't want to have jack shit to do with the stupid fucking imagination. The Artificial Artists and all the other zeros can have a wank with all that. I don't

have time for that shit. I have to write about my life. I'm not talking about anything else.

My case, or as I prefer to call it THE TRUE SPACE, the film I am narrating here: early summer, that at least, moving images, documentary material, glowing and ash, outside and inside. The IceSea is east of Cape Horn, where the Argentine light cruiser *General Belgrano* sank, 4150 metres deep. I know I can't be responsible for the 368 BelgranoDead.

KLAUS says: Exactly!, exactly.

ME: And yet I feel ashamed, and more than that, I feel this burning pain. I sense my guilt.

KLAUS: Outright nonsense.

ME: I hate any kind of flag. Maybe I am chosen. Maybe I should become a saint.

KLAUS Dude, cool down, man.

But ME: I want to do penance.

I cut into my skin. The blood drips. Sun shines on my police station. Why is everything so far away, so hazy, so bright and yet so indeterminate? No Klaus can answer that, nobody can answer that. Maybe love would be something to hold on to. But love –. Everything must have an end. Life makes me so dizzy. I seem to hear a cry. The cry hovers above me. I hear the cries of the insane. No, they are inside me. I beg for silence. Before me, the trains thunder past. Horrible fear, such fear. Then dead silence. Relieved, I take a deep breath. The fear races back into my body with the air, throbbing panic. As soon as a train approaches, I see everything in front of me. The sky has gone dim. Perhaps it will get dark soon.

SHIVER SCREECH HOWL.
If you shout like that, you'll miss the best part, the

TOSSERPARADE, live and in colour.

For that, we must abandon early summer for the winter, for the days before Christmas, when the times get especially tough every year. Yep, it's bad. Detroit is starving. Millions want to work and can't. The threat of the atom hangs over us. But it'll be Christmas soon. So we all want to hold each other's hands. We think of the power of life, we thank the power of the imagination. We feel a reflection coming on. Where adversity looms, strength comes from somewhere and helps to give us peace, to see the positive, to turn everything towards the good. – Today is the GoldenAge of tossers.

And so it is utterly appropriate that Mr B's birthday falls on Christmas day. Mr B looks no less plodding and put-upon than the Christ child, who must bear the guilt of the entire world on his shoulders from birth. Our saviour will now turn sixty-five years old. How will that go? And where will it take us? One thing is certain: In the TosserParade, this Nobel Prize winner, honourable citizen, honorary doctor, and TV star has earned his place as leader of the pack. And he does lead them, un-daunted, painfully aware of the responsibility pressing down on him. But again, the question: To where? To where, Mr B? But of course, that is no question at all, for the TosserParade, as everyone knows, is a polonaise, it circles through the TV studio out on to the countless screens, even through the newspaper culture pages.

And on they go – are you getting the image? – tosser after tosser, each with his hands on the plodding shoul-ders of his respective leader, an arm flies up now and again, one of the tossers waves and glances over, pushes on, galumphing, pushes closer into the camera, right into the middle of my face.

It can befall you anytime, as it did me recently, when

I had the nerve to switch over from *Zum Blauen Bock* to a different progamme with the AnnoyingTitle *On Imagination*. There, KingTosser B, replying to a question from his colleague L, hung his dog-eyed, saviour-like, heavily laden face so long and so insistently in front of the TV camera and thus on my TV screen that in the end, my eyes filled with tears of laughter, I was so amused, I couldn't even write down all the peace-and imagination-platitudes that dropped from Mr B's mouth like hundredweights, all rolled up in one. Did Mr B feel lighter afterwards?, I asked myself. Then I cracked open another beer. Earlier, on Zum Blauen Bock, the mod-erator, Mr Heinz Schenk, had spoken with the same bearing as Mr B, saying this, to be exact: I wish you with all my heart in this difficult time a rueful, merry, beau-tiful Christmas. Rueful, with all my heart, I swear those were his exact words, naturally I wrote it down right away. In the background, violins were playing pensive Christmas melodies. Is the mood catching on? Just a little bit, at least? With that, already, there is something stirring. And then Mr B says practically the same thing, and when, in addition, as on this very evening, Mr Kohl twists that melon of his into the closest approximation of a face for his appearance on the daily news, when this maudlin, clearly irrepressible smile won't stop twitching on the chancellor's face while he adds not a single word to what B and L and Schenk have said, then – yes, nothing less than the truth itself explodes into colossal laughter. Now ain't that something! And naturally we have the TV to thank for that, along with the TosserParade trot-ting around doing its endless polonaise. And our jobless compatriots, whom we think of especially at this time of year, can treat themselves to *Zum Blauen Bock* for a second time the next morning. At worst, the violins in the morning play a little less than at night.

But: someone's missing! Who's missing then? Of course, that tosser G, where is Mr G then? Mr G showed up recently in the culture pages of *Die Zeit* in his typical posture, that is, standing up for peace. That alone is enough for Guido Baumann to come right out on Robert Lemke's progamme *What am I* and say: Am I right to suspect you are an artist? The artist is exposed straight-away. This time Mr G has come up with the *growth rate of immortality*, which is rationalized away deviously from the apocalypse proper, and on account of which you can't even tell whether you want to be an artist or just stand up for peace, so that later, when you are even more senile, it will become worth it, in accordance with immortality and *sub specie*, to become an artist again. Yep, with that, chief tosser B must have had to ask himself whether he too had come up with anything as pathetic as the *growth rate of immortality* in recent days, and whether that tosser G might not be frighteningly close on his heels. B has to ask himself that.

Logically Mr G's standing up for piece comes with a blunder. First he lets slip, with inoffensive stupidity, a notorious understatement in his final paragraph: Answers are past due, he, G, can't give answers either, he is clueless, but still, in his cluelessness he knows that we must find and must do, jibber-jabber and whatnot, and then it hits us: – by disarming ourselves to the point of nudity. Mr G! Mr G! No, please, that will not work, leave your pants on, otherwise, I'll punish you, later on I'll turn you into a ComicBook hero and expose you to certain of Ms Dörte's orifices.

And so the TosserParade continues, tosser after tosser, and now they all wave in their endless polonaise through German intellectual life. (This was the first strike. The continuation I will reveal to you in the advanced level course, where I will go to the mat with Poet E.)

HAPPINESS: You destroy me inside you. You make of my beauty a clump of garbage. You twit.
WELL-MEANING ADVICE: Look, there you have it, and I've been preaching it to you for ages. You can have it that good, for sure! You can be happy.
MS HUMPE: We destroy our happiness, piece by piece, we destroy our happiness.
ME: Destroy destroy.
UNDERSTANDING: My god, we understand the young, they don't have it so easy. But does this have to be so exaggerated, so extreme?
ME: Look people, you don't get it. I can't think about happiness yet. I have to work like a damn mule. I've got to figure out whether there even is a me, thank you.
HAPPINESS: Want a smoke? Got a light?

At my PARENTS', there used to be the coolest thing, in the newspapers, I mean, a regular sex education, bound and printed on special paper that you had to cut open before reading. I used to always peek in through the top. The Otto catalogue I just opened to the underwear section.

Later, at the peak of my long-haired ridiculousness, when there was no more smut, only eternal lovelornness and science, I came upon fused pages of this sort again. But that time, in the institutional library at the Sorbonne, the virgin pages were no longer a lure, instead the opposite, the epitome of ScientificHorror. Thick as a cannonball, heavy in my hand, the hundreds of pages of this prosopographic standard work, composed by a professor well-known in the scientific world who taught at this very same Parisian institute, nothing less than his life's work, the *summum* of his career as a researcher, printed and published just ten years before, and not even all sixteen pages of the first folio had been cut. I could hardly fathom it. In ten whole years, one person had wanted to read five pages of text, and then the work with its many hundred pages was slammed shut, done. Oh science!, I thought, you SufferingLittleWorm in the furthest corner of an imposing cathedral, and I dragged myself millimetrically, full of longing, to that corner, no different from today, yearning for nothing but a happy ending.

Nevertheless nevertheless nevertheless, more than anything else, I would now wish uncut pages on myself. Because now something's coming that's totally private, namely my dream of a year with Mr Achternbusch in that always and everywhere going for the extreme period between Christmas and New Years.

IN THE END: All's well that ends well. In the end, I am the last starving Detroit negroe. I stand in the hot lava like none other. I gotta get it down on paper. That is work. My! If the last true idiot hadn't helped me out sooo much. In the greatest darkness, he was my tenuous light at first and then a swift kick in the arse. Dear true idiot, let me take a deep bow before you, throw myself down with you on to the paper. So.

0.

Christmas Eve is the blackest day of the year. Blacker still is the time between Christmas and New Year. The only thing that keeps it at bay it is workworkwork or something even blacker, such as the products of Mr Achternbusch. Best of all naturally is having both at once, the combination almost gives off a faint, faint light.

So yesterday I watched *The Negro Erwin* and *The Idiot*, one after another in the Arena-cinema, which is deadly cool in the scene right now, why I couldn't tell you, though I am up in the scene 24-7. Later I sat down at Klaus's, had a bite to eat, and as always, the TV was on with no sound.

These TV-images stirred up in me the recollection of a recent public debate about television, where all sorts of well-mannered persons took the floor, and a HeadCultureMummy named D gave an address at the so-called podium, presenting his KnownAcrossTheCountry CulturallyConservative AntiTVRubbish, and naturally, in the course of it, he once more made a spectacle of the pathetic state of the old 68ers. Dreadful dreadful dreadful. And if we have Mr D – this is terrible but true – then we also have Mr

306

Achternbusch again.

Because: ever since there's been a Mr Achternbusch, there's been a Mr D to play publicist, reviewer-crony, and companion. What I can't grasp: how does it not embarrass this Achternbusch parasite to foist the eversame ReviewerGarbage on to the ears of the eversame readership? Has that never embarrassed you, Professor Doctor D?

So he writes a prudish casual dry politically-progressive and thus logically reactionary essay about Mr Achternbusch which he dedicates to some lower-case woman, presumably that's how it's done, lower case, among the progressive German literature professoriate.

So how are you supposed to ever clarify anything to a person like that. All you can really do is insult him: You ProfessorBore, you SomniferousSentenceScribbler, you miserable CultureDefender! No one can help a Germanist, and a politically doughty one at that. He must go down into Hades on his own. Got that, Mr D, begone!

1.
Slob
   Anarchist
   Partisan
   Utopian
   Halfwit
   Nutcase
   Beautiful chaos
   Fabulist-impulses.

This list could go on a long time. With an explanation-and-death-blow vocabulary sharpened over the course of thirty years, the professor inveighs repeatedly against Mr Achternbusch. At that a person like me naturally runs off screaming and crying.

2.

This morning the world is bad.

Late last night, Klaus called to see if we should go to Why Not? and I wasn't too zoned out to get the joke and say why not and have him come pick me up. At Why Not? someone smacked me in the head and today I have not only the usual hangover but also a pain over my left eye on the eyebrow. The terrible thing about Why Not? is it stayed open till 5 a.m. So how can you sit there at the desk at nine in the morning? You know: shivering, buckled over like during a storm, and in a garish orange ski anorak, because the room is so cold.

Outside there's slushy snow, and on the back window of an Audi parked in front of the house, a green roll of toilet paper topped with a stocking cap screams at me nonstop. So what do I shout back? I shout: SHIVERS! MERCY! But the time between Christmas and New Year's knows no mercy. I could prove that to all of you, could do it, for example, with photos. And what else is the world up to this morning? Well: cancer, Kuhlenkampf, moonwalk, Hürriyet, and many other things besides.

– Yesilköy ana-baba günü!

– What's that?

– The Turkish citizens shouldn't always stand on the sidelines, either.

– Right, perhaps THE TURKS are the ideal AchternbuschReaders.

– Excuse me, Professor, sir, could you maybe, could you scientifically clarify this question?

Meanwhile, briefly, I plug in for more –

– and there you have it, Ahoy!, we continue, smack in the middle of

3.
AchternbuschMarch.

Here the esteemed professor laments, in footnote 50 about Mr Achternbusch, which quite obviously has to do with much more than just Mr Achternbusch, that the CSU does not praise Mr Achternbusch. As if you could expect anything worthwhile from morons like a Mr Tandler or even a Stoiber, these unregenerate StateIdiots! As if you could expect the minister-president to lay his official fat paw on your shoulder in recognition. You'd be better off poisoning them with cyanide in their beer, like in that film *The Idiot*. A person could automatically no longer be himself if he officially counted for something with *the* government party. Nothing nothing nothing!, they would crush your windpipe!, OUT!, Mr D, understand!, I must shout it, shout it in your ear, because in your idiotic cleverness you understand nothing.

That makes me berserk, but it's also funny that such risible imbecility, such a sorry lowering of the trousers, such a lowering of the casual blue jeans, should befall none other than a valiant leftist, an upstanding grimly determined CultureDefender and SomniferousSentenceScribblingManOfTheLeft, to a Dr D, that is. Listen up, Mr D, for the next edition, pretty please, rewrite this footnote, aim for a little bitty minuscule bit of reason, which you will have to generate in your brain to start.

4.

The serious thing comes in April. Because a D, in his utterly pitiful state, is much worse than pitiful, is actually ZERO, as one can calculate, prove, and verify mathematically. For that you have to bring in a duplicate, the unserious and the serious, you know, put them together, calculate according to the FirstGradeRulesOfAddition, and there you get the result: Zero.

A D naturally takes himself and his work as unseriously as possible. When some editor or another asks for it, he just dishes out another AchternbuschEssayRehash for the nineteenth time. Logically he is ashamed of himself deep down, and ashamed in front of normal people too. He thinks: Some day the jig's gonna be up. Then he's afraid. But really, he has no need for fear and no need to be ashamed, because it is totally normal for a professor to become something by constantly propagating the same old bullshit. This idiocy is known as a *speciality* among the professoriate and its hangers-on, and idiocy is no less proper to these professors than the casual jeans and long hair these forty-year-old pre-senile fossils don to asperse and attack the state while waiting for it to cough up their pensions. And since you're some-thing of an idiot, since you've just been treading water for years, if and to the degree to which and because you do not take yourself seriously, it really doesn't matter: you can just crank out the nineteenth or twenty-fourth Achternbusch article, shuffling this group of words around again and then letting them fall back on to the paper. A person like that's got it good, one who turns ev-erything into flimflam. A person like that has repeated for years on end: I think, and in reality what does he do? Balderdash, poppycock, horseshit.

But now, now comes the good part! Because *how*, how do people like this create their god-forsaken flimflam? Of course, dead seriously, with such seriously clenched teeth that for some time all I've wanted to do is drive a fist square into their faces, so all those clenched teeth fall right out of their mouths – that, or give them one in the gut. And during the beatdown I would like to sing songs of praise for the Kluge-Gernhardt-Achternbusches.

You, D, you! Get it!

5.

At the Stadtmuseum they showed *The Searchers*. And I was raging and I had to take a break and so I went to the cinema. Mr Achternbusch comes in behind me and he had to sit on the floor, too. Logically he couldn't have the least notion of the tenuous light he cast for me in those mad black days between Christmas and New Year's. The film began amid this cluelessness. It has nature in it, men, love, and duty, it's so perversely meaningless but still, it remains duty. So it's a film about life. The loneliest thing in the world is a lonely settler's house in the broad sandy Wild West with a big blue sky above. It provokes such yearning. And there is no way home but off into the Technicolor night.

Afterwards I thought of my hot, ungenerous tirades against this professor and said to myself: With a film like this, every such tirade, every bit of wickedness, is disgracefully disgraced and dies away in me, and the wicked words should also die away on my far too wicked lips. Then a couple of images appear.

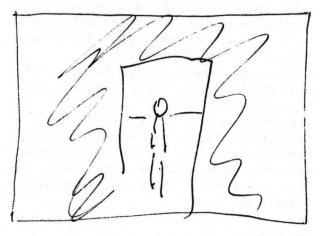

In the final take John Wayne's back says: A man's gotta be alone. I take a deep breath and nod. Ri-ight. There is so much longing.

You have insulted a professor. Go to jail. Go directly to jail. Do not pass go. Do not collect 4000 marks.

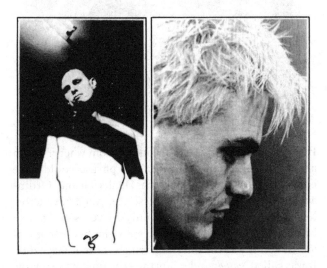

I recognize my wickedness, my guilt. I want to perform active penance.

But then a different strength comes. From where? From above, or else from a phrase. The phrase could have come from Professer Diedrich Diederichson, Ordinarius Emeritus. A clever professor, as you'd have to be, logically, to be an emeritus at only 24 years old, but so he is, they shut his journal down on him because it was too clever. It was the only unboring German magazine. It was called *Sounds* and it was the salvation of Germany. Now we have the 8-year plague of Kohl and nothing but *Titanic*. That fortifying sentence might go something like: On it goes with new cool cult legends and other consolations so strength and dignity may flourish in order – that's right!, Ahoy ahoy! – to lift the world off its hinges.

6.

In this WinterJune I organized a cooking course for all the image- and TV-burners and imagination- and word-PraiseSingers, in brief: for the entire Culture Defender Rabble. We get a large pot, and we put in seven things, precisely these: Achternbusch, TV, Searchers, Sounds, Space, magazine leftovers. We let that stew a bit. Then I stir it energetically and fish out the word space. So: that thing hanging off the fork, what is that?

Space is everything you can use for agitation, enjoyment, LearningSomethingNew, for all stimulation of the senses and the brain. In space terms there's no difference between Matisse, the painter, who makes the humdrum person's turquoise shiver with unease, and the sports spectacle bestowed weekly on the Republic by the ImageFelicity of RummeniggeDribbling and KaltzFlanking. Or take the difference between *Ulysses* and the *Bild-Zeitung*, which, as is well known, are hardly the same thing. What? You don't know Mr Wolfgang Osinski? He told us the story yesterday, the new Dahlke-story, in the coolest TelegraphStyle, the unmistakeable sound of *Das Bild*.

Achternbusch and Diederichsen have something important in common with Osinski and Joyce: they are exquisitely *nibblishly usable* and can be consumed in this way without strain. This is also true of leafing through magazines, whichever magazines are in reach, but even then, you only look at the pictures, that goes for *Wehrtechnik*, for *Stern*, for American *Penthouse* or for the Japanese *Popeye* Ms Rutschky brought me back especially from Japan. Images images images. Accidentally read a sentence and you fall instantaneously into despair. Quickly I stop myself reading, otherwise my brain runs out. Will I have to put myself through this forever?

315

These types, the BrainRunningOutSentenceWriters, who think nothing and write nothing coolly in their magazines, am I really not even allowed to give them a proper dressing-down? If they are editors, they know their readers to a T, of course better than themselves, whom they must not know at all. These are the nobodies who dictate to you what you should write for them. They can kiss my arse. If this is how it is, I'll go back to being a headshrinker.

– Not so loud, kid, not so loud.

Rewind. In order for the nibblish utility to be intelligently useful, every nibble must logically be a pleasure. And pleasure is often what is hyper-newest, freshest, most unstable, furthest from theory. But pleasure is not something you can just pin down: all of a sudden, when you least expect it, an undaunted, vulgar, but anyway clearer anyway more correct outlook-sentence does pleasure good; and it does me good as well. Strange but true. And it can also happen that, sentence by sentence, a correct theory-exertion becomes the true space. There are no rules, just LogicalLogic. So, will every CultureDefender now please cook this, this simple recipe?

And while you practice, I will play you a pretty blues tune – the real, *Negroe blues*. But for that, we must turn to page 3 of the *SZ*, where hunger and poverty in the USA reign.

– That's just awful, at Christmas time to boot,

– True, it always hits the poorest. So what's that on page 3?

– I believe that's a picture of the weight of the world.

– Yeah, from Detroit probably. But why does he look so angry, that Detroit negroe? That is a Detroit negroe, right?

– He doesn't look like a shrewd hungry one, an authentic starving negroe, he doesn't look like one of those.

– No, he probably isn't an authentic starving Detroit negroe. There they have lots of them, and such-and-such a percent are undernourished. But this one isn't undernourished.

– Nah, he's not undernourished, but maybe he's cold. He must be cold, a negroe like that, he must certainly be used to something different, maybe a black Congo.

– Maybe a Congo, or a Togo, or what are the other ones? Anyway, he looks like a sweetheart.

– Yeah, that negroe is a sweetheart, so sorrowful. That thick coat he has on exudes sorrow. It really is beautiful, that something so primal still exists. But when I read that headline, right away it makes me hungry.

– Huh? What's it say?

– Begging for soup and a piece of bread, it says it right there in big letters, and on Christmas, moreover.

– Yeah, we better buy ourselves a cheeseburger and stamp that damn hunger out.

Next blues: Starving Detroit negroes, baseball caps on their heads, poke listlessly at their food in some soup kitchen.

NEGROE 1: The selection here is bullshit!

NEGROE 2: You got that, I'd just as soon eat nothing.

NEGROE 3 (thinking to himself): I'm going up to 34th. But don't tell anyone. They got BAUMKUCHEN over there!

NEGROE 1: A damn scandal, that's what that is!

NEGROE 4: Shut your mouth. What's the pope say?

THE POPE: Jerusalem!, Via Dolorosa – (*thinks to himself*: God All-fucking-mighty! My anus praetor is acting up again something fierce today!) – Via Dolorosa now refurbished.

ME: Everyone's got worries. I've got worries too. For example: Maybe the world sucks.

Third and last blues:

ME, loud, practically urbi et orbi: Hey there, starving Detroit negroes. I'm not the pope, but any chance the Negro Erwin is sitting with you all, it happens I'm looking for him. Hello, helloooo, anyone here speak Bavarian?

ME, softly, to the OTHERS: Maybe he's in the 34th street soup kitchen, because they redid 34th, it's all brand new. They went out of their way to tell us back home. I believe they want to make us jealous of the negroes.

HIM, also softly: That's right. But we've got our Wienerwald in Gauting. So come on! Let's creep on over! It's gloomy here, I don't like that. Best if we go to Rome. I can see it in the pope's face, he looks like he needs our help.

ME: Yeah, let's go. It surprises me though that they already got a soup kitchen on 34th street. I'd also like to be a starving Detroit negroe sometime.

HIM: True. But come on, let's beat it!

ME, loud: See ya, negroes!

Now the pretty music dies away. My!, I say to them, I could play you all sorts of music or paint you pictures about the theme of space while you practice cooking. I'd be happy to do it. But, I'm a poor bastard, I have to write in words, and from my word prison I greet the comrades from *Freiwillige Selbstkontrolle* and the dear SpecialistFuckingPainters up there in Hamburg, far away from here. I salute you! I shout through my prison window and wave longingly.

7.

I have to keep writing words down, but I need to find

318

another tempo. I need to bring this rotten joke to an end.

It's July, and Mr Achternbusch is roaming through nature. I don't like to go out during the day, if I do I get tanned in no time. That's the last thing I need. But I can leave the window open, unlike in the black WinterNow, and the wind blows my thoughts out on to the table. Some of my thoughts are sick thoughts. Does everything, even war, really have to do with me? Could I be turning paranoid? Klaus doesn't understand another word. (*The Film* in early summer). Many of my thoughts are completely normal thoughts. They come along so midsummer fast and fleeting; like (selection) this:

What a Professor D lays out in those loose sentences of his stands at odds with what you comprehend immediately as soon as you see him in the flesh, because D, taken as a whole, is a starchiness, a *StarchSpastic*. A person like that should write StarchSentences and not affectedly loose ones that remain spastic despite everything. Can a person like that really not understand something so simple?

If you wanted to be fair, you'd be better off just packing it in, or else you could lock up his *head*, or *chop it off* and pack it in mothballs. Stuff the hole in the neck with gauze bandages, don't forget that, otherwise the blood will spray everywhere. I saw that more than a few times in my days in the clinic days with the fellow psychiatrists, lots of gauze bandages plugging lots of holes in necks. But that's a whole different story.

Strange: *Out-and-out idiots* are all around me, lambasting me with their stupidity, and still, they haven't been enough. Because all at once I stand up and know who I am and where and what I must say. And I jab. Stab by stab, I jab.

Well, Mr D, for a long time you were doing just

peachy, and then *with one blow* you are an idiot too. But I will not reveal my fencing- and boxing-coaches. Whoever knows them, knows them anyway.

Where? Where does one go here for the latest thing? I don't want to suck any more at worn-out braces holding up ProfessorJeans. And you, take a bath for once!, you.

What do you think, Mr Professor, how long can such vituperation go on? A long, long time, I assure you. We're only now in the midsummer. There is such *heat* inside me, and a white snow falls outside.

And a shrewd *threat* blows through: Mr Professor D, if you direct one more word from this terroristic milieu at Mr Achternbusch, as you did recently again on page 39, the consequences will be bloody indeed. This is the deal: you know those cool-arse helicopters from *Wehrtechnik* with the rotary auto-cannons on the right and left flanks, well, I get hold of one of those, and then, obvs, fly it over the BKA or some other minority group, then I get to spraying, *spray you to death*. And what do I leave on? My sunglasses obviously, I leave those on all casual. So, on into August, keep going with the mess.

8.
Now I no longer know myself. This really must be an illness. It's not normal. I lie in bed all the time, actually it's all I do. August is the most dreadful month of all. If a breakdown comes, logically it's coming in August. The holidays, the summer, which already is no summer, but rather rack and ruin. I suffered a bad attack of gout. I also have a high fever, most likely. Worst of all: the orders they send out over the radio. One time, I heard I should exterminate myself, then I heard I should at last bring order to Lebanon. From across the way, the police station glows. I think ceaselessly of the bomb that's

320

supposed to blow everything sky-high, bring every single thing to an end. I must have fallen asleep. I am a worm. When will I be stepped on? By whom? Was I not unfortunate in love, too? A person like me takes all the misfortune in the world upon himself. Perhaps now, I can only think things that are inwardly destroyed and that destroy me. The time, the year, stands forever still. I wish I were a greyhound. (*The Film* in August).

While I lie there so miserably, Herr Achternbusch is sitting pretty. In a matter of days, he cranks out a clever good book, *Revolts*, for example. If someone picks up a copy, Mr Achternbusch gets a percentage, almost enough for half a pack of smokes. Good old Unseld always skims off the top, but probably not with *Revolts*, probably least of all with whatever there is to be skimmed off the top of New German Mysteries, probably he sticks to the cheap popular- and special-editions and all the classics from near and far. Naturally none of that bothers me one bit, as long as I get to do what I want. I can soap myself up, for example, and then skim that off, as long as the soap bubbles up right. Anyway the cash doesn't matter. I just need it to be *there*, thanks. So you can pick up *Revolts*, for just a few marks, *Revolts* as is well known, will never do you wrong, and then Mr Achternbusch can buy himself another cigarette.

Question: Does he need another two marks? Does he even smoke, this Achternbusch?

District Attorney: Gentlemen of the court, I object to this line of questioning.

Judge: The state's objection is sustained, the question is inadmissible. Court adjourned.

See see see!, what a dumb-arse question. The private life of a person like Mr Achternbusch is absolutely none of your business. I'm not telling you either whether

I smoke or have a wank or pray or when or howoften or howmuch. But respect for others is something the AverageMutt and progressive BrotherhoodIdiot no longer has any notion of. No, the preservation of a *seemly distance* is an extinct virtue that me and my kind have resurrected. And here comes a fab strike. I use it to take out countless birds with one stone. THWACK. From among the countless birds, allow me to name three:

1. I economize on many many pages.
2. The ranger doesn't nab me again.
3. You find out for once how a book like this comes to be.
4. I get to say the lovely title, at least.

OK, four birds, doesn't matter, you should think up the rest on your own. In the interim, I strike through the gripping serial novel now beginning, illustrated with exclusive photos and other images, with the highly auspicious title: *The Pole at Sea, the Poet in his Homeland, and the Pope in the Pfattican.* And now it opens, with a twist of fate, naturally: strike-through.

9.

Had I not deprived you of the first chapter beforehand, you would logically be pleased to find out how this SecretAgentSexAndLoveNovel continues, above all you would be interested in when the Pope comes in and how he's wrapped up in everything, but alas, even a never-to-be-published serial novel appears in instalments, and I shall not offend against such regulations. I'm not some anarchist, like this GermanistComedian, what did I call him again? Oh yeah, Mr D, it's been too long since I railed against him, not once in all of August, but I'm doing it now.

Because now is September, so the annual Culture

Season is back, and here I am again clinging to life: in August you get the struck-through rubbish, in September comes culture. Logically that means crossing paths with culture, which knocks me back several years into the theatre. Before, in those days when I was still as pathetic as Mr D is today – and anyone who can read must know by now I have to keep hammering at Mr D because I must hammer at myself for how pathetic I once was, hence an expiation appears below – back then, I used to go constantly to the theatre, and constantly means: at minimum, every other day, if not every every day. Yeah, that's how it was. Because whatever I like, I do like a madman, and I can think of nothing, absolutely nothing else. And the theatre was such InsanityFun, logically Image- and SpectatingFun, and there burned in me constantly like nothing else the urge to go to the theater as a spectator and a connoisseur. Admittedly I also entered the theatre as a fugitive, though today the fugitive goes somewhere else, not to the theatre. Never! (NB: that was a LyingLie.) Why should I let something of mine be spoiled by an ArtPerson, which a TheatreDirector inevitably is. Achternbusch's *Frog*, for example, I could read alone on the *chaise longue* at home, if I had one, instead I read at the desk, but alone, nonetheless. And I don't have to sit in an uncomfortable theatre chair and stare at some stupid DirectorialArt.

So what, Mr Professor, are we to take from that? That whenever a person strives to make art, boredom and rubbish inevitably ensue. Same as with a signing machine or a fucking machine: you throw your bribe or your coin in the top and satisfaction comes out the bottom, either as a signature or white sap, totally automatic, and logically it's no less automatic with art and BoredomRubbish, which is so noxious it makes my foreskin burn. What art does to a woman, I'm not so sure. Maybe in her case a certain hole grows wider and wider, but really, I couldn't say. And here we go with this, when I wanted to stay all serious in serious CultureSeptember.

Culture is my life. That's why I scream like this. Culture in the narrow sense, with theatre as the PathosHit and literature the BoredomHit, that still interests me as well, though I will only touch it with my very pointy cossetted fingers with their white-glove elegance. That's the only way I do it. Culture in the broader sense, though, the New Fun Painting, non-French cinema (because in most cases French cinema is more exasperating than theatre. – But the Hatter's Ghost, the Hatter's Ghost! – That's a good one, no need to be infallible, I can assert something different tomorrow), TV, logically, every single day, and logically, pop music even more – in the whole of culture, in the broadest sense, I can immerse myself fearlessly, without a net, and often it gives me such a fucking thrill that I thank the Lord God for inventing it.

What would I be without culture?, exclamation point. Maybe a blue Nivea Body Milk squeeze bottle. With HERTIE and DM 3.28 over the top of it. But I'm not, so that means there is culture. Thankya thankyaverymuch.

And so, as we banter here, the days are turning shorter. Already the year is tipping into autumn, which brings golden October, Lexicon of Love, melancholy, merriment, and a pleasant aroma. At night we stand in these brightly lit spaces where the pretty people enjoy themselves, and hey! Take a look! All the nice little boys and girls come past and give you such strange looks. Yeah! The night is rocking there, come on! We want fun, we want to go completely wild!

10.

Now, you think, is where the fun part comes in. But thinking doesn't often do much good. Again, you've misunderstood me. The fun you gotta bring yourself, live. I can't help you with it, despite all these words and countless struck-through images. In October, with Mr Achternbusch, ideally, I await the first snow. The nekkid men at my place running across the TV screen can't bother me, because they're mute, and on the record player, Mr Oakey's crooning, and anyway, they're already gone now. Now they look like workers and they're running through a forest. You see a mountain range, too. There's snow over the peaks.

11.

But that's just a TV snow, practically a lie, the kind that, per valiant Professor D, kills the so-called imagination. I don't know though, Mr D, whether you consider what I write to be imagination, so-called, or dead, or terroristic matter. But I'd like, at the risk of presumptuousness, to be allowed to ask, when's the last time you glided across a piece of paper with the kind of elegance I have shown here. Now we are standing in a discotheque and now we are back on the topic of snow, because I let it fall from the TV screen into my typewriter. The hardest thing is so simple. No need to stare all dumbfounded. You'd be better off reading something clever instead of constantly writing down the same stupid bullshit. And just as I prepare you for Chinese Foot Torture – idiots I torment with particular relish, I like that even better than MinorityDefamation, which I already take such pleasure in – right in the midst of this preparatory phrase, what rescues you is the very thing you inveigh against so tediously, television and nothing else.

I surrendered to television because a naked woman's torso came on, very beautifully she thrust her nude breasts into my solitude, and moreover, she wanted to tell me something. But I had turned down the volume, and just then, a dull sagging dogface muzzled up to me from the floor and reminded me straightaway of a well-known tosser. Then there piped up flute music, and then, now comes the worst part, I saw a girl at a window blowing a melody into a flute. On TV 0.7 seconds passed between the horny woman and the little FluteGirl, in literature that lasts half a page, but this is a crossroads and not a redemption of the kind D is always harping on about. On TV there is a space and in literature it is a mere affirmation, that right away, I was hot for sex with children, a prepubescent child, logically, on TV there's a cartoon that gets the kid all hot and bothered. Hey!, D!, look sharp, here's another danger of television: ChildSex. Rail against it in public, for all I care, maybe you can even get some women to help you, one of those CultureDefenderCunts that come in droves.

You want to know the difference: When you think of TV, you think about the defence of culture, and when I think about TV, I think about sex. I'm a normal person, you're a stupid one. And logically, you are actually the illiterate one. Proof: you need only two pages in your AchternbuschTextlet, dedicated to this lowercase chick, before you wind up alongside the illiterate and his kind, with the *terminological difficulteez*. Those are the professor's porno. They get him nice and in the mood. Then, he spends the rest of the time relativizing himself. A guy like that never manages to blow a load.

Thanks be to God I only know this ludicrous professor from seeing him, and as a SomnolentSentenceScribbler and not a private person. That would really be the end.

Because then I could no longer tell the awful truth about that rubbish of his. Because probably he is, like the majority of these stiffies, a proper nice chap. That reminds me of another StarchyCritic, a bearded one, naturally, eternally jotting down one after another of his likewise bearded, spastically loose sentences. Let's call him Bone Better-BetterNot. Just now I am the good Lord God, that's why I get to christen you with this lovely double-name. To hear a Bone like this blather on about Rohner-Radegast is the same as wanting to be a dog. But even if I were a dog, this wretched Bone would probably be too bland for me.

– When do we get back to something actually clever?
– Now, one beer coming right up.

Truth is, I was just at Wienerwald and bought six beers so I could make it through the rest. The terrible thing is that at Wienerwald, at the one by me anyway, they've only got Hacker, no Augustiner. That, and not television, is what is truly terrible, Mr D. Terrible is a whole different thing from what you think. For example, at Wienerwald they were blasting a sappy rendition of *Only You*, which I would still have been happy to sit down and listen to, because it could have reminded me of the Platters, whose version of *Only You* I danced along to with Klaus soo much, on Christmas Eve, apparently, and with such a longing in my heart. And then? I won't tell you. I could just as well say lemonade or woman or hole, but I'm no exhibitionist. I much prefer being the dear Lord God, who gives out names and metes out just punishments, like the Chinese Foot Torture I threatened you with earlier, my sinful son D, before I switched – hey, you already read that! You pig! – before I switched with utmost care from the TV screen to the very steamy subject of sex, and then brachiated at ease from a NewStarchyCritic like this BoneZero to good beer to the thing that is naturally all really about, to love. From love to beloved Lord it wasn't too far.

– D! Germanist!, stand up, you hippie! How many letters was that from love to your beloved Lord?

– Four, I think, Lord God. But I have to question –.

– Muzzle it, pal! Cut off your hair and beard, put on something decent, and stay on the sidelines a while, maybe have a good think while you're at it!, understood!

– Yes, Lord God, but it hurts so much.

– Muzzle it!, I said, the Chinese Foot Torture hurts worse. And if you don't shut your trap, I'll show you images that will kill your so-called imagination even deader, dead as a motherfucking doornail.

– No!, dear Lord, please please no.

But then the first snow was there, though it didn't snow in November. It was the kind of snow Mr Achternbusch writes about. It was the end, and it looked so beautiful. Dear Nile! Thank you so. You flow true, what happiness I feel. Oh oh. At that I start to sing. I sing the song of praise to bars. I'm never go into any bars. That way I can make a stop at every other Achternbusch sentence. That's where I drink my beer. That's where I find consolation and strength. D-sentences, ZeroSentences, in other words, are shut down for good. Or else they are thrown so wide open that there is nothing inside. I never will stop off at a ZeroSentence, I couldn't if I wanted to. I'd rather be pummelled and run away pummelled. Quite another thing is an Achternbusch or DiederichsenSentence, which I can greet with open arms, say a friendly Hello to, and stop off at right then, when my head is clouded, like a man with a parched throat. Every time I leave, I am fortified. Afterward, I even trust myself to utter a sentence. Suddenly I know

German. That emboldens me.

Yes, my dears, with the slogan PASSION! NEW AND STRANGE written in the biggest letters possible, and the tiny addition *I'll go senile on my own and soon enough*, with these words I spur myself on and once more strike through my illustrated serial novel about SecretAgentWomen, other broads, and the hard, hard duties of men. Weak weak weak, get rid of all that, or no, only almost all of it.

19. THE POLE: Touch yerself! Touch yeeerself!

THE POPE: Heeheehee, do it again, Slurp! Heeheehee, faster!, Hee! While the dream dies away...

20. Yeahyeah, the POLE thinks wistfully, now here lies the Dörteflesh, whoa, that's so real. But the memory, my God!, how lovely. What bliss, back then in the Pfattikan, making fuckyfucky like that. But when the bliss gets most blissful, it soon flies away. Ay! That hurts. And now there hangs here – what can that be then? – something brown and rumpled between Ms Dörte's legs. Yeahyeahyeah.

In the meanwhile, though, in the faraway distance, the poet sits bored and tired...

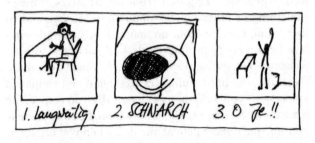

1. langweilig! 2. SCHNARCH 3. O je!!

21. Bored and tired Mr G sits at his desk and observes the Pole.

1. He thinks: What smut, I can think that kind of thing up myself, I've already thought such things before, but I exalted them immediately into art and inscribed them into my bricks. But tomorrow I will stand back up for peace, or I'll scratch something FutureDepressive, perhaps my depressive bard. And all in vain, no more growth rate of immortality! That is the most rotten thing. Then I get so tired.

2. Then Mr G fell asleep at his desk.

3. Suddenly he gets up. He shouts: What! Did I miss the best part? Or...! He stands there and watches how the Pole...

To be continued.

12.

Dumb-arse, now I had to lie again. But still, as far my serial novel, almost totally crossed out and yet not in the least sense at an end, I can't just hang up a notice reading *To be continued* because I have to rush on into December and in reality there is no continuation. Even if, after a few days in my room, enough material for several volumes has flowed forth after a teensy weensy – but only teensy weensy – eruption from my archives. There's something or other you're supposed to respect, and so there is no continuation, no matter how much glowing lava lies on my floor and my desk. Sometimes nothing comes to me but outright lies, and sometimes, more forcefully, the hard truth. Respect, plain and simple. If you respect yourself, then automatically you respect the reader, too. So there is no continuation, because there is nothing that doesn't get flat and dull when you roll it out for too long. And if I bored myself and others rolling out the mess of what had once been a good idea, I ought to be ashamed of myself. But if I gave a shit about this

BeingAshamedOf Myself, I could just as well exercise my learned profession as doctor to the insane. I wouldn't have any money or StarchyCritic worries, but the BrainWorries I wouldn't wish on my worst enemy. The professors you have to struggle against are far stupider even than a Germanist. And worst of all: you must beat everything out of yourself, up to and including your last bit of self-respect, until you no longer know who you are. Even now!, if I think about it, the most vicious fury weighs on me, and wet tears well up inside.

The *End* before my eyes, longing and fear. The glowing lava will turn cold. I will no longer remember how I yearned to reach into it, pull something out, and throw it on to the paper. When I file it away in my archives, it will be frozen matter, nothing more. Without the light of lava, I will sit there and it will be dark and I will be such a toad that even the lowest zero will be a person next to me. That is the normal state of affairs. That will leave me eternally freezing, like a Detroit negroe. No lamentation will help, I will be forced to croak around, it will be back to the old, miserable, unsoundest path of all, and I'll have no choice but to creep forward, blind and millimetrically, ToadStepping, looking for something to hold. There is great fear in me, but longing, too, fear and longing for the *End*.

And you're wrong, dear Professor, the end is not yet there if you still believe you were a person all along and could think and needn't worry with writing amid this darkness and could keep walking in place and scribbling everything down, never changing, just scribbling forever. You may not, idiot. And if you were to try, I'd light up those Cubic Thunder firecrackers I picked up for New Year's Eve and stuff them right in your oral cavity, the fount of those words you let glide on to the paper without cease. That would make a right pretty explosion. In your head, logically, more than anywhere. Then it'd be curtains for your stupid exalted so-called imagination. Maybe that would be worth it. Or would you prefer a trip to a Chinese labor camp? Go! Get gone! Out with you!

Already, the sun's coming up. It astounds me. So it's time. I take out a Hacker, the last Hacker stays in the fridge. Tomorrow I'll buy myself a case of Augustiner. Although actually the Hacker works, too, as I notice now while drinking it down. Tomorrow it will all be different. So I have to look, while I am still alone. No one can help me anymore. A good week ago it was Christmas. For two days I was unconscious, swimming in beer. That was nice. This year was my finest party of all, I believe. This year, the one where I felt the greatest fear, particularly for that black, black time to come. Then Mr Achterbusch plunged me deeper and deeper into this hot glowing lava. What work it was. I didn't give a damn about the devastation around me. I didn't even have food left to eat, and my body stunk. For me that was not normal. I owe it to Mr Achternbusch. For me he was first a tenuous light, then a swift kick in the arse, and that pushed me tripping and tumbling through a dream year and out into the open, yes!, into the open!

That means now: I can live. I have a right. My heart leaps, it dances.

– Somehow I already knew all that.

– Me too, though I'm the one who wrote it.

And so it shall be, dear God said, and cracked open the last Hacker. He took a swig and said: How many times must I explain this to you idiots again! With all your culture, I think you've got fir twigs up there where I have a brain. Everywhere, yes everywhere, I have always torn out and mashed together and devoured the best and nothing but the best, WhatWorksForMe, logically, and nothing more than that. Understand! I don't have to be original. I'm not a weakling. I'm sooo strong. What I need, I take. Then the dear Lord God gulped the next swig of Hacker down into his big beerbelly and lay on his bed.

– Mommy, now comes the story with the whore, where the Lord God woke up said to her God Alfucking-Mighty! That was a hell of a rest.

– No, kids, I have to go to bed now. Now it's finally over.

– Bah! Meanie! We don't want to go to bed yet.

As I said that, my dick was itching. Maybe that's a sign. Tomorrow it will all be totally different. After getting up, I will write down a sentence immediately. I know that already. I am very anxious for it: begin again, now, at the end.

XXXXXXXXX CLOSE HERE XXXXXXXXX

If he woke in the EARLY MORNING, after far too little sleep, as happened often in recent days, if he lay there, dull and quiet, if the chattering of voices kept rising menacingly in his mind, as if they'd never stopped, at that time of year, at the beginning of March, the prodigiously early arrival of morning was a consolation and a relief. He watched how the morning light grew. It should be spring soon, he thought to himself. The relentlessness of year and day was grandiose, and their benevolent power was decisive for him. Time and again everything was new, everything possible for him, everything promised. Yes, this is the beginning. I am not lost. I can win. Whatever I do – onward and upward! – will be good. And the days became longer.

A tranquil QUIET VOICE spoke in him, the voice of the storyteller, clearly audible, and said: Oh, how I would like to be just the lofty, serene storyteller and not the insane hero too.

EXHAUSTION!, yes, the hero is so exhausted, he can't keep it going anymore. How he would like to go home now, again, after all these years. But what does it mean to go back home again? You find it, the hiding place under your childhood home is still there. The Colt is there, the ComicBook, and the old tin can with the two coins inside. You turn over on your belly, you look a long time, propped up on your elbows. Is this what coming home is? The longer you look, the further away the things of childhood seem to lie. There is no going home again. No, the hero must go on, hardly has he rested than the hero must go on, onward, ever onward. And the road ran on and on. And the hero takes up the fight again. Fear and triumph and fear again and the unquenchable longing for warmth, he knows all that, but still, he has to fight on and knows that nothing's good for anything. There is only the end. There's no getting around it, it's always just as risible meaningless and miserable. Thus ends Robert Mitchum in The Lusty Men and later Nick Ray himself in Lightning over Water.

Soon it will be EVENING. And the shadows grow. I may call them my friends. They say, come my boy, off, we must travel on. But the stone at my feet demands I stay. All that is long gone, very long gone. If I remember right, I picked up the stone, stuck it in the pocket of my jeans, and followed my friends into the night.

Lesson Number Two: LONGING. No need to repeat the first lesson, all the punk stuff, the stolen leather jackets, the untold stories about hardness, terror, Freizeit 81, smut and ruin. Anyway there's a sudden cheer, a notable levity, the longing for large feelings, and silk shawls and roomy pullovers. What happened there? Everyone talked everywhere about punk, but through a secret substantiation, its blood had in the meantime long become the wine of elegance. When? How? No idea. I only know, as with every revolt, it must all have happened very fast.

Coloured neon lights glowed bright, Black Out was there for the whole of the fleeting autumn, they played melodious softly saccharine synth, and I stood there, again almost every evening, my lower eyelids a muted red, drank beer, and waited full of longing. The last teenager could see my longing. When he came over, I sensed the dread in my eyes. What is this? I never felt a longing like that before. The last teenager knew well what was going on inside me and toyed with my bewilderment, with a half-glance or a few words made me a fool of me. With sorrow, I pulled on the SteelGlimmering knight's armour of prudence. And once more, I was untouchable. Later, maybe, love will come. Does anyone know what that is? I don't. But maybe that's what it's all about, that and nothing else.

Again I've got FRENZY for everything to come crashing down. Is that what knocked me down, me and my bicycle just now? Or what? The ground is right by my face. Go away!, you black asphalt floor. Why is my hand so damp? I'm tired. A strange flowing red, so what. Must be blood, the thing that's dripping from me, but that can't be blood. Nothing hurts, nothing feels. Bed would be better, but again, so what.

MY BIKE gets around. Last week this late-to-the-game punk slashed my back tyre because earlier I wouldn't let him have a sip of my beer. They can kiss my arse, all these scroungers. I'm not their social worker – or some well-heeled moron. Day before yesterday, I'd just had my bike fixed, this late-to-the-game punk tried to scrounge off me again. I punched him in the face without further ado and then gave him a knee in the pills. Pow, that was it for MrHardcoreToughGuy, there he goes howling and blubbering. My white silk shawl was bloody and filthy from rolling on the ground. What the fuck did I care. To celebrate my triumph, the next day I brought myself a big white studded leather band for my left wrist; looks supercool.

Ayayay, a guy shouted AYAYAY FOR TWO MINUTES into the microphone, then blew the sax like a total dilettante, then shouted ayayay again, and then again blowblow for two minutes straight. That was the summer when all of the sudden we were crazy to death about the saxophone. I laughed myself silly over Lorenz Lorenz's TwoMinuteAy, just as, a year before, the year when we made all those fanzines, I had laughed at his *Loneliness of the Runner Amok*, the most inept pimple-faced fanzine in Munich. Good Christ!, I envied him for his impudence back then. He still makes the best music here today because his stage-coolness is diametrically opposed to his ability to play an instrument. *I was the first James Dean in our apartment block*, he bellowed defiantly, and the horde of nitwit PogoPunks in their stamp-stamp-stupidity sprayed him with beer and almost pulled him down off the stage. I can play along with the stupidity, but to the extent that a punk is indistinguishable from a certain German professor very frequently encountered here, this eternal imbecilic StompingInPlace turns everyone to an ultra-dull hippy. PunkHippies and ProfessorHippies stomp in place side by side, it just happens that each knows nothing of the other.

At the same time, any normal person can tell everything is changing constantly. My envy of Mr Lorenz is practically gone, though I would still love to be a rock star, or at the very least a painter. But only because, if I were one, I would no longer want to be one. Then I would think to myself: Well shit, now I'm a rockstar, any dickhead can be a rockstar, I ought to be a telephone technician or at least a sausage vendor instead. And so it goes. Now the happy ending is close. And Lorenz Lorenz's bandmate Floli already became a twenty-something long ago.

Even BIO BIOLEK was in New York. He brought

back these annoying step-grandpas in jackets with fat stripes, a sex-scandal grandma straight out of the Bild-Zeitung by the name of Marisa Mell, that rock-and-roll fossil Santana, and who knows what all else, anyway just grandmas and grandpas. Still, Mr Biolek is an interesting case, he stands irritatingly somewhere between Wendehals and Simmel, see above. Unfortunately there is no Kröher anymore to talk with about how, with a Biolek on our side, we could use our beloved television to take control of the world. All that is far harder than what the CleverDumbarses on the one hand, and the professional TV-nitwits on the other, commonly imagine.

The last time we were together at the Größenwahn was at the Andreas Dorau concert. Man, hell of a time. The kid had just the right mix: he's scuffed up just right, he's got this stage power he earned with his maladroit weirdness, he's trying to have his own private fun but still entertain people like crazy, and of course, he's set on reaching the top. Pow.

For me all this is totally new. To tell the truth, I have no CoolCultureHeritage, no radio, no Mickey Mouse, no nothing in my childhood, my parents put the kibosh on anything related to culture. But I'm at least half-Viennese and I know no fear, logically that saves me. So here again, there is nothing to lament. When it comes late, the space is that much more gigantic.

The hero is the CONSTANTLY MOVED PERSON. Logically his place is film. The clever film is privileged. It can tell the story of the hero. It starts up, lasts an hour and a half, and snap, it stops. No artboredom, just images images, light, yeah!, the whole of life.

IN THE CINEMA, last time.

You can feel the end coming. A few minutes ago, you looked involuntarily at the clock. Then you said: actually it's not boring to me, this film. Then you sensed the knob on your right ischius. It didn't hurt, but you sensed it was there, without knowing what it was. You looked for a new position. You jerked back and forth, then adopted a very stable but only briefly comfortable posture: chin on both fists and both elbows on splayed knees, legs firm, feet fast on the floor. In this way, between the pairs of shoulders of the people seated before you, apprehended less by your eyes than by your nose, you took the glowing screen into your mind and grounded it directly over four large bones.

Is this really going to end in a massacre?, you ask yourself now, unsettled. You *just* had to identify with the hero, even though he was extremely odd. You don't want to see this blood you see now. Is it spraying out of the hero? What is all this red blood spraying out of? Look sharp, the dreadful image is torn from your eyes, and the black blackness strikes you like a blinding light.

You hear my voice: Finally this goddamn year is over. Everything is open. But then comes the latest: they want to pin something on me at the clinic. All I said was: – Vaginitis, I think that's a nice word, asked: – Might there not be a fissure in the world? Now they're saying I'm sick. I just need a rest. There are times when I throw myself to the floor in my room and lie there like a corpse.

As you've heard me talking, you've seen the black turn to grey. At the end of a deliberate silence you hear that sonorously suggestive voice, the one you trust again immediately, correct, the voice of the storyteller, speaking calmly into the greyness: Maybe everything will be fine. Maybe we just needed to be able to sit down again, to truly relax somewhere, to find calm.

Now the whiteness. At length you see an endless white plain, broad, with a white snow gliding over it discreetly, so near so far so eternal. You look into the light. You hear the music of unquenchable longing.

Logically all I wanted in the cinema was to GET OUT after this final image, I would have been happy to take it with me and keep it for myself, for my life driven through the evening streets. But you stand wedged in among cretins. Not even GoingAlone to the cinema does any good, because once you're out, the whole pack uses its prattle to hack away at your brain, which must be exposed and vulnerable, and everything inside me burns and screams, because the pain runs so deep.

– Was that a crime flick or what?

– What was it supposed to be, then?

– If you ask me, that movie was weird.

Maybe someone else, someone I just didn't happen to hear, said what was obvious anyway: it was a weird-ass crime flick, because of the drugs and the real and imagined chase, and logically it was a film about music and friendship, too, about people like us and the space we have. Sure, and maybe another one said: And the hero reminded me of the *Hatter's Ghost*, with those perverse movements coming out of nowhere, or the voice rising up pointlessly for half a sentence. At times, it made me think of, eh, *Eraserhead*. You know that one? That is a real nasty film about craziness, not just some starchy b.s. like that dumb fuck Schröter makes, what did he call that horseshit of his again? And then the other replies: *Day of the Idiots* is what you're thinking of. That was the bottom of the fucking barrel. Utter mendacity, I wanted to start howling in the middle of the film because it really was just totally dishonest, how he bellows at the top of his voice, just bellows his stupidest lies, when what's needed is the softest and most tentative language.

Now I have got lucky and on my way out, I've fallen in with the true cinemagoers. Those exist, too, logically. The world isn't only filled with dumbarses.

I CAN BOX, just as I'm doing here, and as everyone now knows, I use every means at my disposal: clean brutal direct jabs to the middle of the face, punches below the belt, kicks in the balls, no trick is too rotten for me if it deals the opponent a clever blow. I need boxing for self-defence. I usually don't even fight. I do have to wrestle sometimes.

I announced the WRESTLING COURSE for advanced levels, now it's actually happening. I have selected, as my opponent for this demonstration bout, E, the poet, because he hasn't lost that beautiful *half-courage of puberty*. But now, it's put up or shut up, and his whole courage is on the line.

1. Repeat: nothing produces such intellectual slurry as *values* and *doctrine* (VD). This is a kind of thinking that dispenses with the mind before the eyes have even opened and started to look around. This thinking runs through the world like a blind person, seeing nothing. No: values and doctrine must think of responsibility instead. Hence no truth concerning the world ever pierces it, nor even a bit of curiosity. No, this thinking produces automatically – just as automatically as (whoever was there for the AchternbuschYear knows this automatism already) signature- and fucking-machines – the very same thing, over and over again: valor, indignation, the inanest engaged righteousness

341

and the AbsolutelyFlattestSteamrolled piffle. And in my case, as a sufferer, VD provokes a raging headache against which aspirin can do nothing, nothing works but SelfDecapitation or screaming GROWL GROWL repeatedly. (Quickly now, the homework for the English learners among us: For what would the abbreviation VD be used in the English language? Translate and explain cogently its relationship to the DumdumThinking here disparaged.) Every NewspaperReader is well-acquainted with the slurry this thinking produces, from terrorism-fever to peace-fever, and its famed collateral garbage: environmental pollution, paved-over cities, dying forests, transparent numbered people, starving Detroit negroes, and who knows what else, right, what have *You* for example thought – that's right, you! – about this responsibility slurry lately? I don't know, no idea, you're the one who ought to know.

Good good good. Mr E, who would be better off using his inborn cleverness for thinking instead of as a responsibility-crutch, already understood all that 30 years ago. And it worked out fine at the time, because irresponsibility is the beautiful wild virtue of puberty. In precisely that stage of the late 50's and early 60's, our dear republic found itself defrauded of its beautiful savagery by totally senile diligent democrats and former Nazis now reconciled to the state.

All these Adenauers passed out dextrous handjobs to Mr E and others from every different direction. Must have been cool. Unfortunately I wasn't around yet. But I can read about it, at least. And I recommend doing so highly. Instead of some book railing against the A-bomb or sulphur, the VD-afflicted should pick up one, two, or three early books by Mr E, read them and learn them by heart. Now then: five minutes to think up something cleverly irresponsible. In poor stupid Germany, that would already be a medium-sized revolution. But but, my friend!, don't count your chickens before they're hatched. The story has progressed, and so the sad part has to come now. All right, once again, to the cinema.

2. You sit with me in the little Werkstattkino and black negroes are talking down at us with glowing eyes from the screen. The film is called *The Murder of Fred Hampton* and is a documentary about the Black Panther Party from the year 1970.

– Say, can you see anything?

– Nah, 'cause the black negroes are so black and the film is so black, too. It's shit.

– True, but who cares. We'll listen to it.

– Fine, but it really hurts me to listen.

– Me too, logically, but that's the good thing about it.

Yes, that was the good thing about this film: it jabbed at a sore spot in my heart, how simple and graspable the revolution seemed then, at the same time how laughably naïve all the ideas about bringing it about were. Their arguments were so inept, their strength so vehement. All our sorrow will turn into action. Back then, the film shows it, this wasn't just some gallant phrase, it was one that burned with pain and rage. After the film, I talked to you in the Größenwahn about my own *Soul On Ice*, which burned for the Black Panthers back then as much as Eldridge Cleaver's had. Naïve as it was, it even bought into Mr E's beautiful impudent wild words, without really understanding them. My those were lovely times!, I tell you. I like that, thinking back on them. Yeahyeah.

3. I've got it good: unlike a lot of the oldsters from '68, who had a dustup with Mr E on account of RevolutionMeddling or what have you, I can only be thankful to him. For he taught me the courage of

irresponsibility. And today, in his mid-fifties, with that puberty he's chronicled into a life-principle, he guides me to the next, no less important step: you also need the second half of courage, and that means the *courage of your own history.*

Yeah, he's a gambler, Mr E said once into a tape recorder, but he only played games of risk, everything else is boring. – Bravo!, I shout, down with the zillion culture-bores!, up with the gamblers, above all with the high-risk ones! But: I don't have any use for whoever won't blow up the bank. All the flip-floppers, the chicken hearts, step aside, if you please. Excuse me, Mr E!, please be so kind and step to the side a bit, for me you are half-a-courage too uncourageous.

I'm looking for risk-takers, gamblers who don't just play, but also play to win, whose greed inspires them with the mission to tear the world off its hinges. And so? Playing with such passion, they inevitably come up short. Win or lose, they want to learn for next time. Seldom does WantingToLearn prove useful, but it gives the game the weight of intelligence. Everything else is abstract tosh or mundane like a red brassier.

So logically, Mr E logs every lost game as a win for the simple reason that he bothered to play, like recently, with the inauguration of his journal. He never learns anything new. His whole life, he's only ever been impetuous, out front, and with his brilliant formulations, he's never had to pay for being right. He can write well, but really, so can every other tosser.

In all seriousness, the young person has to say to the old: Mr E, You have only *one* life as a gambler. You're well into your sixth decade and, to judge from your boyish smile, which is praised the world over, you can't keep starting again at zero. It surprises you that no one grapples properly with your newest thought-impulses. Look, I can lay it out for you, and you should try and get it into your utterly clever, hopefully not completely critically intractable head: these provocations of yours nowadays don't so much provoke give people the feeling they're being fucked with. These days, even the lowliest country doctor knows you'll be wagging your hand jovially tomorrow: Tsk tsk, kiddies – the country doctor already hears you calling from the ultra-newest corner of tomorrow – that's truly moving, how you've got all worked up over little old me, that is just dear. – And these days, this senile attitude bores even the lowliest country doctor.

You still don't get it? You no speak German? Should I explain it all to you in Swedish? Because I will learn Swedish right away, that's how important it is to me. So, in Swedish this time: for once, put your money on winning and not just on playing. After thirty years of being in the right, for once be something more than just the most brilliant brilliant chap in Germany. Consider the victories and failures of your story, instead of begging for a private TV channel, like you did recently, with that slender nose of yours jutting out. I too, dear Mr E, am for private TV and hey, you haven't stroked out yet, I'd even support you being irresponsibly responsible for such a channel. I could put in a good word for you. But please! Straighten yourself out, don't just put in more appearances as the eternally ageless aging adolescent, for once, at long last, show up with the *whole of your courage*.

Bam, done, pinned. God Almighty, that was some wrestling match, and with this guy, no less. But I don't need some opponent from another galaxy to fight against; nor am I content to sweat it out with some zero, no, logically, I have to start by dethroning my gods.

345

In this very moment: the PANICKED CERTAINTY, this can't go well, this will come to a horrible end. Must it be so? It doesn't have to be that way, I want to think. But my head is torn away. I feel a dreadful undertow. And I turn against myself in a rampage.

Raspe clearly sensed that CYCLOTHYMIA, raised in this way to a vital principle, would necessarily lead to ever more desolate excesses of exaggeration and truth and so, progressively, to ever greater extremes of despondency, loss of self, and life-exhaustion; hence, like a one-way street, to the destruction of the world and self and finally to catastrophe; or perhaps he just felt pushed and shoved and asked himself: Why is this happening to me? Why do I have to stagger like this? My head keeps beating against a wall. It hurts so much. Pain, please stop.

At times, Raspe suddenly, and without further ado, would look away from the sun for a moment, would catch sight of the clinic, and would immediately want to poke out his eyes with two knitting needles, to poke even further into the thalmic regions, poke away all feeling and then reach the telencephalon and poke his memories to death, till he reached the very back, the medulla, and the last fucking breath ceased.

Then it was moist inside his eyelids. And perhaps Raspe thought to himself: I cannot see those crippling images again. That must be when the breakdown started, no? Over and over, my old patients shuffle in slow-motion through the tender mass of my brain, in a medicated trance. What painful pressure in my head! From just *one* year of my life, grown ancient in that single year. Then the fury burns in me, the fury burns hot. With all my strength I must beat my head against the wall repeatedly, rushing against the wall, rushing head-first, till nothing is left hanging there but bone slivers bloody brain-brown clumps. Then there will be calm, then everything will be fine. Did Raspe really think this? If so, then he must have truly thought he had no choice, that after leaving the clinic and that redemptive year of freedom in culture, he had to go back into the horror, even if it turned him into a prematurely aged, bizarrely rampaging being. Hard to say how much Raspe really understood, what he chose, and what life lived through him, random, unnoticed, and not subject to influence. Sometimes he may have marvelled at his incurably tattered history and longed for the strength to understand it all.

Now he cowers on the floor next to the desk, visibly aged, so dull, dejected, so spent, he, who wanted like nothing else to talk a happy ending into being, now he cowers, beneath the window, logically, his arms holding him together like twine, the most miserable one of all, a sack of flesh.

A person like this has not a single word left. He would like to think, maybe something like this: Kind yellow light, come to me in my deepdark head. I see no happiness for me. I would like at least to have back my harsh German. No one knows my loneliness. Who will sustain me? Who will hold me when I collapse adrift, to where?

WELL NOW, BLABLABLUE! Everyone knows, take a Buchholz in his wild years or Elvis in Jailhouse Rock or whoever you want, everyone knows that the hero is always a weakling, and logically the weakest weakling of all is the authoritarian rebel. You don't need cinema for that, you can have a Raspe of your own. Remember how back then, that was still in the clinic, at night and drunk he pissed inside this Porsche Cabriolet parked in the bike lane, then the owner sleeping in the driver's seat woke up, and both men were shocked and surprised, the pissing Raspe and the pissed-on driver, and then the driver got up slowly and grew taller and taller, and the total shock precluded all escape save a squalid open-trousered few steps of running, and then you lay writhing on the ground, the once so proud brazen into-the-Porsche-pisser begged for mercy and pity from the gigantic pissed-on PorscheOwner, and you, with your ridiculous stab at having a pair of balls, had no self-dignity whatsoever, all you wanted was to keep your teeth intact and-so-on-and-so-forth, I would never dare to tell the story as me. And see how it looks now, totally banal.

What I'm missing – is this true?, is it false? – is the courage of THE CONSEQUENCES OF PATHOS. I'd rather be derided as the sorriest of PatheticLosers than be exalted as a NeverEverWrongWriter who's always right about everything. To be right and sit pretty on the proper side of things, any wanker can do that, but whatever, you don't believe me, I must make something more something difficult of my work, the truth of everything.

I think of SCHÖNE AUSSICHTEN in Hamburg, of Tieck, and of Heaven 17: Here today my tomorrow. And every word burned.

The IRRUPTION OF THE IDYLL into the unstinting horror seems a working hypothesis worthy of testing. But all at once, optimism was Kohl, not Dante. Logically I wanted to scream now: Victory to the green hippies! And it wasn't fun anymore to keep mowing those tossers down. Everything's a giant sack of shit.

348

So what now? Faced with this porcine puerile petulant panorama, perhaps the next strategy for subversion is the flipflop: vitriolic error.

Someday I will finally read DANTE. I have so much planned. I just need the insane strength and total time. Continents lie within me.

How long I dreamt of NEW YORK! Now, when I am here, I couldn't logically care less, I'm so exhausted. I can't do it anymore, can't stumble through the CityNightLights I yearned for so. I imagined a triumph, humming with melancholy. Nothing, I feel nothing, as if my life were not given to me, but in the end torn out of me by the roots.

I BREATHE, breathe, breathe.

What I thought I knew may no longer be called HOPE, but stands before me as a stinking little question, as destitution even, and continues to exude its forbidden bold and craven stench: Am I finally free? Is everything finally one, my work?

Fitzcarraldo Editions
8-12 Creekside
London, SE8 3DX
United Kingdom

Originally published as *Irre* by Suhrkamp Verlag in 1983
Copyright © Suhrkamp Verlag Frankfurt am Main 1983
All rights reserved by and controlled through
Suhrkamp Verlag Berlin
Translation copyright © Adrian Nathan West, 2017
This fourth edition published in Great Britain
by Fitzcarraldo Editions in 2020

ISBN 978-1-910695-31-9

Design by Ray O'Meara
Typeset in Fitzcarraldo
Printed and bound by TJ Books

The translation of this work was supported by
a grant from the Goethe-Institut London

Fitzcarraldo Editions